BLOCKBUSTER

BLOCKBUSTER

Stephen Barlay

WILLIAM MORROW AND COMPANY, INC.

NEW YORK   1977

For Agi with love

Published in the United States in 1977.

Copyright © 1976 by Stephen Barlay

Published in Great Britain in 1976.

Printed in the United States of America.

1   2   3   4   5   6   7   8   9   10

Library of Congress Cataloging in Publication Data

Barlay, Stephen.
    Blockbuster.
        I. Title.
PZ4.B2567Re3   [PR6052.A654]   823'.9'14   76-26909
ISBN 0-688-03127-7

BOOK DESIGN   CARL WEISS

CONTENTS

1

THE MONTGOMERY ULTIMATUM

It was a warm and noisy night. The frogs, the distant church bells, the clattering ventilator at the foot of the bed, and then the telephone. Bucken looked at the digital clock: 0235. Maxine sensed his hesitation, bounced up hard toward him, and caught his waist in a skillful wrestlers' leg lock. That settled it. Let it ring.

The ringing stopped. She did not. Then the phone again. Somebody meant business. He reached out and she cursed him. The Lad sounded desperate.

"Coitus interruptus for noncontraceptive reasons," he said in place of an explanation and hoped against reason that she might find it funny. She swore she would never again sleep with a bloody copper. He swore he would never let her sleep once they were in bed together again. She let him disentangle her long legs, then stood up with him. His lazily stooping six foot something cut her down to size but she could still kiss him on the mouth without any nonsense of virginal balancing on tiptoes.

While he dressed she rolled a cigarette. It always aroused him to watch the fluent dexterity that elevated "rolling her own" into a minor craft, and the contrast produced by slim feminine fingers doing what, instinctively, he would have associated only with hunters and masons of another generation.

As he drove the MGB GT, the only permanent feature in his life since his divorce, Bucken tried to guess the reason for the urgency. Detective Sergeant "The Lad" Hunt had a boyish face and a stack of straw hair, but he was a strictly nonpanicky more-adult-than-most, who happened to believe that even Superintendents of the Special Branch must have occasional moments of privacy. Bucken had handpicked him for an immigration racket investigation, and for eighteen months they shared this mere pretense of an assignment which barely concealed the fact that Bucken had been exiled from London.

Empty suspicions, bitter months of fruitless routine inquiries—but then a lucky break which might buy their return ticket back to the Big Smoke. It depended on the undercover job the Lad had begun a month earlier. He was lining up a deal to run illegal immigrants into Britain in the guise of drama students. A "drama school" was set up as a front in Newhaven, and the deal was promising enough to attract the attention of and introduce Professor Hunt to the big boys in the business.

The omens were good. One of Hunt's first applicants at the academy was soon identified as O'Leary, the pavement artist—a professional strong-arm man from North Belfast, usually employed for violent duties in the street. Covering bank robbers was his specialty, but now he was being used probably as a front man to keep an eye on and befriend the Professor. Bucken knew they had to be careful and devised a rota of meeting places. A brief, no-names phone call would demand an emergency rendezvous, never the same on any two consecutive occasions. If one could not free himself from unwanted company, they would meet at the next place on the list.

This time, it was the turn of a tree near the left foot of The Long Man, the 231-foot chalk figure on the downs above Wilmington, only six miles from Maxine's luxury pad at Seaford. Meeting in an open field had special advantages. Anybody who succeeded tailing Bucken or the Lad would have to fall back here or be noticed. The distance from any suitable hiding place was such that at night, when they mostly met, the recognition of the partner would be well-nigh impossible even with powerful infrared viewers.

8

As Bucken was approaching, he recognized the Lad's much-cosseted World War II jeep under the tree. Behind the vehicle, The Long Man stretched out like the chalk drawings with which policemen mark a murder victim's precise position. It might have been premonition that, this time, gave Bucken an eerie drive across the peaceful rolling downs.

He noticed Hunt only when his headlights had rounded the tree. The Lad was hanging upside down, one ankle tied to a low branch, so that the massive rear bumper of the virtually hand-built jeep would be level with his head. Somebody must have reversed the vehicle hard at him. Perhaps Hunt struggled and that was how, when smashed against the tree trunk, his shoulder and chest rather than his head took the brunt of the impact. Then they must have left him for dead, long before Bucken appeared. He certainly saw nobody leaving. So Hunt must have been early. Too early. Against the rules Bucken had devised. While cutting him down, Bucken only hoped that his delay in answering the first call had not contributed to Hunt's fate.

The sports car gave the Lad only cramped accommodation, but he wouldn't know. Speed was more important than comfort. Bucken drove like a lunatic with waves of curses rising behind him. The smell of blood filled the car. That and wild thoughts of accusations made Bucken drive even faster. Somebody had squealed. And that somebody had to be high up, in the stratosphere of the Metropolitan Police where alone Bucken's plans and Hunt's whereabouts would be known. A nark in the Yard. A traitor. He wished he could cry.

Bucken was used to squealers. Petty criminals would sometimes surprise but never shock him with their softly whispered cheap treachery. Except now, the flow of information, the lifeblood of Old Bill, had been reversed. If Hunt had been followed, he would have gone on, without stopping at the tree. So somebody must have been waiting for him.

But why did they not kill him more simply? Could have shot him. Or knifed him. And it was not the first sadistic, spectacular killing Bucken had seen lately. Somebody was clearly taking pleasure in being original in the choice of weapon and the mode of murder. The similarity seemed significant to some people. But he was not one for fancy theories.

He almost hit the wall as he cornered, skidding sharply into a little alley behind a boatyard, virtually on the doorstep of the hospital. The quiet back entrance was used mainly by dustmen and undertakers, but it was the shortest route to the emergency ward. He carried in the bleeding mess by himself. He softened his usual hurried, heavy gait to give Hunt a gentler ride. He refused any help from the willing but obviously unmoved congregation of porters and nurses. His eyes sought only a doctor, old and cool enough to trust, young enough to move fast. The sight of an Indian whitecoat filled him with irrational confidence. He wanted to believe that some acupuncturistic Oriental miracle was about to be conjured up. Only because of that did he let himself be talked into leaving the theater.

When he was allowed to return, Hunt was lying on a table, tilted head down, with only his toes sticking out and up into the air like antennae at the end of the white sheet that was too short to envelop his bulk. But there was no Oriental elixir. Only the syringeful of juice for painless stupor, and the mere formality of the drips, the soothing words, and the hope that he would go without too much suffering.

The sour hospital air, the musty smell of drying blood, Bucken swallowed hard to drown his nausea. He dreaded infirmity and loathed those womb-warm emergency wards. "Give me a cool, honest-to-god morgue any day," he once mumbled, half-asleep, to Sarah. Must have been a million years ago, between their first and second divorce, after a nightlong session of identification on a slab of cheap stone. She pushed him out of bed and refused to let him touch her for two weeks.

Any memory of Sarah normally freed him from unpleasant thoughts. Not this time. Beyond the acute pain of losing a friend and craving for revenge, his entire system reacted violently against the duty of taking a dying declaration. To feel for the failing pulse, and the weaker the signal grew the harder to squeeze for a statement. To beg doctors to do something. Prolong life. Bring him around. Just long enough to make him talk.

The slow shuffle behind him announced the return of the Jamaican nurse. Bucken did not look up. He wished he knew where exactly they made them so intensely desirable. She was checking the drip. But her eyes were on him. His back told him. His back always knew. He pressed his thighs together. He needed a wash. Did this girl sense the unfinished lovemaking?

The Lad's toes stirred. "Only reflexes," she muttered and turned, brushing deliberately against his knees. Bucken stared at the toes. His last open line of communication. Toes. Fat, hard, pavement-polished toes. If only they could speak. Toes, the whole toes and nothing but the toes. He did not apologize for the bad joke in the presence of approaching death. The Lad would laugh. Would he still laugh if the nurse seduced Bucken on the edge of his deathbed? "Wish somebody did it on mine," thought Bucken and smiled. Only smiles could coordinate his irregular, nose-dominated, chin-strong features, and the effect was infectious. She smiled back. He knew he had to run away.

"Must make a few phone calls. Please shout if anything happens."

The corridor received the first rays of daylight. The milky window panes were filled with the bobbing pin-thin shadows of the masts in the marina beyond.

John Cutter-Smith watched the early autumn sun filter through the cheap, unlined curtains of his maisonette in Elstree. He had had a long sleepless night but enjoyed every minute of it: anticipation was more pleasurable to him than actual events no matter how important. He noted the state of the cupboard: his new suits inside deserved better shelter. Again and again his mind returned to the first visit to Lanelli and Son and the foretaste of a new life-style.

"What do you suggest one should wear on the day of receiving a rather large sum?"

"How large, sir?"

The tailor had given no sign of regarding the question as bizarre or capricious. It made Cutter-Smith pleased with his choice: they obviously shared a genuine respect for the true sartorial problem of finding the correct attire for every occasion.

"Are you a sporting gentleman, sir?"

"No."

"Ah."

That would rule out a betting coup on the racecourse. The question, and the fact that the possibility was considered at all, gave further joy to Cutter-Smith.

"A mere financial transaction of a, shall we say, nonroutine nature," he volunteered to help the Son part of the old firm and to eliminate any further questions. He longed to declare that the payment would be made by the Bank of England itself, but he resisted the urge.

For Collection Day, the decision was made easy by a deep and instantaneous understanding between the two. A plumblue, from the darker end of the spectrum, with virtually invisible pin-stripes. The actual handling of all that money would demand respect. Lanelli the younger would have been badly shocked if his new customer told him that on Collection Day, with that suit, a soft, very wide-brimmed black hat, black gloves, and an overflow of red handkerchief in the breast pocket would be worn.

The other suit to be ordered proved to be a much trickier enigma. Cutter-Smith could not quite explain to the tailor that he would not really rob the Old Lady of Threadneedle Street, he would only ask ... well, serve a demand for the million. In cash. As always, he was only anxious to do the correct things in the correct manner, but there was nothing to guide him. He would have liked something romantic and flamboyant for Demand Day. He dreamed about red velvet, something like his favorite though rarely enjoyed Châteauneuf du Pape, with a pale, flowery shirt . . . but he knew he could never bring himself to order it, let alone wear it in public. Yet why not? This was to be the turning point, after all, the release of the true Cutter-Smith from invisible bondage.

Unfortunately, the discussion remained restricted to nonzip flies and the width of lapel, and he ended up with a medium weight, medium-gray suit which offered nothing to show for the bulk of his savings.

Naturally, the true price had to be kept from Winnie. She would never forgive him. So what? She was in for greater shocks than that.

He turned and stretched and turned again. Too late to sleep, too early to rise. He felt like that all night. Now, at last, with some justification. Demand Day had arrived.

To while away the remnants of the dawn, he tried to visualize the massive silhouette of the man whom he called the Principal. My Principal, to be precise. Where could he be? Would he also toss and turn sleeplessly or would he snore away merrily without a care as if it were to be just like any other day?

His fingertips ran a routine check around his hair, sculpted sideburns and finely pointed beard. The Cypriot hair stylist, known for some obscure reason as the Dodo of Mayfair, had certainly done a great job on it the day before. The trichological examination alone had lasted almost an hour. The result was worth every penny of this once-in-a-lifetime extravaganza. Mother and Winnie would disapprove, of course, but he had waited five decades for that. And the Dodo smiled heartily when Cutter-Smith told him: "No segregation or racial discrimination in my hair—I wear black and white in equal numbers. So no tinting please." It was nice to talk to a man with a sense of humor.

The light now probed the shadow between the wall and the old cupboard. Cutter-Smith could just about make out the shape of the large suitcase. It was leaning against the cracked plaster he would never have to paper again.

Winnie was clearly upset when he brought home the suitcase and asked her casually: "Do you think this could accommodate nine hundred thousand pounds?"

"Did you say nine hundred thousand?"

"Pounds. Only in large denominations, of course. Used twenty-pound notes, to be precise."

"An interesting problem." As on several occasions in the past few weeks, she was obviously considering if this was the right moment to summon some psychiatric assistance. At the age of fifty-two, men should not play such stupid games.

"The size of the twenty-pound note is six and five-sixteenths by three and nine-sixteenths, inches that is, and the normal bank package contains fifty notes. If we double the package, we'll need four hundred and fifty of these extra large bundles. This suitcase would take twenty-four bundles per layer, and therefore nineteen layers would almost fill it, leaving room for, say, six nice boxes of cigars."

"What are you talking about?"

"Just a mental exercise."

"With a suitcase."

"The net weight is, of course, a little tricky."

"The weight. Oh."

"Yes . . . should make about one hundred and ten pounds or something like fifty-five kilograms, give or take a little, depending also on the state of the notes, the extent of normal wear and tear, the weight of dirt and bits of sellotape, but this should be duly compensated for by lost corners and torn edges . . . still, we could average, say, four ounces per bundle . . ."

He was not all that sure about the figures, but an ounce or two would not matter much, and he was ready to take his Principal's word for it.

14

Winnie turned. He peeped down the only slightly plunging neckline of her well-worn nightie. After twenty-three weeks and three days, he would have liked to make love to her once again. But he did not feel entitled to it. She needed rest. And it was all his fault. Or rather the Bank's fault. He could reasonably expect a job to ensure a better life for her. So now they would have to pay. Even if, for once, she would not benefit from it.

He knew that some people imagined he would never make love to Winnie. The thought of sex with a one-legged woman might put off many. But his hand seemed to know better. He decided to dissociate himself from his inconsiderate fingers. But she shook herself free. Knocked out by her beloved Mandrax, she raised a lamely defensive arm, reminding him that good and decent men were not supposed to take advantage of a sleeping invalid. He withdrew at once—and felt ashamed of it. It would not be easy to abandon a lifelong ambition to please everybody quite unselfishly.

He tried to concentrate on the vision of the waking City. If only there were guards in bearskins and scarlet tunics still on duty at the Old Lady, he would proudly ride to the gate with them. But no more guards, not even in battledress, any longer. Just hidden TV cameras. So he would go by tube.

The 100-BHP diesel engine had begun to develop an asthmatic cough in the past few days, but Sergeant Elms was not unduly worried about the patient. It could still gather up strength for a healthy push in a hurry, and the thirty-foot fiberglass hull would then skitter along the peculiar currents where the Thames and the Medway play chase over the Nore Sands. Another round of policing those waters was coming to an end, and not too soon either. The oil refineries on the Isle of Grain were just about leaving the corner of his left eye, so Emma could see the boat now from her bedroom window. His two-man crew—known at the Station as "the two Wilsons, brackets, unrelated"—were ready. One changed course, the other flashed the spotlight twice, telling Emma "no holdups this time." Breakfast would be on the table just as the Sergeant closed the garden gate, deciding, as he did every day, that it needed another coat of paint if it were not to rust away prematurely.

Elms shut his tired eyes for a second or two. He could afford this luxury. The two Wilsons were well drilled to keep their eyes open at all times.

"Skip . . ."

"What?"

"I'm not sure . . ."

"Make up your mind."

"It may be just the trick the sun sometimes plays on us . . . but that buoy on the *Monty* . . . Can you see what I mean?"

"I've got eyes, haven't I?" Elms peered hard into the rising sun: was that buoy light really off, out of order, or simply blotted out by the mightier beam floating momentarily on the water behind it? He only knew for sure that he must never be wrong. Not in front of his kids, not against Emma or the crew. So he had to keep quiet and reserve judgment.

"Skip . . ."

"Still not sure?"

"Nope."

"Go in then and investigate. Find out for yourself."

He hoped he sounded convincing enough, for he never liked to go near the *Richard Montgomery,* the wreck with those thousands of tons of aerial fragmentation bombs lying in less than thirty feet of water ever since the war. The suspect light buoy was, in fact, one of the two which—supported by an electric foghorn—were supposed to warn and keep away ships and tankers, the inquisitive and the suicidal from the wreck.

Elms noted the time—0543. The police launch approached the buoy fast on the back of the tide running out to sea. Another ninety minutes to ebb tide and slack water, but the masts and derricks of the wreck were already stretching tall on the horizon. With the sun behind them, details of the old steel safety nets were finely etched on the sky. The steady breeze swayed them slightly, and Elms thought he could hear the wreck groan and creak like an ancient galley. What would that gentle movement and the strong stir of his propeller do to those bombs below as they corroded away, bit by bit, imperceptibly, every day, like his garden gate?

"Skip . . ."

"Get on to the RT then."

PC Wilson R. cleared his throat.

"You're not going to shout then, are you?"

Elms knew that this was uncalled for. The laddie only showed a healthy respect for the radiotelephone, but he hated that wreck profoundly. He knew it could blow Sheerness and the oil installations on the Isle of Grain right out of the water, could start a tidal wave and—who knows?—set off an explosion up in the Estuary on Canvey Island—and then they could really start bringing in those pocket computers to count the dead and notch up the losses all the way to Tower Bridge.

The light was off, indeed. The laddie was clearly enjoying himself with the running commentary he gave on the RT like a heroic bomb-disposal expert, approaching the deadly enemy and making sure that, when he is blown apart, the next brave man will have at least something to go on.

"That will do. We'll come back to them when we know what's going on." Elms would have liked to send a "delay" message to Emma, but the wreck and the buoy now held all his attention to the exclusion of his doomed bacon—or was it Thursday and therefore kippers today?

As the water was beginning to run low, the railings of the *Monty*'s bridge emerged and birds flew in to rest on the metal nests of the ack-ack. The angle was better now and Elms raised his powerful binoculars without the risk

17

of blinding himself staring into the red disc of the sun. Something was covering the top of the buoy. Something soft, something loose, something that danced in the breeze and masked now this, now that part of the sign on the float:

Warning

DANGER

Unexploded
Ammunition
Keep At Least
500 feet
From Wreck

WRECK

By the time Elms could read it without the binoculars, the police launch was only a hundred feet or so away. He took the wheel and throttled back to let the current carry the boat to the buoy where Wilson S. G., known as the Other Wilson (because he had joined the police a week later) neatly caught a metal hook with the long grappling iron.

A black plastic refuse-collection bag covered the light which was still flashing faintly underneath. Some joker must have done it. The Sergeant could have given him the cat without any compunction. Never mind the Criminal Damage Act 1971—felony: seven years or felony: life. In his book, a prank like that would have qualified for hanging if there was an accident.

"Tell 'em what we found, then. And keep the line open."

Wilson R. remained on the RT, ready to duck when the Sergeant gripped the edge of the bag. You never knew what would be underneath.

Elms had collected a couple of awards for conspicuous bravery in his long service. He had fought a gunman successfully with his bare hands, and saved one of his men when he was a diving instructor. The possibility of a bomb under the bag was a risk he could take in his stride without too much concern. What mattered was that the Station should know what was going on. But that wreck below did worry him. All was quiet now, the boat swung with the buoy, only the waves sounded an occasional cloop. But he could hear the silent moaning of the broken-in-two ship and the rust gnawing away the bomb casings.

The bag slipped off easily. There was nothing underneath that should not be there. The light was in good working order. He radioed for instructions.

"Carry out a visual, then come in."

The visual inspection yielded nothing apart from the fact that the presence of the plastic bag could be no accident. He packed it carefully in case there were fingerprints on it.

"Some stupid bugger," concluded the Other Wilson.

"Hope so." And after a rather theatrical pause: "Better than some villain covering the light and committing unlawful interference with government property in the ensuing darkness ..." Elms was pleased with that. He could tell when he impressed the laddies.

He was also pleased to leave the wreck. To him it was a ghost ship. Perhaps because, as a small boy, he almost witnessed the now-you-see-me-now-you-don't act by this American Liberty ship. "August 1944 ... thirty years now, almost to the day," he mumbled to himself, knowing that the diesel would swallow the sound.

The Estuary had never seen anything like that. Ships, guns, tanks and soldiers to back up D-Day, it was like watching live movies all the time. Elms and the rest of the Sheerness kids knew most ships and their tonnage by heart. The only-a-year-old *Richard Montgomery* was not much to look at, but the lethal cargo fascinated them: there were some eight thousand tons of bombs and TNT in the four holds. She was anchored near the shoal, the Nore Sands, and part of the fun was that the stevedores demanded danger money before agreeing to offload her. And they got it, too. Perhaps half of the cargo was on shore when there was a gale warning. Elms later heard that there was another argument on board about whose duty it was to cover the hatches before leaving the ship because of the approaching storm. There was no time for arbitration and, finally, all cargo holds were left uncovered.

That was when Elms was ordered indoors by his mother. He never quite forgave her for it. When the gale hit the Medway, waves broke through the open hatches. Driven by the force 8 wind, the ship dragged her anchor from shallow waters on to the shoal. Lifted and banged to the bottom, up and into the sands again, the *Richard Montgomery* snapped in half amidships. By the time Elms was back down on the waterfront, there were only the masts and the derricks of the ghost left to stare at.

Since then, Elms had always half-expected the biggest nonnuclear bang there had ever been. It was irrational, really. He had dived in the area and knew there was no imminent danger. He knew about the Ministry of Defence underwater surveys and the bomb-disposal men's verdict that it was safer to leave the freighter alone than to start a complicated salvage operation. But he also knew the risks: the main Thames shipping lane only a mile to the north; the Medway lane between the marker buoys even nearer; the huge tankers with millions of tons of oil passing by; and the jets' shock waves above and the corrosion below and the storms in between and the stupid skin divers—one of whom had already chanced a visit to pinch some brass fittings—and the possibility of careless or malicious interference . . . and now this prank.

Elms would have hated to admit it, but he felt very uncomfortable. And he knew what Emma would say about dumped breakfasts and the housekeeping money going down the drain yet again.

Maxine answered the phone right on the first bell. She did not bother to inquire who the caller at this hour was.

"Listen, burk, you either get right back into my cunt or

screw your sergeant from now on till the first after Epiphany which is a fair way to go by any calendar." End of conversation.

Maxine never missed an opportunity to demonstrate her sound Biblical education, the very best those solemn trustees of her inheritance could buy, and hardly ever failed to impress Bucken with the combination of her angelic face and foul mouth. He dialed Scotland Yard and left a message for his boss, Commander Allerton of the Special Branch, then made a courtesy call to inform the local CID who showed no sign of enthusiasm for helping him. The suspected Newhaven immigration racket and Hunt's accident were clearly Bucken's pigeon—and he liked it that way. Except that once again he was convinced about but had no proof of a top-level leak.

Must be fate, he thought, as he returned to the bilious memory of the first case. Drugs with odd political implications. It reached the point where he could have locked up a dozen ordinary villains right away. But he was chasing the big fellows. The ones with the custom-built catamarans and mink-skinned birds rather than chummy who rides his old bike from one four-ale bar to the next. In the last moment they got away from him. He had no doubt that they had been tipped off. But no evidence. He stubbornly played his hunch—and earned himself an invitation to a caviar-for-starters business luncheon. Throughout, he sensed corruption floating lightly like gossamer all around him. He sat sandwiched between a retired Chief Constable and a retiring Chinese importer, and noticed that there was something barely whiffed in his direction about mutual back scratching and the fat skimmings of crime. Even if taped it would have been no proof. Bucken voiced his suspicions just a notch too loudly. That shook his own position in The Job even with his best friend Rattray, the new Assistant Commissioner. Then came a false accusation of using undue force and violence. A put-up job if ever there had been one. But everybody knew it would stick. Bucken's filthy explosive temper had landed him in a mess before. Rapists and

21

child molesters made him violent. Couldn't help it. So there was no investigation, no case to answer, nothing. "Just pick yourself a partner and look into this suspected immigration affair. Take your time."

He did take his time. He had no choice. And Hunt was his partner throughout.

The three phone calls and the run along the corridor did not take him more than seven minutes. A record, perhaps, but long enough to miss the Lad's death by fifty-five seconds. The coquettish nurse was already tidying the room, preparing it for the next in line.

Bucken grabbed her arm. "Why didn't you call me?"

"I called the doctor."

It made sense. Bucken felt spent and thoroughly beaten.

"I really thought he might make it. At least to talk to you," she said and offered him a cup of lukewarm tea.

"Well, he didn't." He took a mouthful of tea and rinsed his palate hoping that it would wash away the stale bitterness of the night. Apparently, it was wrong to hope for anything. He spat the tea into the wash basin and used his elbow to turn the tap.

The nurse displayed small, firm breasts as she submitted to a wholehearted, well-deserved yawn. "I'll be off duty soon ..."

"A nice thought. Thanks for everything ... and see you sometime," he mumbled as he left. It would be good to touch her skin lightly, anywhere, but then how would he stop there?

Maxine would also have to wait. He must take a good look at the scene at The Long Man, although the local boys would already be there and his mouth was too dry for a long conversation, putting them in the picture and, inevitably, feeding them with a pack of half-truths and lies.

By choice he would have driven all the way to Windsor for a quiet breakfast with Sarah. She would ask no questions and she would sense his mood. She had once met the Lad, too. But that wasn't on. How frequently can one pay unexpected visits to one's twice-divorced wife? He ought to ask some women's magazine about it. It should produce some interesting answers.

Another strong urge was to hit back fast. He had something to go on. Enough to organize a couple of raids and pull in a "sus" or two from each. But suspects were not enough. And small fry were no good. He wanted the big boys and wanted them badly. He must have a private word with Rattray, and then convince Allerton that there had to be a serious leak. Something that was more important to investigate than any immigration or other racket. There were only half a dozen people who had access to his reports filed at the Big House. That must surely interest Rattray. They could breakfast together. Even a rare, warm family occasion if he arrived before the innumerable little Rattrays began to disperse for the day.

As he stepped out into the alley, he wondered if the car had been badly bloodstained. The rear door was still wide open: on the way in, locking it was the least of his worries. Now he was so preoccupied that he walked right into the shotgun waiting for him behind the car.

"Mornin', guv."

The squat, bowlegged man holding the gun sounded quite respectful. It might have been the effect of the nylon stocking he wore over his face.

"With the amount of work you do, my pet, you should be able to afford proper ladder-proof ones," Bucken said with a nod toward the hole that revealed the man's sweaty temple. He half-hoped that the gunman's automatic reaction would be to touch it. It sometimes worked. Not this time. O'Leary, the pavement artist, was a pro who would not let go of the shotgun so easily.

"Wrong size, guv, that's all."

For a second, Bucken thought about a dive for the gun. But the man read his mind: "I wish you did, guv."

"You picked the wrong guy, chummy. I'm no diamond peddler and this is no Hatton Garden. That's more in your line, isn't it?" Through the nylon Bucken saw the eyes move. O'Leary was looking right through him, and now signalled to somebody behind Bucken. Bucken did not

23

turn. It might have been a trick. If he was to be knocked down with the gun, the man would have to do it facing him. But it was no trick. Bucken heard somebody running away.

"Won't be long, guv."

"What?" Bucken edged a little nearer.

"Transport. That's the word, ain't it?"

"Where to?"

"You'll see."

"Tell me, sweetheart. I'm curious." Another inch forward.

"That'll do."

The man was only a good arm's length away. If the barrel had not been sawn short, he would not have been able to come even that far. The only chance would be when the car came. It was bound to attract the gunman's eye for a split second.

Bucken widened his nostrils. His mouth opened. He breathed a soundless "Ha" . . . and another. Ha . . . His whole face was contorted now. Mouth in a half-yawn, gasping for air, cheeks squeezing the eyes into a slit . . . an aborted sneeze, and it still wouldn't come or go away . . . Bucken's hand started toward his pocket. O'Leary slowly shook his head.

"Touch of the old flu, guv?"

"Bloody hay fever."

Bucken's nostrils were twisting once again. O'Leary laughed heartily.

"Hay fever? You have hay fever, guv?" He found it the biggest joke.

Bucken nodded and the sneeze that would not come crumpled his lined, tanned face into a knot. His hand moved again, now upward, where the edge of a handkerchief showed at the top of the breast pocket. He swallowed air now so noisily that anybody knew there would be quite an explosion when that sneeze broke through at last.

O'Leary was shaking with laughter—from shoulders

24

upward. His hands remained steady. A superintendent with hay fever! Bucken gave him a questioning look as he reached for the breast pocket.

"Okay?" His nostrils stretched to the limit, the sound was truly nasal.

"Okay. But keep it nice and slow."

At last, Bucken heard the approaching engine of a car. That was the moment he was waiting for. O'Leary was bound to look up and glance toward it. When Bucken saw his eyes flash in the sunlight, he slowly took a grip on the corner of the carefully placed handkerchief, and pulled it fast into a well-aimed swipe at O'Leary. The bunch of keys, tied to the bottom corner of the handkerchief, hissed through the air in an arc toward the gunman's temple. Blood spurting everywhere was Bucken's last visual recollection. The last sound he heard was a muffled crack at his nape. It blotted out the world and switched off the sun. His spinal eyes had failed to warn him this time.

It was still much too early to get up, but Cutter-Smith could not restrain himself any longer. He quietly slipped out of bed so as not to disturb Winnie, took a battered black briefcase from the top of the cupboard, and settled with it at the dressing table. He spread out four sheets of neat handwritten notes, and pretended to read them. Pretended, because he knew every single word by heart and he only looked at them again and again because the precisely planned, step-by-step timetable of the coming day's events reassured him in moments of weakness, indecision and fraying nerves. By any standard of logic this would be the moment for destroying them.

"But why?"

"It's evidence."

"For what?"

"My guilt."

"But that won't be a secret. There's nothing here you won't do or actually tell them anyway."

That was the trouble all the way. It was impossible to argue with the Principal. Cutter-Smith could recall every detail of their brief meetings in the darkness of the motel off the M1, only a few miles from his home in Elstree. He sometimes woke up at night hearing quite clearly the whispering, always whispering, voice, the words of reassurance, the ready answers to every conceivable question, and the tone of total conviction even when the logic was arguable.

"Now why should you worry about the evidence, Johnny? May I call you Johnny? Oh, good, we're partners, after all, partners in the perfect crime which is not even a crime as far as your role is concerned. After all, you'll be a representative. My representative. What's criminal about being a rep? All right, you'll be demanding money with menaces. True enough. But even the menace won't come from you. You don't say that *you* will blow up the Sheerness marker buoy. You say that somebody may do that. At thirteen-forty-five precisely. You only inform the authorities. You perform a civic duty. And for that you deserve a modest reward. A commendation. A medal."

Cutter-Smith longed to boast about it all to Winnie. To somebody. But the Principal was most adamant on this point. Nobody must know about anything before the operation began. Once it started, everybody could be told about it freely—there was no way to stop the machine.

"In today's 'big crimes,' in kidnapping for ransom, hijacking, skyjacking, threat with a stolen atom bomb, bank and money-in-transit robberies, the terrible, insoluble problem is how to get away with the lolly once your hostages, airplane, whatyoulike have been released, blown apart, take your pick. Few countries would offer them asylum even in political cases, so they try their tricks, put their faith in some idiotic dream such as parachuting into a jungle; and, even if they succeed temporarily, they must remain on the run forever.

"But you, my dear Johnny, you won't run. You won't need a hotel, I mean a hiding place where criminals try to sit it out and sweat it out, chewing their fingernails to the bone, irritating and sometimes killing each other. Not you, Johnny. You can stay at home or move house if you like, buy a pad in London or a penthouse in Rome if that's what you and Winnie fancy, and just send a change of address card, out of sheer courtesy, to C.O., I mean Scotland Yard, every time you change residence."

"But why?"

"They'll insist on that."

"Then I shouldn't do it."

"Come on, Johnny, don't let me down, I have absolute faith in you. After all, I chose you of all people as my partner. Of course Old Bill will maintain an interest in you. And why not? The cops visit you and drink your pink gins or pink champagne, by then. A friendly chat? Questions and more questions? Why not? You won't have any secrets. For once you've passed on the money, there will be nothing to connect you with me or with the threat. But the threat will remain. And that gives you security. Forever. Should they do anything to you, a terrible revenge will follow inevitably. Because our bomb, dear Johnny, is a perennial, like a geranium. Until plucked, it will come on and go off at will forever.

"That's what you have to impress upon them. The eternity of the threat. The fact that they'll be the prisoners of their own past inaction and present impotence wrapped in the safeguarding of their false public image. Whereby the simple opportunity for the perfect crime arises."

But that was what the Principal never seemed to understand. That it was the very simplicity of the plan that gave Cutter-Smith an almost physical pain of frustration. It left him with the emptiness of thwarted dreams, finding his flights of fancy still stuck in the mud.

He never even tried to explain it ... to explain that, when you first go in for crime to take revenge on life and prove yourself, then yes, it is an appealing idea to rob the Bank of England itself and humiliate the guardians of the Old Lady. But you do not want to sneak in through the back door. You do not want to pinch the Old Lady's purse like any common pickpocket. You want to kick the door in with guns blazing. Or let the grappling irons catch the miniature columns of the first-floor balustrade, so that a solitary, desperate, hated and feared man could scale the windowless screen wall that guards the acres of banking halls. What an awe-inspiring sight for the Lord Mayor of London, as he looks out of the window of the Mansion House! Or perhaps a long, lonely, and arduous tunneling job with stunning precision, leading right into the lowest of the three vault floors. Or a single-handed commando operation pulling off what has always been regarded as the impossible, by landing in the superb and impenetrable Garden Court by parachute.

Unfortunately, most of the exhilaration was doomed to come from inside his own pressurized skull, racing blood and overflowing adrenalin. And above all, from the ultimate proof that he was not a kindly and exploitable remote-controlled puppet, but a man with his own will, capable of doing something evil, for once, whatever the pattern of the past.

"No, we won't have any problem with the cops, I can assure you," the whisper flowed on.

Cutter-Smith nodded. Always nodded, he would recall ruefully. Too impressed to disagree, too worried to voice agreement. But once, having downed two ultralarge pink gins, he was unable to resist the temptation to find the element of deadly risk for himself.

"Aren't you afraid that I might tell the cops?"

"N-no ..." Did the whisper grow hesitant? "Too late to *stop* the process. Delay, well, perhaps ... I'd need a new frontman."

"Would you kill me?"

"It may take time to find a replacement."

"Would you kill me?"

"Besides, the sheer disappointment would really upset me."

"What if I let the police loose on you? I mean when we have another meeting or something?"

28

"You wouldn't have the opportunity."

"Are you watching me? Are others watching? How can you be so sure?"

"I am."

"So, would you kill me?"

"Look, Johnny, I don't want you to do this under some sort of duress. Just as I didn't want someone to come in with me purely for the money. I needed someone who was not a criminal."

"This will make me one."

"No, it won't. And you know it. Your first motive is not gain. They owe you the money. They used you when they sent you to Uganda. They used you in Brunei. You could still sit there, virtually a deputy finance minister, if you didn't help British interests and if you didn't trust Britain's promises to look after you."

"How did you find out?"

"Didn't they tell you not to worry, Mr. Smith? With your contacts in high places, Mr. Smith, you could land the job of your choice. Didn't they tell you that the Governor of the Bank of England was greatly indebted to you?"

"The Governor and the Court knew nothing about this, I'm sure."

"Makes no difference. You still want your revenge on them, don't you?"

"How do you know?"

"You told me. And that's why, to please you, I agreed to the change of plan so that you could approach the Bank rather than the Treasury or the police in the first place."

"They shouldn't have done it to me."

"I know."

"Like hell you do." He rolled the angostura gently around the glass—a joyful memory from Brunei where he had acquired a taste for sweet life and bitter liquids. "As if you knew the difference between being good and bad."

"I know."

"You know nothing." The glass now was reddish misty, ready for the gin, and the shadow that was the Principal,

29

never mean with his measures, filled it up for him. He would not even know how much gin it needed. How would he know the perverse ecstasy of planning and savoring truly wilful disobedience for the first time, particularly if this teen-age rebellion had been delayed for four decades? A prolonged childhood of trying and trying harder to please. Only because once, only once, he brought home a disastrous school report at the age of ten, and his parents were still in a state of agitated fuming when Father happened to suffer the first stroke which would soon lead to another and would eventually make Mother a widow at thirty-two. "You argued too much," was her verdict.

He held out his glass for another drink.

The shadow shook his head.

Cutter-Smith blushed. Which infuriated him. Here we go again ... I'm trying to please. Red face apologizing for my drinking.

Mother was always easily pleased—by everybody else. By women friends who giggled with her for hours on end, by men who came to discuss her numerous charity projects sometimes well into the night, by the twins who joined the Salvation Army and married the right good men—but not by him. He was responsible for Father's strokes, and he lacked the true goodness of heart, and his falling in love with and marrying a disabled girl were merely an attempt "to demonstrate virtue under false pretenses," probably the worst crime in Mother's book. And not only that. She soon convinced Winnie, too, about this nonsense. That he stuck with her for years and years was not acceptable as proof of loyalty or love. On the contrary. And she continued where Mother had left off. With the incessant scolding for being a careerist yet not doing enough for his wife, for being materialistic but not looking after money, for being unpatriotic yet too easily exploitable by anybody British, and with never, never laughing at his jokes and so denying him the opportunity to learn what was or was not really funny.

30

Yet he was proud of having the strength to joke about his life. "My weakness is the strongest link in our marriage," he would remark with rather pleasing results particularly among those who heard it for the first time.

Now all this would come to an end. Winnie would have to go. If she felt that he took advantage of her, if she found him a through and through evil man, so be it.

Rustling sound brought him back to this early-autumn dawn: his hands were furiously crushing the sheets of the timetable. Pity. He had drawn it up with the orderly precision of a neat financial brain and the loving care of a parchment-copying monk.

The list began with "Arrival at Bank Station, appr 1130" and in brackets: "Take Central Line for greater regularity and reliability; leave by Bank exit; proceed to main gate, Threadneedle St."

Although this was at the very top of the page, Cutter-Smith had squeezed in two more points in pinhead print above it: "0815—office" and "1130—Court assembles."

The rest of the long timetable was uneven in detail. The 1135 entry mentioned only the laconic instruction "Doorman, official and—or letters." The eight-minute walk to follow it described, however, the route with great precision, allowing extra time for "Call House of Commons (list of telephone numbers attached)" on the way, from "box at Royal Exchange Bldgs—1139 appr."

The time was 0630 Thursday. The old bank-rate day. The traditional weekly session of the Court. The day he chose. A quick glance down another list of "things to organize." The hired car booking. The private detective. The suitcase. Delivery of detector kits. All duly ticked off. Letters to write—letters to take. List of phone numbers. Checklist completed.

He packed away most of his sheets in the briefcase, clipped together the papers to take, and tried to lengthen this umpteenth dry run. But apart from burning the list of "things to organize," there was nothing else to do. Activities would soon give way to worrying thoughts,

31

passivity would grab his stomach in an ulcerous cramp till 1130.

Winnie was still asleep. It would have been good to wake her up, hold her hand, and talk to her. He knew it was madness, but with the slightest encouragement he would have told her all, whatever the Principal would say or do about it. Even though he sometimes had a feeling that the man could read his thoughts and perhaps had the bedroom bugged. Luckily, Winnie showed no inclination to wake up. He would have to make his own breakfast if he wanted to leave early.

Perhaps it was stupid to go first to his office for a short visit on a day like that. He had warned them in good time that he would have to be away on very important family business and they agreed to it. Yet he had to go in. Wearing that new suit and letting the entire Planning-Programming-Budgeting stew. Particularly Mr. plain-Smith, his immediate "superior with the inferior mind"—a joke that usually went down well with junior and even senior staff. Let him see the suit. And may he be reminded on reading the Cutter-Smith proposals, already on his desk for over a week, that the Council's PPB should, in fact, be known as PPBS, with S standing for System, a vital element which Mr. plain-Smith tends to forget, at his own peril.

What makes him head of the Borough Finance Department directly under the Chief Financial Officer anyway? This inept, ignoble ignoramus may go on treating it as a never-ending source of merriment that Cutter-Smith should only deal with *cuts* in the budget when comprehensive planning is put into operation via the medium of PPB or rather PPBS, but he will never fully appreciate corporate management concepts or, indeed, be able to deal personally and in style with the Bank of England in the course of a major transaction.

"What happened?"
"You were coshed or something."

"Don't say." Bucken recognized the nurse's voice and opened his eyes.

The pain did not bother him unduly, but his head weighed a ton. He tried to touch it but a massive blob of bandage was in the way. "Must look like a cartoonist's model for the crazy motorist. When did they put it on?"

"You gave us plenty of time. You were out cold for more than an hour."

Startled by the loss of time, he tried to sit up. Now it hurt.

"You must take it easy."

"Is it bad?"

"You're lucky. Only seven stitches and a bit of concussion. Want a drink?"

He tried to nod but that turned out to be the wrong idea. "Please. Make it a Scotch."

She ran the tap. "You looked a real mess until we cleaned you up."

"Did you bathe me?"

"Not yet." Her eyes laughed.

"Hey, you're supposed to be off duty."

"You changed my mind."

"Thanks."

She held his head while he sipped some water. It began to hurt more.

It was odd how slowly it all came back. As if his mind refused to ask the more important questions first.

"Did he get away?"

"Not the one you messed up. Ugh."

"Come on, let's have it."

"I get the doctor and a cup of tea for you."

"First tell me." The light was too much and made him blink.

"I'll draw the curtains."

"You just talk." He closed his eyes.

"Not much to tell. When you left, I was also ready to go, and because you went through the back exit, I thought you might be waiting, so I went that way. I saw you raise your arm, and I remember how surprising it was that you

33

waved your hanky. There was much blood and then I saw the other man behind you and then he hit you on the neck with something. You and the masked man went down and then I screamed and ran back for help. By the time a porter came out with me, a car just picked up the man who hit you. They left you two there on the road."

"What sort of car?"

"Black."

"What make?"

"I don't know. I had other things to think of."

"And the man who hit me?"

"You want to know what make?"

"Sort of."

"White. Very small. I don't know how he reached up to crack your head."

"Blond, dark?"

"I'm not sure. I saw only his back."

"You're a great help."

"That's what your colleagues said."

"Where are they?"

"Next door. Trying to question the other man. But he wouldn't talk. And now you must not talk. I call the doctor."

Bucken was not pleased but, with Hunt dead, local CID involvement was inevitable. He looked down at himself. He was covered by a blanket and a sheet. His jacket and shirt had been removed but he still had his own trousers on. His eyes followed the creases in the sheet. His bare toes were sticking out at the far end.

"Is he conscious?"

"Yes. But you must rest now." She was at the door.

"You're very beautiful."

"Sssh."

"One more question."

"If you must."

"Have they taken away the shotgun or is it still here?"

"What gun?"

"Christ."

"What are you talking about?"

"Didn't you see the shotgun?"

"No."

"Didn't you see that the masked man was threatening to shoot me?"

"He was behind the car with you. I saw no gun."

"Not even afterwards on the ground?"

"I didn't look. And you promised only one question no more."

"I must see him." He tried to sit up and, for a second, he thought he would faint again. His vision was blurred and the furniture swam in a wavy pattern. The throbbing was bad, too. It helped to clear his eyes. But no sensation of the true upright. She made an effort to keep him in the bed, but his feet were already dangling over the side. "Help me."

"Back to bed at once or you'll be in real trouble."

"I am already. Help me. I must talk to O'Leary."

"Who?"

"The man."

She did not want to risk struggling with him and force him to exert himself even more. "It's stupid, but wait until I get you at least a wheelchair."

She had lied to him: instead of the wheelchair, she brought back the Indian doctor.

"Get back to bed. Please." He sounded very, very tired. He should have been off duty eight hours ago, but his colleague had not turned up.

"I must go next door."

"And I forbid you. You're my patient."

"Then I discharge myself."

"You will sign the form that it's your responsibility?"

"Yes."

"All right. Nurse will get you the form. Until you sign you stay in bed." He was too worn out to be concerned. A dozen more willing patients were waiting for him anyway. His walk there and back down the corridor amounted to a welcome rest from people and injuries.

35

Bucken's balance and vision were better now. He tried to convince himself that the shotgun must have been seen by the nurse and picked up by the local CID men. If not, he was in greater trouble than ever before. If he was merely threatened by a masked but unarmed man, there was no justification for the damage he must have inflicted with that bunch of keys.

The nurse returned with the forms and a wheelchair. She had the good sense not to argue any more. He signed it all without reading the small print. She helped him into the wheelchair, put a blanket around his shoulders, then opened the door to wheel him out into the corridor.

"I may remember seeing that gun or whatnot if it's important to you ..."

"Not that important. But thanks for the thought."

The local CID Sergeant who had already questioned O'Leary briefed Bucken in the corridor. "He can hardly speak but he dished up a likely story, guv. He says you attacked him."

"You didn't find his shotgun?"

"Didn't know he had one. His story is that a rich junkie picked him up and was going to pay him for a one-off job. They wanted to come into the hospital and while chummy frightened the hell out of everybody with his monkey face in the stocking, the junkie would grab some drugs and blank prescription forms."

"But no weapons."

"No."

"I'm going in to see him."

"The doctor is very shirty already with us and chummy wants a lawyer."

"To hell with them all."

The whole right side of O'Leary's face seemed to be held in one piece by bandages. His right eye was covered, too. His chin was firmly held in position. According to the Sergeant, he had several fractures in the temple, cheekbone and jaw, lost a couple of teeth, and his face was cut right open from the temple all the way down to his chin.

"I hear we have your shotgun."

O'Leary stared at the ceiling with his one free eye.

"I think your best bet is to come to some understanding with me, chummy. There's going to be a stink because of the killing of my Sergeant." Bucken tried to sound convincing, but he knew he was rushing it in despair.

The pavement artist slowly turned his head a little toward the detective, and motioned him to come nearer.

"A right old pair we must look," said Bucken as he wheeled himself to the bed.

O'Leary could not move his jaw at all and even to whisper required a great effort matched only by Bucken's as he forced himself to stand up and lean over the bed. His head was throbbing again badly but, this time, his vision and balance did not abandon him.

"You sleep well, guv?"

"What's the joke, sweetheart?"

"If I were you, guv, I'd sleep lightly, very lightly from now on," he croaked. "You can expect visitors."

"I like visitors. Will they bring me presents?"

"Of a sort. There's a contract out to get you."

"Thanks for telling me." O'Leary must have been hurt more than he thought. This "warning" was his revenge to make him worried. Or was there more to it?

"Somebody wants you badly. It's worth a packet."

Judging from the attack on Hunt and then on himself, Bucken knew that it might be true. At any given time, there were at least half a dozen such underworld contracts out for gunning down troublesome policemen. Bucken knew all the other likely names on the current list. He would be in good company. But a contract was not his only worry at the moment. Best to drive to London right away and meet it all head on, he thought. Which was not the most appealing metaphor in the circumstances.

He had no doubts at all that he must warn Rattray about the leak and his own predicament before doing anything else. But it was not simple to make the decision and call him privately at home.

37

They belonged to the same year's police intake. They had become great friends during initial training at Peel House although their backgrounds differed sharply. Rattray's father, a retired general, profoundly despised the Police as a career, while Bucken's mother was suitably impressed by her fatherless fifth son's choice of a job and hoped that it would keep him out of prison—a reasonable assumption in London's postwar dockland.

The two young police constables discovered one another in a small, windowless back room, where gas masks and other oddments were stored, and where the storekeeper, an ancient copper, would let the young recruits enjoy "a glimpse at the unseemlier aspects of the visual arts for a modest consideration." The rumor was that the pictures, at that time a real rarity, had been borrowed from "official stock"—Scotland Yard had always been the largest collector of pornography, waiting as evidence for trials.

The similarity in their tastes was restricted to the two-dimensional—their girl friends and wives were more different than their backgrounds—but their friendship survived some of the severest tests, including the discovery that Rattray would become one of the true high fliers of the year's crop: he would be hand-picked for accelerated promotion, his spell on the beat would be shorter than anybody's, he would waste the minimum amount of time in any rank, and would be sent from course to course to emerge as a trained leader of men.

In that storeroom, among the gas masks and the naughty pictures—full-frontal nudity had not even been invented at the time—the two dreamed about running the Force one day. Bucken opted for detective work in the CID, Rattray was steered toward the top in uniform.

And then it happened. Twenty-one months before that early-autumn dawn, Rattray was appointed Assistant Commissioner/Crime, only two steps removed from the top of the entire Metropolitan Police. Both men took meticulous care to ensure that all their official contacts were correct, without any trace of favoritism or intimacy, even though, by that time, Bucken was the godfather of Ron and Timmy, the two Rattray boys, and the favorite adopted uncle of the girls, too. They knew that with great caution their friendship could probably tiptoe across this latest minefield laid between them, and the unwritten rule was "no private matters to be mentioned in the Big House" and "nothing about the Force" outside.

Yet the circumstances did not help the survival of their friendship. Under an ailing, weak Commissioner, marking time, there were serious disciplinary problems, the Force was riddled by infighting between plainclothes and uniformed potentates, questions in Parliament about police brutality and corruption, and the entire police at a loss concerning the role to play and the way to play it in modern society. No identity, no true morale, no *raison d'être* to hand down to new recruits. On the back of genuine social reformers and demonstrators with a cause, ruthless troublemakers and criminals were clamoring for fuller protection from police powers—but nobody paid much attention to the human rights of policemen.

Rattray was ready to fight it all. Stamping out corruption and brutality was his first target: without the clean name of the police he would never be able to deal with the accusers and the silent politicians. And just when he started, Bucken had run into a "spot of trouble" over the drug case. A carelessly dropped remark in anger: "I know there is corruption at the very top because the biggest villains are better informed than even the Commissioner"; and Bucken was sent on that wild goose chase around the coast. Even though it was an official assignment through the proper channels, it was known that Rattray had been the prime mover. Old hands regarded it as a betrayal of a friend, and a way of getting rid of anybody who might be seen as the new Assistant Commissioner's weak spot or even pet. Rattray's popularity took an immediate deep plunge, and when Bucken failed to resign to show what he thought of all this, colleagues began to misinterpret his loyalty and dedication: he must be afraid of the big wide world outside. Perhaps he would not get a decent job in industry or bank security because the necessary references would not be forthcoming . . .

Since then, their strictly private meetings became more and more spaced out, with no invitation to a "spot of Peel-housing," their code for a quiet chat over a jar, in the last eight months. Bucken visited the children whenever he could, but talked to Rattray only in front of the entire family. He knew about the AC's lonely struggles, but he had his own battles to fight. His plan was to squeeze some results out of the impossible and, by bringing the immigration racketeers to justice, leave the Force with a bang rather than a whimper.

So it was not easy to make that call now, and he considered himself lucky when Timmy answered the phone.

"Are you coming to play with me, Bucken?"

The little voice was full of surprised joy and genuine expectation, and reminded him of what he might have missed by not having a family. But he wondered if any father would receive a reaction like that to an unexpected call.

Timmy then gave way, reluctantly, to his mother, who alone still insisted on always reminding Bucken that he, like other mortals, also had a first name.

"Hullo, Quint, are you in town? Come and eat."

"Thanks, Mu, perhaps later. Is the great man around or is he already slaving away?"

"Neither. He took the day off and went down to the coast last night with Ron for a spot of fishing."

"Which coast?"

"Broadstairs? Ramsgate? Somewhere around there. Is it that urgent?"

"Yes."

"Your best bet is to come here. He'll phone home later on because Timmy's been poorly for a few days. Come and play with him."

"I'll try."

40

"Be here for lunch if you like. I have a special guest."

"Who?"

"Guess."

"I'm in a hurry."

"Sarah."

"Oh."

"Don't you want to see her?"

He touched the bandage. "I'm not sure. Perhaps not today."

There was a long pause. "Quint?"

"Yes?"

"Why don't you go back to her?"

"Ask her over lunch. And tell me when I get there."

He swayed as he put the receiver down. It must have been quite a crack. He was not sure if he was fit to drive the sixty miles.

Gordon (one-L) MacDougal was not looking forward to this Thursday. His driver had been taken ill and he was late; his wife was suffering her seasonal bout of social migraine (she ought to be prosecuted for wilful sex evasion); he was constantly blinking as a result of too much morning light being incompatible with his monu- mental brandy hangover; and he was bored and irritated by the prospect of going through the motions of argument, reasoning, reluctant headshaking and tooth-sucking until the obvious and inevitable decision to raise MLR again could be taken. In other words, from the moment his flagstaff figure had emerged from the car, the rumor spread in wild gusts around the City that the Deputy Governor of the Bank of England was not in the best possible mood.

The scheduled meeting with the new Chancellor offered another source of gloomy expectations. "The chap is a confirmed monetary illiterate," he had declared over dinner at the Reform the previous night, before the cause of his eventual hangover was reached. "I strongly suspect the man believes that a Treasury Bill is a stock character out of a Western, and he won't last long enough to learn that in the City gentlemen prefer bonds." Which was appreciated by all his tablemates as a delicately delivered innuendo on the Chancellor's known budding interest in the latest influential blond bombshell from the Australian political anterooms.

On his way home he had noted the full moon. Another foreboding, he knew. Ever since he had occupied his first seat behind a counter in a more ordinary bank, he had made it his duty and privilege to observe mankind through the bulletproof glass partition, and he safely concluded at a very early stage that the full moon brought out indeed the full range from right old ravers to the bemused potty ones. They came in such numbers, in fact, that he used to believe there was a direct routine jump out of the loony bin into the bank.

As he now crossed the main hall, he could already spot the first of the breed. The well-groomed little fellow with the pointed beard. Standard lunatic—even familiar. Not poor, quite obviously not, judging from the well-cut medium-gray suit, but probably somewhat feeble with that reverential manner toward the towering top-hatted gatekeeper in pink tails. The Deputy Governor was pleased to believe that he could script that conversation at the gate with a telepathic precision. "When I take over as Prime Minister, I hope I can rely on your full support and cooperation"—and the pink coat would give him every reasonable assurance to keep him happy until the next full moon. But other cranks would follow, and Kirby and his security chaps would have their periodic field day, sending him memos which he would mostly refuse to read: "It's not for me, old boy, wrong man, I'm afraid, it's for MacDougall, as you'll see . . ."

It was 1129 when Cutter-Smith surfaced from Bank station on the corner of Princess and Threadneedle

Streets. He could clearly envisage the Governor and the Directors gathering under the chandeliers in the pale-green-and-white grandeur of another age, the Court Room. He had about six minutes to kill. It made no actual difference, but he liked to stick to the plan. He crossed the road to the island, looked up at Wellington and admired the horse as if that was the purpose of his visit. He rested for two minutes on a bench, wondered if the evening paper posters would carry his name in big, big print in a few hours, then studied the massive, dirty-sand-colored building—his target.

The blind screen wall with the black gates, the balustrade on top, the other entrance in midair leading from nothing to nowhere and supported by two topless stone ladies and four males, three of whom displayed a full view of chipped genitals.

He then presented himself at the main gate. The porter was polite but firm.

"Can you tell me what it's all about, sir?"

"I'm afraid I can't, but it's most urgent. A matter of life and death."

"I understand, sir."

"I insist on seeing somebody on the Governor's immediate staff at once."

"Perhaps you could write in, sir."

It was no good. Nobody of substance would listen to him. But it had been foreseen that they might treat him as a crank. And it was expected that the greatest problem would be to convince everybody that this was no joke. So contingency plans were ready.

"All right, you'll be held responsible."

"That is understood, sir."

"You will also be responsible for delivering this letter to the Governor, and this one to the Cashier's Department, without any delay whatsoever."

"Without delay, sir."

The pink coat took the letters, held them gently by his fingertips, just a touch worried that they might explode at

43

any minute. His eyes were already on the plainclothes security guard hovering in the background. The guard shook his head almost imperceptibly—no, there was no need to detain the visitor, just get his name as a routine.

"Perhaps you'd care to leave your name and address, sir, in case they wish to contact you urgently ..."

"The name is Cutter-Smith, as may be seen together with the address on the back. Good day to you."

As he left with an air of somewhat hurt dignity, he knew that the letters would be delayed for bomb-screening, and then absorbed in the mass of internal mail for hours on end—by which time somebody might get hurt near Sheerness.

Unhurriedly, he sauntered along Threadneedle Street, stopped at the old shirtmaker's—by appointment to Their once-so-impressive Highnesses the Amir of Afghanistan and the Maharajah of Patiala—to see in the reflections in the window if somebody had followed him. Nobody paid any attention. He passed the nostalgic little office of the Commercial Cable Co., stopped at Bendicks and mentally chose a huge box of mints to buy on Collection Day, and flirted with cigars and expensive wines on display at Green's in the small square behind the Royal Exchange. That's what life was going to be like.

He sat on a bench until the telephone near the fountain became free, then called 219-3000.

"Houses of Parliament."

"Forty-five-forty-five, please."

The Prime Minister's secretary answered without any delay.

"My name is John Cutter-Smith. I must talk to the Prime Minister immediately." His voice was authoritative but he did not expect miracles. He was wondering if a tape recorder was already switched on and if security men were already listening in.

"Could you tell me what it's all about, please?"

"Naturally. If I cannot talk to the PM, you'll have to act or take the responsibility. I have demanded a million

44

pounds from the Bank of England or else a remote-controlled bomb will explode the *Richard Montgomery* wreck at Sheerness. The likely consequences are probably known to you, but full details are in the letters which I left at the Bank and which, I suspect, are not getting due attention. I strongly advise you to follow this up without delay. Good-bye."

"Hold on, you must ..."

He put down the phone and dialed the same number again. This time he asked for 4141. The Leader of the Opposition was also unavailable but the secretary was more impatient.

"If you keep interrupting me, you'll never know what this is all about and you'll be held responsible." Cutter-Smith liked to be in command of the situation.

He followed this up with a quick series of further calls to 4400, the Government Chief Whip, 3654 for the Lady Members' Lounge, and 3712 and 3714 for the underground car park entrance and exit respectively, leaving messages everywhere that the PM and the Leader of the Opposition should contact their private offices immediately on a matter of national emergency.

His last call went to 5311—Security Control. The way they answered the telephone, the questions and careful spelling of his name, the petty delaying tactics to give a chance to engineers tracing the call, told him all he wanted to know: those messages had created bedlam. First there must have been complaints to the switchboard: why had they put him through at all? What? He knew and asked for the correct extensions? How come? Then it must have dawned on them that if it was a hoaxer, it had to be a well informed one. Keep him on the line during the next call. And check with the Bank, of course.

Cutter-Smith rang off at once. He knew they were beginning to take him seriously. He would not give them an hour to conduct some inquiries, and then the next step.

He strolled down Bartholomew Lane, stopped to glance toward the Stock Exchange, then turned the corner into

Lothbury, the back of the Old Lady. Will anybody ever draw a cartoon: The Mugging of the Old Lady by Cutter-Smith the Younger?

He cherished the old print he had once picked up in Portobello Road. It was a fair reproduction of the original James Gillray cartoon—"Political Ravishment or The Old Lady of Threadneedle Street in Danger"—in which an old hag shouts "Murder! Murder!" although Pitt the Younger, both Prime Minister and Chancellor in 1797, tries to take only her precious gold, not her remaining life.

Seeing himself as the budding hero of the mugging cartoon, Cutter-Smith diverged into St. Margaret's Close, the barely three-feet-wide alley that led to the modern building tucked away behind the church—the club of the Bank. He used to dream about that club, while waiting for a decision and answer to his application. He planned to become a very active club member. He planned to be a typical Bank man. He came to this spot several times only to study Bank men's deportment, their gait and choice of clothes. He learned to appreciate the variations in medium grays. Now he came to say good-bye to a dream.

He returned to Lothbury, spared only a casual glance for the tall, metal-barred glass gates and the inner courtyard and more pink coats beyond, then cut through Tivoli Corner and completed his round by descending to Bank station once again. It was a pity that this was the full extent of his commando raid.

Only three stops to Holborn, then a five-minute walk to Bloomsbury Square, and down the ramp, along the route cars take into the underground garage. As if looking for a parked car there, he followed the spiral all the way down. He had already been down there so many times that he knew every crossing point and every exit, but the structure of two spirals running over each other like top and bottom edges of a corkscrew never ceased to amaze him. Just one final check for Collection Day: yes, after repairs, Levels No. 6 and 7, the bottom layers, were open to the public once again, providing parking space for 455 cars and allowing drivers a fairly long run in the dark.

The cars were parked on both sides, like spikes facing the walls, leaving a wide enough space in the middle even for mad, speeding drivers who enjoyed the constant turn and the screeching noise their wheels could produce in the peculiar acoustics of the spiral. Blue numbered parking slots on the way down ... an opening on the right after Blue 60, another after Blue 136, leading to the other spiral, the yellow one, where traffic flowed upward ... Yellow 394 and up for residents only ... from Yellow 430 more headroom ... then one more good turn and the barrier ... with a little extra parking space outside before the ramp up to the Liverpool Victoria Insurance Offices ...

On his way back to Holborn, he had a quick cup of coffee in the restaurant in the Sicilian Arcade, made sure that he had a friendly word with the manager and a waiter who were by now beginning to know him as a regular customer, and then returned by tube to the Bank.

He made no attempt to find out if anybody followed him. It did not matter any more. He would concentrate on killing time.

2

THE MUGGING OF THE "OLD LADY"

Bucken was in a hurry. Lunch with the Rattrays and Sarah. He could then talk to Rattray and warn him discreetly about the leak. And, more selfishly, he would seek his advice about this fight with the "unarmed" gunman.

The Jamaican nurse was still fussing with his bandage. "Can I give you a lift?" he asked without much conviction.

"You shouldn't drive, you know." From the bottom of a pile on her instruments trolley, she produced the bunch of keys at the end of the knotted handkerchief. "Is that yours?" He nodded. "Picked it up when we brought you in."

"Thanks." He stuffed the tinkling weapon down his breast pocket with routine precision so that, finally, only the edge of the linen showed.

"Shall I wash it for you? There's blood on it."

"You're a darling, but not now. I must run."

Run to pacify Maxine, run to reach London in record time, and run before he would ask the nurse's name, let her cook his breakfast, and give her a chance to make him forget that his entire career if not his life might come to a sudden and unpleasant end.

It was a warm morning but he felt shiverish. While examining the police chalk marks around the dark, dried patches on the road near his car, he slipped on the ancient calf-length trenchcoat with the wide collar that turned up by itself without any encouragement from him. In a flash he saw clearly for the first time the full, sentimental value of that coat, and realized that he ought to drop it and run from it. As he ran from all possessions. Besides, he had never actually owned a coat before that. Once he borrowed one as a child. Otherwise, his mother had declared that a coat was not an essential garment for masculine males—and Bucken agreed.

When the immigration ghost hunt began, the coast was ruled by bitterly cold gales, and Bucken was perpetually frozen stiff as he made it his duty to pound the seafront day after day, night after night, and familiarize himself with all the inhabitants and visitors of his new manor.

Then one night the Lad came up with the coat. "Found it," he said. "Somebody must have thrown it away."

"Or lost it."

The Lad shrugged his shoulders. "Borrow it for the night."

At dawn he spread it on a chain fence—and in the evening, when it was snowing, too, it was still there. For a year, Bucken never took it home. Just dumped it near the marina and used it when it was cold or raining. He knew that once the Lad had it cleaned. But they never spoke about it.

He wore it when he first met Maxine. She came in from sea so fast that her fourteen-foot speedboat, capable of doing thirty-two knots, mounted the landing stage and tossed her overboard. Bucken and the Lad fished her out. "Is this Casablanca, then?" was her way of saying thanks, as she hung on limply, without contributing the slightest bit to their effort.

"I don't know about Casablanca," Bucken snapped, "but it certainly isn't the Moon. We have gravity here, you know."

"Ah. Humphrey Bogart, I presume." She examined the full length of the coat and the wearer as she came up level with the men. "I'm cold." He unbuttoned the coat. "Wouldn't dream of it," she said. "Let's share it."

"Here we go again," he thought. It was easy to spot that she was what he called a "drip-dry girl"—roll her in dust, motor oil or a haystack, soak her thoroughly in rain or sea, then let her dry, and she will be good as new. But he could not foresee that she would be the end of an era by driving all other girls away from him for a full five months now.

How that era had begun at all was still a mystery to him. He had to acquaint himself with all the comings and goings around the harbor, and because at the beginning everybody was a potential sus, he watched men, women, beasts and floating objects, fishermen registered with customs and excise, unregistered fishermen, pleasure boats, those who reported "going foreign" and exposed themselves to "anything to declare," and those who obviously managed to get away with the odd bottle of contraband. He was more interested in passengers, and the berthing master always tipped him off—in vain until recently.

As a young PC he never went short of spare and crumpet, later he had his fair share of steady girl friends, and finally Sarah, but he always had to "work for it" and "talk and joke my guts out for getting it"—until that six-berth cruiser came in. He had to search it, and to this day he wondered what was hidden on board or what else made that incredible model girl virtually seduce him. And if that was a miracle, it was certainly not a solitary one. Suddenly the marina was teeming with those drip-dry girls who, apparently, all wanted to sleep with Bucken between their guest appearances, he imagined, on the pages of some glossy magazine.

He could never work out how in rotation they always managed to pack the harbor bars and fool about on the tied-up boats. Some worked, some whored, regularly or temporarily, some were rich, some lived off the land, but they all had plenty of time, a good selfish sexual appetite, and an unselfish habit of passing him around like a particularly tasty concoction just out of the shaker—here, sister, have a sip, it's divine.

"I must be some fetish, a belated sexual discovery at forty-two," he once told Rattray, "but I'll be damned if I chase them away only because their motives are unclear to me."

It sometimes looked to him as if an entire "shamelessly and frighteningly young generation of women" had decided that Bucken of the Port Authority was Experience personified, Experience to be shared by all, Experience with The Sad Smile being the only true gateway to Living.

Maxine, of course, scoffed at it all: "It's the coat, Bucken, that automatic turn-up collar that does it. But the magic is theirs as they hail the day that sees it rise ravished from their longing eyes. Alleluya, alleluya! Until I stuff that coat up their pussies and teach them to hail the Virgin Mary for a change."

She appeared on the scene at the right time, when the sexual miracle was beginning to wear thin, and when he even offered the Lad a share of the coat. Over a bottle of freshly confiscated brandy—somehow, a friendly customs officer had failed to register the seizure—Bucken once told the young sergeant in a third-degree (philosophical) drunkenness what Maxine's arrival had taught him: "The disadvantage of men is that we have no honorable, socially and sexually acceptable excuse for saying 'no' without shame to somebody so eminently desirable, because the implications are too disastrous for the ego and male reputation."

Now the Lad was dead, Bucken had no intention of saying "no" to Maxine, and Bogart's coat failed to keep the shivering in check.

Maxine knew it as soon as he had opened the door. She failed to swear at him and even her "joined the Sikhs or something?" came out halfheartedly as she stared at his bandaged head and the coat. The room was hot and she stood there topless, in front of the vast expanse of the picture window. He concluded, "You must be mad," in a friendly tone. "You seem to forget that the flat is overlooked by the entire figure-conscious staff of the Inland Revenue."

"I'm not mean."

He tried to go on and on, about her curtain phobia, but it was no good. It was just delaying all the inevitable questions while his kneecaps were slowly emulsified by the effort of standing up. Sarah would now make a cup of coffee, sit down, and wait. And wait. She would know that all that was to be said would soon be said. Maxine was only twenty-five and never bothered to learn words like patience or restraint. Yet now she leisurely proceeded to roll a cigarette while he took off his coat. It was a pleasant and reassuring sight which he always found sexually exciting. She held out the unfinished cigarette and he dutifully licked the edge of the thin paper. If only he could sleep now for a few minutes.

She lit up. The usual opening of the floodgates to questions and more questions. The tip of the cigarette opened up like a fast-blooming rose and a speck of glowing tobacco detached itself. She did not flinch as it fell on her thigh and turned into ash. He could not understand the delay. What happened? Where have you been? How, when and why? He was dying to tell her.

"You ought to have a nap."

A miracle. "You think so?"

She nodded.

"Ten minutes then. You wake me up. Promise?"

It had happened only once before, on the day of the unexpected and disastrous run on the pound in New York, Frankfurt and Zurich simultaneously, that anybody chanced to take upon himself the Governor's eternal wrath by disturbing the Court. When now Kirby, the security chief, decided to do just that, he had at least the Prime Minister's full backing which would count, he hoped, as some degree of exculpation. Yet he sought to reduce his guilt by addressing his note to Deputy Governor MacDougal instead of the chief himself.

The massive pink coat whose ill fate it was to deliver the note wished he was back with the paras making only a drop into well-guarded enemy fortifications. As he opened the heavy mahogany double doors and entered under the pillared arches, he knew that, in the sudden silence, his gentlest considerate shuffle on the 150-color carpet sounded like mindless squarebashing which might produce immediate cracks in the fine wedding-cake decoration of this hall of halls. And the full gauntlet had yet to be run. Along the vast expanse of the mahogany table, behind seven directors' chairs, under another seven men's gaze from the far side and four more pairs of eyes at the two ends.

While MacDougal glanced through the note, the hapless pink coat retreated: was he meant to leave or wait for the floor to open and swallow him? He saw that Grandma, as the Governor was generally known in the square mile of pound sterling, questioned One-L MacDougal with a slightly raised eyebrow. The note was passed to him. Foreseeing even this eventuality, Kirby had kept it as brief as he could: "PM requests (yes, that would impress them, requests, not commands or something foolish) immediate attention to matter of national security." (A masterpiece, Kirby thought, as he treble-checked the spelling of the Deputy's name.)

National security did not qualify for an interruption of the Thursday morning session, but Kirby's idea of letting the Deputy deal with it was acceptable. The shrinking pink coat had survived his mission.

Kirby was waiting outside the door. Although he would usually succumb to the temptations of prevarication and candy-floss sentences, his briefing about the Sheerness threat was now so efficient that it reinforced MacDougal's firm belief that only true emergencies brought anything out of such flabby ex-policemen of beat-pounding stupidity.

The PM, in consultation with the Leader of the Opposition, wanted a full report without delay, treating the threat as something much more sinister than a mere hoax. He insisted on restricting information about the threat to the barest minimum number of people on a carefully considered need-to-know basis. That was how at Scotland Yard, in the absence of the Commissioner and Rattray, only Deputy Commissioner Carron and Commander Allerton of the Special Branch heard about it. Both were quick to appreciate the political problem beyond criminal and security implications: on the brink of elections, the PM and his opponent, his predecessor and likely successor, might have to bear considerable blame for lack of foresight and the wrong kind of caution demonstrated by leaving the wreck unsalvaged to this day. They would have, of course, impressive answers to embarrassing questions in the House. They could refer to several underwater surveys, expert evaluations of the risks of action and inaction, the staggering costs of raising the ship, and the tremendous logistic problems of moving entire towns and industries out of the vast danger zone perhaps for weeks. But even perfectly valid answers would not prevent a scandal. Any leak to the media would further complicate the problems not only by stirring up unwelcome publicity but also by inducing thousands of sightseers to jam the roads and pack the shores in and around the Isle of Sheppey, connected to the mainland by a single bridge.

Kirby's room was guarded by detectives and his own security men. His secretary had been evacuated, thus creating an empty room to act as a buffer and prevent even accidental eavesdropping. Not that there was too much to overhear. Allerton was busy grilling the doorman who could remember quite clearly the "caller in question" as being between forty and sixty years of age, nondescript appearance, "not very tall, but then not too short" with a "moustache or beard or other hairy facial feature" ... in other words, virtually nothing.

"And he had the letters on him."

"Yes, sir."

"At about ... ?"

That was the opportunity MacDougal was waiting for.

"Between eleven-thirty-four and eleven-thirty-five, give or take a second or two," he declared, and with that he took the stage. "Smallish chap, very neat, with pointed beard, wearing medium-gray suit."

"Were you there, sir, I mean ..."

"No, I'm not on gate duty, so to speak," he said with a guffaw, "but I was passing by and I happen to have an eye for character."

At last the letters had been recovered from the internal mail. One requested the payment of a million pounds within twenty-four hours—"details as set out in the letter to the Chief Cashier"—and threatened a devastating explosion "on Sunday, at thirteen hundred precisely, with a seventy-two-hour countdown starting at thirteen hundred today." The writer also offered to "further expound the relevant facts in a personal discussion with duly appointed officials if this can be arranged in confidence, because it would be most unwise to allow certain irresponsible elements to gain access to such explosive information."

"Bloody pompous mugger," muttered Allerton with an apologetic gesture toward MacDougal.

The Deputy paid no attention to him. "Seventy-two hours? Seventy-two and a half, in fact ... Surely, any site can be fully protected from an attack by then."

"The bomb must already be in position in the wreck. In the calls to Parliament, remote control was mentioned." Allerton was openly pleased to score.

"Then it's a matter for bomb disposal. I used to have a few very good chaps attached to my regiment during the Malayan emergency."

"Bomb disposal under water may not be that simple, sir. Besides, it's an ammunition ship, where even the search for a bomb may be an unduly dangerous operation," said Allerton, blindly exposing himself to the easy riposte which would put him in his place:

"I don't know about you, Commander, but I usually leave such technical trivia to the experts who are trained

55

for that and no more. Besides, it is my clear impression that we're dealing with a hoaxer."

"A clever one, if I may say so," volunteered Kirby though halfway through he wished he had not.

"Clever? Then why volunteer to talk to us? Why supply his name and address? I have no doubt that both details will turn out to be correct."

"We're already checking that," said Allerton, "and I agree, it's probably the man's real name. But that's just what worries me. He's sure of himself. He's not afraid of arrest."

"Because he's mad. It's the full moon that plays the tricks on them. Tomorrow, he'll cry when he thinks about this mad moment. But, today, he's firmly convinced that he can run away with a million under his arm."

That was the trap Allerton waited for. The Deputy had not yet read the second letter, to the Chief Cashier. Perhaps he thought it was some technical trivia.

The letter dwelt at great length upon the subject of demanding only £900,000 strictly in "used £20 notes." It warned strongly "against any numerical order or markings of any kind, including visual, chemical or electronic identification processes." Luckily, the Chief Cashier's office was busy preparing the Bank Returns for the Thursday publication ritual, and so the letter had remained unopened—a fact which not only reduced the number of people privy to the proceedings, but also spared the Cashier's ulcer from a potential untimely perforation. For that letter also explained how the notes should be assembled with the help of the Issue Office under him, and suggested that the Government might consider raising the cash by issuing some Treasury Bills, the cabinet's IOU's for short-term loans—as if the Cashier had never heard of all this before.

"Why only nine-hundred thousand pounds?" asked MacDougal when reaching this point and growing very bored with the technical details.

"Because, lunatic under the influence of the moon

though he may well be," replied Allerton, "he does not propose to run for it. The remaining one-hundred thousand pounds is to be transferred with no strings attached to an account with the Hanover Square branch of his bank. And he does have an account there under the name of Cutter-Smith."

The pause was noticeable only to those exceptionally sensitive to the rhythm of repartee. "Which only goes to show," said MacDougal, "how right the PM is when he insists on regarding the case as one of considerable gravity." He was not Deputy Grandma for nothing.

It would have been difficult to add anything else to that—except that Kirby was not exactly cut out for bearing the weight of meaningful silence: "Which leaves us with the task of preparing the various specialist reports, while it would be most advisable to locate our suspect without further delay."

Kirby? Kirby ... Kirby ... MacDougal was more convinced than ever that nepotism was not yet dead.

Almost opposite the Bank, on the right of Mansion House, Cutter-Smith strode a short distance down Walbrook. He stopped, facing a tall Victorian blue metal stand, marked Police Public Call Post No. 61 for free use, promising that "advice and assistance" would be "obtainable immediately" and that "officers and cars respond to urgent calls." On that Thursday, no call could be more urgent than his.

"Listen to me, and listen carefully," he said to the desk sergeant who answered the phone. "Are you taking notes?"

"Your name, sir ..."

"There's no time. Ready?"

"Carry on, sir. I'm ready."

"Good." He looked up but could not see the Bank. Pity. "Then listen. You must contact the police in Sheerness, Isle of Sheppey, without delay. They must send out all boats they can commandeer to form a circle of about two hundred feet diameter around the No. 1 marker buoy at the *Richard Montgomery* wreck."

"Could you tell me . . . ?"

"You're wasting time. Have you got it so far?"

"Yes, yes . . ."

"They must not go nearer and they must not let anybody enter the circle. For that buoy will blow up at thirteen-forty-five, sixty-one minutes from now, precisely. Thirteen-forty-five, understood?"

"Hey, what's this? Are you IRA or something?"

By that time Cutter-Smith knew that officers and cars were about to respond to the call. The Sergeant suddenly could not hear well. Could you spell this, sir, could you repeat that, sir? They would soon pick him up. But at least he tried to give them extra time by impressing the urgency upon the Sergeant.

"You must understand, this is serious. I'm trying to help. You must alert Sheerness at once or you may cause damage, injury or even death. But there will be no trouble if you do as I say. It's a controlled, limited, warning explosion. Plays only a minor part in the demand made this morning to the Bank of England."

The more he said the crankier he sounded. He did not mind. He wanted the Sergeant to keep him on the line.

"At last," said Cutter-Smith as he felt a not too heavy hand on his shoulder and turned to face a couple of officers. "Yes, I'm willing to assist you in your inquiries, I'm ready to answer any questions even under oath, but first, if you wish to make yourselves popular, take me to the Bank of England and ask the Governor or the Chief of Security if they wish to see me."

The full moon does it, thought the driver of the patrol car, wondering what made them go for the Bank. He never thought that the head of the Special Branch would almost hug him for letting curiosity get the better of him and asking the Bank doorman if anybody wished to see the bearded chap in the car. Just for fun.

"So what's the shit you want me to clean up this time? If a window is broken you call me. If a paperbag goes pop you call me. If the fart is stuck sideways in your arse you call me. And you call me late, too. What was it to be? Thirteen-forty-five?"

"Yes, sir." The Detective Inspector at Sheerness held the receiver a good six inches away from his ear. He knew that Chief Inspector Walsh, a former mine clearance diver of the Navy, had been having a tough time lately.

"So what do you want from me? A telephone diagnosis? I'm a fucking explosives wallah not a fucking witch doctor, you know. It's already thirteen-o-three and I'm thirty fucking miles from you with fucking holidaymakers laid from end to end in between."

The Inspector waited patiently. The short outburst would not only cool the bomb-disposal man but also give him time to think.

"I've no private helicopter and I'm not the Wright brothers or the fucking birdman of Alcatraz. So listen. You still have a diver-geezer by the name of Oaks or Pine or something botanical in your outfit?"

"Elms, sir, Sergeant Elms."

"Good. I used him once on a job."

"He's already on his way to the station."

"So am I. You can call me in the car, on PC, Papa Charlie three. Got it?"

The blame for the eighteen minutes' delay since Cutter-Smith's first call could not really be put on any one cog in the wheel although the Inspector was hoping to find a suitable culprit. His most likely candidate was the station Sergeant who took the original call from Post No. 61: a light buoy and an old wreck did not seem to be very significant targets to the City man, he suspected a hoaxer, and anyway the patrol would soon pick chummy up. More delay because of that garbled message that they would take him to the Bank of England instead of the nick, and then the line was bad, and the Sheerness man insisted, "You've got to be joking, that's an old ammo ship, dead dangerous, you've got to be joking." A young DC remembered seeing some "interference with light buoy" report in the morning, and wanted to look it up before tracking down the Inspector—another few minutes gone— and then the nearest bomb-disposal man had to be chased from pub to pub in and around Canterbury.

Elms did not find it funny when they woke him up, and the breakfast in his stomach seemed to shrink into a heavy, sticky lump of dumpling when he heard for what job he was about to volunteer. If it was serious and not a prank, it should be something for the Navy.

On his way out to the wreck, donning the old dry suit, he spoke to Papa Charlie 3.

"What sort of fucking visibility can you expect?"

"Nowt to nothin', sir. Just all the muck the tide can bring."

"Christ." Walsh watched the motorcycle escort trying to clear a path for him on and off the road along the grass verge. Normally he shouted and swore a lot but bombs and threats and the risk had long ceased really to excite him below the surface. Mostly it was just a job to do, a job he knew inside out. But this was different. It not only embittered him in a figurative sense but also actually filled his mouth with bilious saliva. For years he had warned and warned all conceivable authorities about the *Montgomery*. One day, some fucking fool ... This might be the day.

"Elms, are you there?"

"Sir."

"Listen. I want you to be very careful."

You could say that again, thought Elms, and rechecked his air bottle. His eyes scanned the estuary where another boat with younger professional divers of the Kent Constabulary might appear at any moment.

"Rule number one. You don't touch anything."

"Impossible, sir, I can look for the stuff only with my fingers."

"I mean if you find anything. It may be attached to the anchor or the anchor chain or the buoy itself or even a separate float tied to the buoy. You're looking for a sealed box or a tube, probably not very large. It's unlikely that just touching it lightly should set it off or else the waves would have done it for you. Besides, it's said to be timed, so probably you're okay."

"Thank you, sir." He slipped his hand through the eye splice at the end of the short line that would connect him to the PC of some diving experience who volunteered to help—if the professionals could not arrive in time.

"Will you have a DUCK set down there?"

"No sir. Wouldn't even know how to use that phone."

"Fuck. You'll have to use your lifeline to send a signal as soon as you find something."

"My buddy could . . ."

An amateur radio man would have heard a fine selection of four-letter words even though Walsh tried to be brief, saying, "No buddy-diving this time, you go down on your own. I don't want any line entangled with that anchor chain."

"But the regulations . . ."

"Fuck the regulations."

No good, sir, they will only multiply, Elms meant to say but did not. "As you wish, sir."

"What would be your normal emergency signal?"

"Four Bells."

"Why not cymbals, trumpets and farts?" He always disliked the expression short, sharp bells as opposed to long, steady and distinct pulls. "Okay, devise something different to signal if you locate anything suspicious. Then come up at once and report verbally. Is that clear?"

"Yes, sir. We're about fifty yards from the buoy now."

"Right. Stop at thirty and swim the rest of the way.'

Still no sign of the divers. Elms sat up on the edge of the boat. "Two pulls if I find something on or near the anchor, three pulls if it's on the chain, four pulls if it's on the bilge of the buoy itself," he suggested, but the Inspector in the boat disagreed, perhaps only to show authority: "If it's on the buoy, you just surface."

Elms bit on the mouthpiece and jumped into the water.

He swam on the surface to the buoy and watched several boats spreading out on the horizon to divert all traffic from the immediate neighborhood. The tide was already running high—it must be 1320 or so. He checked it on his borrowed diver's watch and felt pleased to be almost dead right. 1322. If the phone call was not a hoax, and if this buoy bomb was really a small one intended to be only a warning, the villain must have planned it carefully: at high tide the *Monty* would be least vulnerable. But Elms failed to gain reassurance from the thought.

He gave a long pull on the line, just to inform the Inspector that he was going in, then he ducked. The tide carried a lot of sand but visibility was better than he had expected. He could see his hand as he reached out toward the buoy and almost right away he spotted it: a piece of sealed tube, attached to the bottom of the buoy in a messy maze of wires. Kind of scaffolding pole, he guessed, and noted that, at one end, a watch-size rubber disc was attached by a cable which passed through the seal.

A couple of minutes later he was back in the boat waiting impatiently to get through the heavy radio traffic that dirtied the air between him and Walsh. "The disc may be the timer," he ventured to comment as he made his report.

"Your big fat arsehole is the timer," mumbled Walsh without anger, and noted yet another worried look from his driver—yes, yes, radio traffic was there for all to hear, so what? "If it's a timer, why isn't it inside the tube? Would be easier to seal." And why was it fixed to the buoy itself? To reduce the risk of setting off the ammo in the wreck? And was it there for all to see?

"Listen, Elms. I'm transferring to a motorbike but I still might not make it in time. So it's all up to you when you go down once more. Right?"

"I'm with you."

"This time you can take your buddy. Check if there's any cable or line running down the anchor chain from the device. If not, and only if you're quite sure that there's no connection, fasten a couple of tow lines to the buoy. Do it so that if we tow it slowly, the buoy will have a fair chance to stay upright. Got it?"

"Yes, sir."

"Good man. Then go down as far as the anchor and release or cut the chain. Whichever is less shaky. Under no circumstances are you supposed to touch the device. Is that clear?"

"Yes, sir."

Walsh wished he was there himself. "Repeat it."

Bloody fool. "I'm not to touch the thing."

"Get on with it. And let me speak to the Inspector."

Walsh insisted that the tow lines should be at least fifty yards long, that the paddles should be used rather than the engine to keep the speed down to a minimum, and that everybody taking part in the operation should pray once the towing had begun. He would have preferred to lend them his mascot, a small piece of Belfast concrete, too.

The buoy was still on tow when the Inspector noted 1345. The second hand just tripped over the 5 on his watch when he heard a ridiculously faint "puck." The buoy shook and, held by a rope, keeled over. The damage seemed minimal. The device was gone. If no precautions had been taken, the buoy would have just floated away from the wreck and sunk.

The Inspector decided that nobody should go near the scene until Walsh arrived. Elms suggested that the diver unit should eventually search the area for parts of the device before the retreating tide could carry them out to sea. Which earned him an officer's approval dressed in the old "that's just what I thought" formula.

The heat of a pale sun failed to penetrate London's only genuine Wren church licensed to sell alcoholic beverages. A small crowd was already gathering around the altar area occupied by an Australian string quartet, while a large crowd was scrambling for beer and salads in the crypt below.

An impressive matron of pink silver hair and bejeweled

spectacles dragged a hapless old man from arch to arch exclaiming each time, "Now isn't that neat, honey? Isn't that neat?" He nodded but that was not good enough. "You tell me, honey, isn't that neat?"

"Neat it is, honey, that's right."

"Lucky we heard about these snack concerts at all. I'd say we're the only tourists here, today, what do you say, honey?"

"Neat. Very, very neat, I'd say."

A regular or an observer of sharper eyes and ears might have disagreed. He would also have noticed that in a corner of this political no-man's-land, sandwiched between Conservative and Labour party headquarters, a pantomime of The Truly Fortuitous Meeting was played out by two tall, distinguished, but otherwise nondescript and certainly nontouristy gentlemen. They kept close but well beyond the suspicious limits of a huddle, pitched their voices low, smiled incessantly and spoke mostly toward the walls which were too thick to have ears.

They, too, were glad about the opportunity—anywhere else, reporters and other gossips might have attached undue significance to the urgent meeting of two men who shared a declared interest in matters of security but served on opposite sides of the mostly eighteenth-century square. While one was the current Prime Minister's confidant, the other still hoped to return to No. 10 with his master.

"How kind."

"Not at all, not at all. It's to our mutual, even national advantage to act in concert, no pun intended, of course. Have you reached any conclusions?"

"No, but anything spectacular is to be avoided, I'd say. May I assume that this would not differ substantially from your own reaction?"

"That, I suppose, would not be an arguable presumption ... provided of course that we're fully informed about developments."

"Naturally."

"It may, of course, turn out to be a hoax."

"Indeed."

"And if not?"

"Well, that's the point. Not only the coming political events but also national interest may necessitate that we comply with the demand. Temporarily, of course."

"Via confidential channels, I suppose."

"Indeed. For it could be rather embarrassing to our distinguished predecessors ..."

"As indeed to our successors. So may I take it that you propose to declare the subject untouchable, no matter what, on either side?"

"No political capital to be made of it, to be precise."

"Quite. Provided we're kept in the picture."

"Naturally. Another drink?"

"No, I think we'd better face the music then, wouldn't you agree?"

The four detectives, one of them a young woman, worked methodically. Winnie was plying them with tea and even put out the half bottle of Christmas-leftover sherry hoping to find out what exactly they wanted. They had produced a search warrant but she did not quite believe that they were police. They had told her that a wife was not compelled to say anything but she could hardly keep quiet.

"Yes, he insisted that it should be kept in the bedroom. It's quite new, as you can see. It's the biggest suitcase we have, and he said it would hold nine hundred thousand pounds. Is that why you are here? Has he done something silly?"

"Wouldn't know, ma'am, just a job to do. Hope we won't disturb you for long."

"I don't mind. If he's done something stupid, it's only right he should pay for it. Mind you, I sort of half-expected something like this."

"You don't need to say anything, but if you do, we may have to use it in evidence."

"I'm not surprised. Not at all. At his best he is a sort of Jekyll and Hyde. You know what I mean? He does try to be good, I'm not saying he doesn't, but then deep down, you know, he just can't help it. I mean arranging all that money-smuggling out of Africa and all that. And you want to know something? I don't think that he was even paid for it. He just did it because his inclination is to be on the wrong side of the law. That's what I think. Or he's mad. Perhaps I should have taken him to a psychiatrist, but then it's not easy, I mean what would it look like if I, as his wife, complained that he was mad? These things get out of the bag around here in no time you know. Just as I could tell you a thing or two about the neighbors. If you had time, I mean."

They were in no hurry. Part of their job was to remain there as long as possible. The telephone line was already being tapped by special authorization. They had to stay with Mrs. Cutter-Smith to prevent her from making any move that might help her husband or those who were behind him. But they disliked the job utterly for they had been kept in the dark. Search the ground-floor flat. Pick up any addresses, notes, telephone numbers, look out for weapons and explosives. Bug every nook, use the full range of miniature transmitters the Yard can supply. But no reason given. Crazy to work like that.

"When will he be back?"

"Soon, we hope."

"Where is he?"

"Couldn't exactly tell. Helping with our inquiries, that's all."

"What's it all about?"

"Wouldn't know, ma'am. Honest."

"More tea?"

"No, thanks."

"Spot of sherry then."

"Not just now, but thanks all the same. What did you say, where was the money to come from?"

"Me? I didn't say anything. He never told me. Will you be long?"

"Hard to tell."

She picked up her walking stick to emphasize her disability and limped to the kitchen. One man accompanied her.

Through a haze, Bucken heard the gentle purr of the new bedside telephone Maxine had just had installed and saw the silhouette of her naked figure emerge from the bathroom. With all the venetian blinds down, he was not sure if he was still asleep or not.

"No, I'm sorry, he still hasn't shown up ... Yes, of course I'll get him to call you at once ..." She now noticed that his eyes were open and winked at him. "Yes, I fully understand that it's very urgent."

Bucken turned and his head hurt. He slowly raised his hand, and the feel of the bandage wiped away the fog from his mind like a magic wand. In a fraction of a second, he saw the Lad hanging, the Lad dead, the Jamaican nurse, O'Leary with the gun, O'Leary with the wound, the whole sickening night simultaneously. He tried to grab the phone but Maxine was quicker. She replaced the receiver and jumped into bed with him.

"Are you all right, dear?"

"Was that call for me?"

"Can I get you anything?"

"Who was it?"

"Are you hungry?"

"The Job?" He looked at his watch: 1718. "Christ. Was that your ten minutes?"

"I'll get you a drink. Scotch? ... All right, they want you urgently. It's always urgent if they want you. Can't you be sick or enjoy a dash of privacy?" And as he was already dialing the local police: "We, too, have some unfinished business here, you know." Then shrugged her shoulders. "All right, they've already called twice, but you never even stirred. You weren't asleep, you were out, cold, what was I to do?"

Listening to the commotion at the other end of the line

as they tried to find the senior CID man on duty, Bucken struggled to keep a straight face: she began clowning, wriggling like a lovesick monkey.

At last an Inspector was on the line: "Your London chief is raving mad at you. Where have you been?"

"What's up?"

"A chopper is waiting for you at the old airstrip. How soon can you be there?"

"Is it about Hunt?"

"They don't send Naval helicopters to prevent a Sergeant's death let alone investigate it, do they?"

Bucken had a thirty-second wash-and-brush-up and asked Maxine to give him a Scotch and dial Rattray's home number at the same time.

Muriel answered the telephone and did not sound pleased to hear his voice. "You never turned up."

"I'm sorry."

"None of my business, Quint, but Sarah was really looking forward to it."

It was hard to ask about Sarah in front of Maxine: "Er, still there?"

"Sarah?"

"Yes."

"Of course not, and if you want a friend's honest opinion ... well, never mind. But if you want my work-addict husband, the answer is no once again. You should have married him, you know. He put Ron on the train alone while he flew to London. Didn't even call me."

"Did you say flew to London?"

"Some helicopter picked him up. You'll find him in the office, I'm sure, by now."

Maxine was in an equally hostile mood when Bucken prepared to leave: "I'm sure it was some CID bigwig who invented Immaculate Conception to prove that there was no need for police officers ever to spend the night at home."

*

68

During the short drive—with flashing lights, siren and incessant wheel-screeching—from London's heliport to New Scotland Yard, Bucken removed and stuffed into his pockets most of the bandages to avoid the standard "here comes our hero" treatment. He was also anxious not to give Commander Allerton the idea that he might use his injury as an excuse for anything that had happened.

Whatever in comfort and facilities the new building could offer, Bucken disliked the lot. He was convinced that the revolving triangular nameplate was only the leftover of a TV commercial, and that the entrance hall, which lacked only piped-in background music to qualify for a second-class hotel lobby, would never impress or sufficiently frighten anybody brought in for a friendly questioning. But he was wrong about the bandage: Allerton did not even bother to ask about the wound. He was tenser and terser than ever when he briefed Bucken about the *Montgomery* job, ending with his usual nonquestion:

"Okay. Any questions? Lots of questions. Naturally. It's for you to answer them."

"You said the bomb in the wreck was radio-controlled."

"That's right."

"Can't we jam it? We could flood all possible wavelengths. There can't be that many under water."

Here was another pleasant opportunity for Allerton to score by using the initial information he had already gathered from the Admiralty Experimental Diving Unit's underwater communications specialists in Portsmouth. "As I understand it," he said, "the transmission to the bomb could be in ordinary speech or, more likely, by telemetry, which is electronically coded information. Probably, the message is only a simple code telling the bomb to go off or kindly refrain from doing so. As you suggested, we can, indeed, surround the entire area with an electronic shield which is a field of high level random noise, but the risk is that some of the noise might accidentally trigger off a defensive device that could detonate the bomb. Are you with me?" Allerton was enjoying himself. It was not often that he could tell Bucken something new.

"How about some physical shielding that would only keep out any transmission?"

"Possible but a vast operation. As you may know, though you're not supposed to, we've tried something like this with oil drilling platforms in the north. Hell of a job and totally unpracticable. Besides," and the smile of a mental orgasm flooded his face, "besides, my boy, you've failed to grasp the evil bloody genius of the plan."

Allerton paused for effect and Bucken was growing exceptionally impatient. "Which is . . ."

"Which is that the bomb is timed to go off on Sunday. If we decided to pay up, chummy or the whole bloody gang will send out a message telling the detonator to spare us. This will be some time between tomorrow noon and Sunday, presumably."

"At which point we move in."

"If we want to risk an explosion in retaliation, that is. They merely switch off the timer and, so they say, it would then reset itself for another countdown over some pre-determined period. Admittedly, they'd have to keep switching-off-resetting weekly or monthly, but that's not too hard work for a secure million, is it?"

"We could detect the code by listening in."

"Yes, we could, by placing a vast number of hydro-phones on the bottom all over the Estuary, but anybody who devised the receiver/decoder would have been idiotic not to include a small programmed package to respond to a different code every time. Extra cost? Couple of quid."

"So you think we have a specialist behind it."

"Not necessarily. The whole timing/coding mechanism, just a handful of electronic circuit chips, could be put together by a good telephone engineer or a decent telly repairer—if such a creature exists at all—for less than a hundred pounds. Transmitter? One of the commercially available diver-to-diver models could be adapted by a conscientious schoolboy, though he would have to cut down quite a bit on tuck to save something like a grand."

"Where could the transmission come from?"

"Anywhere within up to a mile. So the trade says. That would rule out transmission from land—except perhaps the tip of the Isle of Grain or Sheerness—and necessitate the use of a boat which could be noticed in the vicinity. But how do we know that they have not anchored any number of receiver-retransmitter stations on the bottom in the Southend-Shoeburyness-Sheerness triangle? Problem: the transmitter would have to be under water—dangling innocently even from the end of a fishing rod—and the signal would have to travel in a straight line, avoid all the deflections and bounces that may reroute the message. Because if the coded signals arrive at fractionally delayed intervals, the receiver may get confused and give the wrong instruction to the detonator. Mind you, that would be mainly our concern, not theirs, I suppose, after the payment of the million."

Bucken looked out of the window. From high above, the town and the Thames looked too toylike to be seriously threatened. "And the threat could go on forever," he said.

"And longer."

"With perhaps a demand of ten million next time."

"A possibility which has not escaped my attention or stretched my imagination beyond its limits," quipped Allerton and produced a sheaf of technical literature and typed notes. "Bit of bedtime reading for you, son, except that there might not be much bedtime for you just now. We're a bit pushed, you might say."

"Then why . . ." Bucken meant to ask why, if there was such tremendous urgency, he had not been paged nation-wide any earlier, but he chose to keep quiet when Rattray entered wrapped in a whirling cloud of cigar smoke. Allerton watched the two men and they knew it: while the Commander only disliked Bucken and probably envied his talent, success and ardent disinterest in office politics, he simply hated Rattray who was a full decade younger, higher in rank and a much better politician than himself. Ever since he and most of the Yard had the impression that Rattray was letting an old friend down to show off impartiality, Allerton stood up for Bucken as much as he could.

Only a couple of weeks earlier, the Commander had even ventured to hint that Bucken could turn to him if there was any further nagging from Rattray. The implication was that Bucken was not without friends at C.O. and unfair treatment of officers was not necessarily to be tolerated. But Bucken chose to ignore the message. He could handle his own friendship or even professional relationship with Rattray or anybody else. Except that right now he had to shake off an irritating little suspicion that he might be wrong after all. Rattray wore an open-neck shirt and took care to appear cool and correct, even contemptuously formal, as if to make up for the lack of his customary armor of business suit, white shirt and the inevitable polka-dot tie—an old police college graduation present of more cheerful days from Bucken.

"I'm sorry to hear you had an unpleasant experience this morning. I hope you're better now." And before Bucken could answer: "Concerning the job in hand . . ."

The phone rang and Allerton excused himself. As soon as the door was shut behind him, Bucken turned to Rattray. "I must talk to you."

"Go ahead."

"Not like that. It must be Peel-housing. Where can we meet?"

"You mean right away?"

"Even that is too late."

"Yes, yes, I know. Losing Hunt must have been an awful shock."

"It's not that. Not even my own troubles."

"If you pull off this job, you can forget about your own troubles. The PM and the whole nation will be indebted to you."

"Fuck the lot."

"Charming."

Bucken heard somebody move in the outer room and

72

grew desperate to fix something with Rattray before Allerton returned. "You don't understand. It's The Job I'm talking about. The future of the Yard is at risk. There's been another top-level leak. Something goes on inside here and if we can't pin it down now . . ."

"You have proof?" Rattray's interruption sounded not only impatient but also cold and unfriendly.

"No, and I won't have it without your help. It's way above my head. It must be."

"All right, we'll discuss it later. After this bomb job."

"That's another thing. Why am I transferred to this?"

"You ought to be flattered."

"I ought to be chasing Hunt's killers."

"You're too involved emotionally. Hysterical, I'd say."

Bucken started toward him. Rattray sensed the threat but his voice remained calm: "You see what I mean?"

Bucken was on the verge of hitting him. It was only now that he noticed how thin Rattray was. And the pallor of overwork. Perhaps ulcers. It would hurt even more if he punched him in the stomach. Later Bucken could not recall how far he was into lunging at Rattray when a whisper stopped him with a paralyzing effect.

"And, Quint . . ."

Was it the third or fourth time in the long history of their friendship that Rattray used his first name?

". . . take care of yourself, will you?"

The door opened and Allerton detected the tension at once. "Anything wrong?"

It would have done no good to deny it. Rattray was quick with an answer. "The Superintendent is not entirely happy about being taken off the Hunt job."

"And the immigration racket," added Bucken.

"You wish to file an official complaint?"

Bucken looked at Rattray who lit another of those pungent near-black cigars.

"I'd better leave you to it," said Rattray and turned toward the door.

"No . . . I'll, er . . . I'd better get on with it, I suppose,"

73

mumbled Bucken and looked at the papers Allerton had prepared for him.

There was not too much to go on. The two letters to the Bank, the notes and timetable found in Cutter-Smith's flat and pockets, the reports about the telephone calls, contrasting statements from various bank employees who, judging from their recollections, could have talked to a dozen different blackmailers that morning, and the reports from Sheerness about the covered buoy and the minor explosion.

"We also picked up some ashes and a few only charred bits of paper at the flat," said Allerton. "The lab is still working on these but it appears from them that a car has been hired for a few days from tomorrow, a private detective's services have been retained—we're trying to contact him—and there seems to be something about a bug-detector specialist, but they can't yet make head or tail of it."

Bucken kept nodding toward Allerton and glancing toward the papers. He was, in fact, itching to meet the man.

"And now, as for some technicalities . . ."

"Whatever you say, Fred," Bucken interrupted his chief, using his first name as always in private, and with that tried to reassure him, that despite his protests and impatience, there was no personal animosity.

"Yes, but you must know. Because the operation is rather unusual, to say the least, we must improvise. I'll be acting as anchor man and you'll report to me and the PM himself if and when required."

"I'm honored."

"He's expecting your initial assessment at midnight and final recommendations at zero seven hundred tomorrow. Apart from that, it's your show. You have an entirely free hand—do as you like."

Bucken stared at him, waiting.

"I mean I'm not authorizing any illegality or extreme methods. If there's a scandal, let the politicians handle it. We want no part of it. And you'll have to account for the

74

prisoner, of course. And if he's damaged in transit, I hope it will clearly be attributable to an accident."

"You think it's that serious?"

Allerton nodded. "And we're backing you with everything we have. A bunch of specialist advisers have already been pulled in. Most of them are Military, but it's our show with their staff. They'll stay at C.O. until this is over, but preferably, they will not know what it's all about. I'm in charge of certain contingency measures: the Estuary traffic is already limited and under control, an emergency evacuation center is being organized at Sheerness, Navy divers and mine-disposal men are on their way, and, in the morning, the Bank will have two sets of ransom money prepared—one marked, one unmarked."

"You're ready to pay?"

"We expect a recommendation from you. Your background, diving and general experience have cut you out for this job."

"And you deal with Hunt's death."

"I'll put a million men on it."

"On my way up, I recorded a report on the immigration racket. I hope the noise of the bloody chopper didn't drown my voice."

"I'll let you know, son. And by the way, you have the sole use of the chopper." He made it sound as if he was lending Bucken the crown jewels. "Any questions? Lots, of course. Answer them. And good luck."

The sun dropped behind a big black cloud and Maxine suddenly felt the chill. She had only five more pages of a thriller to read, but she decided she would not catch cold for any bloody copper's secrets and revelations. She was about to dress when the bell rang.

"Who is it?"

"Flowers, miss."

She did not stop to think why the muffled voice addressed her as "miss" through the closed door. She embraced the opening door so that she could reach out for

75

the flowers with her left arm as she hid behind the panel. She was convinced that her own "bloody copper" wanted to apologize for the night and the rush with the flowers. But there were no flowers. A hard push on the door caught her off balance, and by the time she had a chance to look up, the door was closed and two small men with their round heads in stockings stared down at her. She tried to jump up and run but one man neatly tripped her up. Although bruised on the side and slightly dazed from bumping her head on the parquet floor, she tried to grab a rug to cover herself.

"You don't need that," the smaller of the two mumbled in a soft voice without anger, and stepped on the edge of the rug. He spoke with an accent but Maxine could not decide what sort. "Where's Bucken?"

She now stood up slowly and stared back at the two without making the slightest attempt to cover herself. "Ask the police."

The second man nodded toward the first who now slapped her face with explosive force. The move was fast and effortless, hardly visible at all, but made her fall and slide on the rug into the room. "Where's he?"

As an answer she sprang toward the first man's leg and bit his calf through the thick cloth with such ferocity that the man cried out. She did not see when the other hit her on the head from behind.

A bucket of water returned her to consciousness. Her hands and feet were bound and her mouth was taped.

"Where is he?"

The men freed her hands and gave her a piece of paper. She wrote: London.

"That's better. When is he coming back?"

She shrugged her shoulders.

"Where does he live in London?"

She shook her head. They hit her again but it did not hurt.

"What's his address? Please."

When she wrote nothing, the second man nodded

toward the open kitchen door. The first man carried her to the kitchen and dropped her on the floor. "We'll make some dinner for Mr. Bucken." He spread a fair lump of butter on her feet and sprinkled it with several spices from the rack at random. He then opened the oven and lit the gas.

"What's his address?" He handed her the paper and the pen once again.

She wrote "Scotland Yard."

He moved her nearer the oven.

She wrote down his Bayswater address.

"Thank you. Please tell him that we were here and we should like to see him soon. Or we'll see you soon ... if you're lucky."

Unhurriedly, he turned the control to "low" and the two of them moved her feet halfway into the oven. She could not scream. She wriggled desperately and forced her body into an arch, and they let her drop. Only the melting butter scorched her skin.

"Don't forget to tell him. Please."

The small office was tucked well away behind Victoria Station. Apart from the frequent ads run in the evening papers—Smart Young Man in uniform opening the car door for Mr. VIP—there was nothing lavish or glamorous about PLS, Pimlico Limousine Service, of course, and Sandra had worked there long enough to recognize a truly important customer when she saw one. Her agile, never-resting jaw tried to mash a biscuit, help her gulp the last of her tea and make room for the words offering a seat, all at the same time.

"Did you say three cars, sir? Three?"

The fat man nodded and he had all her sympathy. Sandra knew what a bad toothache was like and more: with a hugely swollen face like that, the poor man was not only unable to speak properly, but he would probably have grave difficulties with eating or even drinking anything. Behind his handkerchief and upturned collar, held protectively over the whole of his left face, she once spotted the troublesome lump, as big as half a peach.

"With uniformed drivers, sir? On Monday?"

Another nod. No, he definitely could not eat anything. Which made her want to chew even more. The biscuit was down, but there was one more in the packet, its edge just about visible, and Sandra struggled not to take a bite.

"A whole fleet then," she said and saw the man's desperate attempt to smile bravely despite his suffering. He was not to know that the three cars did not represent a Fleet but The Fleet, for the only other car PLS owned was already hired as from Friday. Business was picking up and Sandra decided to ask for a raise. If only she could grab that biscuit and stuff it in her mouth without offending the customer. Her tongue wiped her teeth collecting the last few crumbs to chew.

The man whispered a few instructions and Sandra wrote them down. He was blinking all the time behind thick pebble glasses as if having difficulties with his vision due to that terrible pain, presumably.

He paid cash, in advance. He had the right amount already prepared in an envelope. As he turned to go, her jaw began to chew even before her hand had a chance to deliver the biscuit. He suddenly turned to whisper: "Good-night then."

"M-mm sm."

The visible corner of his mouth definitely smiled as if the pain had eased for a second.

Outside, he stopped at a pillar box and scribbled on the edge of a sheet full of notes: "Phase I completed. Hope for the best. Hope I'm right." He slipped it in an already-addressed envelope and posted it to a Mr. Waltheof Stockton-Wright, c/o Mailers Ltd. Sandra saw him go down the stairs of the public lavatory almost opposite. She then concentrated on the biscuit.

3

LONDON NO MORE?

Bucken was pleased. He could not fault the blackmail plan in any detail. It could be a real challenge if Cutter-Smith came up to his expectations. It was not yet eight o'clock when he finished reading through the reports and various notes, giving him more than four hours to prepare his first assessment.

When he introduced himself as the man in charge of the investigation, Cutter-Smith looked utterly calm and bored. He liked that. It gave him the first clear objective—he had to rattle his quarry. He just stared at the meticulously dressed little man, the carefully manicured fingernails, the tidily knotted tie, for a long three minutes, and noted how those smallish white hands slowly smoothed out the accidental creases of the trousers at the knees from time to time. He decided to call him Smith.

"Tea?"

"Please."

When it arrived, Bucken stood up to take the tray, and was about to hand a cup to Smith when, accidentally, he tripped. The tea splashed from the correct angle for maximum effect on jacket, shirt and trousers. It could not hurt—Bucken knew that tea at C.O. was never hot—but it achieved what he wanted. Smith was disturbed by the warm wetness and the possible stains. Bucken showered him with apologies. He even tried to help cleaning the suit with his own hands and saw Smith flinch. The type who is upset by the physical touch of strangers. It was not much, but it was a start.

"Now tell me all about this idiotic demand you dreamed up."

"Idiotic?"

"We'll see."

"I've already told several people and it's also in my letters to the Bank." The stain on the jacket was spreading.

"Tell me again."

"Why?"

"Because I'm in charge and I want you to."

"Then don't waste time. The ship may blow up and then they'll blame you."

"Listen, Smith . . ."

"Cutter-Smith is the name."

"And I don't give a damn, sweetheart. I don't care what your name is, I don't care about the ship, I don't care if you blow a million people out of the map for there're too many of us for this island anyway. All I care about is to see you locked up for a long time or even dead if there's a nice opportunity." He noticed that Smith was now cleaning the suit faster and more furiously. Good. "So start singing, my pet."

"And then you'll let me go home?"

"We'll see."

"Am I under arrest?"

"It's just prevention of terrorism."

"I'm not a criminal, you know."

"No, you're just rotten through and through."

"I'm not! I'm not!"

Why is he protesting so violently? "You're rotten, Smithy, plain rotten. We'd better get you a good lawyer."

"I don't want any."

"I know. Why?"

"Because I'm not a criminal. I'm trying to help you to avoid an explosion and for that you will pay me and let me go home."

"We may also simply throw the book at you with charges of conspiracy, an accessory before the fact, threats of causing malicious damage, preparing explosions, interfering with shipping, threatening to destroy a wrecked vessel, not to mention a waterway and towns and industrial installations around it. Shall I go on? Threats to **cause** burns, to maim or disfigure or disable just one person or cause grievous bodily harm unlawfully and maliciously by explosion is a felony and you can get life for that alone."

"I'm not a malicious person."

"The merest interference with that buoy can put you away for seven years."

"It was a warning."

"It's felony to unlawfully and maliciously remove or conceal any buoy or installation for guidance of seamen. Seven years, sweetheart, and that's just for the plastic bag cover on the light, without the explosion. Do you know how seamen react to acts endangering their lives? Do you know how many seamen there are at any given time in a British jail? Do you know how they will treat you for all this? I hope they'll also rape you."

"You're wasting time, officer, with threats about which I've been warned."

"By whom?"

"My Principal."

"Who's that?"

"I don't know."

"We'll get it out of you."

"More threats?"

"If you like."

"No good. I can tell only what I know. And what I know cannot tell you anything about my Principal. He's too clever for you. You can torture me or kill me or inject me with truth drugs or what have you. Or hypnotize me. I'm ready. I'll sign a permission. But it won't help you. And if you don't pay in time, the bomb will just go off."

"Where?"

"In the *Montgomery*."

"What sort of bomb is it?"

"I don't know."

"But it's timed."

"Yes."

"Then how can we stop it if we pay?"

"You can't stop it. Only my Principal can."

"So he's willing to appear on the scene."

"I don't know. But I do know that he managed to set off the small warning bomb and blow up the buoy under your nose."

"How do you know?"

"I've guessed. Otherwise you wouldn't have taken me seriously, would you?"

"Yes I would, 'cause it's my job to take every fucking bastard like you seriously." He stood now, peering at Cutter-Smith from a menacing height, and his fist came down on the table fast but with great precision, almost skinning the little man's nose. He saw that chummy was frightened. The threat of any violence or even of the merest physical contact may rattle him when the time comes. But Bucken knew he was blindly groping about. "And I'll tell you how seriously we take you. I'll fly you to Sheerness and take you down to the wreck."

"No."

"Oh yes, and if necessary, you'll be locked up in a diving bell sitting right on top of all that ammunition. If it goes up, you go up with it." It was just whistling in the dark. But Cutter-Smith froze and seemed to lose interest even in the teastains. "If you kill a thousand people, you'll make it a thousand and one."

"If I'm not home by midnight, there'll be another warning."

Bucken pounced and caught his shoulder. His fast questions aimed to eliminate thinking time. "What warning?"

"Like the first."

"Another explosion?"

"Probably."

"Where?"

"Somewhere on the Thames."

"Where?"

"In London."

"Where exactly?"

"Don't know."

"Come on!" He shook him and felt that his quarry was shivering. "Come on, tell me."

"I can't."

"I'll get it out of you."

"I don't know. I honestly don't know."

"Rubbish."

"He never told me."

"Who?"

"My Principal."

"Who is he?"

"I don't know."

"Liar."

"Honest. I never lie. I can't lie. He told me that this is the strength of the plan. My ignorance. Like my weakness is the strongest link in the chain of my marriage. I know nothing so I can't reveal his plans. But because I never disappear, he can protect me from the background."

"Okay, Sheerness it is." Bucken always meant to go there and have a quick look around, but now he pretended to use the trip only as a serious menace. He picked up the phone and asked for the office where a dozen detectives were waiting for any job he might have for them. He knew they were furious because they were kept in the dark. He disliked the procedure but he had strict orders. He gave instructions to have a car with escort waiting for him and that the chopper should be ready to fly in half an hour. Cutter-Smith winced at every word as if lashed.

Bucken knew he had nothing else as yet with which to rattle him any more. It might even be true that this front man was the worst liar in town. But then perhaps he might not yet be asking the right questions. He decided to change tack.

"You know something, I might even believe you."

"Thank you."

"You're stupid to lie. And your Principal, whoever he may be, probably knew that, too. For it's quite a plan he's dreamed up, I grant you that."

"That's why I went along with the idea myself." Cutter-Smith relaxed a little and sought refuge in renewed rubbing of the stains.

"But he didn't think of everything."

"Oh?"

"How would he know that you're not freed by midnight?"

"I don't know."

"Would he call you? Or have the house watched?"

Cutter-Smith looked a little startled and turned away.

"For I don't mind telling you that we have your home under observation, there're men stationed in the flat, questioning your wife, others are checking every bit of your background, interviewing everybody you know and might have seen in the last few months, and we have your telephone tapped, needless to say, with special teams ready to trace any call within seconds."

"Can't be done."

"What?"

"Tracing calls that fast."

"How would you know?"

"My Principal told me."

"But how would he know?"

"He seems to know what he needs. Like extension numbers in the House of Commons."

"Okay, perhaps he'll call you at midnight and put the phone down at once when you're not there to answer. He'll then set off another explosion. Okay. And suppose, just suppose, we decide to pay you the million. How will he get his share?"

"I don't know."

"What will you do with the money?"

"I've hired a car as from tomorrow. With a chauffeur. I'll put the money in the boot and drive around a lot. I've taken a few days off from the office, you know. I might even resign. I can imagine Mr. plain-Smith, that's my boss, when he hears about that."

"About the money."

"Yes, everything."

"I mean what will you do with the money in the boot?"

"Nothing. Just wait. Until the Principal makes his move, sends me a message or takes it all. I've no idea."

Bucken hesitated. It seemed best not to press him too hard with the question of the handover. If the Government decided to pay up, the cash could be the only guide to finding the Principal, and if Cutter-Smith was too alarmed, he might mess it up. He began to gather up his notes and tried to sound perfectly casual:

"Your main problem is, of course, how *you* will get away with it. I mean once the money is safely handed over to your Principal and the Sunday lunchtime deadline is passed. If he is honest, he'll switch off the time bomb, somehow, and even if we fail to catch him then, you'll have no more protection. We can just take back your little bundle and put you away for a neat fifteen years or so."

"You're wrong. As long as he's not caught, I'll enjoy his protection."

"Once the time bomb is switched off?"

"It can be restarted, you know."

"By remote control? Ridiculous."

"I trust him."

And I almost believe you, thought Bucken, and hated the idea of developing an unhealthy respect for the Principal. "You want the money tomorrow, but the explosion deadline is only forty-eight hours later. He needs time to prepare for his next move."

"I don't know."

"Why did you hire a car?"

"It's more comfortable. Besides . . ."

"Besides what?"

"My Principal wanted me to."

"Why?"

"He didn't say."

"You're a liar."

"I'm not. I can't lie. But my memory is exceptionally good. I can remember every word he said."

"Did he want you to hire a private detective, too?"

"Yes. Major Skinner of I.I.I."

"Why?"

"To guard me. He said, 'We don't want anything to happen to that nine hundred thousand pounds, do we, Johnny?' He called me Johnny, he said, because we were partners."

"What did you call him?"

"Nothing. I mean, I had no name for him."

"So what did you want from that private detective?"

"Just to watch me. Follow me or rather that hired car with the money wherever we went. He'll report for duty in the morning together with the chauffeur."

"Who paid for all this?"

"My Principal gave me the money but I insisted on paying ten percent myself. We were to be partners, after all, and fair is fair. If only the Bank and the Government played fair with me and gave me the job I deserved, they wouldn't be in such a mess now and wouldn't need to pay. But this will teach them. This will."

Bucken registered the man's growing excitement but found it hard to decide if he was a paranoiac. A psychiatric examination might be useful at some stage. On the other hand, there might be some genuine grievance and a motive of revenge involved. If so, he wondered how much the Principal could know about that. Perhaps by the morning there would be some background reports. He was so lost in his thoughts that he hardly noticed that Cutter-Smith was still talking.

"I mean it's all their fault, isn't it? They're the criminals, the Government and all. Why didn't they do something about that wreck? I mean in time. Now it's too late. Now the threat is permanent. They'll be 'the prisoners of their own past inaction and present impotence wrapped in the safeguarding of their false public image. Whereby the simple opportunity for the perfect crime arises.' That's exactly what my Principal said."

A mixture of anxious self-justification and some official report-writing vernacular. A banker? Civil servant? If the front man's memory could be trusted. But then this kind of excellent memory could be a reason for choosing him in the first place. One of the reasons.

"Why did he choose you of all people to be his partner?"

"He had faith in me. Absolute faith."

"Did he say that?"

"Yes."

"So he must have known you."

"Of course." Bucken was pleased: Cutter-Smith had walked into this neat little trap without thinking. He watched him closely for any signs of a worried man realizing a mistake. But there was virtually no reaction. No sudden fright, no lip biting, no landslide of words to camouflage the slip of the tongue. Was he really that naïve? The perfect pawn? The perfect choice?

"After all," added the pawn, "he must have made his choice somehow. And if he didn't know me ... I mean, how would you choose a partner?"

"That's just it. How did you choose him?"

"I didn't. I just accepted him. He just happened to me like most things in my life."

"You'd never seen him before this scheme began?"

"Not before, not ever. He was always in the dark. I'm ready to show you where we met, if you like."

"Would you recognize his voice?"

"No. He always whispered."

"I don't believe you. And I'll chase you and chase you until I find out the truth."

"You can question me any time. I won't run away. I'll be at home. As my Principal assured me. I don't need a hotel or ..."

"A what?"

"Hotel. Means hiding place, he said."

A banker or civil servant using crooks' slang? Or was the Principal only a contact man, a cutout, carrying messages from an organization to the front man?

What bothered Bucken even more was the apparent lack of effort by Cutter-Smith to cover his tracks. Why did he not try to burn all his notes? Why did he not make a better job of burning others? Was it a mistake? If yes, why would he discuss the car hire and the private eye so readily? Was it that he knew none of this would help the police? It was an infuriating thought that he might be right.

Major-Generous Brammel never dreamed he could get out of it legitimately. His twin daughters were about to have a "technicolor, Cinemascope monster of a double wedding to some sheepmen in Nevil Shute country," and his wife kindly planned to turn his six-week special leave into "a round-the-world social extravaganza of visiting and entertaining every wretched soul who ever had the misfortune of knowing us."

"Now you know me from the old Hong Kong days," he said to Deputy Commissioner Carron, "and you know that I'm a generous man, because one's men don't grant one nicknames for nothing, and I'm surely generous enough to grant utmost favors of time-wasting to my own family—against my better judgment, that is—but my, my, was I pleased when the panic button was pressed and I was summoned to run this little show for C.C.C. or M.A.C.C., whatever the case may be!"

Brammel was not pleased at all that his carefully calculated light chatter failed to induce dear-old-boy Carron to part with any information the General did not already possess. He never really cared for any liaison, let alone cooperation with the police because, as in the Hong Kong days, he firmly believed that public disturbances and civil emergencies were best dealt with by one force only—police or the military—rather than some mishmash command. But, yet again, he had to live with it, hoping that the best-dressed copper, as Carron was known, was equally in the dark about the true purpose of this totally unexpected and unrealistic exercise. Having his anchorman seated at a screened desk in the Ministry of Defence Operations Room while he himself was working at Scotland Yard of all places?—quite, quite unacceptable. And he found scores of other irregularities also incomprehensible.

He was to work under the C.C.C. umbrella but the Civil Contingencies Committee had not been assembled even for an initial briefing session. He saw no ministers but his own who was annoyingly tight-lipped about the objectives: an underwater bomb or nuclear device of unknown destruction potential had supposedly been planted by some terrorist organization off Sheerness, somewhere between the Kent and Essex coast; in cooperation with the police, Brammel must assess grades of risks in an area of up to ten miles radius; establish a command center and draw up plans for a probable three-stage evacuation of the entire population of this vast danger zone. Just for good measure he was to see if industrial installations could be protected at all; assess the necessity of total diversion of shipping from the area; use SAS antiterrorist units—already on a three-minute standby at 22 Special Air Service Regiment—as a spearhead task force at his discretion; and prepare for red alert any other troops to carry out standard M.A.C.C. (Military Aid to the Civil Community) duties such as providing transport for evacuation, maintaining essential services, building temporary bridges, directing traffic, and flying in disaster relief as the situation might develop.

Impressed he was but enchanted he was certainly not. He repeatedly emphasized his unselfish openness with Carron, and wondered if his failure to elicit reciprocal generosity was due to the other man's orders, ignorance or meanness.

In fact, it was a mixture of the three. The best-dressed copper knew about the original threat and ransom demand. That he was to keep to himself. Beyond that, it was infuriating not to know what further moves were being made. He had no good excuse to require up-to-the-minute news, and as long as he was tied up with Brammel, he would have no opportunity to make his informal inquiries, from Rattray or others more directly involved.

"I understand you want to use Bexley for your HQ," said Carron.

"That's right. It would give us an overall outlook on the entire area with readily available facilities. I propose to use the already existing temporary fallout center which can easily be activated. Unfortunately, the more permanent underground control complex, one of the five from where Government could continue to function if London was blasted out of the map, will not be completed for another couple of years or so, potential nuclear enemies please note, eh, what?" Brammel stepped to the enlarged map of the area already on the wall. "But the main problem is the location of my direct front-line command post."

Carron suggested the Sheerness police station but Brammel perhaps did not even hear it.

"There's a wreck here, opposite Sheerness."

"Oh, yes." Carron tried to sound unconcerned.

"Some old ammo ship. What? We'll have to check."

"Oh, yes, it's the *Montgomery,* I believe."

"Ah. That explains it. A possible purpose of the exercise is therefore to foresee and deal with risks arising from interference with the wreck directly or indirectly."

It was Carron's turn to be impressed. It seemed idiotic to keep the whole story from the General, but it would have been embarrassing to admit that he knew it all the time.

"In which case," continued Brammel, "we could use existing risk assessments for a starter." He made a note. "Now then, I understand we're talking about the movement of something in the order of half a million bodies."

"People, you mean. How long were you liaising with the Yanks in the Far East?"

"No, no dear boy, I meant bodies when I said bodies. We then may have to differentiate between live bodies and dead bodies for the purpose of slightly different requirements for immediate transport needs, depending on how much time we have to save lives by evacuation or by removal of potentially contaminated mass. Whichever is

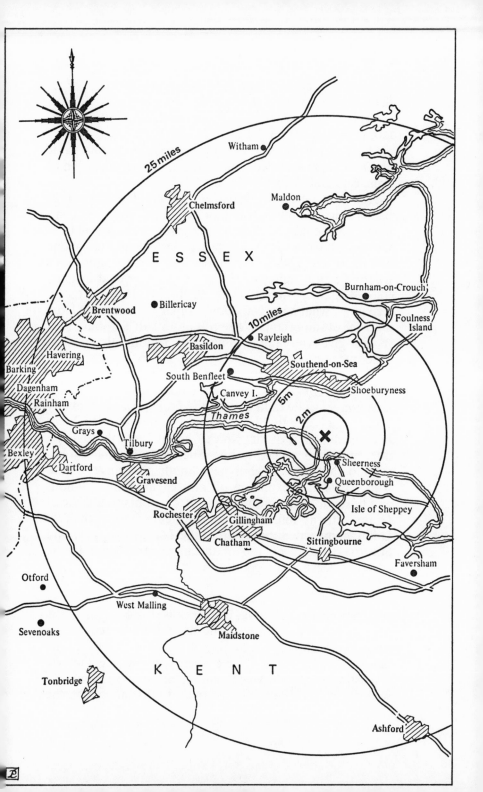

the case, I want my command right in the center . . . er . . . the Sheerness docks?"

"There's a seafront amusement park, facing the wreck, too. How would that do?"

"Fine. What we must avoid at all costs is causing panic and a possible stampede out of the area or an invasion of sightseers and picnickers."

Just as a joke, Carron suggested that the three huge pantechnicons forming Brammel's mobile reinforced command post, could be disguised as circus vehicles, but the General did not laugh. He just picked up the telephone and instructed a somewhat startled duty officer in the Ops Room that the pantechnicons were to be covered by gaily colored circus posters. "Don't ask stupid questions. Lions, elephants, what have you. Don't forget some trapeze lady, that's most important. We're rolling in half an hour. That should give you ample time, yes, I think that's most generous of me."

He returned to the map and, with his pair of custom-built giant compasses, he drew circles of two-mile, five-mile and ten-mile radii around the *Montgomery.* "Nobody who puts a bomb in this area would be foolish enough not to take advantage of that wreck," he muttered through the thin gap of his sucked-in lips. The ten-mile circle threatened to obliterate Shoeburyness, Southend, Canvey Island with all its vast explosive oil and chemical installations and the country's largest methane storage plant, the Isle of Grain with its refineries and petroleum harbor, half of Gillingham and Sittingbourne, the Isle of Sheppey, and Sheerness sitting on top of the imaginary bomb in the center. "Doesn't look good. What?"

Leashed to a roof hook, Bucken was straphanging in the open door of the Wessex. The downdraft stirred by the rotor blades threatened to blow away his first meal of the day, yet he would not have been sorry to see the two disgustingly cold, shriveled hamburger sandwiches make a well-deserved descent into the river. In the moonlight, the

Thames looked the usual strip of silver foil reflecting local authority tastes here for yellow, there for blue street lights, but in his mind's eye the river was red and orange. Burning. According to the initial risk assessment prepared for him at C.O., in certain tidal and cloud conditions, the *Montgomery* explosion might set the river and London ablaze.

Such a catastrophe would not surprise him—his natural pessimism had been nourished by the free use of this helicopter. Bucken always held that, short of miracles, the Metropolitan Police would receive twentieth-century facilities only if the capital would otherwise face extinction. It was peculiar that a threat like that should be represented by a tea-stained vertigo victim whose screwed-up eyes he constantly felt on his back.

He wished to God his opposition were a hard professional criminal, any clever gangland brain, anybody against whom the traditional main police weapon—information received—could be used. The rate of crime detection was unsatisfactory anyway, but, without informers, many more major cases would remain unsolved. On this occasion, however, he could not even hope for tipoffs. Particularly if the Principal worked alone. He opened a can of beer over Purfleet.

"I've had nothing to eat or drink since they brought me in," shouted Cutter-Smith over the engine noise.

"You wish to lodge an official complaint?" Bucken drank thirstily. It was cruel, he knew, but he was in a cruel mood. Which reminded him of Sergeant Hunt.

The totally unnecessary brutality with which the Lad had been murdered seemed less exceptional these days than it would have been only a year or so before. Most of the ruthless beatings and torture appeared to be internal affairs of the underworld, one villain doing it to another. And always somebody trying to skim the cream of criminal takings. In the past few months alone he had come across several cases. The chummy who pulled off quite a good burglary and was then tortured by "unknown attackers" with a red-hot poker for a "one-grand corner

93

from that beautiful tickle as a token of friendship." Chummy lost an eye but kept silent to preserve the other. Then the container theft specialist who, allegedly, would not offer "friendship money," and was fished out of the river minus feet and arms. Then the small-time smuggler who first refused to pay, forked out a hefty sum when forced, and was still tortured almost to death for his "reluctance" to be friendly. Bucken found him on a boat and took his dying declaration—"they offered me police protection, they did, trust me, guv, they said Old Bill will look after me"—but the wretched creature could give him no useful clues. His hand had been nailed to the deck.

Coincidence, some people thought. But Bucken did not believe in coincidences. Or in lucky breaks. He found them too unreliable partners and they worried him: when luck deserts you, you're worse off than before, he used to warn the Lad over and over again. Except that now he felt like praying for some luck without which he would never get anywhere with Cutter-Smith. And even then, where was the guarantee that the Principal would not be tipped off by somebody high up?

He stared silently at Cutter-Smith, then threw him what was left of that wreck of a hamburger and a can of beer.

For quite some time Bucken had felt as if he was working and living in isolation. He could not put a precise date on it, but the final stage was reached at the time of Rattray's promotion. Bucken began to disagree with some new prevailing factions of opinion among his colleagues. The response to his efforts, the echo of his reports, his successes just as much as his failures contributed to the sensation of being used and cheated. A lifelong deal that never really came off.

He used to grumble about the endless waiting and waiting for selection, for promotion, for the openings to step up into higher ranks long after the qualifying exams had been passed, for police college places, for transfers to the Yard. Now he was infuriated by the speedy system that seemed to favor deskmen. Why should he ruin his private life, mix with villains, cut corners in a good cause, and risk losing his temper or merely expose himself to false complaints of violence and bribery, when quick promotion and the plum jobs went to coddled yes-men anyway?

More and more he heard from Rattray that perhaps he was one of the old-fashioned detectives who believed that law enforcement should not be mixed up with social reforms—and the more he thought of it, the prouder he grew of his unfashionable attitude. Oh yes, in some parts of London, scores of people felt grateful to Bucken for all sorts of help, even small cash loans out of his own pocket. He closed his eyes to many petty crimes, helped stray kids, drunkards, old lags just out of jail and their families when he put the men away yet again for a stretch, but he helped some because of plain compassion without social conscience, and helped most with an unashamedly open motive of selfishness: one day they might give him a tipoff, one day, they might stop a knife destined for his back. During their last Peel-housing session at their favorite "we serve breakfast all day" café in the Strutton Ground street market near the Yard, he had told Rattray: "You say it's my *duty* to help all citizens. You say we're now the most essential and largest body of social workers. If so, that's where I get off. I'm a detective. I'm not a masochist and I'm not a professional target man for demonstrators, reformers and villains who play golf with my higher-ups. Okay, if that's the job, I want out."

Cutter-Smith finished the sandwich and the beer. Perching on an uncomfortable seat, he was at a loss over what to do with the empty can so that he could hold on to something, anything, with both hands.

Bucken wished he could classify the man. He would know instinctively all about an East End newcomer raising his first pint to West Ham in the Blind Beggar. Or chummy who was turning up in the old Singh's café in Cable Street where Bucken had learned all about gambling. Or the type he could safely escort to that horrid

Leman Street station which used to have gaslights in his days, and push him through the "wicked gate" for the night, knowing full well what to charge him with in the morning. He would have no problems with Mr. Smith if he were a bottle-fighting Saturday-night tough from the Duragon Arms, a gangland boss of the East End, a smoothy of the West End, a fraudsman, a con man, a heavy, a forger, an art-specialist thief or even an educated, sophisticated "political," well-versed in legal loopholes in his favor. Bucken had been around, there were few types new to him. But this man was one of them. He must have been selected with great care as a nobody, no-type. How? How would the Principal know about a man like that at all?

The lab was still working on that charred note referring to bugs. Bucken moved over to Cutter-Smith.

"Were you afraid of being bugged?"

"What?"

"Bugged!" They had to shout but the Sergeant who belonged to the helicopter crew wore earphones and could not hear them.

"No."

"Then why did your notes refer to bugs?"

Cutter-Smith hesitated and Bucken grabbed his shoulder. That did it. "I had bug-detector training so that I could check the hired car. I mean he showed me how to use the things."

"Who is he?"

"The private detective. You know, he calls himself Major Skinner, but he's retired, of course. He also sells and hires out detectors."

"Did you buy something?"

"No. Hired everything. You know, you saw the notes. It wasn't really important to burn them but I thought . . ."

"Refresh my memory."

"My Principal thought that there was no need to burn the notes because you'd see the equipment anyway when he delivered it."

"The Major?"

96

"Yes."

"What equipment?"

"The bug detector to stop anybody secretly trailing me and the money, and the detector kit to check if the money had been marked somehow. It'll all come in the morning."

"Nobody said we'd pay, sweetheart."

Cutter-Smith shrugged his shoulders. "I'd be sorry if there had to be an explosion. Honestly. I'd be most distressed."

"You don't know how sorry I'd make you."

"I'm not a criminal."

Bucken nodded toward the Sergeant who had signaled that the Wessex was approaching Sheerness, then turned back to Smith to ask as casually as at all possible when shouting at the top of his voice: "What did you say, how would your Principal know if we decided to pay?"

"I said nothing."

"Didn't you?"

"You didn't ask."

"I'm asking now."

Cutter-Smith sucked in his lips and Bucken sensed a touch of defiance. He must not let it develop. He grabbed the man again, only this time he lifted him out of his corner, pushing him right up to the door. He was still strapped to the long lead and he knew he was strong enough to hold the much smaller man, but at the moment, he did not really care whether he dropped him or not.

"How would he know?"

"Please." He closed his eyes and began to tremble violently.

"How would he know?" Bucken edged him further out where the downdraft could be felt.

"I'd have to tell him."

"How?"

"On the phone. He gave me the number ..."

Noticing the twitch of terror on the Sergeant's face, Bucken tried to produce a half-smile of reassurance. He hated himself for what had just happened, he hated the idea that it had been witnessed by an outsider, but he had

97

no time to dwell on it for long. As soon as they landed, he called Allerton to give him the telephone number although he could not believe that the Principal would be caught out just like that.

"That's very odd," mumbled Allerton.

"What?"

"The number sounds familiar . . . We'll soon find out . . . And . . . er . . ." The Commander was not sure if he should tell Bucken about Maxine. After she had called the local police and they telephoned him, he himself spoke to her and made sure that she would get urgent medical attention and police protection, as suggested by the local CID.

"Any news about Hunt?"

"No, not yet. Linley's handling it."

Bucken frowned. Inspector Linley was the archetype he disliked—a fast-rising desk detective, just back from a two-year secondment to Singapore or some place like that. As if an organization or disciplinary job in the Far East would teach him how to catch immigration racketeers or any other thieves. "I see."

Allerton decided against saying anything about Maxine. Bucken could do nothing just now and it would only divert his attention from the case in hand.

While waiting for the telephone number to be checked out, Allerton told him that a special message from the PM authorized Bucken to investigate the case "by any legal method," freely, and apparently, he would act "with the full blessing of the leader of the Opposition," too.

Bucken smiled. He always thought of the two great men as the puppets Pinky and Perky on a seesaw. Now he envisaged them rising and sinking, into power, out of power, but blessing him in concert all the way. He heard Allerton grunt at the other end.

"Fred, are you there?"

"Yes . . . er . . . "

"You got the number?"

"Yes."

"Well, come on, for God's sake."

"It belongs to Carron. His home in Harrow."

"You mean the Deputy? Christ."

"I'll call you back. Try to get something out of Smith."

Bucken tried, but he seemed to know nothing about the number or its owner. And the detective believed him. He would not have the bloody cheek ...

"All I know is that I must call that number. I don't know who will answer. I swear. I only have to say that Grandma and Old Bill agreed to pay. Then put the phone down."

"Grandma and Old Bill?"

"Yes. I know that Grandma is the Governor of the Bank. Old Bill must be the Treasury."

Bucken did not bother to correct him. Old Bill meant police in the underworld.

Brammel's traveling circus had already left London by the time the relevant reports and other documents were assembled by the Ministry, but the gist of it all was radioed to the General. Surrounded by a maze of radars, all the paraphernalia of communications equipment and batteries of scramblers, he was alone in the windowless armored section that could be used for briefings, and stared at the hugely blown-up projection of the Sheerness area map. He called his Minister to obtain authorization for moving massive air, sea and ground transport formations into the area. If the exercise was to be realistic at all, there should be not a second to waste. Even without possessing the full details of the risk, he wanted sandbags to go up everywhere, TV and radio announcements to warn the population, police cars and crowd-control motorcyclists at main road junctions, and preparations for an evacuation job that would dwarf the memory of Dunkirk. Using an exclusive wavelength, it took him only seconds to trace the Minister to Downing Street where a conference with the Prime Minister was interrupted without much ado.

Brammel derived no pleasure from mysteries and the irregularities of working without precise chains of command and communication not only vertically but also horizontally. Direct reporting to the Minister was flattering but unsatisfactory. The man knew nothing but the politics of defense. Was this then a political exercise in emergency handling?

His proposal was listened to and turned down. An impassive voice reminded him: "The job is to assess, plan and prepare, no more. Keep me informed at all times, will you?"

And if it was merely an exercise for the politicals rather than the military, why have him on the move at all, why actually alert some units, and why not play it out to the full in the games room?

The dispatch rider caught up with the circus near Rochester. In the remaining twenty miles to Sheerness, Brammel grew convinced that if there was just a grain of reality in this exercise, and even if he disregarded the "unknown destruction potential" of the traditional or nuclear device supposedly in position already, London or a substantial part of it might be wiped out by dawn.

The latest available official assessment was dated 1973. MoD salvage divers had examined the wreck, found it still in two parts and, although rusted, in a "generally sound" condition, in some thirty feet of water, a mile and a half away from Sheerness, and about seven hundred feet north of the Medway Approach Channel, between the two major tanker routes. The divers were not permitted to enter the wreck which was deemed too dangerous to touch, and could not therefore produce up-to-date information on the state of the explosives and the extent of corrosion affecting the casings.

The report referred to various specialist and scientific reviews of the situation. There were warnings that careless skin divers or irresponsible pranksters, malicious acts by some terrorist organization or even shock waves produced by low-flying jets could trigger off "the largest non-nuclear explosion" on record. On the other hand, it appeared that the risk of digging through the layers of silt settled on the wreck would be too great to attempt fuller exploration. On balance, the Government reaffirmed earlier decisions that the wreck should remain undisturbed because an accidental explosion was extremely unlikely but a salvage operation would require a vast evacuation and could cause tremendous and widespread damage within an up-to-ten-mile radius.

Brammel then noticed a discrepancy in the charts determining the relative position of the two broken parts of the hull. Was it due to an erroneous measurement by the first or the last survey or had the strong currents caused some movement during the intervening two decades?

The file also contained several references to independent assessments of and public reactions to the risk. When Bernard Braine, the MP for Southeast Essex, tried to establish who had at least the authority to deal with this known menace to public safety, the Ministry of Defence, the Home Office and the Board of Trade played Ping-Pong with the question of responsibility, and the game ended with a glorious love-all score. Local and port authorities as well as shipping had apparently learned to live with the bomb and even love it as a well-known landmark and titillating tourist sight.

As he read on, Brammel found that the consensus of expert opinion was against the likelihood of a spontaneous explosion: the safe shelf life of pure TNT (some 1,500 tons of it in the holds of the *Montgomery*) was known to be "extremely long" because of its stable molecular structure, but nobody could guess just how pure the Trinitrotoluene inside those bombs was. In that last year of the war, American bombs were not produced to last long on the shelves and be safe from growing dangerously unstable. It was even found to be an advantage to allow certain impurities because adulterated mixtures intensified the explosion. The very thick steel casings of the bombs, well protected by paint of excellent quality, could resist the incessant salt bites and remain safely watertight in the wreck for centuries. Yet there might be just one faulty casing . . .

He found a lengthy treatise on the detonation of fused and unfused bombs (arguing the mere probability that most of the *Montgomery*'s bombs were unfused); and another one on the chemistry and likelihood of the potential breakdown process of the sixteen, mostly nitrate-based, wartime bomb fillers (with reference to the chances of TNT crystallization, and to the fact that crystalline TNT could weep more readily from the casings and that it could be exploded by even slight surface friction).

The movement of the wreck itself or the constant slow shifting of the cargo, induced by the rotting away and collapse of wooden cases and racks, could make a bomb slip and explode, but this was considered to be a minimal risk and specialists doubted if this would have the force underwater to detonate all the rest of the cargo.

Brammel came to some newspaper clippings. It appeared that the authorities and the public had been duly warned in forceful terms on several occasions. The by now defunct *Wide World* magazine had run a detailed exposé in 1964. The *Sunday Times* produced a thorough investigation in 1971. Both quoted Major Hartley, holder of the George Medal for gallantry and one of the world's most experienced bomb-disposal specialists, who firmly advocated a cautiously planned salvage operation without any delay. Brammel chose to take his word rather than the famous "consensus of expert opinion," the red-tape formula for compromise.

The factors of hazard assessments, collected in the thick, strictly confidential file, varied a great deal. Heavy fallout of shrapnel, cracked structural walls, collapsing weaker walls and roofs in the vicinity, broken windows and swept-off roof tiles at five miles or more, light to heavy damage to oil tanks and industrial plants, and considerable damage to ships nearby were predicted. It was pointed out that if a tanker, one of those 100,000-tonners, was passing by when the bombs went off, pollution of the Estuary and the whole of the Southeast would be the least of the authorities' problem—flames could spread like bushfire along the surface of the water and threaten to incinerate the entire coast and the fleeing population.

The more pessimistic forecasts emphasized that a simultaneous explosion of all the cargo would cause a tidal wave which would sweep up both the Thames and the Medway, and might drown scores of villages, towns, and low-lying parts of the capital. If the wreck blew up at low tide, when there was least water above to act as a buffer, the effect would be even more devastating. The ultimate risk depended on the weather. A heavy and low cloud ceiling would not only prevent the dissipation of the shock waves into the atmosphere, but it would also bounce the blast back at an angle toward the area surrounding Sheerness. Canvey Island, storing usually some 120 million gallons of crude oil, gasoline, and highly explosive toxic chemicals, would be a prime victim of "the bounce" and the cause of an incalculably devastating chain reaction that might hit London with an unforeseeable force.

Brammel knew that he was reviewing the most extreme possibilities. But he retained a healthy respect for chain reactions ever since he witnessed the near-total defeat of an entire battalion by an enemy, inferior in fire- and manpower, purely because the cowardice of one man had started an unstoppable panic. In his book, "pessimism" was defined as "realism based on minimal expectation of luck"—and luck figured only as an occasional bonus in moments of desperation, such as this blessed, out-of-the-blue emergency exercise that saved him from that dreadful social globetrotting at least temporarily. He glanced at his watch. His wife must be airborne by now. He was hoping that the exercise would last long enough to excuse him from joining her until the wedding itself.

"Coming up to the bridge to the island, sir," reported the driver through the speaker.

Brammel swiveled around and reached up for the viewer of the miniature periscope in the roof. The incredible width of the view through the fisheye lens brought the dark panorama of the island into the timeless and shadow-free glow of his command post. Brammel switched over to infrared, and peered into that all-green world. It seemed amazing that the bridge survived the weight of his traveling circus.

Brammel knew that in a true emergency he would simply have to disregard the Minister's instruction to restrict himself only to planning at this stage. Worried by the real hazards, and in order to increase the realism of the exercise, he decided to ignore his orders and pull in some bridge engineers. Otherwise he would see no chance for a meaningful evacuation attempt by road.

He scanned the marshland along the narrow, treelined road. "Sheppey welcomes careful drivers." A starless sky. Pregnant clouds hanging menacingly low. He radioed the ops room and urgently asked for a steady flow of weather reports and forecasts for an area of twenty miles' radius. He would have to be ready for a "bounce" in what he named *blockbuster conditions.*

For the first time Winnie was angry. She had had quite a lot of trouble lately with her artificial leg—"The love of the job was gone and craftsmanship went with it the day they permitted a fitters' strike at Roehampton," she complained to anyone who cared to listen—and the long presence of the detectives in the flat prevented her from removing it for a while and giving the sore stump a chance to heal. When she now decided to put some ointment on it and rest it in the bathroom, she discovered that the woman detective would want to accompany her and stay with her. After her long and bitter complaints, a compromise was reached: the detective would turn her back but stand in the open door. In this way, Winnie had at least found a captive audience for her customary tirades against "this cruel, blasphemous and uncharitable world that catered only for the mad drivers who would run down more and more of us, children of this age, and produce more customers for Roehampton so that the fitters could hold society to ransom."

104

She had just begun to expound on what the world owed to its disabled victims, when the telephone rang. The detectives were anxious that the call should be answered at once, but Winnie refused to show herself without the leg and the wire would not reach into the bathroom. After some infuriating haggling, the three men agreed to line up facing the wall and the woman detective, with her eyes shut, helped Winnie to the telephone.

The whisper on the line was hardly more than heavy breathing.

"Speak up, will you? Who is it?"

"Is that you, Winnie?" The whisper was now just audible.

"Who is it?"

"Lis-ten care-fully. This is an ur-gent mes-sage for Johnny."

"I won't listen if you don't speak up."

The detectives in the room crossed their fingers hoping that Winnie's insistence would keep the caller on the line long enough for the tracers. She had promised to cooperate. In the basement, at the junction box, the tappers were recording every word, but the man with the headset swore loudly: this hyphenated, robotlike whisper would deprive the speaker of his usual accent, and probably resist all attempts at voice-print identification. The tapper touched the wire with a screwdriver: perhaps the noise would force the caller to raise his voice.

"I can't hear you. It's a very bad line," shouted Winnie.

"Just tell Johnny that he should not worry. I know they are still kee-ping him and af-ter mid-night there will be an-other warning." He sighed.

"What warning? It's this noise again."

"An-other war-ning as pro-mised. That should teach them."

The tappers had the modest satisfaction that the noisy line had forced the caller to produce a louder whisper. The effort, in turn, induced a slight rattle in his throat. A touch of bronchitis perhaps?

The tracers were swearing. The call was too short. They

105

knew it was a local call, from somewhere in the Westminster-West End area of some three square miles.

It was such a peaceful scene. A tug chugged along the Sheerness quays merrily, her master quite oblivious of the turmoil of bombs and divers below the familiar warning buoys. On the horizon, some clumsy old tramp ship, laden right down to the Plimsoll line, dragged herself along, sending short impatient blasts to somebody somewhere. Bucken could have sat there watching it all through the periscope for hours. But a police launch interrupted the view. With her searchlights sweeping the water, she barked at the tug, urging her to give a wider, more respectful berth to those buoys. This was just one of Bucken's problems: his duty was to avoid causing a big upheaval on the waterfront. Whatever the risk, he must not draw bingo players' and one-arm-bandit artists' attention toward a more realistic gamble. He had an increasing suspicion that, somewhere at the top, political considerations were trying to wish away the threat.

General Brammel suffered yet another insult when, on ministerial orders, he had to surrender his command post to some Superintendent from Scotland Yard. He meant to clear out at once and it was only by chance that Bucken still caught him there.

"Could you please tell me why exactly you've brought this traveling circus in here?"

Brammel tried to size up Bucken. The question was polite enough. The chap seemed earnest enough. "I don't quite see, frankly . . ."

"Sorry," Bucken interrupted, "you're quite right. It would be none of my business in normal circumstances. But these are not normal circumstances. I'm not quite used to acting on direct orders from Downing Street."

Brammel explained his duties. Bucken listened intently, and hesitated only for a second. "Can I ask for a favor, General?"

"I have no choice, I believe."

"Stay with me. Please. You'll listen to things which only

106

I am supposed to hear, so you will take some responsibility for getting involved, because this request is in direct breach of my orders. But I may need urgent help in some corner-cutting. What do you say?"

Brammel knew for sure that this was no exercise any more. And that he was facing no fool of a policeman. A huge smile, the first since discovering his release from global marital service, slowly overflowed his face. "I'm not too bad at bending the rules myself. What?"

Bucken smiled with him. It gave him a breath of warmth to find an unexpected comrade in pulling faces at authority. He tightened the Bogart coat around the waist. He did not even realize that he was still wearing it.

He first listened to a brief report from Elms and then another from Walsh, the explosives wallah, whose shriveled face with innumerable smile grooves appealed to him, and who asked for permission "to volunteer a theory."

"Shoot."

"Wrong word, sir, if you don't mind. Even a loud fart, no disrespect meant, might trigger off something awful around here. I think that the banger on the buoy was not the full story. It's only a hunch, you understand, but it was too professional to stop at that."

"Why? Because of the precise timing as predicted?"

"Nope. That's easy to arrange. It's what Elms reported. Sounds like the bomb itself being in the tube and a receiver transducer in that rubber disc connected by cable. I mean if it was a timer, why not build it in the tube or a slightly longer piece of scaffolding? No reason whatsoever. But! It would have a detrimental effect on the clear reception of some underwater signal which, I believe, detonated the device. Now, if it's just a nasty little joke, why go in for such elaborate arrangements? Why cover the bloody buoy at all? And if it's just a prank, then why not stir up maximum publicity? No, it was all kept very quiet. As if there was something else to come. As if this was just a test or something. Now ..."

"Okay, okay," Bucken cut in impatiently. "You know

107

something about these signaling devices. Are you a specialist?"

"Worse, sir, a fucking enthusiast. It's my hobby."

"Good. Stick around. You're relieved of all other duties for the time being."

"Except that . . ."

"On highest government orders. And I mean the PM." Bucken was beginning to enjoy his special powers. It would have been even more fun to use them for starting an immediate evacuation despite the possibility of making a fool of himself with a false alarm. He still had to wait for the return of the Lieutenant Commander whose team of eleven clearance divers, all with full underwater demolition and bomb-disposal training, had already begun an initial search of the wreck.

Bucken tried to call Maxine yet again only to tell her that he would not be back, perhaps not even be in touch that night or the next day. There was still no answer. Sarah, if they were remarried, would sit at home in a situation like this, sit and wait and worry. And then divorce him once more, for the third time. Maxine also worried, but wanted him to share the feeling. She might have gone to a friend. Was the job worth losing them both and everybody else who would not fit into his distorted world of two categories—those who would steal a bike and those who would stop them?

Allerton came through using a sophisticated scrambler supplied by the Army. He told Bucken about the whispered warning given to Winnie. They agreed that it must have been a reference to the second small explosion Cutter-Smith had mentioned to support the main threat. Patrols would be out in force on the river throughout the night. It seemed unlikely that the explosion could be prevented. But the question was: how would the caller know that Cutter-Smith had not been released? Was he guessing? Had he some way of watching the flat?

"We have the entire area under surveillance," said Allerton.

"How about checking the residents, too?"

"Thanks, Bucken. Would never have thought of it."

"How about that telephone number?"

"It's been decided that we let the call go through. I mean if we decide to comply with the demand."

Bucken was astonished: "You mean to say that you won't warn . . ." He stopped. If this was the decision at C.O., in order to clear the Deputy Commissioner, perhaps he should not mention Carron's name.

"You didn't finish the sentence."

"I'm not alone. But you can't be heard. I'm using earphones."

It worried Allerton, but Bucken was not in an apologetic mood.

The young Lieutenant Commander in charge of the divers did not bother to peel off his weedy black dry suit before coming to the command post. After a quick scrutiny of the General and the two civilians, he chose to turn to Brammel who directed him with a light gesture toward Bucken. "Well, I've no idea who's running this show, sir, but we've been going up and down like yo-yos for a couple of hours without really knowing what we're supposed to do."

"I understand you took part in the last official survey of the wreck," said Bucken.

"Whatever it was worth, yes, We were not to enter and . . ."

"I know. But I'm told you might be able to say if anything has been disturbed down there."

"Rubbish. I beg your pardon, sir. What I meant was that probably you don't fully appreciate the conditions. I mean we're working in virtually total darkness, mostly with eyes closed."

"Can't you use torches or something?"

"It would make it even worse. The sand and general muck suspended in the water would only disperse and bounce back the light and blind you even more. Near the surface, on the bridge deck where the ack-ack mountings

109

are, you know, the circular gun positions that are sometimes visible at low tide, you may get some light on a
bright day, but that's all."

"I don't understand. When some university students
played a hoax for the sake of a rag charity . . ."

"Nineteen-sixty-nine," interrupted Brammel.

"Whenever it was. But I know that a survey was carried
out immediately with the specific purpose of establishing
if the wreck had been disturbed, and as a result a report of
unequivocal reassurance was published."

"Not by us, sir. We did spread out a wire mesh over
Number Two hatch to keep idiots out of this most
dangerous hold, but only in 1970!"

Bucken stared at him. And then he knew. Politics.
Bloody politics. "So if I told you that there was reason to
believe that a bomb or something had been planted down
there, what would you do?"

"I'd pray, sir," the young diver said without any
hesitation.

"Which is what I suggested to Elms in the first place,"
chuckled Walsh.

"You mean there's not a chance of locating the bomb, if
there is one, by dawn?"

"Not unless you believe in miracles, sir," said Walsh,
and the Commander offered to put his money on success
in the year 2000 or beyond.

Brammel sensed that Bucken was not ready for jokes.
"For the purpose of this little exercise, we'll have to treat
the Superintendent's supposition as a serious threat." he
said, and turned to his files.

"Sorry. Have you ever done any diving, sir?" asked
Walsh.

Bucken answered with the halfhearted nod that brought
back not particularly treasured memories; the water
pressure gave him a severe pain in the ear and he had to
overcome a constant panic of claustrophobia despite
excellent visibility.

"Where?"

110

"Off Jamaica."

"Oh. That doesn't help much. You see, here we'd have to search only by hands. Palm by palm." He thought the *Montgomery* was about five hundred feet long—which was an overestimate of the overall length but only by fifty-eight feet six inches—and suggested that "this should be considered in terms of the average hand span being, say, some ten inches. And that's only the hull, working once along its full length. And the hull is the easiest part even though it's completely covered by barnacles which would cut through rubber gloves and flesh with equal ease as you paw it gently to avoid setting off something accidentally or activating some anti-interference device. Then you'd have to dig into the sand and silt that had built up all around the hull over the years, and again, you'd be digging with your fingers."

"And we haven't even thought about the really tricky parts, all that clutter between masts and derricks and various deck levels," added the Commander. "With due respect, sir, where would you suggest we start? In the holds, tanks, cabins, stores or shaft tunnels or where? It might take years if we're lucky."

Brammel was bored with hearing only about difficulties. He put a file in front of Bucken. "I have a feeling that you'd prefer to start thinking in more positive terms, Superintendent."

He was wrong. Bucken was slowly drifting into a defeatist mood. He knew that Cutter-Smith must be sensing victory by now. He was grateful to the General for giving him pieces of paper, at least something to cling to. Perhaps a platform from where to fight back. Eventually.

The file contained some basic information about the *Montgomery* and a photograph taken during her brief lifespan. Bucken learned that the Liberty ships were a mass-produced type, "built by the mile and chopped off by the yard" as all-purpose cargo steamers. Basically, it was a British stopgap design at a time when U-boats sank cargo ships at a faster rate than the yards could build

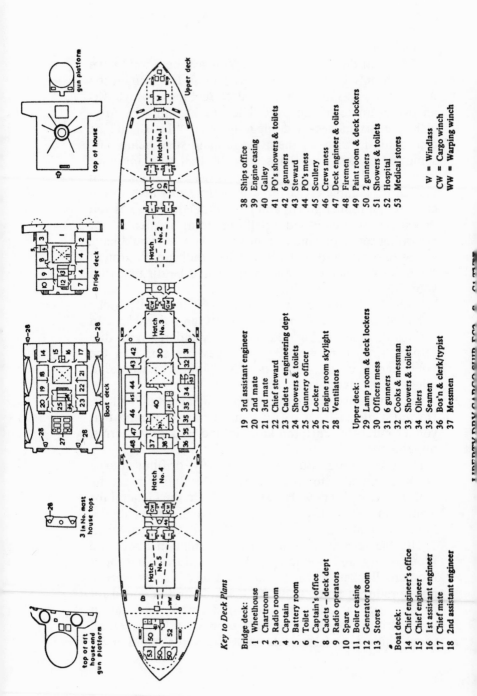

gun platform

top of house

Upper deck

Bridge deck

Boat deck

3 in No. most house tops

top of aft house and gun platform

Hatch No.1

Hatch No.2

Hatch No.3

Hatch No.4

Hatch No.5

Key to Deck Plans

Bridge deck:
1 Wheelhouse
2 Chartroom
3 Radio room
4 Captain
5 Battery room
6 Toilet
7 Captain's office
8 Cadets – deck dept
9 Radio operators
10 Spare
11 Boiler casing
12 Generator room
13 Stores

Boat deck:
14 Chief engineer's office
15 Chief engineer
16 1st assistant engineer
17 Chief mate
18 2nd assistant engineer

19 3rd assistant engineer
20 2nd mate
21 3rd mate
22 Chief steward
23 Cadets – engineering dept
24 Showers & toilets
25 Gunnery officer
26 Locker
27 Engine room skylight
28 Ventilators

Upper deck:
29 Lamp room & deck lockers
30 Officers mess
31 6 gunners
32 Cooks & messman
33 Showers & toilets
34 Oilers
35 Seamen
36 Bos'n & clerk/typist
37 Messmen

38 Ships office
39 Engine casing
40 Galley
41 PO's showers & toilets
42 6 gunners
43 Steward
44 PO's mess
45 Scullery
46 Crews mess
47 Deck engineer & oilers
48 Firemen
49 Paint room & deck lockers
50 2 gunners
51 Showers & toilets
52 Hospital
53 Medical stores

W = Windlass
CW = Cargo winch
WW = Warping winch

LIBERTY DRY CARGO SHIP EC2-S-C1 TYPE

1 Stores
2 Fore peak
3 Deep tank No 1 (P & S)
4 Deep tank No 2 (P & S)
5 Fuel oil settling tank (P & S)
6 Machinery space
7 Refrigerated rooms & storerooms (P & S)
8 Fresh water tanks (P & S)
9 Deep tank No 3 (P & S)
10 Thrust recess
11 Shaft tunnel
12 Tunnel recess
13 Shaft tunnel escape trunk
14 After peak
15 Steering gear compartment
16 Void space

17 5-ton boom (P & S)
18 50 or 30-ton boom (CL)
19 30 or 15-ton boom (CL)

Double-bottom tanks:
20 Fuel oil or ballast tank No 1
21 Fuel oil or ballast tank No 2 (P & S)
22 Fuel oil or ballast tank No 3 (P & S)
23 Void space (P & S)
24 Reserve feed water tank No 4
25 Fuel oil or ballast tank No 5 (P & S)
26 Fuel oil or ballast tank No 6 (P & S)

P & S = Port & Starboard
CL = Centre line

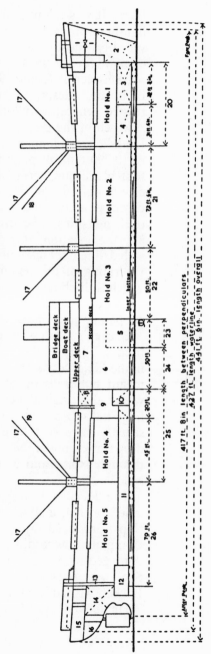

(Drawings from *The Liberty Ships* by L. A. Sawyer and W. H. Mitchell.)

them. It was adopted for the American emergency ship-building program as a type that could be assembled speedily, mostly by unskilled labor, to satisfy the vast demand for the transport of men, mixed war materials and oil. Between 1941 and 1945, some 2,800 Liberty ships were built and, despite their simple crudity, they became trusted general workhorses to carry anything anywhere.

Much of the essential data was meaningless to Bucken. Length, gross tonnage of 7,254, net tonnage, deadweight of 10,700 tons, displacement, speed of up to eleven knots, four-blade nineteen-foot propeller, single screw, the poverty of equipment, lack of radio direction finder and gyro compass, accommodation of crew and gun crew in a three-deck midships superstructure and in a single deckhouse aft, the location of refrigerated food stores, clean and soiled linen rooms, engineers' stores, hospital, et cetera, the rating of the booms, number of steam-driven cargo winches, lifeboat specifications, the reduced anchor chain length due to steel shortage, location of tanks, boilers and propelling machinery. . . .

Bucken's depression darkened by the second when he tried to apply all this to the two maps of the Liberty ships in the file. Every single line, every level, every little square meant hundreds of additional hiding places. The holds where the original bomb load would be stored seemed huge halls of potential horror. No. 2 hold was the largest: seventy-three feet long and some thirty feet deep. The deep tanks under No. 1 hold ... shaft tunnel running through No. 4 and 5. Half a million cubic feet of bale space. . . .

The *Richard Montgomery*. Built at a yard at Jacksonville, Florida, in 1943, as No. 7 of the eighty-two Liberty ships produced by the St. John's River Shipbuilding Company. According to American records, she was damaged by enemy aircraft and sank on August 20, 1944. She was regarded as CTL—Constructive Total Loss. Bucken wished she was.

He looked up. His gloom had already spread to the

other three faces. But this time it was Walsh who tried to push a lifebelt his way: "Okay, it's an immense task. Hopeless, if you like. So here are two suggestions. One is to use police divers as well as the Navy. Normally our chaps won't have anything to do with explosives under water. So we'll have to ask for volunteers because they have more experience than the Navy in searching for odd objects with their hands in low or no visibility. My other suggestion is to follow standard police procedure both on the deck and in the holds."

"Which is?" asked Bucken.

"We drop a shot weight at the end of a line and from there the diver pulls along a bottom line with a bottom weight. They work along that line, then move the weights and work their way back. Takes ages but with a bit of luck ..."

"You've never been down to this wreck, have you, sir?" asked the young Commander with the slow, aching wisdom of old frustrations.

Walsh shook his head. He knew the risks. Divers might get disorientated easily in the holds. They might unseat a door and get their lifelines clipped. Loose cargo, rotting racks, rickety crates with bombs might trap them. No matter how slowly they moved, they might disturb a sleeping eel in some cozy nook. An attack by the eel, quick evasive action ... and something might be pushed accidentally. "Well, we've got to start somewhere," he almost shouted as if reaching the crescendo of an argument.

Bucken's facial muscles began to reassert their authority over the drooping flesh and jaw. "Okay, let's then start with putting that bomb into that ship, shall we?" And seeing their surprise: "If you wanted to do it, how would you go about it?"

"Depends who I was." Walsh already loved the exercise. "I mean, am I a diver? A foolhardy professional or shit-scared amateur? Do I know the Estuary and do I really understand bombs or do I just toy with them like you play with your balls in a hot bath? No disrespect, of course."

115

"Good questions." Bucken was quick to decide that, for the time being, he would look for the simplest solutions for the various problems rather than the best ones that would require a true specialist in each field. The use of specialists would indicate a big organization behind Cutter-Smith. Bucken chose to believe that the Principal who had dreamed up the perfect crime would go for the perfect execution and reduce therefore not only the number of stake holders but also the traditional range of potential traitors, nonthinkers, panickers, show-offs and other dangerous associates. So if he had to do all or most of the chores himself, he would probably be a jack of all trades ... an expert at nothing. "No, you're not a professional diver ... You'd take some inevitable risks but try to limit them ... You must have some basic knowledge of explosives and perhaps underwater communications ..."

"The sort you can pick up in libraries?"

"Okay."

One possibility was to row a small boat to the wreck on a dark night after the police patrol had passed, and simply drop the bomb package, hoping that it would settle in some sensitive part of the wreck. But this seemed too chancy. Not a course for the man who had set up the warning explosion on the buoy and—which only Bucken knew—devised the method of demanding the money.

"Any other, more elaborate procedure would make it imperative to wet your feet," said Walsh.

Bucken agreed. He saw Brammel fade discreetly into the background, listened to the ideas and reasoning of the two bomb men, and for the first time, began to visualize the Principal—a well-spoken whisperer and natural user of slang, a lone shadow on the waterfront. He looked at Walsh's strong, fleshy yet agile hands with the sausage fingers and nails thick enough to act as emergency screwdrivers, and he was sure that the Principal's hands would not be like that.

A boat, yes, he would need a boat to approach the wreck because the powerful currents would be too dangerous—unless he was an exceptionally strong swimmer. But even a small dinghy would create problems. He would have to dodge police patrols as well as the radar coverage maintained by the P.L.A. Thames Navigation Service. At the wreck he would have to tie the boat to a mast and take the risk that the boat might also be spotted by anyone while he was below.

No. Must discard the boat. He would have to be a reasonably good swimmer. An inflatable life jacket would help. At the wreck, before the dive, he could deflate it and, with the aid of a spare pressure bottle, blow it up for the return journey.

Perfect timing would be of paramount importance. That as a challenge would appeal to the schemer he was. For the dive, he would need calm conditions. Slack water or top of the water. Low tide, especially an ebb tide at low water, would give the easiest access. Tide charts would help him choose the right day and hour. If then he used the last, slower moments of the seaward running of the tide to help him drift down to the wreck, he would have fifteen or even twenty minutes of virtually no currents disturbing his dive, and the returning young flood would give him a free ride back toward the shore.

What if he missed the masts? The tide would not have the speed and strength by then to carry him far out to sea. He could also take the precaution of swimming with a rope tied to a tree or something in a direct line above the wreck on the island. Once at the wreck, he would discard the line. But if he was not at home in the Estuary, he would need expert advice on all this. From whom?

Then the dive. Walsh and the Commander were in perfect agreement that the use of professional dry suits would be out. Although for an amateur it would be reassuring to keep all the water out and wear warm woolies for the dive, it would be impossible to put on and peel off the strong rubber outfit without assistance. A wet suit, the sort used for recreation by amateurs, would be more suitable. The water enveloping the driver underneath the suit would soon be warmed by the body and, on a summer night, would protect him sufficiently from the cold and cramps for the short dive.

A single-cylinder aqualung with demand valve and contents gauge would be enough. Even the most inexperienced and slightly panicky diver would get a good thirty minutes' air out of it. Twin cylinders would give him an extra margin of safety if anything went wrong. But the extra safety would have to be weighed against mobility: with twin cylinders he might have to risk almost twice the chance of getting hooked on or trapped by some structure.

Mobility. Fins would help him greatly to and from the wreck but they would probably be a hindrance below. Swimming along the deck or in the holds would be more dangerous than trying to walk and drift slowly. On the way down, a mast or a derrick could guide him. If he tied a line to that at deck level, it could be his landmark to return to and his guide to the surface.

Bucken suddenly knew that if he ever wanted really to understand the Principal and formulate some meaningful advice to the PM, he himself would have to dive to the wreck. A prospect that gave him no pleasure.

Brammel took a call from an outside guard: a Naval diver wished to speak urgently to the Lieutenant Commander. As the call was heard by all three of them, Brammel merely hesitated for a few seconds so that Bucken would have a chance to give or refuse permission without a General losing face. "Go and see him, then come back right away, will you?" Brammel pressed a button and a steel door opened to a blast-proof outer airlock that worked like a submarine escape hatch.

Bucken watched Walsh. He could virtually hear the brain cells clatter away like an old cash register in the bomb man's balding skull. "If this was not just an exercise, what sort of bomb or package would you look for?"

Walsh's immediate answer showed that he was also thinking along this line. "I would presume that our joker would be the same as the originator of the afternoon fireworks with the buoy. If so, why should he take the trouble to devise different systems? After all, only his target and the amount of explosives would differ—he could use the same detonators and timer or electronic trigger. Now then. If I was right, and Sergeant Elms's observation concerning the watch-size rubber disc proved to be correct inasmuch as it is connected to a tubular structure, we'd probably have the outward appearance of the bomb in question."

Bucken itched to interrupt him. Why the hell did senior policemen tend to develop this report-writing vernacular and use it as soon as a serious conversation about crime had begun? Only a twinkle in Walsh's eye prevented him from making a hasty remark—perhaps the older man was only pulling his leg. "Okay, I buy it so far. You suggested that the rubber disc might have been a receiver for some radio signal. Where does that lead us?"

"Perhaps to the likely position of the bomb. Because on underwater wavelengths you cannot transmit along a curve or bounce the signal into a closed space such as inside a wreck. The receiver therefore would have to be approachable in a straight line, on the outside, on the deck or fixed to the hull, with a cable leading to the bomb consisting of one or more pressure-type boxes or, even more likely, some scaffolding which could house explosives and electronic circuits if necessary, and which would be easy to seal with some readily available resin or rubber solution around the cable entry spot."

It was an impressive piece of reasoning and Bucken acknowledged it with a thoughtful "Mm."

"Which leads us to bloody nowhere," added Walsh. "But it's a start. Any package inside the wreck with a cable attached . . ."

A buzzer interrupted. The Lieutenant Commander had returned. The steel door slid aside to show him looking haggard and wan. "I don't know what sort of an exercise this is, but my chaps have just found a long and wide hole in the mesh over Number Two hold."

Ten minutes later, standing on the waterfront, the scene did not look peaceful any more. Bucken had no more hope that this might be a hoax of some kind. The Principal or his specialists had taken no chances and were reckless enough to enter the wreck.

He had left Cutter-Smith locked in a patrol car under guard, and now it did not improve his mood that he found chummy sleeping peacefully. "Get out. Out, out, out." He was angry with himself. He should not let the man sleep. If he is tired, he might make mistakes more easily. As might he himself.

The divers' van proved to be a comfortable home from home with changing, washing, resting and first-aid facilities. Of these, Bucken needed only the changing compartment but it took some convincing—and flashing his unusual authority—to persuade the Commander to let him dive and be his buddy.

As Bucken squeezed into the neoprene rubber suit, the cellular spongelike feel of the material brought back his unpleasant memories. An uncomfortable dive . . . a heavily weighted body in an advanced stage of decomposition. Then he wished there was less perfect visibility.

"The tide is coming in quite fast. We'll use the opposite side, sheltered by the wreck."

Bucken nodded in agreement.

"What is it you really want to know?"

"Must get the feel of the conditions. The chances for a successful search. And I want to get to the hole in the mesh."

The diver shrugged his shoulders. "If you must." Then after a pause, as casually as he could: "Any health problems?"

"I'm slightly overweight, Who isn't?"

"Heart?"

"Ticking, I suppose."

"Don't worry about air. You have a J-valve there which makes it harder to breathe if you're running out. Then just open it fully and get out. It won't happen, but I'm just telling you . . . Can you clear your ears?"

"Hope so." Bucken picked up the face mask and nose clips. He used to have some mild sinus trouble which caused the pain when he had dived before. But since then, no more sign of it. There was a fair chance that it would leave him in peace. After all, he was not going to any great depth.

Bucken arranged that Cutter-Smith should be in the Naval launch taking them to the wreck and that he should stay there, guarded by Walsh, throughout the dive. The effect on Cutter-Smith was unmistakable, and just before boarding Bucken whispered to him: "I know it's a crude way, sweetheart, but we're going to look around down there and you'll be sitting right on top. If we go up, see you in hell."

"You have no right."

"A-Ten branch will be delighted to hear from you. They love villains who disapprove of our professional conduct. But that's tomorrow. Tonight you sit it out ... unless you have some last-minute information for me to change my mind." But chummy had nothing to say. Bucken guessed the quivering lips were on the verge of crying. He had no pity for the man and felt like completing the job with a punch that would shove a few teeth down his throat, but the launch was waiting.

Bucken was a little uncertain on his feet carrying the almost fifteen pounds of belt weights and cylinder. The Commander checked his belt with the strap going over his shoulder where he now attached his one-and-one-quarter-inch lifeline to a loop. "You know how to tie a bowline?"

Yes, Bucken remembered. He knew this was something every diver would do only for himself—and he also remembered that any sailing man worth his piece of rope must pronounce bowline as if dropping the "g" from bowling. They went over the lifeline code of emergency signals once again.

They cut the engine and all radio traffic, and paddled the last hundred feet to the wreck. On the seaward side of the mast, they slowly slipped into the water, feet first, hanging on to a rail. The Commander checked their buddy-diving line, the short rope connecting them with spliced eyes around their upper arms. It was one long pull—are you all right? Bucken's instinct was to nod "yes," but then answered with one long pull—yes, okay.

They used a ladder leashed to the derrick with the port and starboard five-ton boom between No. 2 and No. 3 holds. Bucken descended slowly, not to get entangled in some rope or old safety nets, but the instant loss of visibility came as a shock despite his preparedness as soon as he was below the surface. He concentrated on his ears: would they hurt? At about ten feet down would come the test. But there was no trouble, his sinuses seemed to behave themselves. Only his mask was squeezing his face a little.

Bucken was still holding the ladder as the Commander joined him on the deck, but claustrophobia began to close in on him. It was cold, too, and in his mind he used this as an excuse for his shivers.

The Commander was leading, pulling, shifting him gently, giving him the benefit of his constant reassuring touch, but a sensation of loneliness was growing. How did the Principal put up with it? Had he ever been down there? Was he a diver or just reckless?

They were moving along the side of the hull now. Bucken knew that his bare hands were already a mess. The hard crust formed by barnacles cut his palms and fingers in parallel lines almost every time he gripped some part of the wreck to drag himself along. The mask was squeezing harder. His ears were throbbing. The pain was not yet bad enough to warrant a four-bell emergency signal to his buddy, but it added a great deal to his discomfort.

The unexpected bumping into "things" was the worst. When something live brushed past him, he wished he knew a little about marine life. The thought of touching eels made him squirm. Never, never again would anything force him to visit the wreck. Never. He swore to himself.

He heard the faint noise of a propeller. There was no

way to tell how far it was. He only hoped it was far enough.

It was then that he bumped into a body which made him jerk backward quite violently. He knew it was one of the guards posted by the Commander near the gap in the wire mesh, but in the darkness he could not control his instinct. He remembered the sketches of the wreck quite clearly. He remembered the route they had agreed to follow during the dive. But he had no idea where they were. If this was disorientation, it was a dreadful way to die. The pain in his ears grew worse. He tried to blow out and clear it. He ought to have mentioned that sinus trouble to the divers and let them keep him out of the water. Now he only hoped that his eardrums would not burst.

He touched the mesh; the edges of the hole were quite clean and straight. He knew that they would pause there so that the Commander could cut a small sample for a lab examination, but Bucken had no doubt that the gap had been cut deliberately. As he moved on, he bumped his head against something. To avoid the obstacle he tried to swim and bumped again. Disorientation had reached a point where he began to lose the sense of the vertical, too. He was not sure if he was moving or even standing the right way up.

Structural features and various objects he tried to feel with his fingers. Everything vaguely tubular, every piece of rope and cable implied the threat of setting off an explosion. And the most infuriating thing was that he had no idea of what he was handling. Any of it might have been the bomb—what a triumph if he found it.

His mouth was dry—the earache almost unbearable. He felt sure his drums began to bulge dangerously. Another long pull questioning him on the buddy line. The temptation to answer with the four bells. He knew that the Commander was also waiting for his decision: should they try to get through the gap in the mesh and descend into the hold? The temptation to say yes. Perhaps the bomb

123

was dangling only a few feet below them. Perhaps they would feel the cable, pull up the bomb and be heroes. Perhaps they would just disturb a trembler and set it off.

The buddy line tightened and held, then let go. A pull. Long, steady, distinct and unhysterical. Another. And two more. "Time's up. Start ascent." Bucken had no idea how long they had been. He was grateful that time running out had saved him from making the decision about entering the wreck.

Major Skinner, the private eye with the lopsided face between flapping earlobes, was not flattered by the unexpected visit, even if the head of the Special Branch himself was his near-midnight caller. But he did not try to hide anything. He had no reason to.

"It was about a fortnight ago that this geezer, I mean the client, called. I can look up the date, shall I?"

Allerton shook his head. He wanted to be away as soon as possible. He was allergic to private eyes and phony Majors, and this one in mauve and yellow pajamas disgusted him.

"As I say, he came himself and wanted to be trained in the use of a bug detector and our goods-marking antitheft kit for which we're also agents," he said not without pride. "He paid cash and we trained him."

"Who's we?"

"My junior partner, I mean wife ... er ... girl friend, let's say."

"Let's. Did he give his name right away?"

"Yes. Then he paid for a day's hire of all this equipment in advance."

"When's the day?"

"Tomorrow. Tomorrow it was, that is, until there was this stupid telephone call about half an hour ago."

"Who called?"

"He said he was Cutter-Smith, you know, the client himself."

"Half an hour ago, you said." Allerton knew that

Cutter-Smith could not have called from Sheerness. "Did you recognize his voice?"

"No. That's what sounded so stupid about it. He said he had a throat infection."

"And he was whispering throughout, is that it?"

"How did you know?"

"Standard symptom, I suppose."

"He was also having difficulty with saying more than one syllable in one go. But he said that the equipment would not be required, I could keep the money for that, which was very nice but of course I was offering a refund because it's not our practice to exploit the client if unforeseeable circumstances . . ."

"Anything else?"

"The rest of the arrangement is still on. I mean that we'll have to provide sort of bodyguard duties from tomorrow morning." He hesitated. "Do you . . . I mean does the police have any objection? I mean we don't want to get involved with something illegal and if we could be of any assistance . . ." His voice tapered off under Allerton's gaze. It was difficult to imagine the slight, pajama-clad senior partner in I.I.I. providing bodyguard services even to himself. "We are to report for duty at oh-nine-hundred hours," he added trying to sound very martial. "If that's okay with you, sir."

"Do you know what your duties will be?"

"No idea. But we made it a condition to be paid at the end of every day in cash."

"For tax purposes?"

"No, no, it all goes into the book. It's only that you can't imagine what sort of tricks clients can get up to."

Allerton could imagine it. Judging from the combined bedroom and head office of I.I.I. "Just go ahead and report for duty at oh-nine-hundred as arranged. And do me a favor, don't mention our little conference to the client."

Five minutes before midnight, Bucken sat alone in

Brammel's command post. He was connected to Downing Street within a few seconds, and his call was answered without delay. He was right to imagine that some tall, distinguished gentleman under a silver sheet of hair must have been waiting with a hand permanently poised over the receiver of the scrambler.

"Superintendent?"

"Yes, sir."

"What's your advice?"

"Well, it appears that for the time being ..."

"Cut it out, will you?"

"We'll have to pay."

"Right. Just what our expert panel thought."

Bucken was itching to ask who those experts were and why was anybody else consulted if he had the job exclusively, but satisfied himself with a lifeless, "I'm pleased, sir."

"Good. Prepare a summary of your reasons for recommending this course of action. You'll be here at seven A.M. precisely. The PM might wish to hear your report personally. You understand?"

"Seven A.M., sir, and I'm familiar with the address."

His voice had a sharp edge, and a slight pause at the other end of the line indicated to his greatest satisfaction that the impudence was not lost on the PM's security adviser. But he was wrong.

"The address, yes, good point, Superintendent. Make it ten to seven, and report at the entrance of the Cabinet Office in Whitehall. Use the third door from the corner. Good night."

Pity. It would have been nicer to wipe his shoes on the old scrapers and bash the door with the brass lion-head knocker of No. 10 itself. With that mild disappointment around his lips, Bucken fell asleep for fifteen minutes. Then he snatched another five minutes in the car, and a final ten minutes aboard the helicopter. Feeling quite refreshed, it was sheer joy to wake up his prisoner who had also reached the state of falling asleep anywhere any time.

126

"I have news for you."

Cutter-Smith looked up—only to turn away quickly from the picture-postcard view below. He was on the verge of throwing up, but he fought the urge and managed to mutter: "I know. You'll pay."

"And you know why?"

"Because you must."

"Wrong. Only because that way we'll catch your Principal. When he collects the money."

"He must have thought about that."

The chopper dropped a foot or two and Cutter-Smith swallowed hard.

"Accidents can happen," said Bucken.

"I know. And I can't even try to warn him."

Bucken very much hoped that he would try to warn the Principal. "What will you do with your share?"

"Nothing until my Principal has received his."

"Nothing?"

"No. Just play truant, let them miss me, but stick to routine, go for long walks, perhaps buy a few luxuries, eat in my favorite restaurants and . . ."

It might have been the thought of food that did it. With Cutter-Smith going violently sick, Bucken just about scrambled out of the way and could not resist wishing him "bon appétit."

"I have a weak stomach," Cutter-Smith apologized. He was still trying desperately to clean himself when Bucken released him at the heliport.

"How do I get home?" he shouted after the detective who opened the door of the waiting squad car.

"Walk."

Bucken did not realize that Cutter-Smith might have to do just that: no cab driver would take him until he discarded the foul-smelling jacket of the special demand-day suit. The two detectives, whose job it was to watch the suspect, invented a great variety of swear words for the Superintendent because they had to pick up and preserve that jacket in case it was needed as evidence.

*

127

Thames Division of the Metropolitan Police had its busiest night since the inauguration of the first Marine Police Office in 1798. In addition to the usual patrols—carried out by thirty-six duty boats with 100 BHP diesel engines and three twin-screw launches—the seven stations mobilized every floatable craft to cover the fifty-four mile river beat extending from Staines Bridge to Dartford Creek. They even borrowed a dozen launches from the Port of London Authority and the Kent and Essex Constabularies. Lookouts were posted at every conceivable vantage point to scan the river and the shores with army-issue night viewers. The entire operation was controlled by all the top brass the Division could muster (hurt and infuriated by being kept in the dark about the full purpose of the peculiar exercise) and, to add insult to injury, they were personally supervised by Assistant Commissioner Rattray, Deputy Commissioner Carron and Commander Allerton—with the Commissioner himself expected to put in one of his rare guest appearances.

The boats were instructed to keep away from the shore, give a wide berth to any buoy or ship at anchor, reduce engine speed to the barest minimum, refrain from any use of the two-way radiotelephones—and apprehend virtually anybody on sight ("Charge them with loitering or something similarly suitable") for stopping and staring or fiddling with any device or refusing to cease fishing or any similar activities.

By twenty minutes past midnight, twenty-seven suspects were helping the police with their obscure inquiries. Every one of them was brought to Commander Allerton at Divisional headquarters at Wapping, and only he had the authority to release them. Most of them were soon freed with not very convincing apologies. Allerton felt depressed: it seemed most unlikely that the whispering telephone caller would show up in person anywhere on the river after the open threat—unless he failed to realize that Cutter-Smith had known and given away the rough location of the second explosion. The strongest probability was that the threat would never materialize or else it would, but somewhere else. There was also a fair chance that any device would be controlled by a timer which required no personal presence or triggering by underwater transmission. Yet even this eventuality had been catered for: naval units with hydrophonic equipment were monitoring the underwater wavelengths along the river.

Fifty-seven minutes past midnight, Duty Boat No. 16, manned by an Inspector and two Constables, approached the white sculpted front of the new Metropolitan Police boatyard, separated from the old Wapping Station only by a small park. Riverview offices, overhanging the Thames with concrete legs in the water, hid some of the lookouts who now followed the progress of No. 16. She passed the yard and drew level with Wapping Station. The Inspector looked toward the shore and saw the long black catwalk, leading to a decrepit police landing stage, tremble and topple. He later swore that a leg went first, that the water around it humped up, and that he heard no explosion. The first two observations were eventually confirmed by technical experts, the third was meaningless because the sound of the small explosion—hardly registered by the hydrophones—would be suppressed by the engine of No. 16.

Divers of the police Underwater Search Unit—already on full alert at their Wapping base—were in the water within seconds of the explosion. They would scour the entire area, try to prevent anything from floating away, and clean up the riverbed as no underwater stretch had ever been cleaned before.

Bucken heard about it on the crackling police car radio as he was driven toward the West End. It seemed pointless to go to Wapping right away. There was nothing for him to do there. He asked Allerton how serious the explosion was.

"Nothing. Non-event. So tiny that if anyone were on that catwalk when it happened, he would have his feet wet. That's all. Quite ineffectual."

Ineffectual? Bucken had his private views about that. It

happened under the nose of the police once again. But he asked only about surveillance facilities—and found that anything he wanted would be available.

"Any other questions?" asked the Commander.

"No. I'll try to snatch a few hours' sleep."

"Er ... yes ... do that." Allerton could not bring himself to tell Bucken about Maxine. He would find her in his Bayswater flat anyway. Under police guard. "I'll see you after your Whitehall visit. There'll be time to work out the best way to hand over the money."

But Bucken was not yet ready to go home. He sent surveillance units to Elstree, left his car with the driver in the shadow of the Regent Palace Hotel, then walked down to Piccadilly Circus, along the by-then half-dead Shaftesbury Avenue, to the Professor's all-night hot dog stall in Wardour Street, on the edge of spreading Chinatown.

The Professor was an odd mixture of a chum and a squealer, but if he was an extraordinary friend for a detective, he would be an even more exceptional snout, too. The Soho legend was that he used to teach in Vienna before becoming a refugee from Hitler, and that many City bankers still regarded him as one of the great financial brains of this age. Allegedly, some tycoons could be seen consulting him any night. Nobody ever bothered to check the details or to cross-examine him as to why he had become a hot dog seller, but it was an accepted fact that it was not worth knowing what the Professor did not know about the movement of money, fortunes and small sums, legal and illegal transactions in London and in other money capitals as well as in the tax havens of the world. In a flat school-masterish tone, considering principles more than practicalities, he would always be ready to advise anyone who cared to ask him, showing no favors to financiers, villains or the Fraud Squad—if the legend was to be believed.

Bucken had known him for years when he happened to hear that the Professor was applying for naturalization. He volunteered to be one of his referees. Later he was warned that it might be inappropriate for him, as a Special Branch officer, to give the Professor the necessary references, but the old man valued the gesture itself, and the casual offer earned Bucken a friend. The Professor would still refuse to put a finger on anyone, but in his quiet impersonal fashion, he would sometimes drop a hint or two which Bucken could interpret and use or pass on to others. Tonight, Bucken needed every crumb he could pick up. There was a fair chance that the Professor might soon hear something about the fate of a hot million. Or else he might already know something: clever crooks sometimes established a reputation of legitimate wealth or gambling wins well in advance of the day of pocketing their criminal profits, so that any suspicious connection between a crime and their good fortune could be avoided.

The ageless old man's white coat and rakishly angled cap sparkled in the streetlights. His long, childishly thin arms shot up to express delight and greet the detective who shouted from a good thirty yards away: "Vee gates, hare Professor?" Bucken's polite *"Wie gehts, Herr Professor?"* sounded as German as the old man's answering "Vat vill yoo have, mein friend?" could be accused of being English. But they understood one another.

Luckily, the old man had no other customers. He could talk as freely as he wished. This meant, however, that Bucken would have to play chess, and halfway through his second night's vigil, shivering despite the warmth of the Bogart, he did not feel up to it. Still, it could not be helped—and he would lose anyway. The Professor whiled away the long nights' loneliness with working out chess problems in his head. For his customers, he had two small magnetic boards fixed to the outside of his stall, where he could not see them. His greatest moments were when he could find two good opponents to play blind simultaneously. If the customers left leaving the games unfinished, he would just remember the positions on the boards—and new opponents could continue where the others had left off.

The Professor opened the lid and submerged himself in steam for a few seconds, only to surface with a double hot dog soaked in hot English mustard—just the way his "shtupid detective" friend liked it. "Come, come, you avoided me for ten months, but there is something quite wonderful for you." This could be it, Bucken hoped for a moment. "A variation on a Nimzowitsch-Capablanca endgame which they played in New York in neunteen twenty-seven. Which do you want to be?"

Bucken tried not to show disappointment and chose to be Capablanca—or at least a variation on him—and moved his black Pawn to K4 attacking a Bishop. "Ach, you think you are clever? Then how about Rook to Queen 1, what?"

"Mm. My apologies to Mr. Capablanca."

"While you think, you must also look at the other board. It is an interesting Queen gambit play, a little like Belsitzmann played against Rubinstein in Hamburg. No . . . Perhaps Leningrad . . ."

Bucken decided against a devious approach—off the board. "Listen. I don't usually ask direct questions, do I?"

"No, it could not be Leningrad. Not in neunteen-seventeen or eighteen . . ."

"You sometimes give me a hint or two, and I sometimes tell you something that may help some small fry keep out of the way when the heat is on for something big. Right?"

"It's your move."

"Pawn takes Bishop."

"You are mad. Shtupid."

"Maybe, but I really must ask for a favor. It concerns a million. A feather bed may already be prepared for it. Can be anything. Some transfer, a big legalization coup, a trick to convert it into some foreign currency or just resting. And I must know."

"How much?"

"A million."

"Chickenfeet."

"Feed. Chickenfeed."

"Makes no difference. Queen to Queen 4."

132

"I'm willing to make an exchange."

"What? Queen for Queen?"

"Information."

"You must be very desperate. But I don't do business with you. You are mein friend. And what I tell you is more important than your . . . ach! It must have been Hamburg after all!"

A car had stopped. The Professor served two young customers. Thugs, really. Bucken was ready for a fight. But they left peacefully. The detective was always amazed that the Professor was not mugged once a week. Perhaps he had too many influential friends in the underworld.

"Where was I?"

"You said it must have been Hamburg, after all."

"Oh, yes. That my news is more important than your chickenfeet million. Because too many people say that business is good, very good, and will be very, very good, because the police is in their pocket. And they get the tipoff from your Scotland Yard, you know. That's what they say."

"Who says so?"

"Come, mein friend. You know me better than to ask things like that. And I don't know those people. I only know the gossip, what's the word, rumor? But even old crooks are crying because somebody is taking the cream from every job as a sign of *friendship*. Skim-off, that's what they call it. And they take now more away than the Krays and the Richardsons used to take."

"Poor, poor villains. It breaks my heart."

"It should, mein friend. Because the money is for protection—*from* the police! And then the money must go *to* the police!"

Bucken felt a lump in his throat. Yet another reference to leaks and corruption at the top. Chickenfeet. He saw the Lad's feet sticking out from under the white sheet. "Rubbish," he said without much conviction.

"Please yourself, mein friend."

"You must tell me more to convince me."

133

"I never must anything! Never. You understand? But I don't like when people say that the police is in their pocket. The last time I heard that was when I had to run away because the Nazis really had the police in their pocket. And now it's the Chinese."

"I thought you like the Chinese."

"I do. Wonderful people. But they have the Tong. You know the Tong? The Triads? I think somebody uses them on hire or what."

Bucken could only nod. The way the Lad had been killed would just fit the style of Tong thugs, members of the secret brotherhood that might still be controlled from somewhere in Hong Kong or Singapore, with possible branches everywhere else. He forced himself to say "Rubbish" once again only to bait the old man. "They might terrorize a few Oriental grocery shops or restaurants, and blackmail a wretched gambler or a prostitute, but they've never been big in London."

"There is always a first time. And there were other police forces in their pockets, remember?"

"That was in Hong Kong."

"Please yourself."

"Thanks anyway. And please, please keep an ear open for that million."

Another three moves later, Capablanca's carefully built position was in ruins. The old man was still trying to remember the location of the Belsitzmann game—"It could have been Berlin, you know"—when Bucken said goodbye.

"Remember the Triads and look after yourself." He never accepted money for hot dogs from his friends and those whom he regarded as true, professional and full-time vagrants.

Bucken had stopped shivering. He credited the mustard with it. He first opened the Bogart coat, then took it off, and finally, as he cut through Windmill Street, he just let it drop on the pavement at the entrance of a nightclub. A stripper or a drunk might treasure it on a cold night. For him, it was the end of an era of partnership. Perhaps he ought to buy a coat one day.

"All right. Out. Your time is up." No, that's too crude. "Sorry, darling, it just didn't work out. And it would be even worse from now on. Because you wouldn't want to live with a bankrobber, would you?" Wrong again. Why should Winnie have the satisfaction of refusing to put up with it? She must go. Because her husband, her master, says so.

Cutter-Smith was chewing, tasting words all the way home. Harsh words like "wretched cripple," succulent words like "I declare you a marital failure." Failure. "You're the failure, not me, no matter how many times you call me a failure. Those who fail to comfort a loser should not benefit when the tables are turned. So winner takes all and there will be nothing left to share. Hard luck, darling. Find yourself a good man. A feeble goody-goody." And if she tried to drown his usual meek protestations against the flood of motherly scolding, even a firm "fuck off" might be in order, for the first time since he left school, only to show that he was now outside her marital jurisdiction.

Winnie must go. Preferably tonight. Or why not leave her? Just walk out. Taking only the suit for Collection Day. "Come back! Come back! Please come ..." "No. It's all yours now, whatever it's worth. I'd help you with more, but of course you wouldn't dream of accepting any juice squeezed out of the fruits of crime, would you?"

From the rear window of the cab he noticed that a car followed him all the way to Elstree. It did not matter. He also noticed long shadows in the street: some detectives tried to make no secret of their presence. It would have been pointless.

The flat was in darkness. But Cutter-Smith knew that Winnie was there, waiting. She would not take her sleeping tablets—that would deprive her of the pleasure of asking him what he thought the time was. Better be bold and attack. No cautious shuffling—the gait of the winner and all lights on. Yet he was wrong. She was asleep. Even though he saw her tablets and water prepared at the bedside but untouched. For the first time in about ten years, she was tired enough to enjoy natural sleep. Not even the lights disturbed her. And he did not quite know how to wake her. He dropped a shoe hard on the floor, but when she stirred, he placed the other shoe quietly on the carpet.

He sat down on the bed and looked at her face. He still found it beautiful. The blanket followed the curves of her body, and he had long forgotten that it was not perfectly normal for a woman to have one leg. Only his recent thoughts reminded him to call her a cripple. But it seemed unfair to wake her up with it. He climbed slowly into the bed, moving inch by inch not to disturb her. It was hard to wriggle free from the years of binding habit.

He closed his eyes and tried to sleep. But Mother appeared on the screen of his eyelids. "The false pretense of being virtuous seems to be over, Johnny. You're no good. You've never been good. You're fishing only for an excuse to leave her." I love her, Mother. "Lies! Lies!" I love her. "Love? Taking advantage of her is what you call love?" I married her, didn't I? How many men would have married her? "A million. Any man. If she wasn't an invalid." But she was, Mother. She still is. "And yet you plan to leave her—see?"

It was no good. But he could not sleep. The best would be to sneak away and only write to her. No, he had to say it to her face. He had to tell her that it was not his fault. That now she would not need to put up with him any more. "It's only what you always wanted, Winnie. I now admit that I'm bad, rotten to the core as you always said, and I even give you the final proof by leaving you as a criminal ... I'm mad. I can't say all this. I'm apologizing. What for?"

He tried to decide when to tell her. Not before collecting

the money. Until then he would not be a real criminal. Besides, there would hardly be time for a long talk—if she wanted a long talk. It must wait until the afternoon. He lightly caressed her hair, and she smiled in her sleep as if she liked it. His air intake began to grow and grow until his chest seemed to reach a state of permanent expansion. His stomach muscles vibrated with an inner belly laugh and he had a throbbing erection. It was exhilarating to be a winner.

4

COLLECTION DAY

For once the shower mixer attachment of totally independent will worked in Bucken's favor. It changed the water temperature with unpredictable frequency on a full scale as if it were calibrated from "scald" to "ice," and so helped the detective to cross the threshold between a sleepless night and another dawn with renewed vigor.

By now he had the impact of the initial shock behind him. Maxine was asleep, in the combined gentle care of a tranquillizer shot and a woman police officer who at last told Bucken about the attack and the injuries, which were not serious. When the WPC left, Bucken sank into a chair, next to the bed, and spent the remaining few hours of the night in a semiconscious slumber, his mind racing freely between the alternating courses of marrying Maxine first thing in the morning or leaving her forever and concentrating on revenge. Luckily, she slept through his dilemma as well as the arrival of another WPC to take over from him, sparing him the agony of major decision-making. After all, he could not marry her because Sarah was his wife whether they were in a state of divorce or not, and he could not set out on a mission of personal revenge without breaking the lifelong stranglehold of duty. It was only in the first few minutes of his fury that he failed to trust his fellow officers whose job it would be to track down the attackers with compassion (it concerned a colleague's life) and integrity (despite its concerning a colleague's life). It was only on his way to Whitehall that his doubts returned and accused him of being a phony and a self-deceiving cheat, but by then it was too late.

The Cabinet Office building appeared to be asleep, but when he pressed the polished brass bell, the door was opened without delay by a security guard and a secretary—he had been expected. In the street, No. 10 appeared to be just a few steps away from the corner of Whitehall. Inside, along a web of underground corridors, he suffered such a strong disorientation—not unlike his feeling underwater—that he thought the girl had lost her way to the internal side entrance to No. 10.

"Didn't you know you could walk all along Downing Street inside the buildings, all the way through Number Ten and Eleven and Twelve without seeing daylight?"

She sounded too chirpy for his liking at this hour of the day, but her wiggling tail made it a forgivable sin. She led him through a door into a red-carpeted corridor. "Here we are." He glanced toward his left and saw the main door. It gave him an acute sensation of being on "the other side" where prime ministers disappear from the telly cameras. Turning right, she led him into the antechamber of the Cabinet Room. Bucken would have hated to admit even to himself that the place somehow managed to overawe him. Yet there was not much to look at. A bare round table covered by black oilcloth, a sofa and few chairs which *per se* would not increase the pulse rate of a country auctioneer who was ignorant of their history, and hat and coat pegs around the walls. But then he noticed the gothic script assigning each peg to the holder of a ministerial post.

"I'm one of the Garden Girls," she said in a sweaty attempt to chat him up. "You know, I work in that maze of offices which overlook the garden which gave us its name. I do filing, actually." She looked at her watch. "The PM starts the day in three minutes." She nodded toward the double doors leading to the inner sanctum. His reverence level began to rise once again. And he could not quite understand why he felt so embarrassed by this peculiar sense of occasion. Perhaps because No. 10 and the Cabinet Room conjured up visions of Pitt and Churchill rather than the current political midgets, of war rather than a bomb scare, and of a whirlpool of gold braid and epaulettes rather than a cop chatting up a Garden Girl. Or perhaps it was one of the rare occasions when his own importance impressed him.

At seven o'clock precisely, a tall and distinguished gentleman entered. It was a pity that alcohol, probably good wine, had embroidered such an intricate pattern in red on his nose. "Thank you, young lady, that will be all. You hold yourself in readiness, Superintendent."

As the door opened and closed, Bucken caught a glimpse of the huge Cabinet table covered in green baize cloth, some two dozen chairs around it, the clock on the far side between windows overlooking Horse Guards Parade, the french window in the corner leading down to the garden, and the right shoulder of the PM seated in front of the fireplace under Walpole's picture. All the other chairs were empty, and Bucken tried to guess if he would be offered a choice of seats. But less than two minutes later he was told that he would not be required to report to the PM in person. Pity. And relief.

"The PM has authorized me to wish you good luck in your predicament."

"Thank you, sir."

"You'll carry this considerable burden by yourself in the national interest."

"Crap." Fortunately, it sounded "Durp." Bucken cleared his throat once again for emphasis.

"It is, of course, a highly irregular situation and you now have the opportunity to back out." And without any pause: "But I'm glad you don't wish to. I understand you want us to pay. What's your immediate plan?"

"I only want to avoid the explosion and gain time. Beyond that . . ."

"The plan. Your plan."

"We'll watch the money mainly by using that private detective, already employed as a bodyguard. But beyond that, we'll play it by ear."

"Oh."

140

"I can see certain leads to follow up if we have the time, but of course our best chance is to make our arrests when the meeting is arranged and the dough, I mean the cash is handed over."

"Our arrests and our chance? I thought you understood that without my personal permission no other officer is to be made privy to the true purpose of your inquiries. Allerton will coordinate, but you won't submit written reports and you won't be required to come here ever again. This is because the case is handled by the police, confidentially but through the usual channels, without our participation. Is that clear?"

"Perfectly, sir."

"In other words, the PM has never, never been involved or even informed. Is that how you understood it?"

"I follow you."

"Good. If anything goes wrong, though I'm sure nothing will, you'll have to be held responsible, I mean for any foolhardy decision or single-handed action that might invite disaster, and of course I can't promise you rewards or promotion or anything like that, you understand. So at least enjoy your freedom and make the most of it. You can reach me on this number." He held up a slip of paper. "Will you remember it?"

Bucken nodded. "And your name, sir . . ."

"What? Oh, yes. Yes. Call me Wade. Michael Wade."

By the time Bucken left the building through the back door, an Inspector White from Special Branch had already introduced himself to Major Skinner of I.I.I.

"With reference to the earlier visit paid to you by Commander Allerton, I am to ask you for a special favor." He dug his nails into his palm and forced himself to add: "Sir."

"I'm always anxious to help the police." (I bet you are, thought White, but said nothing.) "Is it in connection with this bodyguard job?"

"Yes, sir, but don't ask me what exactly it is because I myself wasn't told."

"So what can we, I mean I.I.I. do for you?"

"I believe you drive an old Cortina estate car. Is that correct?"

"Yes."

"Has it ever been seen by your ... er ... client?"

"No, I don't think so."

"That's good. Now what exactly is your duty going to be?"

"As far as I know, Mr. Smith, Cutter-Smith as he wishes to be known, will have something exceptionally valuable in the boot of his car possibly for days or even weeks. We're supposed to guard that boot day and night."

"And you have the necessary personnel for that, sir. I mean three shifts every twenty-four hours, relief men to allow the officer on duty to answer the, er, calls of nature, et cetera, et cetera ..."

"Mm, well. We would ... mm ..."

"Quite. We understand. And that is where we would come in. You see, we could supply you with a faster and later version of your car, and officers who could share the long hours of duty with you. Because we understand the contents of that boot will indeed be valuable, and we wish to keep an eye on it ourselves."

Major Skinner felt he was growing in stature by the second. "I see. You want to come in on this with me, under the I.I.I. umbrella, so to speak. Mm. Well, I don't see why not. I mean no ethical considerations would seem to preclude our cooperation. The client's interests, our main concern, would be even better served, and our integrity, any private detective organization's chief asset, would come through unscathed. ... And if we use your car, will you also supply petrol and shall we be exempt from parking fees?"

The Bogart coat awaited Bucken at the reception desk of the Yard. Would it never go away?

"Who brought this in?"

"Old Jock, sir, you may know him as the Lord of the Lies," the Sergeant said.

Of course he knew Jock. Most London cub detectives learned interrogation on him. The old man claimed to have lied his way out of every police station within a couple of square miles around Victoria Station where he slept on cold days: vagrants, sleeping rough, were chased by the police only at night. So he slept in the morning. "Did he say anything?"

"First he only said that the Professor had sent him with the coat, but when he was already at the door, he remembered a message which must be in code, sir." The Sergeant consulted his notes. "Here we are: 'Tell Superintendent Bucken that it was Warsaw and not Berlin'—does it mean anything to you, sir?"

"Oh, yes." The Sergeant seemed impressed so Bucken decided to reaffirm a little of his old reputation at C.O. "It's a reference to Belsitzmann in nineteen seventeen," and walked to the lifts leaving a baffled Sergeant trying to pin a little criminal history on the memory of the hapless chess player.

Admittedly, he, too, was perplexed by the reappearance of the coat. How did it find its way to the Professor? How could the old man be so sure that it was Bucken's when this was definitely the first time that the detective had worn it in London? Questions that would have to wait.

He found that his old room, next to Allerton's, had been reallocated to him. That pleased him. There was a report on Skinner: he turned out to be an ex-major indeed—but of the Salvation Army. The traffic controller of the Yard TV Center was waiting to see him. A message from the Bank of England about the assembly of cash for unspecified destination. A series of receipts to be signed by him acknowledging that various sums, amounting to a million pounds, had been paid to him over the past seven years for obscure research and charity organizations.

"I hear that, finally, you made your decision," said Allerton.

"What decision?" Bucken disliked the emphasis on "you" and "your" decision.

"That you want to pay."

"Oh, yes."

"I fully understand. But as it was you who advised the PM . . ."

"The PM has not been involved."

"I see what you mean."

"But you have."

"Oh, no, my boy. I was not involved in making the decision. You had a free hand. So you'd better make sure that the money is not wasted or lost." Allerton paused. "But I'll bloody well try to back you with everything we've got."

"Thank you."

"You may retain the use of the chopper and requisition any number of cars."

Bucken had less than thirty minutes to make essential arrangements for the surveillance of Cutter-Smith and the money. In that half hour, his secretiveness managed to generate more resentment among his colleagues than a lifetime's good comradeship could undo.

He had made his most pressing decisions by 0820. He had left instructions for the WPC in his home to phone him as soon as Maxine was up, and her call caught him on his way out.

"She's awake, sir, but she refuses to talk to you."

"All right. Just give her the receiver whether she wants it or not, then leave her alone in the room."

Bucken knew that if there was one object in the world Maxine could not resist, it would be a telephone. She would talk into it—or throw it. Expertly.

"How do you like your girls? Rare or well done?"

"I just wanted to tell you how sorry I was. I really am." He sounded like that, too.

"How is your head?"

"My what?"

"Head. You know, the hairy growth on the top of your neck to stop your tie slipping off in the wind."

Bucken touched the wound. It was still throbbing but he had forgotten about it. "Never mind my head, love, it's bad enough to hear that you can't take better care of yourself. Now why the hell would you warm your feet in the oven on a nice day like that?"

He could not promise what time he would go and see her. He begged her to wait. And he really meant it. He wanted to see her. Perhaps more than he wanted to sit with Sarah. Which was odd.

"All right, I wait, but you must let me get rid of this pious bride of the Metropolitan Police," she demanded.

"She may stay in the other room. But don't kick her out into the rain for God's sake." Sarah would insist on having company. Preferably male company. She refused to be alone day or night in any circumstances.

Chief Inspector Jeff Walsh was waiting for him at the wheel of a Jaguar. "It was good of your boss to let me borrow you and I appreciate it that you didn't mind," said Bucken. "What's more, I needed you because you can recognize a bomb scare when you see one, and you were recommended to me as an excellent driver despite the fact that you're stone deaf."

Walsh did not turn to face him. "I'm a lousy driver."

"Rubbish. But you're stone deaf, Jeff."

"As you wish, sir."

"They call me plain Bucken, but you may use Quint, if you wish. And you have twenty minutes to hit Elstree."

Walsh shrugged his shoulders and switched on the engine. "It's your funeral," he mumbled and started the Jag as if he meant to leave its rear behind.

At twenty to nine, the breezy village street was as quiet and deserted as always. The milkman noted that the large electricity board van was still parked there but he attached no significance to it until that madman of a driver in a Jag (Allerton's best) burst into the silence of the street with the engine roaring and the tires sanding the curb around the corner. It stopped only to allow its tall passenger to jump out, and then disappeared through the entrance of a lumberyard.

"No wonder those bloody electricity bills go up and up, nonstop," the milkman muttered.

Bucken knocked and the back door of the van opened. Once inside, he positioned himself in front of a pair of powerful binoculars. Passersby would never notice the lenses hidden in the dots of the two i's of "electricity," but he had a perfect close-up view of the door to the Cutter-Smiths' ground-floor maisonette. A detective seated next to him was about to film the still grumbling milkman—a record was to be kept of everyone who appeared in the street. Another two detectives sat in front of an instrument board and three large tape recorders—one running, another ready to take over as soon as the first stopped, and a third on standby. Several of the volume control knobs were marked—bedroom 1, living room, kitchen, bathroom, bedroom 2, hall, main door (external), telephone. The well-placed bugs were not supposed to miss a suppressed burp.

"Nothing much," reported the senior man to Bucken. "They were up at six thirty-seven and she swore that he was trying to poison her or to imply that she was mad because she must have taken her pills without which she would never be able to sleep. Since then she's been calling him names and he mostly refuses to answer. He's been dressing himself for about the last, oh, fifty, fifty-five minutes, and she likes it less and less."

Bucken moved over and put on a pair of spare earphones. He disliked Winnie's voice and that made him sympathize with the husband. She spoke like those amateur actresses who never quite grew out of the ever-so-successful school adaptation of *Alice in Wonderland* for open day.

"So you don't want to talk to me."

"I told you, Winnie, dear, I have a lot to say, and I will say it tonight."

"If I'm still here."

"If you're still here."

A cupboard door squeaked, but her voice soon drowned

146

it. "So you bought a hat, too! So that's where the money is going. What? Answer me!"

"I've told you. Everything I'm going to wear is brand-new, and that includes the hat."

"It looks terrible."

"I promise I'll soon throw it away."

"Like that brand-new jacket?"

"Like that brand-new jacket, dear."

"What are you up to? You want to rob a bank?"

"Didn't the police tell you?"

"No."

"Then, apparently, it must be regarded as utterly confidential."

"I'm only pleased that your poor mother didn't live to see this. It would have killed her seeing you in prison."

"I do not intend to go to prison."

"Criminal. Bank-robber. Murderer."

"Thank you."

She must have run out of words: she began to sob hysterically. "Tell me, Johnny, please tell me, redeem yourself at least in my eyes, tell me that you can't help it, that they're using you again, you're blackmailed, you're doing it for your country . . ."

"Nobody is using me. Not any more."

Bucken was called back to the binoculars. A Cortina had just parked in front of the house under surveillance. Bucken took a good look at Skinner and Inspector White. He did not like the arrangement, but it seemed the best in the circumstances. The private detective's presence gave the police a tailor-made cover for sitting incessantly on the suspect's tail, but it was just a little too convenient—it gave him no choice. If the private eye's car were cut off in traffic, Cutter-Smith would notice it. Following behind the Cortina the police car itself would be cut off. He would have to use motorcyclists at least from time to time. He asked for an extension cable so that the earphones could reach him while standing at the binoculars.

"Major Skinner reporting for duty, sir." The "main door

147

(external)" knob needed some adjustment. Now it was loud enough. "And that's my best operative, Mr. White."

"I thought you'd be on your own, Major," said Cutter-Smith.

"Never, sir, never. It's elementary to have a partner as a backup in bodyguard assignments."

"You have all the equipment?"

"No, sir. You said you didn't want it."

"Did I? When?" He sounded alarmed.

"You called me last night, didn't you? I'm glad your voice is all right now."

"Oh, yes. Yes. Was I whispering on the phone?"

"Don't you remember?"

"Oh, yes. Yes. Good. Will you wait in the car then? We'll be leaving soon."

Two minutes before nine, another two cars arrived. The maroon Triumph 2000 with the uniformed chauffeur told its own story, but Bucken asked for a quick check on the car hire firm through the registration number. At this stage, it seemed pointless to involve the chauffeur who, for all he knew, might be an accomplice himself.

The other car, a battered Renault, was more of a puzzle and a full checkout was started immediately. Its driver, a portly man in a two-sizes-too-small tweed hat, unloaded a small suitcase and a large briefcase and carried them to the door.

Bucken turned the "main door (external)" volume to full blast.

"Mr. Smith?"

"Cutter-Smith, yes."

"Don Downes is the name. Delivering the gear you or rather your colleagues asked for."

"Oh."

Downes put down the briefcase and checked a note. "I hope I got the right address ... your man was a bit of a mumbler with that toothache ..."

"Oh, yes. Come in."

Bucken found the hall and living room microphones much more satisfactory.

"You know how to use these things, I suppose."

"Let's just check it ... Mm, yes, these are the types I know ..."

"Yes, your poor man said you'd know these models. I was, in fact, a little worried because there are so many different types these days, and every Tom, Dick and Harry pretends to be a main dealer, but we can of course supply and make and we're main distributors for several of them."

"Yes, yes, thank you. Anything to pay or sign?"

"Just this chit, please. I'll return it to you with the deposit when you don't need the stuff any more."

"It may be days or weeks."

"That will be fine."

"Don't leave it with him," Winnie shouted from the bedroom. "He's a criminal! He's a criminal!"

"Well, we don't like snooping or poking our noses into the client's affairs ..."

"Don't worry, Mr. Downes, the equipment is safe and purely for defensive purposes."

"Yes, that's what I was told originally. We don't like to get involved, you know ..."

Shooting out of the lumberyard, Walsh caught up with the departing Renault easily and almost managed to ram it, too. A little extra fright could only be useful to Bucken, he thought, as he persuaded Downes to wait with him.

Bucken still had a phone call to make. "Is that you, Smith?"

"No. Must be a wrong number," said Cutter-Smith and put the phone down. He was lucky not to hear what Bucken thought of that. Then the call came through again.

"Superintendent Bucken here. Is that you?"

"Who do you wish to speak to?"

"Cutter-Smith," he said through his teeth.

"Mr. Cutter-Smith speaking."

"Listen. The arrangements have been made, but it would be more convenient to hand it over in a flat in Cheapside. Quite near the Bank and nothing cheap about it."

"No. Won't do."

"It's actually owned by the Bank and it's rather grand for it's mostly used by the Governor for official entertaining."

"I believe I've specified every detail. It's got to be Grandma himself in the Court Room, and that's that. I'll be there at noon. The rest is up to you."

Bucken took it out on Downes as Walsh drove them toward the Yard. "Who was the man who hired the equipment?"

"I don't know."

"You like to deal with strangers?"

"I'm in business, it makes no difference."

"As long as they have the cash."

"As long as they have the cash."

"And this man had cash, right?"

"Yes."

"I suppose we'll find the amount in your books."

"Well, as a matter of fact . . ."

"You cook the book monthly, I know. Describe him."

"Very tall and very fat. I remember quite clearly. And had a dreadful toothache."

"Which made him whisper all the time. Right?"

"How did you know?"

"So you remember nothing about him."

"I remember everything." Downes sounded thoroughly insulted. "I may not be a cop, but I'm connected with the security industry. I remember he came last week . . . on Tuesday, gave me no name, said he was acting on behalf of Mr. Smith which sounded a phony but apparently wasn't, he had the toothache with a big lump in the face, he was sweating profusely . . ."

"Wasn't all that hot last week."

"No, but he wore a heavy overcoat."

"Bet it was really flash," remarked Walsh. "Large checks or something like that? He'd want you to remember that instead of his face."

Downes suddenly remembered pebble glasses: "Yes, he

had to clean them several times because the heat he was generating must have made them foggy . . .”

But Bucken guessed that the overcoat was not to bear sole responsibility for all that sweating. Probably the “big fat man” was not fat at all. The padding would account for all the sweat. Cleaning the glasses would give him a chance to shift that “lump” in his mouth before it gave him a real pain.

A call came through on the radio for Bucken. The teletappers had sent a message to Oscar Victor 2, the call sign of the surveillance van: “Suspect has been trying repeatedly to get through to Harrow number as expected but there is no answer.”

So Cutter-Smith was trying to report, according to his instructions, that the payout had been agreed. The tappers were using impulse recorders which registered the numbers dialed by Smith. But the surprise would have been if there was an answer: Deputy Commissioner Carron had spent the night at C.O. and his wife was still in hospital after an emergency appendectomy.

By the time Bucken reached the Yard, Downes's background and criminal record had been checked out: one conviction for fraud eight years ago; now a partner of electronic gadget manufacturer, handling the trade side only; lately of international reputation as supplier of bugging, tapping and concealed recording equipment.

“You're in trouble, Downes, and don't try to deny it.” said Bucken. “Help us and I might be persuaded to forget things.”

“I supplied only defensive equipment. As I told you, I delivered a bug-detector set and a comprehensive kit for marking goods electronically and chemically as an anti-theft measure. Nothing illegal in that.”

“All right, we're going to check your books right away. Shall we?”

He became most cooperative when Walsh took him to “Hefty” Solomon, the Yard's own electronics wizard whose job would be to assess the limitations of the detector and come up with some counter countermeasures.

Another message from the teletappers reached Bucken outside Rattray's room: Cutter-Smith was still trying to contact that Harrow number, but in the meantime had called his bank manager and told him, later in the morning, a hundred thousand pounds would be paid into his account; ninety thousand pounds of that he wanted transferred to his deposit account, currently standing at £4.55. The rather flabbergasted manager wanted to know where the money would be coming from, and "suspect" assured him that it was all perfectly legitimate.

"Why did you want to see me so urgently?" asked Rattray as Bucken entered. The air in the room was already hazy from the cigar smoke.

"Because of Carron. Why did you want to let the call go through?"

"Not that I have to answer that..."

"Yes, you do, I'm acting under direct orders from Downing Street. Remember?"

"Just don't let it go to your head. Do you have your orders in writing?"

"No. And I also know why. If anything goes wrong at any stage, a comparatively junior man will be blamed and told to piss off. Perhaps an error of judgment by his superiors to leave it to him. But that him is me, and I don't like it."

"I'm sorry. I really am."

"I'll add your sympathy to my reduced pension."

"As a matter of fact, I tried to talk others out of it. You had enough on your plate as it was but they wanted you and I had to admit you were the best man for the job."

"Thank you. So will you tell me about Carron?"

"Yes. Letting the call go through was the quickest way to clear him of any suspicion."

"I don't see the reason for being suspicious at all. Only an idiot would make such an obvious arrangement if he was involved."

"That's how the Commissioner saw it, too, but we

wanted to make his innocence visible to all and sundry. Except, perhaps..."

"What?"

"It's only that the call wouldn't need to go through at all. I mean if somebody tapped the line the way we did, a dial counter would give him the same information, that chummy did try to call the Harrow number, and that's what matters."

"Brilliant idea."

"Sorry that I only thought about it now."

"I'm going to score, Ratts." Rattray stiffened as Bucken used his name normally reserved for Peel-housing. But Bucken just went on: "For I did think about it and I had that line fully checked and cleared. Physically and electronically."

"Oh. I didn't know."

"Perhaps it was one of the arrangements I made but forgot to mention to Allerton."

On his way out, at reception, the Sergeant stopped Bucken. There was a telephone call coming through for him. The officer in charge of the surveillance van reported that "suspect has just left the house carrying large suitcase, and wearing dark blue suit with faint stripes; outsize red handkerchief in his breast pocket, may even be a red scarf because it's so big; black soft hat with very wide brim, black gloves, black shoes. Cortina glued to tail."

Bucken was now in a hurry to check the final moves at the Bank, but the Sergeant stopped him.

"Lucky you got that message in the morning, sir."

"Why lucky?"

"Well, I mean in the circumstances..."

Bucken was not sure if the Sergeant was trying to say something or merely find out what the meaning of "Warsaw not Berlin" was. "What circumstances?"

"Didn't you hear, sir? The Professor is dead."

"Dead?"

"And a messy job, too. You know, where he usually parked his stall..."

Bucken did not hear the end of the sentence. He rushed out and shouted "Gerrard Street" as he jumped into the car. Walsh made another of his flying starts. Hefty Solomon, waiting in the car, remained totally unruffled by the sudden jerk, and rattled off his report on the capabilities of Don Downes's bug detector:

"Quite a sophisticated job, sir, what we call in the trade an autosweep. What I mean is, it can give an automatic and continuous sweep of each frequency band within the ten to seven hundred fifty Megahertz range, which is very good and covers most popular and convenient frequencies for clandestine transmissions. It will detect and latch on to any strong signal, modulated or otherwise, and also has a built-in line and mains tester. Are you with me, sir?"

No, Bucken was not with him. Why would anybody kill the Professor? And why just now? "Oh, yes, Hefty, please carry on."

"What didn't I mention? Yes, it has a chopper circuit and a very high-gain amplifier, it can measure the signal strength of a detected transmitter, i.e. bug, and so help to locate it, and you can tune off the chopper and listen in to normal modulation on the speaker. There's of course a jack socket for recording."

Listening to this electronic gibberish was part of the ritual of keeping Hefty happy. "What I want to know is whether the bastard can detect the presence of our bumper bleepers or not."

Hefty began his answer with one of his famous mysterious smiles. That was all Bucken wanted to know, but he had the grace to let him carry on and enjoy his moment of triumph. "Well, yes, it would detect all our regular stuff, but I happen to have a little darling on me, what we'd call a Special in the trade, sort of one-off job . . ." He produced a tiny metal cube from his pocket and just demonstrated its magnetic base when Walsh zoomed into Gerrard Street and barely managed to spare the lives of the two young PCs whose job it was to keep irate drivers and pedestrians away.

Near the Post Office ran a narrow passage which the Professor always used as a shortcut to the yard where he would park his mobile stall for the day. This time the stall never reached the end of the alley. The walls were stained—a random spray of big brown patches, intermittently still damp. The acrid stench of drying blood reminded Bucken of the Lad, the emergency ward ... only some thirty hours away. The Sergeant's "a messy job" aptly described the scene. The Professor lay in a contorted position at the foot of the wall as if trying to retreat into the cracks of the old brickwork. His mouth was thickly taped from ear to ear. Whoever had done it was not after a quick kill. Some answers were probably required from the old man. About Bucken? Did he oblige? His right-hand fingers were cut off. There were several body and facial injuries—long, deep cuts—but, according to the initial medical assessment, none of them would have killed him outright. It was the cumulative effect, the shock and profuse bleeding that finished him off.

Bucken found it odd that the murder had not been discovered until eight o'clock in the morning, but the old Chief Inspector from West End Central told him that newspapers had been piled on top of the body. Somebody needed time to get rid of the inevitably bloody clothes and the murder weapon which might have been some sword or large and heavy knife, even a bayonet.

"Or a parang?" Bucken suggested.

"What makes you think that?"

"The wounds ... This part of Soho ... Admittedly, the parang is Malayan and the people here mostly Chinese, but many from Singapore ... Anyway, it was just a thought." He did not feel like telling the Chief Inspector in charge about the attack on him, Maxine and the Lad, about the Professor's suspicions and vague accusations, about some Tong executioners' indulgence in rather crude, preferably Oriental weapons, and about the thickening web of haunting thoughts and vexing implications that would need much more pondering time than he had been

155

able to spare in the past thirty hours. But he did tell him about the peculiar recovery of his coat, and they agreed that Bucken should see Jock as soon as the old liar was found.

On the way to the Bank of England, Hefty Solomon completed his impromptu lecture on bleepers. He suggested the use of his Special not only because it operated just beyond the range of the bug detector, but also because it worked with remote control: "To locate a small piece of dead out-of-place metal on a car would take the customer ages even with luck. So we could activate this little darling only when you really needed it, in an emergency when you're losing the customer and must give chase." It made sense and Bucken accepted the Special. But the goods identification kit proved to be a more serious problem: it contained a comprehensive range of marking techniques and equipment for recognition and protection. How could the money be marked in a way that would remain undetectable to Cutter-Smith?

A call came through from Oscar Victor 3, one of the cars following Cutter-Smith's hired Triumph and the private detective's Cortina: "After some aimless drive-around, caravan proceeded to Town Hall where suspect alighted." Caravan was the correct expression: Bucken had organized a relay of different cars and motorcycles to escort chummy. Inspector White, posing as Skinner's "best operative," sat in the estate car with the bodyguard himself. This car had also been equipped with a powerful police radio but Bucken's instruction was not to use it except in an emergency to avoid monitoring and arousing suspicion by the gang that might be watching the front man.

Skinner, instigated by Inspector White, volunteered to accompany Cutter-Smith into the Town Hall and provide continued protection, but his offer was turned down. "Suspect only wished to make courtesy call. Observed by a plainclothes officer, he then proceeded to the Borough Finance Department where he was greeted by some handclapping and catcalls. An agitated discussion took place with two men, and suspect then left waving to staff in a mocking manner. Officer is still in the building awaiting instructions if he should make inquiries about the exchange that had taken place."

"No, not at this stage," answered Bucken though he dearly wanted to know if chummy had already grown confident enough to resign.

Walsh began the last lap toward the Bank, and Bucken made his final checks on the radio: the fleet of cars was positioned all around the area; every driver and officer had the full description of Cutter-Smith, the chauffeur, the maroon Triumph and the estate car; a call to "India 99," the police helicopter already on standby—yes, it could be airborne without delay and join the pack. Oscar Victor 3 reported that "suspect's motorcade heading southeast"— the City, presumably. Bucken had less than an hour for the decision about the money.

Walsh dropped him at the main entrance, and a swarm of pinkcoats descended on him immediately. He was asked to wait a few seconds for security chief Kirby which annoyed him. He stared up at the dome, down at the mosaic floor, and sideways toward the banking halls from where muffled echoes bounced off as in a swimming pool. A splash of cash instead of water, he thought, and decided that he would dislike Mr. Kirby who kept him waiting and who was, presumably, responsible for all the plainclothes security men vainly trying to look very natural and busy. His impatient, empty gaze fell upon the black columns.

"Finest Belgian marble," he heard.

"Just what I always wanted to find out."

"What? Oh. The name is Kirby. Would you like to come with me?"

Well, what else? He knew he would not like the man.

The corridors were deserted. Bucken only hoped that not everybody in the building had been made aware of the situation.

"Just one spot of snag, old man."

157

"Bucken is the name. Superintendent that is. What's the snag?"

"Grandma won't play."

"Who?"

"Are you joking?"

"I'm not in the mood. Who's Grandma?"

"In banking circles..."

"I'm not a fuckin' banker, just a bleedin' cop, and so were you at some time."

"Sorry, old man. It's the Governor. If he won't play, it can't be helped." Kirby looked at his watch. "By now he's in Zurich, I suppose."

"The PM must be informed."

"It's done. But it's too late. The Deputy will have to deputize."

"It's his funeral.... And yours. You'll have to tell chummy that only the Deputy will perform the ceremony."

In the anteroom of the Court, a specialist from the Home Office Forensic Science Laboratories was waiting for them. He started a slow and slurred monologue in the middle of a sentence and kept noisily adjusting his upper denture after each brief dribble of words. That's all we needed today, thought Bucken, who knew the man and also knew that any interruption would only be regarded as a signal to go back to square one and start again with greater clarity. What eventually transpired only confirmed Bucken's worst expectations: identifiable paints marking the money would be visible to the naked eye; invisible chemical markings could be detected by ultraviolet light and radioactive markings would trigger off Geiger counter signals; the kit delivered by Downes contained suitable equipment for the detection of any of these.

"Anything else you can suggest?"

"Some invisible transfer dye perhaps (clutter, clutter, suck) which may mark the cash or the door handle or container (clutter, clutter, suck) and will remain indelibly on the hand or gloves for at least twenty-four hours (clutter . . . would not click, disappointed sucking) but I'd have to know more about the circumstances (more sucking) because I have here all the necessary stuff (clutter, clutter, at last, and suck)."

Bucken told him to wait in another room, then asked Kirby if the money was prepared.

"But of course, as you wished, old . . . I mean Superintendent. A million in used notes and extra large bundles as demanded, a million in new and old notes mixed and much of it marked in invisible paint, and I added a million in brand new ones in case you'd need it." With great panache, he pulled on a plastic sheet and uncovered three tall trolleys not unlike those used in hospitals to transport dirty linens.

Bucken swallowed. Three million pounds in cash looked less realistically desirable than the change from a fiver that had paid for a beer. The brand new "loaves"—fifty thousand pounds' worth of twenty-pound notes in each machine-wrapped and machine-sealed polythene package untouched by human hand and produced by a virtual replica of bakery equipment—were useless for his purpose. The mixture already marked was too vulnerable to detection. Could they gamble on some marking and possible discovery? Could they risk a last-minute hitch in the handover and so deny the gang the opportunity to switch off the detonator? Bucken knew he could telephone the man who called himself Wade at Downing Street. But it would be no good. On his own advice, he had been authorized to pay and use it as a bait. Too late to back out. Pity.

"Very thoughtful of you. Thank you. But we'll use the unmarked used ones," he said and picked up a few bundles. Two grand each. He examined one and dropped it on the pretty table.

Kirby winced. "If you don't mind . . ." The security man quickly picked up the money and gently wiped the polished surface. "Chippendale. One of the only two oval desks ever made." And as he followed Bucken's eyes still

159

searching for some other piece of furniture he could use: "I'll hold it for you—the sofa is Sheraton."

It was out of sheer spite that Bucken selected fifty bundles at random and let Kirby hold them. "No need to be generous," he said, "we were asked for only nine hundred thousand pounds."

As Kirby's luck would have it, Deputy Grandma One-L MacDougal arrived just in time to see him in this idiotic pose, weighed down by a hundred thousand pounds. "What are you doing, Kirby? Can't you put it down somewhere, for God's sake?" He then turned to Bucken and handed him a sheaf of documents. "It concerns the cash, of course, so you'll have to sign for it. Mere formality."

"I've already signed the papers."

"I know but . . . er . . . Kirby . . ."

"Sir?"

"That will be all, I suppose, unless the Superintendent wishes to ask you something else . . ." And to Bucken: "We thought Mr. Kirby could arrange the reception of the party and see them up here via the Governor's offices and his private staircase. It's highly irregular, of course, but it appeared best to avoid any great procession along the usual route."

"Suits me fine, yes."

"Then see to it, Kirby, will you?" And when the door was shut behind the man with the armful of money: "We'll have to speed things up if possible, because it's MLR day as you must know, and I'll have to deal urgently with the Treasury Bill tenders if we do not wish to delay the announcement. As for these documents, well, I'm sure you know why I didn't want to discuss them in front of Kirby."

"I hate to disappoint you, sir, but I've no idea. I've already signed the receipts for the money."

"Which is why you have to sign these at once unless you wish to find yourself in a, say, highly embarrassing situation. How can you receive ex gratia grants or financial

160

assistance for certain special projects by a paper organization if you're not a member of the imaginary board of that company, not even on paper?"

Bucken glanced through the documents. Some purported to be parts of an "old correspondence" offering him a seat on the Eclampsia Research Advisory Council ("something to do with pregnant women and epilepsy, nothing to be ashamed of," explained MacDougal) and a directorship of the International Swamp Ecology Federation ("rather hush-hush, I'm afraid"), while some other, similarly antedated, papers would authorize the Treasury to include "the above-mentioned sums under certain other relevant headings in the annual Treasury Estimates." Bucken hesitated.

"You fully appreciate, no doubt, that this is purely for accounting purposes," said MacDougal and only his eyes explained what he meant: go on, sign it, ignorant bastard, we cannot balance the books without proper receipts, and we cannot publish the figures unless this item of "payment of a million to blackmailer" is suitably camouflaged.

Bucken signed them all. The last two letters were his resignations from the Eclampsia Research Advisory Council and the International Swamp Ecology Federation. MacDougal took the papers with a stiff bow, presumably an appreciation of Bucken's ephemeral yet invaluable services to the nonexistent bodies of governmental altruism.

Security men came to collect the two trolleys with the unwanted millions, and a pink coat delivered the message that the "visitors" had arrived.

Cutter-Smith's Triumph and Skinner's estate car entered through the tall gates in Lothbury, and were directed to an inner yard where they parked under the eyes of Walsh and Hefty Solomon. Cutter-Smith did not wish to be accompanied by Skinner, and was delighted when Kirby cleverly informed him that, by special permission, he would be able to use Grandma's private stairs to the Court Room. Bucken had his moment of pleasure when

Kirby introduced chummy to MacDougal and said, most apologetically, that "due to entirely unforeseeable circumstances, only the Deputy Governor was able to be present." That "only" had badly stung the man. Bucken was ready for any reaction from Cutter-Smith—except that he would be all smiles.

"I'm delighted to meet you again, Mr. MacDougal." He held out his hand. "It's still one L, I suppose."

"Again?"

"You can't remember. What a shame. But it's understandable. In your long years of service, I must have been just one whom you left behind with a ruined career. Brunei. Does it mean anything? You came to see me."

"Oh, yes. Now what was it about?"

"Some special favors. Thought I'd break the law, Britain would be grateful. Eternally grateful, yes that's exactly what you said."

"But of course. I remember now. And I think I saw you this morning at the gate . . ."

"Pity you didn't remember me when I wrote to you for the job you promised."

"I'll make inquiries. Must have been some administrative error. We can still correct it, I'm sure. If we came to a mutually satisfactory arrangement, we could compensate you most generously for any injustice or loss of income, and of course, whoever kept your letter from me would have to bear full responsibility."

Cutter-Smith was not smiling now. He looked infinitely sad and his voice was hardly audible. "You signed the letter, I'm afraid, sir. I still have it. You assured me that it was some mistake on my part. That you never came to see me in Brunei. That you never received me on behalf of the Treasury where you worked at the time. That you would never ask anybody to break the law of a friendly country, not even in Britain's interest . . ."

"Of course you must understand . . ."

"I do. And I didn't mean to bring it up."

MacDougal hesitated. He would hate to apologize. To

admit a mistake. But the temptation was great. It could be a tremendous triumph if...

Bucken tried to help: "Couldn't we discuss this perhaps over a spot of lunch?"

"An excellent idea, old man. Shall I arrange something?" Kirby volunteered.

"Some smoked salmon? Glass of champagne?" MacDougal suggested.

"If you wish, gentlemen," said Cutter-Smith without raising his voice, without a triumphant smile, without making a meal of his moment of revenge. "Some snack would indeed be nice while you take me to the Court Room and we attend to the actual chores of handling the cash." And as he saw more hesitation on the Deputy Grandma's face, he added: "I'm really sorry, but it's too late. I'm committed and I never go back on my word."

Cutter-Smith carried his brown suitcase, Kirby pushed the trolley with the £900,000, and MacDougal and Bucken walked behind them through the highly polished mahogany double doors that had remained inviolate to robbers, gatecrashers, eavesdroppers and even uninvited prime ministers for so many years.

MacDougal and Kirby winced painfully as their tormentor dropped his suitcase on the long table with total nonchalance, took out the bug-detector and marking-identification kits and placed them next to the case, then asked Kirby to help him lay all the money on the table, and generally proceeded with the perfect calm and certainty of the man who had rehearsed the scene a million times in his dreams.

"You know something?" He threw another sad smile toward MacDougal. "At some stage even my own wife thought that I was a criminal and that I was only trying to whitewash myself by these stories about breaking local regulations for Britain's sake. She actually thought that I was rotten, that I had tricked several African central banks and effected illegal money transfers for my own gain. Especially after your letter..." He glanced at his watch.

"Oh, well, I'd better get on with it." He noticed the large old clock over the mantelpiece. "It's two minutes late."

"Can't be, sir," protested Kirby. "As you know, it's a Tutet. Like the one in the anteroom."

Bucken felt like slowly throttling him. At the moment, he was not quite sure who had most of his sympathy: he was sorry both for chummy and MacDougal.

Cutter-Smith worked with great speed and efficiency. The way he handled the bundles revealed not only dexterity and experience, but also the emotional detachment of the pro. He flicked through a few bundles at random to get the feel of the notes—yes, they seemed used ones all right. He put the Geiger counter in the suitcase so that each bundle going in would be checked automatically. Next he took a bottle of lacquer and a marker crayon out of the kit. With these he drew invisible lines on a sheet of paper. Kirby, MacDougal and Bucken watched him in silence, and the entire scene grew more and more humiliating for all three of them by the second. Cutter-Smith seemed to have forgotten about their presence altogether. He removed a small portable ultraviolet lamp and connected it to the powerful battery in the kit. He switched on the lamp and held it above the paper sample he had prepared. The invisible markings responded with an immediate brilliant fluorescence. Completely absorbed in the test procedure, he nodded to himself with satisfaction.

Kirby cleared his throat. "About the snack we discussed . . ."

Nobody reacted. Cutter-Smith opened a bundle. He spread out the twenty-pound notes on the table and ran over them with the ultraviolet beam. There was no glow. He gathered up the notes and produced a handful of rubber bands from his pocket: he had been prepared for a quick remaking of the bundles. Unexpectedly, as if only continuing a train of thought, he turned to MacDougal: "She told my mother, too, about those transactions and reinforced her belief that I was born to be a criminal. Do you realize that my mother refused to talk to me on her deathbed and died condemning me for being rotten to the core?"

There was silence until Bucken could not stand it any longer. "Very touching. But of course the dear soul was wrong, wasn't she, my pet? You're an upright citizen never ever deviating from the path of honesty!"

"This is different, I can assure you."

"Is it, my pet? Is it? You want a mirror? You should see yourself right now."

"I'm only living up to everybody's expectations. Your expectations, his expectations and her expectations. One can't live against one's reputation forever. Sooner or later you become what other people think you are."

For the first time, Bucken hated the Principal whose devilish scheme also subjected him to the humiliation of being captive audience for a criminal's philosophy.

MacDougal tried to run away from it: "Well, I suppose I won't be needed here any more . . ."

"Please stay," said Cutter-Smith with quiet authority. "It was a condition that Grandma should be here in case some urgent decisions must be made. You should be glad that I accepted you in his place."

"This is ridiculous." MacDougal started toward the door.

"All right. Then keep your money." Cutter-Smith began to gather up his gear.

Bucken had to stop any further development of this crazy situation: any moment now, they would have to beg chummy on their knees to take the bloody ransom. "Enough of this nonsense. Okay, we don't like each other. But we're caught up in this, we're forced to play—and that goes for you, too, chummy, if you don't want your Principal to kill you. So stop bickering and get on with it."

Nobody argued. Cutter-Smith worked hard and frequently wiped his forehead with the large red handkerchief which seemed to be just the right size for the job. Twenty-four bundles made up one precisely fitting layer

165

on the bottom of the suitcase. He then stood the geiger counter on top of that and continued the packing. He sampled about one in every eight bundles, but sometimes he packed in twenty without any tests, sometimes he tested four in a row. Occasionally, he glanced through a bundle to check if any numbers ran consecutively. But there was no hitch. Now and then he picked out a note and stuffed it in his pocket. Bucken wondered if this was to be a petty theft from his Principal. If yes, he hoped the Principal would take revenge in due course.

All the four hundred and fifty bundles in nineteen layers were soon in the case. That left room only for a piece of thick sponge—already cut to the correct size, equal to six bundles. Cutter-Smith looked up: "Didn't even need to count the money—it's enough to measure the volume. Thank you for being so cooperative and reliable. But then, what else would one expect from the Old Lady of Threadneedle Street?" With a rubber solution he sealed the case all around.

He asked for a telephone and called his own bank. Yes, the money had been duly transferred. Yes, only ten thousand stayed on the current account. He was sweating profusely and stopped many times on the way down Grandma's private stairs, but insisted on carrying the 110-pound suitcase without help.

The yard seemed deserted: only the two cars and Skinner with his man witnessed the arrival of the suitcase. Cutter-Smith heaved it up on the edge of the Triumph and let it drop gently into the boot. He did not bother to lock it. He then packed his equipment on the back seats, took out the bug detector and gave the car an almost inch by inch checkover. Skinner watched him with an obvious touch of pride: whatever the client was up to, he had paid for training, and trained he had been in the use of the detector. He also checked the inside of the bumper with his fingers. But Hefty Solomon's silent little darling remained unnoticed behind the rear axle.

Cutter-Smith put on his wide-brimmed black hat and

instructed his chauffeur to drive around and around the building until they met somewhere on the way. With that he walked out of the Bank into Lothbury. The two cars overtook him. Police cars were watching him. Cutter-Smith was followed by two plainclothes men who would soon report to Bucken that "suspect walked back into Threadneedle Street..."

Cutter-Smith expected a sense of tremendous exhilaration, an irresistible gush of exuberance that would urge him to walk tall or run like a dog chasing flies. Instead, he felt empty. A spent force. No triumph. Despite the surprise bonus of MacDougal's presence. There was not much to do, just go through the motions as planned, follow the daily routine already established. He knew that the Principal must be watching him and the money somehow. He also knew that the police would not be far behind. He did not care. It seemed none of his business any more. He would have to start reshaping his life, particularly after that nasty exchange in the office in the morning (they would never really understand the true difference between PPB and PPBS). But first a final decision about Winnie. She would have to go. Then the spirit of the true Cutter-Smith, with all his murky ways, would be released from the bottle.

He called the Harrow number from a public telephone. He noticed that somebody was craning his neck as if to see what number he was dialing. He did not mind. There was no answer. He tried it once more. Still no answer. The Principal said it would not matter. So he walked on.

His car, tailed by his private detective, passed him. The chauffeur slowed down, ready to pick him up. He waved them on. He went into a branch of Barclays Bank and took three twenty-pound notes out of his pocket. The cashier changed them into fivers without any fuss. It seemed there was no special alert to check twenty-pound notes. He strolled on, looking for other banks. He disliked the sight of foreign banks mushrooming everywhere. Mitsubishi, Nova Scotia, the Dutch Algemene ... in his

167

book, at least the City should have remained all British. He visited another three banks to change twenty-pound notes, £360 in all. There was no difficulty anywhere even when he changed eight notes at the same place. The cars passed him again as he returned to Threadneedle Street. His name was not headlines in the evening papers. At Bendicks he bought the largest box of mints on display. He never understood why Winnie adored them. In the small square, at Green's, he bought a box of cigars for seventy-five pounds. It was like spending Monopoly money. He flagged down his chauffeur.

"Bloomsbury Square."

Walsh was driving less than half a mile behind, well out of sight. A detective sergeant in a Volkswagen sat right on the tail of the Cortina. He radioed to Bucken every turn the Triumph and Cortina made. He would soon make a positive handover by nods of recognition to a man and a girl in an open sports car. The rota was well organized. From time to time, Bucken switched on the remote control unit to test the bleeper under the Cortina. The signal was perfect.

"We're using more fucking cars on this fucking chase than the Red Army could line up for the pleasure ride from Stalingrad to the Rhine," grumbled Walsh who was rather sore, like many other officers involved, about Bucken's secretiveness concerning the true nature of the job.

"And you haven't seen the half of it yet," said Bucken who was busy calling India 99. It came in at last: yes, the pilot of the helicopter had the Triumph in view. Bucken was not sure if he himself was in the right position. Perhaps he ought to be aboard that chopper. Perhaps he ought to sit with Oscar Victor 100, the call sign allocated to the officer working for him at the television traffic-control center of the Yard. His problem was soon answered by a call from Oscar Victor 100: "Suspect's car turned into Southampton Row and we lost it from our screens."

"What do you mean lost it?"

"Sorry, sir, I'm monitoring everything we've got in the area, but the system has holes in it. I'll be back to you as soon as we pick them up."

Bucken switched off. "Fuck the system."

"It will only enlarge those holes, sir," said Walsh.

The driver of the sports car reported that the Triumph had turned into Bloomsbury Square and was about to enter the underground car park. That could be the pickup, thought Bucken. He ordered all cars in the area to converge on the sleepy square, and be ready to seal off all exits. He radioed Inspector White in Skinner's car to go in with the Triumph and stick to it as close as possible. Walsh drove him right up to the entrance of the car park. Bucken rushed in with the two officers in the sports car. The helicopter began to hover above the British Museum with a clear overall view of Bloomsbury Square. What worried Bucken most was that he would lose radio contact with the private detective's car and would not be able to pick up the bleeper signals either from underground. He identified himself and asked the attendant at the cash desk how many exits there were.

"What do you mean?"

"How many places are there where you can leave?"

"You can't get your car out?"

"I've no car inside."

"Then what do you want?"

By the time he had established that there was just one exit for cars and pedestrians, and another one only for pedestrians, Walsh came running after him to report that Cutter-Smith had been seen leaving the car park on foot. In a couple of minutes, the panic was over. The Triumph had been parked deep down, almost at the lowest level. The chauffeur had been told to go and get some lunch but be back in an hour. Skinner and White had had the Triumph in sight all the way down except for a few seconds when they had to pick a ticket out of the machine to open the automatic barrier while their charges began to turn and turn slowly along the ever-spiraling ramp. Just for good measure, Bucken tried the boot of the Triumph. It was open, and the suitcase was there.

He left Skinner and White guarding the Triumph—as required by Cutter-Smith—while he returned to the surface. He realized that he might have attracted too much attention and he would have to avoid that in the future. So he must devise a system by which all entrances and exits of any car park would be quickly controlled. This square was a relatively simple task. Inside there was one-way traffic: one spiral down, another one up, with gaps to cross from one into the other, but only one exit. The square itself was also a one-way system, with enough heavy traffic in the surrounding streets to preclude a fast getaway attempt. Right now, there was nothing left but to wait: officers, who were watching Cutter-Smith, reported that "suspect" was about to order a meal in a small restaurant in Sicilian Arcade where he appeared to be known as a fairly regular customer. Bucken was a little puzzled. How would he get there on weekdays in his lunchtime? Perhaps he came in the evenings. Or weekends. Did not seem important.

When Cutter-Smith left, the headwaiter confirmed that "señor with the sort of goatee? yes, know him, he's what the Yermans call stammgast, you know. I wor-ked in Yermany, not enough yobs in Alicante in win-ter, yes comes to din-ner, but sometimes yust coffee. And lunch every weekend, yes, in last two months, yes?"

The convoy, with the revolving team of tailing cars supervised from the background by Bucken, set out toward the northwest, but progress was slow. Cutter-Smith seemed to be in no hurry, stopped to buy some bread and again to feed the ducks in Regent's Park—Bucken immediately pulled in an extra half dozen cars as reinforcements—and then had a word with Skinner:

"I'm going home now for a short rest, and then perhaps to dinner. The Triumph will be parked outside my home overnight, but the driver will be away, of course. Have you made arrangements for the continuous guarding of the car and that suitcase in the boot?"

170

"Naturally. According to the letter of your original instructions, sir. At I.I.I., the client's wish is law."

"How about the night? Will you hand over the job to some of your other men?"

"Not tonight, sir. One of us can always take a nap in the back, and frankly, I prefer to handle important assignments myself. If it goes on too long . . ."

"I don't know how long I'll need you."

"We'll see, we'll see how it goes, sir."

"Suits me. As long as the car is watched incessantly."

"It will be, sir. Some of my operatives will always be present." Skinner made it sound as if he had an organization as big as the Metropolitan Police behind him. Which was not far from the truth at the moment. Cutter-Smith paid him cash for the day's work and gave a fiver as a tip to Inspector White who was so shocked and surprised that through some mysterious twist of thought acknowledged it with "any time" instead of a more conventional thank you.

Winnie was away. Cutter-Smith invited the driver in and, monitored by Bucken in the surveillance van, offered him a can of beer. Later both men were overheard snoring.

Bucken called Maxine (who refused to talk to him but swore with reassuringly robust health at the woman PC looking after her), then tried to pick Walsh's brain for information on underwater detonators, tremblers, timers and all the paraphernalia of infernal machines as well as the risks and prospects of a successful search.

At half past six Winnie arrived home, kicked the driver out of the flat, and refused to talk to her husband.

Ten minutes later, a call came via the Yard radio center: a Chief Inspector from West End Central was on his way with a character named Jock. Bucken arranged to meet them around the corner, out of sight but within earshot of the surveillance van.

A car was not the ideal place for Jock's interrogation: although he spoke with a faulty silencer and his r's whirred like a mistuned engine, all the windows had to be rolled down because cleanliness was not one of his many virtues. It was obvious that the Professor's death had badly upset him.

"Och, Superintendent Bucken, it's good to see you, I'm sure. I'll do anything to help you because murderers are no friends of mine."

"I'm sure they are not. So let's cut it brief, I don't want to keep you long, my pet, and let's stick to facts—not even white lies this time. All right?"

"Aye. You've known me, sir, for long many years, and you know I've kept to the straight and narrow, aye, and I can stand here with my head up like any other honest citizen of these gallant isles, because the good Lord rewarded me with lengthy absence from the nick."

The Chief Inspector grew very impatient, but Bucken knew they had to listen to the preliminaries if they really wanted Jock's help. And in his own good time, with minimal gentle prodding, the old vagrant came to the point.

Apparently, Jock was about to receive his free hot dog when a young Chinese waiter brought the Bogart coat to the Professor, saying something like "your friend lost it." Bucken knew precisely where he "lost" the coat: he had walked away from the stall and turned a corner before dropping it. The Professor or anybody else around the stall could not see it. The only possibility was that he had been followed. If the young Chinese or whoever else it was did not shout a simple warning to Bucken, it could only mean that he wanted to know who the Professor's acquaintance was and use the return of the coat as an opportunity for finding out.

"Could you describe the man?"

"No, sir, the good Lord has punished these people by making them look alike."

"Would you at least recognize him if you saw him again?"

"Aye. Because I know where he works. He's a waiter. And he's new in London because he said he'd never seen snow in his life."

It emerged that the Professor was reluctant at first to acknowledge his acquaintance with Bucken, but after a short conversation, by which he had probably convinced himself that the young Chinese, a newcomer, was no danger to him, he asked Jock to deliver the coat and the message to the Yard. That might have been his own death warrant.

"But surely, sir, you must remember all this or at least what the Professor himself told you."

"I never spoke to him after my coat had been lost."

"Och, you were out that night then, sir. He must have spoken to somebody else because I was there when he called you from the corner."

If anybody, Maxine would have taken the call but she must have forgotten to mention it. In any case, the Professor would not have said much to her.

"It's essential to find that man," Bucken told Jock. "Will you help us, my pet?"

Jock was not particularly keen on the assignment, but at last agreed to point out the young waiter from the darkness of the Chief Inspector's car. Bucken would have an early opportunity to interrogate him. He was itching for action, physical action, and he knew that this might bring the worst out of him. But he could not help it—and he did not care too strongly about it: two friends killed, Maxine and he himself attacked in less than forty-eight hours, and still just sitting on a puppet's tail was too much for his natural inclination for active detection.

The men in the surveillance van were brewing up, and Walsh had already spread out some cod with double-portion chips for Bucken, when Cutter-Smith succeeded in persuading Winnie that they should go and dine in town. What she did not know—and what would have been meaningless to Bucken—was that the Savoy would be their destination. They had had lunch there on their wedding day and dinner when visiting London as unofficial guests of the Treasury. Since then, Winnie had always longed to go there, and he always had to repeat, "Can't afford it, you know perfectly well we can't afford it." "You mean you

173

can't afford it," was her usual answer. When he now quietly said "Savoy" to the uniformed chauffeur, she knew that all the nonsense he had half-hinted at in the past few months had become reality. He must have committed some filthy crime. He was a criminal after all. And she was shocked by the fact that she felt impressed by him for the first time.

Walsh, who managed to secure a table next to them, was bored by the conversation he overheard, but enjoyed his fillet steak particularly because he knew that Bucken was eating his cold fish, from a three-day-old *Daily Express,* in the car, watching the boot of the Triumph.

Halfway through a bottle of champagne Winnie was suddenly drunk, without any previous progressing symptom of intoxication. She became chirpy, coquettish and ready to laugh at the slightest provocation. She began to flirt with the man at the next table and enjoyed his shyness and obvious embarrassment—Walsh just did not know what to do with himself. The last thing he wanted was Cutter-Smith's attention, let alone a fight with him. But Cutter-Smith was far from being annoyed. In a way he was grateful to Walsh, the champagne, the Principal, the Savoy: everybody and everything that might have contributed to Winnie's mood. Her cheeks began to color, and a touch of perspiration added a faint glow. Her severely back-combed hair loosened, a curling lock freed itself and fell into her face, and she did not care.

She leaned forward so that she could whisper to her husband, and with an irrepressible girlish titter she reminded him of a trip to Djakarta: a young man dining next to them in a restaurant had eyed her so intently throughout his rijsttafel that half his food ended up on his immaculate white tuxedo; when they left, he noticed the limp and the artificial leg; his face then made her cry. Now the memory seemed incredibly funny. She could not stop giggling.

Cutter-Smith was fighting back his tears. This was the girl he once married. He always knew and admitted to

174

himself freely that she could marry any man she chose if she had two real legs, and that he could never marry somebody as beautiful as Winnie unless there was a snag. He was a realist and he selected the compromise most acceptable to him: a lovely girl with a forgettable disability. If only he could have ever told her all this. It was too late now. She would have to go, as planned. But not tonight. What would a day or two matter?

An hour later, the entire caravan returned to Elstree and prepared to bed down with varying degrees of comfort. The chauffeur ordered a cab—he was free until 0930. Bucken pulled in reinforcements for the night and surrounded the area with carefully hidden surveillance, defensive and chase units as well as a squad of marksmen: he was prepared for any commando raid or even military-style offensive. The helicopter was grounded on the old airfield nearby, with the pilot in a sleeping bag underneath. If the Triumph with the money in the open boot were hit at night, the police would have a choice: they could fight and arrest even a heavy armed raiding party, or they could tail them hoping to find all their associates.

At half past one in the morning, Jock identified the Chinese waiter in Soho. The Chief Inspector let the old vagrant go, picked up the suspect, and radioed Bucken that they were on their way to meet him. This was against regulations but luckily the Chief Inspector was at an impressionable age (near retirement) and Bucken was determined to claim a piece of the action.

They transferred to another car and Bucken drove them out of the village. He parked under some half-dead elms near a reservoir, and told the boy to get out. He already knew that chummy was frightened, but would not say a word, not even his name, on the way out. Now the lonely spot implied unknown menace to him.

"You have no right to bring me here."

"We didn't bring you," said Bucken. "We found you

here. Wandering." He hit him hard just under the heart. "You seemed to be in pain." He hit him in the stomach. "Dazed. Doubled up. So tell us what's wrong, my pet."

The Chief Inspector was not impressed. He would have forced and held the boy's head under the water just for starters. But Bucken was already digusted with himself. It was the first time that he had hit anyone with cool deliberation. He turned away. The boy refused to answer any questions. Bucken thought about the Lad, Maxine, the Professor, but could not bring himself to turn into a torturer. If only the boy were cheeky or aggressive. The Chief Inspector's face clearly showed disappointment: the Superintendent was no help to him, it was a wasted journey, and if pressure was needed, he would know better how to apply it. He volunteered to help. Bucken turned it down.

The old detective knew nothing about Bucken's troubles among which a possible disciplinary action over the beating up of an allegedly unarmed pavement artist was only one, and could not really care. He wanted to lock up the boy, charge him with something, go home to his four faithful cats, and put off the boring thoughts of murder and retirement until the morning.

"Well, I'd better go and take him in now, sir," he mumbled, "or I'm sure to get a rocket from the Commander."

His last words were lost in the high-pitched desperate outburst from the boy who had only half-heard the sentence but picked out one word clearly enough: "No, no! No rocket! Don't get no rocket! Please!"

Bucken's brain would often beat the computer procedures at recalling facts or making the right associations, but now those obscure relays in his memory bank took a good few seconds to produce the right contacts and come up with the picture of suspects being tortured by police in Hong Kong. Oh, yes, sticking fireworks up the arse was one of the more unusual but successful techniques of obtaining cooperation over there. He now learned that this had been done to the Chinese waiter's friend and this boy would not wish to share the experience.

The floodgates were suddenly open. He began with his name, Lau, and the admission that he was an illegal immigrant. He had been smuggled into the country by some Chinese criminal organization which also supplied him with papers to obtain a work permit. He had to hand over 70 percent of his wages and tips every week, but he could make up for the loss by running errands for the organization. The Tong? He would not know or would not say. But he claimed that torture and painful ways of death ensured loyalty and enforced discipline. And by a simple reasoning exercise Lau proved himself a realist: the organization might discover his disloyalty and might kill him—the police were already prepared to shove a rocket up into his bowels. Therefore he would side with the police in return for protection. He offered a deal though he seemed to have little for trading. But then he almost casually mentioned something that provoked the old detective to jump at his throat:

"I don't know how they do it, but they call it the skim-off. You know, people must show friendship and give them a big share from every big crime money. Very clever. And they know where to look for big crime money and big criminal because Scotland Yard tell them."

That was the point where Bucken had to rescue him from certain death by strangulation.

"You fucking yellow bastard!" the Chief Inspector yelled. "I'll teach you to respect the integrity of the British police!"

While Bucken fought to restrain him, Lau tried to run for it. But Bucken had an eye on him, too: he stuck out a foot in time, and Lau's dash ended in a dive into the barbed wire fence surrounding the reservoir. Which did not leave him in a presentable state as a true volunteer on the witness stand for the prosecution.

Bleeding profusely from an intricate pattern of facial cuts, he was now keen to answer any further questions, but he had little more to offer on the factual side. He claimed repeatedly that the connection between the organization and high-ranking policemen originated in Hong Kong. And Bucken knew that lately there had been a major influx of senior ex-Hong Kong detectives at the Yard. Carron was one of them. Allerton another. Even Rattray did his short stint there, helping to set up an anticorruption squad. And come to think of it, Linley, the deskman who took over Bucken's immigration racket investigation, had once been seconded to Singapore. Bucken wondered if this old Chief Inspector had tried to kill Lau because he felt so deeply insulted by an accusation against the police? Or did he feel threatened?

"Were you watching the Professor?"

"Who?"

"The old man at the hot dog stall."

"Yes."

"Why?"

"I don't know. It was a job for five pounds."

"Who gave you the job?"

"Don't know. Never seen him before."

"Don't give me that!" Bucken raised his hand.

"Honest, sir, I swear, I swear!"

"You got the five pounds?"

"Yes."

"From the same man?"

"Yes."

"Where's it?"

Lau hesitated, but seeing Bucken's slow leaning forward, he produced the five-pound note. Bucken searched for something to wrap it in, and found a length of bandage from his head wound: he must have put it in his pocket on his way to Allerton's office. "You'll get it back." He hoped to find some useful fingerprints on it. "What did you tell the man?"

"That you went to see the old man."

"And?"

"That you played chess."

Bucken bit his lip hard. He should have noticed that

they were being watched. "Did you hear what we talked about?" Lau looked away. "Did you?"

"Yes."

"And you told the man about it ... Yes or no? ... Inspector, get the rockets from the car ..."

"Yes, I told him."

"Good. That makes you a cool accessory before the fact. And the charge is murder."

"He said nothing would happen to the old man. He said he just wanted to know."

"The old man is dead. Would you like to see his body? They cut his fingers off. Now the question is: are you willing to help us find the man?"

"Yes, sir."

Which did not mean much. Lau would never identify the man. The risk to him would be too great.

They returned to the surveillance van and Bucken arranged that one of his own men should accompany the Chief Inspector and his Sergeant. He claimed that Lau was dangerous. But in fact, he wanted to make sure that Lau would reach the West End nick. Alive. His own doubts made him feel sick. It was nauseating not to trust an old colleague. But right now he trusted no one.

Walsh watched the party's departure. Lau's face was a sight in itself. "I don't understand what these modern tattooists find so attractive in abstracts. I'm all for the old-fashioned shriveled mermaid on the Petty Officer's balls."

Bucken stared at Walsh's shoes for thirty long seconds. "Fuck the Principal," he concluded at last.

"Is that an order or mere advice, sir?" And when Bucken resumed that gloomy silence, he added: "Matter of fact I almost did just that. I mean to the principal violinist appearing at the Flower Ball in aid of the Distressed Gentlefolks Association in Chelsea Rectory Garden. No, sir, I'm not a regular patron or a much-sought-after escort for pink-cunt debutantes. My appearance was more in the nature of a fucking bomb hoax ..."

Bucken left him in charge at Elstree with the instruction

179

that anyone approaching that money bag in the boot must be detained for questioning. He knew he was taking a tremendous risk by leaving the scene, for it was for him to sit it out and make all crucial decisions such as those concerning the use of firearms, but Rattray would have to know about the accusations against high-ranking officers at once so that Lau could be brought to the Big House without delay.

Mu did not even try to pretend that she was not badly upset by Bucken's visit at half past three in the morning. Having herded the children back to bed, she left him in the hall and went upstairs with the light, breezy movement of the sleepwalker. Three minutes later she was down again and steered Bucken toward the kitchen. Politely offering a cup of tea was her second nature which would not be suppressed by sleepiness or anger.

"Will he be long?"

She shrugged her shoulders.

"Should I go and give him a shake?"

"Won't help. Already gave him his pill."

"What pill?"

"The one that wakes him up." And seeing Bucken's astounded expression: "Didn't you know? Of course, you don't Peel-house so regularly any more."

"Didn't I know what?"

"He's on tranquilizers. And stabilizers and whatnotizers. He can sleep only with those white tablets and can wake up only with the yellow ones."

"How long has this been going on?"

"Few months. He's always busy and always tired, he smokes like a bloody chimney and coughs between puffs at night. He has no time for the children and this aborted fishing trip was the first for . . ."

The water began to boil and it was too late to silence the kettle. As Mu burst into a bout of furious activity, the door opened. Bucken expected Rattray. But it was Sarah.

"Anything wrong?" He was pleased to hear her genuine concern.

"No, nothing. And hello. Didn't know you were here."

"Is that why you're late? You were expected to be in time for lunch."

"Two days ago," added Mu and left with a cup for her husband. "Help yourselves!" The Rattray household was already in full swing.

Sarah looked numbed as she did on every exceptional occasion when circumstances forced her to spend the night shivering in a bed on her own. Her elegant figure disappeared completely in the thick folds of a huge angora blanket she always used as a dressing gown. Bucken quickly poured out some tea for her and she grabbed the mug with both hands. Only then would she look at him. Her eyes emitted a shimmering glow which latched on to its target like the heat-seeking device of a missile, and the instant effect was what Bucken called semen curdling. He felt it and she knew it because her lips toyed with a soft smile.

"I'd love to see you." He hesitated. "Perhaps lunch . . ."

"Give me a ring."

"Or dinner . . ."

"Can be arranged."

Arranged. Of course. She would have to tell her friend, boy friend, man friend, lover—Bucken could never bring himself to ask. Knowledge would not alter the fact that Sarah never lived alone if she could help it. She called it an illness. She was born for companionship. Oddly enough the thought did not hurt him as much as usual. But he had to pocket his left hand to shift his suddenly too tight pants surreptitiously because her eyes were still glowing at him, causing an erection which he did not want her to notice. Though he knew that she would.

"Make it an evening," she said. "Come over if you like." Her voice was quite flat, the invitation sounded as innocent as he would want to make it. And her tone remained perfectly matter-of-fact when she added: "Any evening." But the implication was clear. The continued story of their life together. Resign or find a desk job or do anything to ensure that you spend the night with me, every night, and then there won't be any more friends, boy friends, lovers, nobody but you, you bastard.

He found it peculiar that in the presence of Sarah, his mind should stray repeatedly toward Maxine. Maxine who might leave him without warning at any time. And if she did, she would never return. But until she did, she would wait for him. All night. Any night. Alone. Which was all wrong somehow. It was Sarah who professed to be entirely monogamous. Perhaps that was why she could not bear loneliness. While Maxine claimed that infidelity was natural and meaningless, that love could be shared by many, and that even whoring (yes, love, fucking for thirty pieces of silver, never mind the inflation) should be morally acceptable—a statement which once made him blush in front of the Lad. But she would wait. Perhaps masturbate and wait. The mental picture was lit up by Sarah's eyes and the combination was almost too much for him. He was afraid he would erupt like a teen-ager in sweet dreams.

Rattray's arrival saved him. Sarah smiled and offered to leave them. They accepted. On her way out, she touched Bucken's face just with her fingertips which were hot from clutching the mug.

Bucken found it disconcerting to look at his friend: once a serious contender for a place in Britain's Olympic pentathlon team, Rattray now smoked one of those dreadful cigars hungrily, his tall, sinewy figure held in an arc, almost doubling up and balancing precariously on groggy legs, his normally alert, penetrating eyes shrouded in the opaque emptiness of a near-blind dog's eyes.

"Are you all right?"

"Will be in a moment."

"You look ghastly."

"We'd make a fine pair."

Bucken began to talk about the Professor's warning and

182

the Chinese waiter's allegations, but Rattray, recovering fast, interrupted him: "It's the second time today that you've broken the rules."

"The first was yesterday." Yes, Bucken knew only too well that Peel-housing meant "never talk shop in private" but he was desperate. "The Lad's death was caused by grassing in reverse. Now all this about a nark at C.O. or worse."

"Don't get hysterical." Rattray knew that this hurt most. Bucken could be called anything but hysterical. Yet he used the word for the second time. "Have you got proof? And I mean hard evidence, not gossip."

"It's not for me . . ."

"Of course not. You dislike the dirty work, don't you? You despise a rogue cop, but you prefer to let the rubber-heel mob do the dirty work for you." His voice was full of venom and Bucken tried to explain, but Rattray would not let him. "But it's grossly unfair, you know. They have enough on their hands as it is on the seventeenth." And seeing Bucken's surprise: "Oh yes, you were away. A-Ten has moved up to the seventeenth floor because they needed more room. And you know why? Because they're handling some thirteen hundred serious complaints against the force right now. And because they got rid of more than a hundred bad apples last year. That's why. And then you come with vague allegations in the middle of the night. Furthermore, you come to me privately, behind Carron's back . . ." He could not hold down a burst of violent coughing any longer, but he would still not remove the cigar from the corner of his mouth.

Bucken was tempted to exploit the opportunity and answer him, but it seemed unfair. His words might not even be heard. Besides, how would he even start to explain that he did not feel like going through the usual channels because the accusation was too monstrous, and he could not cut corners by approaching directly the Deputy Commissioner, the man with overall supervision of A10 Department, because Carron, too, was ex-Hong Kong? In his present mood, Rattray would find the mild insinuation ridiculous or else might even go wild and explode Bucken's thinking aloud into an official allegation against a superior. He tried to soft-pedal: "Look, I'm not saying that there's anything to it. And I'm not saying that I'd be profoundly shaken if it turned out that somebody or other had his palm oiled a little. But this sounds like greasing. And if nothing else, it needs clearing up."

"Right. Provide some evidence and I'll back you."

"It's not for me to rubber-heel on any colleague."

"Are you seeking a transfer to A-Ten?"

"No."

"No. You prefer to supply the tipoff. Just to keep them sweet. Especially now that they might look into that O'Leary affair."

"It was self-defense."

"He was unarmed."

"You take his word against mine?"

"That has nothing to do with it. It doesn't matter what I think. It's a question of facts. Evidence. Just what you seem to overlook completely. What happened to you? Are you mad? Think, Bucken, think. You'd already be suspended if this *Montgomery* job hadn't come up."

Bucken's lips began to tingle as they did after a dentist's injection. He was not sure that he could move them if he tried. But why try? What's the use? Rattray would not listen. He had not listened for a long time. Did he want his resignation? He could have it. But he must ask for it. Or was it to be only in the wake of Bucken's biggest failure? The wild goose chase. The prospect of success—and then the transfer to another hopeless task.

Rattray was staring out of the window. The coughing had left him almost trembling, set up for any sucker punch, ready to be counted out at will.

"You ought to see a doctor."

"And you ought to back your allegations."

"I really mean it."

"So do I." He lit another cigar, letting the butt of the first burn out slowly on a saucer.

Walsh welcomed Bucken with the good news of no news. Near the surveillance van a post office cable-maintenance tent was set up—a few of the men at a time could snatch some sleep.

Cutter-Smith was up at seven o'clock and gave Winnie breakfast in bed. They made love noisily and gurgled a lot of sentimental nonsense. Bucken was not sure if he was more embarrassed than bored or the other way around.

At 8:55, Cutter-Smith gave the Triumph the onceover with the bug detector, carried the money into the house and, while Winnie was in the bathroom, checked the waterproof seal, then cut it open. Bucken was pleased with himself: during the Savoy dinner, he had arranged the installation of two hidden remote-control cameras, so now he could watch the scene with reasonable clarity. Cutter-Smith made a few spot checks with the Geiger counter and the ultraviolet lamp, then resealed and examined the suitcase with the bug detector. By the time Winnie came out of the bathroom, he had replaced the suitcase in the boot. Once again he was wearing the dark blue suit, the black hat, the red handkerchief in the breast pocket.

At 9:30, the chauffeur reported for duty. At 10:00 o'clock, Cutter-Smith took his wife to his bank, drew a thousand pounds cash, then went on a Knightsbridge shopping spree. They spent £3,057.50 on clothes, a fur coat (she refused a second fur coat and he laughed) and some old-fashioned costume jewelry. He arranged everything to be sent to Elstree in the afternoon after the clearance of his checks. The chauffeur drove around and around until they reappeared ready to go on.

At 1330, the Triumph, followed by the estate car, followed by Bucken's surveillance team, approached Bloomsbury Square. While the Triumph was parked, watched by Skinner and Inspector White, the exits were blocked. Cutter-Smith gave ten pounds to Skinner who was to get some lunch for his "colleague" and the chauffeur. He and Winnie had lunch in the Sicilian Arcade.

After some rest at home, they returned to town and parked the car in the Hilton garage underground. Bucken's well prepared procedure worked without a hitch. The couple went for a short walk, then back to the Hilton for dinner. At night, Cutter-Smith sent the chauffeur home, and paid Skinner cash for the day's work. He seemed unconcerned about the suitcase: he knew that Skinner and his man would be on duty through the night, he must have suspected that the police, too, would be watching, and he did say it was none of his business what happened to the £900,000, Bucken recalled.

The Sunday program was rather similar, with a long walk instead of shopping, lobster at a fish restaurant near the Elstree airport (it was a good opportunity for Bucken to let the chopper land and refuel), early dinner in the Sicilian Arcade, followed by the silliest show in town. Winnie laughed heartily.

The Triumph was in a multistory garage in Soho and all was under control. Bucken used the opportunity to slip away and see Maxine. She had refused all day to talk to him on the telephone. He found her fully recovered from the shock of the leg burns, and he hoped to pacify her. But the prospects were proved to be bad when he found her packing a small suitcase. She did not believe in moving completely out of any place. She had clothes and shoes left behind in almost every house she ever stayed in. "You know how it is, I might come back and then it might be useful."

Yet the way she kissed him and the way she fussed over his head wound suggested that all was well. "Shall I help you with your packing?" she asked.

"Packing?"

"The cruise. Down to Naples or beyond. Remember?"

186

"Oh yes." That marvelous invitation from one of her wealthy friends. He promised to squeeze a couple of weeks' leave out of Allerton even if he had to report sick or resign. He would then fly home and perhaps rejoin them a month later if possible. The rest of them would stay aboard a couple of months or so. One of the girls owned an island somewhere in the sun.

"I see." She knew it all along. So now she was sad but not surprised. "Here," she threw down his car keys and began to roll a cigarette. "Some copper drove your war wagon up from the coast. I've never seen so much blood under one sunroof. Who did you deflower in there?" Then she tried to retract it. "I'm sorry."

He helped her to shut the suitcase and hoped that he did not look too despondent. "I bet I'm even sorrier."

She put her arms around his neck. "I wanted to fuck you so much on that boat that by the end of the fortnight they'd have to unscrew us." And she was about to start, too. And she paid no attention to the WPC who knocked and entered without waiting.

"Excuse me, sir, urgent call in your car."

He was halfway down the stairs when she yelled after him: "I'll cable you from Naples when we get there. Join us or after that I won't guarantee my virginity!"

The WPC was pleased to see the end of this assignment.

Walsh had called because the caravan was about to move on. Bucken caught up with them on the way to Elstree. Once again, the chauffeur was released and asked to report back at 0900, Cutter-Smith paid Skinner for the day, and Bucken supervised the surveillance arrangements for the night. He called the underwater search unit and asked for divers to stand by: that rubber sealing around the suitcase might also be useful to the Principal if the money was to be hidden under water. But Bucken's main problem was the flagging alertness of the surveillance team. Normally, a twenty-four-hour "follow" job required eighteen men in three shifts with all the car-changing facilities of the Yard's reserve pool—if the suspect had no reason to believe that he was being watched. The moment that chummy had the slightest inkling of being tailed, the job became harder and harder, sometimes impossible. In any case, time was entirely on chummy's side. He could strike anywhere at any time. His only risk was the meeting—the moment of the actual handover. He might use intermediaries. He might attack in force or stage an accident. Bucken felt confident that the police precautions were foolproof, yet he could not sleep much as he tried again and again to spot the weakest points.

The morning routine was by now quite predictable. Breakfast in bed for Winnie, checking with the torch, the geiger counter and the bug detector. Apparently, it never occurred to Cutter-Smith to check the flat, too, for bugs. He ordered a cab to take Winnie to Roehampton, and arranged to meet her for lunch at the usual place. He said he might go and see someone in the office. She made some remark about his clothes. She disliked the suit and the hat, and she thought the red scarf looked ridiculous. He said he was bored with his old clothes and he would see his tailor perhaps in the morning.

He later visited a continental real estate agent inquiring about luxury apartments in Florence, then sat for a couple of hours with Lanelli Junior and ordered a dozen suits. The Triumph approached the Bloomsbury Square garage at 1327. Skinner's estate car sat right on its tail. At 1328, the automatic barrier let the Triumph go through, then came down only to be lifted again by Skinner taking a ticket. The delay was no more than twenty seconds.

As the two cars disappeared, Oscar Victor Two, a Detective Inspector in a Volvo, notified Bucken and took up the usual surveillance position on the corner of Bedford Place from where both the entrance and the exit of the underground car park could be watched. Oscar Victor Five, a motorcyclist, dismounted in front of the Victoria Insurance building, right at the edge of the exit ramp, and began an everlasting round of feverish inactivity with an all-too-shiny spanner. Walsh parked the Jaguar, Oscar Victor One, in Russell Square and left to pick up some sandwiches, while Bucken called India 99 and instructed the pilot to use the lunch break for refueling.

These simultaneous moves did not quite take a minute. So it must have been at about the same time that Skinner, having passed the barrier, tried to catch up with the Triumph. This was the only period of no more than twenty seconds when he would not have Cutter-Smith in sight because of the slight delay and the corkscrew structure. He could not go too fast, however, because Inspector White had to look out for the Triumph which might have already parked anywhere. Before he could complete the first turn, a van and an old Mercedes pulled out from the parking slots on both sides at right angles to his path. Idiots. They were really asking for trouble. He hooted impatiently, but the two drivers stepped out of the cars instead of moving out of the way. White pulled down the window and shouted at them. They came over to the Cortina and prevented White and Skinner from opening the doors.

White blew up: "Police! Get out of the way!" He tried to fork his identity card out of his pocket but the man on his side misunderstood his intention and grabbed his hand.

"Don't do that, old man, or I might have to smash your face in. Don't you know that it's a serious offense to impersonate an officer of the law?"

In desperation, White switched on his transmitter though he knew he would not be heard above ground.

A couple of turns further down, the Triumph had just reached parking slot Blue 60, beyond which on the right was the first opening that gave access to the yellow upward spiral. A towering, fat and bearded Sikh in his traditional green turban stopped the Triumph. He wore the car-park attendant's usual yellow coat. His hand signal indicated that the driver should turn right. The lower levels must be closed again, thought Cutter-Smith. The Sikh guided the Triumph into the first free parking slot, Yellow 396, normally reserved for local residents.

Cutter-Smith did not want to wait for Skinner. By now

he knew that the detective could be trusted to be right behind them. As they walked toward the stairs, he told his driver to be back from lunch by three o'clock.

Two minutes after Oscar Victor Two, the Volvo, had taken up its usual position, a maroon Triumph appeared on the exit ramp. The Inspector leaned forward to peer into the slowly moving car. By then, Oscar Victor Five had also spotted the car. Uniformed driver and the passenger's unmistakable attire—the dark suit, black hat, huge red handkerchief in the breast pocket ... the Inspector radioed Bucken without delay. Chummy must have changed his mind, he reported.

"Any sign of the Cortina?"

"Not yet. Must still be at the cash desk."

The Triumph reached the top and turned toward Great Russell Street. Both the Inspector and the motorcyclist stared down the ramp, waiting for the Cortina. It must have been delayed because a Mini had slipped in between them.

The Inspector started his engine. Bucken wanted him to allow the Cortina to take up its usual place behind the Triumph: "But don't lose it from your sight. Where is it now?"

The Inspector looked up: "Just rolling into Great Russell Street, going slowly, waiting probably ... hey! They changed the number plate! He surely can't hope to ..."

Bucken did not hear the rest of it. His blood pressure began to rise and he yelled into the microphone as if trying to cut out the radio altogether. "Tail it. Don't you lose it! Oscar Victor Five, Oscar Victor Five! Go down exit ramp and investigate!" He moved over to the driving seat. As he pulled away from the curb with a racing start, he called Oscar Victor Seven and Eight, and two foot patrols whose job was to tail Cutter-Smith and the driver if and when they left the garage by the stairs.

The motorcyclist was running down the ramp, dodging two cars of no interest—his eyes glued to the dark exit point where now another maroon Triumph appeared.

Uniformed driver and conspicuously dressed passenger. He stopped for a second only to stare at the number plate: a different one. He turned and raced the slowly moving car back to his bike. As he switched on his radio on top of his gas tank, he saw the Triumph turn left. He had difficulty getting through to Oscar Victor One because Bucken was busy ordering all units in the area to converge on Bloomsbury Square, telling India 99 to return at once no matter how low on fuel the pilot was, and talking at last to the foot patrols: "Return to car park at once. Oscar Victor Seven to enter by stairs, Oscar Victor Eight stand by at the entrance."

"You mean we stop tailing suspects?"

"What do you mean?" Bucken managed to avoid hitting a low-flying Chevrolet and turned the Jaguar into Blooms-bury Square.

"The two are about to cross over to Sicilian Avenue."

Bucken was about to ask if they were sure they were tailing the right men, when he half-heard the motorcy-clist's panicky calls and himself noticed, too, a maroon Triumph turning left and left again in the Square—and then yet another maroon Triumph, also with unmistakably obvious driver and passenger, emerging on the exit ramp.

"Seal car park at once. Oscar Victor Seven and Eight, detain both suspects and return them to their car. Oscar Victor Five enter garage via exit ramp and investigate. Oscar Victor Two! Stop Triumph and detain passengers. All cars in the area. Seal car park, stop and detain the two maroon Triumphs just leaving the Square."

As he parked his car, running it into the curb, the various units arrived with screeching tires and brakes, and the men sealed the Square, according to plan, with military precision. The entire operation did not take more than two and a half minutes from the moment of the first Triumph's appearance. Yet it might have been too long. Bucken was dying to go down and check the position himself. But it was more important for him to control the next moves.

India 99 was now overhead. He told the pilot to look

over the entire area in case he could spot somebody with a heavy bag, suitcase, anything that might weigh about a hundred pounds. It was unlikely, but he had to try.

Oscar Victor Two reported that the first Triumph out of the car park had just been stopped: the occupants were not the original driver and passenger although the description of their clothes was identical.

The other two Triumphs were also spotted and about to be stopped. But what Bucken wanted to hear from anyone was the make, color and registration number of any other car that had left the garage in those crucial two minutes.

The motorcyclist did not need to run far down to find the Cortina held up by some obstacle that looked like a single long object in the semidarkness. He saw a big burly fellow straighten up from Skinner's window and take a menacing stance, still holding the door. The motorcyclist swung the spanner and brought it crashing down on the man's head. The attacker on the other side tried to run but Inspector White reached out and held him through the window.

A few seconds later, the garage was swarming with plainclothes police. Bucken joined them. As he ran past the Cortina, he took in the scene there at a glance and shouted, "Hold them."

He reached the gap at Blue 60 and noticed Cutter-Smith on the Yellow ramp. He crossed over. The original Triumph with the correct registration number was still there. The boot was shut. Bucken opened it. The suitcase was gone.

They stood in stunned silence. Cutter-Smith kept repeating the obvious—"It's gone. It's gone."

The moment Bucken had dreaded all along had arrived, and he knew that he would have to pull himself together and start thinking fast. He tried to block out spurting thoughts of self-inculpation. Bucken's aim had never been total prevention: he baited the man and the bait was lost. How? He saw three possibilities.

The first was that somebody had simply walked out with

the suitcase. Unlikely, but if so it would mean the use of a car parked nearby or an arrangement for having a "flop," such as a girl friend's flat or a specially rented room or some other hiding place where the money could be cooled while the heat was on in the neighborhood. Worth checking strangers, new tenants and unoccupied premises in the area, and also residents with a CR file or known to C11, the Criminal Intelligence Section.

The second possibility was that the money could still be underground. It might be hidden in a car or even a cavity in the wall. There had recently been some building and repair work carried out at the lower levels—that would have been an ideal opportunity to prepare an easily accessible cache. Checking that would require a monumental search of the car park that held 455 cars and offered immense time-wasting wall surfaces for the minute examinations that would be necessary. His instinct told him that the money was not down there any more, but that was no evidence. A search would have to start without delay. Meanwhile, the place must be sealed, everybody and every car must be thoroughly searched when leaving, names and addresses must be taken and checked before anybody could be permitted to go.

The third possibility was the most likely one: the suitcase had been picked from the Triumph, transferred to another car, and driven away between the more significant departures of the decoy cars and suspects. The motorcyclist remembered that one of the cars was a Mini. The cash desk attendant remembered "a smallish, dark, sort of ordinary car." No, he did not pay much attention to them. Yes, he knew this was not very helpful. He was sorry. But he could offer one item of positive assistance: there were no attendants working underground; he certainly did not see a yellow-coated Sikh in a green turban, but a bearded driver had indeed left the car park a few minutes or so earlier—he remembered because the man wore a blue denim cap which the attendant thought had gone out with the Beatles.

Bucken was now sure that the Principal or one of his men had been down there, and that, by now, the beard and the cap would have long vanished. But the existence of a "flop" nearby was still a fair probability.

While the search operation began, Bucken escorted the entire herd to the Big House. A quick series of initial interrogations outlined the basic pattern of the meeting. Its main feature was that the operation could be simply called off at any stage until the actual transfer of the money. The true risk was therefore reduced to less than thirty seconds. If the "Sikh" saw any problems or guards or unexpected observers, he might just walk out without putting on the yellow coat.

Cutter-Smith appeared genuinely surprised but could not suppress a smile: the Bank and the authorities had been fooled, the Principal had been right once again. If anything, the snatch strengthened his faith in the protection promised by the Principal. He now demanded to be set free at once or else . . .

The original Triumph with the driver had been hired from Pimlico Limousine Service by Cutter-Smith himself. That Bucken knew from the start. Now the other three drivers told him that they, too, worked for PLS and only Sandra, the girl in the office, would know who had hired them. The assignment—"some film work or what"—was to pick up three identically dressed passengers at Bloomsbury Square and drive them from the underground car park wherever they wished to go.

Sandra told Bucken what she knew about the client: a fat man with a toothache. Yes, she would be available for questioning any time.

The three "passengers" worked for a male model agency. One of them, who spoke with a nasal drawl, happened to be in the office when "a mad American, who was the assistant of a film producer, came in with a big, big pile of cash and a lovely job for three. . . . Yes, amigo, of course I know he was mad, I mean with that jacket like a checkered flag under a glazed chintz cape which is the latest ladies' fashion in Paree, and that accent, well, amigo, I could tell you stories about accents like that, but what I actually mean is that I can surely detect an American... The job? Oh yes, simple and lovely. Cinéma vérité, if you know what I mean, amigo. He actually said it could lead to bigger things.... Well, he wanted us to imagine taking part in a big con. You know, a little criminal but clever. Dress specified, just as you see us now. We were to meet the three Triumphs underground. Pay the parking fees at one o'clock, then wait just outside the cashier's kiosk. Bit cramped but not too bad. He warned that we might be filmed at any time by hidden cameras. So the idea was to behave naturally. Eventually, an Indian or something in a turban would give a signal and then we were to drive out, slowly, and proceed to the British Museum where the producer might meet us. If not, we were to repeat the exercise on Tuesday.... Can't remember, amigo, the financial side is handled by Jeremy who would accept anything—probably cash or check or sweet little kisses...."

The two men who stopped the Cortina owned Spartan Guard Security Services. Bucken knew the company: they would be out of business the day any licensing was introduced. They assigned reasonably presentable ex-convicts to guard cash deliveries; they often employed temporary labor even for the most confidential or high-risk duties. They accepted this job on the telephone—with half the cash fee through the mail in advance. While one owner was still nursing the damage done by the spanner, the other told Bucken:

"Like I says, there was this geezer on the blower, calls himself Cutter-Smith and he wants guards, see? So I says our terms is cash on the nail, always, see, and he says that's okay with him, but it's hard to get his meaning sometimes 'cause he whispers 'cause he says his throat's playing up, see?"

"All right, all right, what was the job?"

The caller claimed that his wife had him tailed by some

private eye day and night. He wanted to give him the slip for a few hours, and the Spartan Guards were to help him. The two owners were a little suspicious—"You never know what you get yourself into in this business, if you know my meaning, sir"—and quietly checked the setup. They found that the Cutter-Smith address in Elstree was correct, and that the man was indeed tailed by "a Major Skinner who goes in for such jobs." After the cash had arrived, they received another whispering call giving them the place and time for cutting off the tail. The instruction was that if the maroon Triumph and the tail did not turn up on Monday, they were to be ready for it again on Tuesday. They found it most unfortunate that quite unwittingly they had interfered with the law, a sentiment which was shared fully by Bucken.

5

THE RECONSTRUCTION OF
A PERENNIAL BOMB

The evening brought rain but Bucken was ready for a long walk and too determined to care. The only difference it made was that he stopped at Reception and, watched by an astonished duty Sergeant, unfolded a suspicious-looking bundle that was his coat.

This slight delay might have contributed to his missing a fairly ordinary sight way down at the far end of Victoria Street—a tall figure leaning over a pillar box and scribbling an additional line at the end of a longish letter. "Phase 2 completed. So far so good. Hard to see anything going wrong now." He put it in an envelope, already addressed to "Waltheof Stockton-Wright, Esq. c/o Mailers Ltd.," and posted it.

Bucken turned up the wide collar of the Bogart—it just touched the top of his ears and reminded him of Maxine rising from the water, and Maxine packing. In the morning it would hurt a lot more. Right now, he was punch-drunk, too groggy to try and roll with the blows any more, and relieved by the final bell—he hadn't much more to lose in any sense. There would be an inquest on the operation in the morning. He would have to go to Downing Street. They might give the follow-up job to somebody else but it seemed unlikely. Then they might suspend him for the alleged attack on O'Leary. And for the unauthorized dive to the wreck. And for the loss of the money. And for . . . how many times could they suspend him?

But there was a positive side. The Principal had shot his bolt, and presumably he would now want only to preserve the status quo. Unless he tried to make a second demand, which would be a much greater risk, the initiative would begin to shift to Bucken. And the Superintendent looked forward to that. The hunt had already started. Before he left the Yard, he had already made numerous arrangements. Although his men had still to be kept in the dark about the true nature of the crime under investigation, there was something cozy and reassuring about starting those dull routine inquiries which carried the promise of a rainbow around every corner. Bucken visualized the Principal, sitting on his million—well, minus 10 per cent—biting his nails, staring out of the window, and reacting with a jerk to every noise that might pre-announce the arrival of the police.

It was a dream with nothing to substantiate it, and Bucken knew that. Yet it made him feel light and euphoric, walking on air, rising, rising, until it hit him that the pilots who flew too high without air supplies would suffer anoxia, and the lack of oxygen would convince them that they were safe to fly higher and higher ... which made him plunge into one of his deepest depressions.

"I might be drunk," he thought, and could not remember how much of his usual office rum—a cheaper bottle than his favorite Bacardi for the bottom drawer—had been finished off in the course of that bloody hopeless afternoon. "To them it's just a bloody job. Only I live it full time. Allerton running home to his dying wife. Big deal. Rattray running home to Mu. Another big deal. Why the hell does he love that clinical lady who'd probably disinfect her hands every time she fingered his private parts ..." Bucken knew that he was actually mumbling and giggling but couldn't care less. "Private parts, my foot. Would she fire a shotgun in the bog to camouflage every fart?" He laughed and felt like crying. Not a good marriage in his terms, but for one reason or another it seemed to be working for them. Love? How would even a close friend know? Loyalty? Certainly. Like Allerton's.

And undoubtedly more than what he could give to his women in return for what he never had from them. "Loyalty. Big deal. Yeah. Go on, Bucken, sneer at them. As much as you like. But you're the one always alone, not them." He smiled again. It was going to be a night of heartwarming self-pity. He opened the coat and let the rain wash his face and sneak under his collar. An aid to more effective wallowing in his lukewarm misery.

He had a Bacardi in the Rose and Crown, and another in the Tudor, and so worked his way toward Hyde Park Corner, wet and warm, smiling sadly, when it hit him: he had a tail on. He did not turn to look, there was no rational indication, he just knew it. He sobered up that instant—he always claimed that it was a matter of willpower and that you could not be a London detective without being able to hold your liquor and more than your fair share, too.

He was careful not to steady his gait or give any sign that could warn the tail. Questions and answers flashed through his mind: who, why and what to do? In eight seconds he decided that it could be a villain chasing the contract on Bucken, or some rubber heel from A10 doing the groundwork for some disciplinary charge, or a hound set loose on him by the PM. Whichever tailed him for whatever reason, he decided not to react. Not yet. He could easily slip away but that would warn the tail that Bucken had been alerted. (He always drew plenty of reassurance from the fact that he had never been driven to using his last resort, the perfect disappearing trick through "the door that led nowhere"—a location he had kept up his sleeve since stumbling on it as a young constable on his dockland beat.) He could pretend ignorance of the tail and employ his "advanced drunkenness" to maneuver himself into a position where he would at least identify the tail; but if the opposition was good, this, too, would be a warning. So he chose to do nothing. That would give the tail a false sense of security, a taste of success—anoxia—yet with one element of risk: sudden death. For if it was a contractor, an attack might be imminent. Bucken suspected that, with his sudden transfer, O'Leary's mob might not be all that keen on his death any more. But what if they had not heard about the transfer? Bucken had to know for sure. He turned into the park.

The traffic zooming north between his path and Park Lane drowned any footsteps behind him, and he was determined not to look. He felt his ears grow longer and longer in an effort to pick up any audible clue, while his hunched neck, back and shoulders made an uncontrollable attempt at disappearing in the folds of the coat.

He reached Speakers' Corner and felt the temptation to cross over to the lights of Marble Arch. He resisted it. So far only a shot could have dealt with him. It was unlikely that a contractor would attempt that in the open. If it was to be a blow or a stab, it had to wait for a better opportunity. He turned left, deeper into the park, and continued along the riders' path parallel to the Ring and Bayswater Road.

By now he was sweating profusely and the rain could not wash away the heat. Inside the park, this seemed the longest mile he had ever walked. Occasionally he heard the crunch of too-cautious footsteps behind him. Then somebody approached, running. Bucken pulled his jaw muscles tight. His neck trembled in anticipation of a blow. He trusted his instinct to warn him in the last second. But the runner came at a too-slow and even pace. A keep-fit fanatic, he decided, and hoped he was right. A sprightly septuagenarian passed him. "Should get him for indecent exposure," Bucken thought as he watched the old man's wet, skintight gym suit. Then he heard the steps again.

Bucken could not stand it any longer. He staggered to a tree, pretending to be sick. Now his own footsteps did not interfere and he had a limited range of vision behind himself. The tail approached and would have to attack or overtake him . . . now.

A man passed him. Bucken knew he had never seen the face but he guessed that it belonged to a not very experienced detective. The gait, too, seemed to say "look, look, just strolling." Even stopped to look up at the sky as if the rain had failed to provide the required information. A10. "My behavior should give him something to report," Bucken thought. The picture of a vomiting drunk would conveniently support any suspicion. He kept up the pretense all the way home and, for good measure, bought a bottle at his local off-license. He looked forward to his first decent sleep since this case had begun.

The corridors of the block were deserted. He never understood how all tenants managed to avoid each other most of the time. There was a thin yellow strip at the bottom of his door. The light in the flat was on. Bucken was furious. A10 was welcome to conduct any investigation into his affairs but if it was that serious, they should at least let him know. His heavy footsteps echoed as he approached the door. He would ... He never finished the thought. The light went off. There was to be no confrontation or argument. They wanted to get out clean because, obviously, they had no search warrant. Beginners, Bucken concluded.

He waited until the automatic switch turned off the lights outside, then put the key into the lock and kept fiddling with it, as if having difficulties, even when the door was already open. He then kicked the door hard enough to knock down anybody nearby and lunged forward with a flying tackle into the unknown, hoping to reach the point where somebody might still touch the light switch. He landed on bare flesh. Maxine screamed, Bucken swore at her, and the bottle, smashed against the wall, sprinkled them with glass and Bacardi.

They made love hungrily on the floor, fell asleep, and woke up shivering past midnight. Somehow they made their way up to bed without letting each other go, and talked in the dark, still rolled into one.

He did not ask and she did not explain why she had returned. They were free agents and loyalty was not contractual. Bucken wondered how he could ever envy anybody. As they were lying on their sides, facing each other, she tried to roll a cigarette behind his back.

"Are you in trouble?" She sounded quite casual.

"What makes you ask?"

"Don't know. Are you?"

He shrugged his shoulders.

"Do that again." She moved her shoulder.

"Why?"

"It was nice."

"Lecher."

"You didn't answer."

"It's the job. I've got a pretty impossible case."

"Quit then. The offer is still open. We go fifty-fifty on everything I have."

"Thanks."

"You know, no strings attached."

"I'm delighted. And deeply touched."

"You accept?"

"I accept the compliment. Not many men in their forties receive offers like that from incredibly desirable crumpets like you."

"What have you against money? Even the two of us could never spend all of it."

"Well, I suppose . . ."

"Suppose what?"

"It's never too late to start a new career."

"You mean it?"

"Why not? Don't I even look like a gigolo?"

"Get stuffed."

"Lot Twenty-three, stuffed gigolo; made of copper; real collector's item; authenticated by many users."

"How many?"

"Are you a serious bidder, ma'am?"

"All right, I'm serious. If, and I say if, you loved me, and if you not me had all that money, and if you offered me half, and if I accepted it, would you call me a whore?"

"No, but I'm a male chauvinist pig."

"Does that make me a sow?"

"Yes, but only if, and I say if, you love me and if you're not a queer swine."

"Which reminds me. Rattray phoned."

"What did he want?" He tried to move away and rise but she clung to him.

"I'm not accustomed to being left half-way. You won't make a habit of it, will you?"

"It could be urgent."

"It isn't."

"What did he want?"

"Peel-housing. In other words, he needs something from you."

"He's my friend."

"Oh, sure, as if I were fighting Joe Frazier. I'd always be on the receiving end."

"What have you got against him?"

"Nothing."

"Then leave him alone. And if you must know, it's me who let him down rather than the other way around. It was me who lost touch and didn't know until yesterday how overworked and ill he was."

"You lost touch? Wasn't it he who sent you to that Newhaven shadow-boxing show, bless his fucking soul and the Virgin Mary, or else we'd have never met?"

"But he had a reason."

"Sure. His own career."

"He had more than that in mind. And, at the time, I was ... well, an embarrassment. Almost a liability if you like."

"And you call that a friend."

"That has nothing to do with it. Peel-housing must be kept separate. That's the deal. And if I ever had to make a choice, The Job would come first."

"And that's how you landed this shitty case. What is it?"

"Wrong again. He tried, in fact, to keep me out of it."

"You didn't answer."

"And you know something? I think he tried to keep me in Newhaven because of you. Because he knew that I'd want to stay with you."

"Rubbish. He and Mu want you to go back to Sarah. Because she'd never take you away from the job. But you didn't answer my question. Mind you, I shouldn't be

203

surprised. Not any more." She shrugged her shoulder again so that her breast would stroke his chest.

When at last total exhaustion knocked her out, Bucken staggered to the window. He spotted two men in a Saab which was parked in a vantage position to watch both Bucken's MG and the entrance of the block. Bloody A10. Pity it was too late to phone Rattray.

Rattray's call woke him up soon after seven in the morning, but there were no apologies: "I had to make sure that I caught you at home."

"Now you did. You could have asked your boys outside, too."

"What boys?"

"I thought you were still in overall charge of A10 inquiries. Of course you might be too busy to remember every tail you put on some obscure superintendent fresh from the sticks."

"Don't be daft. I'll look into it. By the way, I hear that Chinese waiter you picked up the other night had some unpleasant accident while talking to you."

"He ran and tripped over some barbed wire."

"Oh, I see. Well, I'll try to make everybody else see it the same way."

"Thanks. You're a real pal."

"That has nothing to do with it. And you know it. So don't try to be sarcastic early in the morning. You're on too important a job at the moment, that's all."

"Am I still on it? Despite the fuckup yesterday?"

"Nobody could have prevented that. But you have to find the man and the money."

"Now wait a minute. We're talking shop. I thought you wanted Peel-housing."

"Never mind what you thought. You have a meeting this morning and I want you to press for something that I consider vitally important."

"Can't you press for it yourself? You'll be there."

"There's been a change. You go in to represent The Job

on your own. And you'll have to convince them that the wreck must salvaged without any delay. It's absolutely imperative."

"They won't play, Ratts."

"Make them. I mean if you agree with me because . . ." Rattray's voice grew weaker and disappeared in a thunder of coughing.

Bucken waited patiently. He heard Rattray swallowing something in big gulps. "You were saying."

"Yes." The voice was now weak. "Make them play, Quint, because the risk is too great. The bloody thing may go up any time."

After a long ritual fight with that hysterical shower unit, Bucken was ready to leave, but the two men in the Saab were still outside. He reckoned that, even if they were amateurs, they would also have somebody at the service entrance at the back of the building. He decided a lesson in professionalism should only do them good. Maxine was delighted to help.

She left by the main door, carrying a bag of laundry, and took the MG. The Saab did not follow her. She returned a few minutes later, stopped in front of the block and hooted three times. Bucken appeared in the window, gave her the thumbs up, and waved to her, indicating that she should come to the back entrance and that he would be down right away. As he withdrew and shut the window, he observed that the driver of the Saab swallowed the bait and followed the MG slowly, at a safe distance. Bucken gave them two minutes, then went down and left through the front door.

He presented himself at the reception desk of the Cabinet Office and, once again, the chirpy Garden Girl came to guide him along the corridors to No. 10. Mr. "Call-me-Wade" greeted him with a "how good of you" and led him toward the stairs this time. "I hope you haven't eaten yet, because I've arranged some light working breakfast for the two of us," said Call-me-Wade, but Bucken hardly listened: although he was now well prepared for a severe outbreak of embarrassing reverence, once again he found it difficult to counterbalance the effects of the building and the special treat with his usual healthy skepticism.

In the two-up-two-down where Bucken was brought up, three brown-blue clay ducks in full flight adorned the staircase, and he used to tease his mother that perhaps she was wrong in her firm conviction that the ducks must be positioned to diminish in ascending order. Along the stairs of No. 10, the wall was lined with the pictures of all former Prime Ministers, leading up toward the current PM's predecessor. Bucken wondered if they, too, diminished in ascending order.

He knew that the "light working breakfast" might be designed to set him up for a heavy-handed con, but he could not help feeling that such were the occasions when men might be told that "your Queen and country need you," and even cynics might volunteer with a gesture of glorious lunacy. He was not sure that he could refuse the call of the bugle.

Call-me-Wade led him fast along the first floor corridor, fingering lightly the doors they passed: "The White Boudoir, Pillared Room, the Small and Main State Dining Rooms, as you probably know, a bit too grand perhaps for just the two of us, so I'm afraid we'll have to suffer somewhat, shall we say, more cramped conditions."

The room itself, borrowed probably from the Church Appointment offices, and the breakfast—coffee, buttered buns and cellophane-wrapped biscuits—were nothing to write home about, but when your country needs you . . .

Bucken's opening apologies for the blunder were brushed aside with a grand gesture. "We're quite capable of reviewing all merits and demerits of your case, I can assure you, and on balance what you refer to as your 'blunder' may well be the only viable proposition to avert disaster."

"You mean by giving in?"

"If you wish to choose those words."

"It's not a matter of choice, sir, it's a matter of facts."

"Quite, quite. On the other hand, you will perhaps agree that politicians cannot always afford the luxury of making decisions based merely on the facts of the actual case. There're overall political and social considerations, respect for expert advice and regard to consensus of opinion which, like the departmental point of view, may appear to lack logic but always is wiser and more comprehensive than individual brilliance, if I may paraphrase the thesis expounded by no lesser authority than Lord Bridges."

Bucken felt slightly dazed, but this seemed his first opportunity to insert the beginning of a sentence "concerning the salvage of the *Montgomery*..."

"Precisely. I knew you would see it our way. Now had it not been possible to deal with this preposterous demand in absolute confidence, we might have been in the unenviable position of 'giving in publicly,' to use your expression, or to fight a costly and still potentially disastrous battle. So I'm pleased that, if I read you correctly, you're proposing to let sleeping dogs lie, so to speak."

"No, I'm afraid you don't read me at all, sir. What I am proposing is an immediate salvage operation and complete evacuation of the entire area, of course."

"You have considered both the cost and risk, I presume."

"Not the cost, sir."

"Not the cost. Oh. Not the cost and not the interruption of traffic in the Estuary and not the general upheaval leading to a potentially disastrous panic."

"General Brammel..."

"I hope you haven't taken the liberty of discussing your investigation with the General."

"No, sir, but..."

"Good. The General has unfortunately manifested, let's say, an excessive zeal by concerning himself with matters beyond his terms of reference."

"An application of individual brilliance?"

"What? Well, we'll put this down to the tremendous

207

pressure under which you had to perform your duties, shall we?"

"Forgive me, sir, but I won't apologize for what I said. The General had a job, mock or no mock exercise, and he would have let you down if he failed to consider all relevant factors, put two and two together and prepare a full assessment of the situation."

"Well, the exercise is over, and from tomorrow he may attend to his numerous family commitments."

"Is it over, sir? Are you sure we won't have to face another, perhaps even bigger demand? And what then? Send in a yes-man you cannot rely on or assign another brilliant individual who will soon have at least an inkling of what it's all about? So why not leave the man in charge? I mean the devil who already knows."

"Mm. And you are a mere superintendent? I must say I envy the Commissioner. The Metropolitan Police must be absolutely bristling with talent. Or do I take it that they might require more tact and political sense for further promotion?"

"I'm perfectly prepared to resign from this assignment, sir."

"Are you, my dear Bucken? Are you really?"

Bucken hesitated and stared out of the window. This was The Call. This was when sane men should stand up and go. Go? Run. He looked at Call-me-Wade. "No, sir, not really."

"Good. That's what I was led to believe about you. And your coffee is getting cold. Biscuits?"

"About the salvage, sir. Expert opinion . . ."

"*Some* expert opinion, Superintendent. Some. While the overwhelming weight of the majority opinion comes down against disturbing the wreck."

"There's the question of corrosion."

"But the indication is that most of the bombs are of the aerial fragmentation type in heavy casings which will corrode at a slow rate that can be ignored."

"That is the indication. We don't know."

"No. But the risk is so minimal that the earlier decisions

are still justified. And that goes for the other risks, too. For God's sake, grant us credit for having studied the hazard at least as thoroughly as you have!"

"And now you, your experts, your government and your predecessors, all of you, refuse to admit that you were wrong. Or that you might have been wrong. Or that we now face an unforeseen new situation."

"You mean the hoax?"

"I mean the interference with the wreck. I mean the fact that the protective net has been cut and the microscopic examination has proved it." Bucken produced an already pocket-worn enlargement and tried to smooth it with some embarrassment. "We have no idea what might have been dropped through there and how dangerous it is."

"Precisely. Which leaves us with a nasty hoax plus your hunch, if you like. But I'm afraid we cannot afford the luxury of backing hunches with the nation's wealth. Yet, on the other hand, you're most welcome to produce the missing evidence one way or another."

"I'll try."

"Which brings me to the main point of our meeting. On expert advice, the PM has categorically forbidden any diving, search or remote control operation inside the wreck. Outside, you may proceed with due prudence and caution but must avoid public attention, not to mention outright publicity, at all costs. Monitoring of transmissions will be carried out as a naval exercise with underwater listening devices, et cetera, et cetera."

"Even that involves an element of risk, sir."

Call-me-Wade searched Bucken's face, and smiled when the message reached him loud and clear. "All right, Brammel stays put. If you feel happier."

"Thank you, sir. At least we'll be prepared if evacuation becomes inevitable."

"And that's exactly what should not arise. We must not force their hand. It's as simple as that. You must not antagonize the opposition to the point where they'd try to retaliate. What are your chances of tracing those banknotes?"

"Minimal, but we'll try because they could lead us to the villains."

"Quite. And you will, of course, continue your routine inquiries, if that's the correct expression. But you see, Mr. Bucken, the art of politics, like the art of trawling fish and the art of battle command, rests on the ability to recognize the moment when, sadly, your losses must be cut in order to preserve your reserves. In my humble and purely personal opinion, this point has been reached concerning the bomb hoax. If we had any guarantee that there would be no further money demand made on us, I'd recommend the instantaneous cessation of hostilities. Alas, this is not the case. But you will have to proceed with utmost secrecy, using only Allerton for any liaison that may be necessary with me and your commissioners."

"Will you require a copy of my progress reports, sir?"

"Copy of what? Nobody wants any written reports from you. What for?"

"If and when we bring any of them to court . . ."

"Court? What court?"

"I mean even the most routine, meaningless progress reports are usually required by DPP as evidence. We can of course keep them strictly confidential until then."

Call-me-Wade stared at him hard for the longest fifteen seconds Bucken had ever lived through. He then smiled with a total lack of warmth, gaiety or reassurance. "Mr. Bucken. You don't quite understand. It's my fault. I apologize. I failed to make it quite clear that this is now a security case and would never go to court. If your tenacity and good fortune happen to lead us to a serious suspect, the final investigation will have to be a, shall we say, internal matter. We certainly cannot afford the luxury of publicity, or, indeed, the exposure of government weakness in a case which may then be regarded as a precedent by some foolhardy copycats of blackmail. If therefore our internal inquiries led to some informal convictions, there would be no need to burden the Director of Public Prosecutions with extra duties because our most distinguished coroners would be quite capable of clearing up

210

the odd fatal mishap that might occur here and there." He stood up. His face showed no reflection of thoughts about murder. "But please, please, do not hesitate to contact me for consultation and guidance on the number I gave you— if it's an absolute must."

Half an hour later, still wandering aimlessly up White-hall and around and around Trafalgar Square, he kept telling himself, "I should have resigned there and then." Yet he knew he would never run away. Beyond duty and loyalty and a flowery mishmash of sentiments, the case was now a professional challenge, the Principal was his private enemy. Yet he envied the Great Unknown Amer-ican Detective who, he imagined, would now start schem-ing to arrange a well-timed leak that would lead to a ruthless cleansing operation, a combined new Watergate CIA affair, in which gradually all secrets would be uncovered, gathering momentum all the time until ... until what? Did it work there? Would it work here? What would be achieved? Besides, he knew he could never start it. Not with training, tradition and instinct telling him clearly what is and what is not done. He had never been a deep enough thinker to consider fully if the guiding light of the "it's not done" principle was or should be ex-tinguished, but he suspected that in some cases it might not illuminate the correct path. So he drew his conclusion: "Balls."

The Photofit pictures amounted to a complete mess. After hours and hours of painstaking interviewing, projec-tion, re-interviewing and reprojection by two specialists in Penry Facial Identification Technique, the Principal ap-peared to have short, dark, blond, silver and long, black hair, brown eyes and blue eyes, wearing/not wearing spectacles, clean-shaven, bearded, with and without moustache and long sideburns, having a very prominently protruding upper lip and/or "normal mouth but one tended not to look because of the dreadful scar and the badly stained, foul-smelling teeth," and the victim of

211

chronic toothache (one side of the face covered, the other side in constant contortion due to obvious suffering) which must have bothered him over a period of at least three months—if the witnesses were to be believed.

The composite pictures only convinced Bucken what the Principal was probably not like. But even in that he would not necessarily be right because the pictures so thoroughly contradicted each other that even a true likeness might have slipped in somewhere, only to increase further the range of possible suspect types.

All the descriptions referred to a fat or heavy man which did not help much: although it is difficult to disguise real bulk, people tend to give indefinite descriptions by failing to differentiate between plump and portly, corpulent and massive, truly fat, flabby bodies and natural heavyweights—while, on the other hand, any of these may hide a thin man who can easily "put on weight" by generous padding in a two-sizes-too-large suit.

The first point of real value emerged when Bucken compared the Photofit pictures: none of the witnesses had mentioned a double chin, one of the features almost impossible to disguise or produce properly, convincingly and without the constant risk of a slipup. His second valuable observation was that all descriptions implied "a large face"—presumably a long face with fairly prominent cheekbones which might be conveniently fattened as required by packing the inside of the mouth along the top and bottom gums with anything from a couple of pieces of chewing gum to more professionally molded rubber fittings. Finally, it also seemed beyond doubt that the Principal was a tall man.

Bucken re-interviewed all the witnesses—the receptionist at the motel where Cutter-Smith claimed to have had his meetings with the Principal, Sandra at the Pimlico Limousine Service, bug-detector dealer Downes, Jeremy and the would-be actor from the male model agency, and the chauffeur. These lengthy talks yielded few useful details but convinced Bucken that the disguises bore a professional touch: it seemed that the Principal's aim was always to look positively like somebody else rather than the negative approach of trying to look unlike himself. Striking, dramatic, and disgusting features were applied—including a bad limp, scarred lip, stained teeth—because these, together with loud and conspicuous clothes and easily adaptable accents, provided another factor of disidentification: the characters the Principal impersonated would mostly be remembered by these obvious elements of initial impact.

The motel receptionist remembered "quite clearly" that the room was always booked by "a Lufthansa pilot who spoke remarkably good English." Unfortunately, the soft lighting and the pilot's cap prevented him from taking a good look at the face "but then one is not supposed to break the rules of discretion: once the room is yours, and provided that it's a double, you come and go, unseen, as you wish."

Downes claimed to be able to recall everything about the man: very tall, very fat, pebble glasses, sweating, flashy overcoat, swollen face and toothache—amounting to nothing.

The "mad American film producer" who appeared at the model agency spoke "with a touch of Texan," was dressed for effect and had a "quite dreadful scar on that superbly protruding upper lip."

The chauffeur who drove Cutter-Smith's car remembered a "big, fat, bearded immigrant in a turban ... what immigrant? wog immigrant, that's what. Of course I know that he was black or yellow or brown or something. No, I don't think I saw what color he was, not in that dark tunnel, but it stands to reason, don't it? He had to be a blackie 'cause white wogs who come here wear crowns not turbans, don't they?

Bucken tried to interview his witnesses in their "natural habitat" and in Sandra's case his extra effort paid off. He observed her for a while from the street and noticed her constant compulsive munching. Detectives, who had watched her for the past couple of days, confirmed that most of the time she had nothing to do and, apart from eating, she passed the time staring out at passersby. When Bucken talked to her, she immediately remembered the big-time customer who had booked a fleet of cars: fat man with toothache, his face protected by handkerchief and upturned collar of coat, thick pebble glasses, voice reduced to a whisper. She was convinced quite unshakably that "he wrote something leaning over the pillar box outside, then posted a letter, and went down to the gents opposite."

"Were you busy at the time?"

"Busy? You must be joking." She offered Bucken a cup of tea.

"So you were just reading after he'd left."

"No, I wasn't. I was just finishing a snack."

"Ah. That's how you had the chance to see him going down the stairs to the loo. You wouldn't remember which way he went when he came up again, would you?"

She swallowed some tea and chewed a biscuit as if her life depended on it. "Funny that you should ask. I don't remember him leaving the loo at all. Even at the time I thought it was funny. I mean I was watching him because I guessed that a man like him would drive away in a Rolls. But I never saw him again."

"And nobody else left the loo while you watched."

"I wouldn't say that. I mean there are always some people coming and going there. But not him. He never left. It was funny."

"You wouldn't remember the others who left, would you?"

"No."

Bucken was grateful. He was now sure that the man who had booked those cars was not fat at all: he would shed all surplus weight in the public lavatory, pack it in the briefcase, and walk out a slim man. That was why she thought she never saw him again. Might have been the Principal. Whoever he was, he might have been a disguise expert himself, but there was the odd chance that he had sought specialist advice somewhere. Bucken assigned two detectives to the chore of listing and visiting all disguise specialists and theatrical makeup artists in case one of them remembered a tall stranger perhaps with a peculiar whisper—or an even more peculiar voice.

But disidentification techniques were not the only skill the Principal needed to pull off what appeared to be the perfect crime. Bucken therefore listed the fields in which chummy would have to acquire at least a certain degree of expertise or enlist specialist assistance.

No. 1 on this list was the *Montgomery*. It would be vital to know everything about the ship, her history, last cargo, layout, et cetera. Who would have access to details outside official sources?

No. 2: Life and traffic in the Estuary. Tidal conditions. Police patrols in the area and around the wreck. Natural cover for regular visits to Sheerness.

No. 3: The behavior and potential effectiveness of bombs and explosives under water. The risks of placing explosives in the wreck. The work of underwater detonators. The construction of remote-control time/detonator device.

No. 4: Diving. Equipment and technique suitable for given tidal conditions. How to approach the wreck without being noticed by police or passersby?

No. 5: Remote-control technique to activate, stop, reactivate time/detonator by some brief coded signal. How could suitable sonar-type equipment be built or purchased?

No. 6: Cutter-Smith. How and why was he chosen?

Bucken regarded each of these as pores through which he could sneak under the Principal's skin. Once inside, it would not matter that the man was faceless. He would know what made him act the way he did, how he would go about protecting that million.

Bucken was reluctant to commit himself to any particular theory, but he was willing to bet that this was a single-handed job "purely because it was possible to do it alone, without the risk of accomplices and without the need of sharing out the loot."

Allerton disagreed. He thought that one of the major

criminal brains must have been behind it, and a half dozen or more specialists were employed in the execution. But Allerton would not debate the subject. He was not supposed to get involved, and he liked it that way. He raised no objections to Bucken's rather excessive demands for scores of detectives to check every conceivable aspect of the Principal's preparations, Cutter-Smith's moves and all radio traffic in the Estuary, because, he said, "I have orders to back you and provide you with all facilities, but it's your show, son, and your head on the block, and frankly, I don't want to read your reports and don't even want to be told about your progress or the lack of it."

"There won't be any reports, Fred."

"You mean not in the usual form? All right, I'll make some special arrangements for you."

"I was told no reports at all. Not a word."

"But that's mad!"

"I know."

"So how do you intend to cover yourself? What if one day DPP comes back with some tough questions? What will you say? 'Sorry, sir, you have to take my word for it and trust my memory?' Is that what you have in mind?" Bucken tried to interrupt him and at least imply that nothing was ever supposed to go to DPP, but Allerton would not give him a chance. "All right, this is a special case. But what if one day—in all good faith, I grant you that—you exceed the invisible limits of your unlimited freedom? What if there's serious complaints against you? You want to have nothing to fall back on, nothing to prove that you did have the authority to do this, that and the other? Wait, I haven't finished yet. Because there's something else, perhaps the most important of them all. What if, at some stage, you suddenly lose your grip on the case? Good way of putting it, don't you think? Lose your grip on the case. But I spell it out for you that accidents do happen. Especially in a case like this where, in my humblest opinion, you're up against highly organized crime and villains who mean to hang on to that pretty pay packet for a good day's work. Who will then pick up the threads and how? Will the poor bugger who takes it over from you start all over again?"

It made sense, of course. While Bucken was ready to cover up for or even play the whipping boy to the PM, Call-me-Wade, Allerton and anybody with the flimsiest claim to consideration in the national interest, he was not prepared to let all his effort, however little it might achieve, go down the drain the moment he bumped into a lucky contractor's stray bullet.

On a routine investigation like the immigration racket, he would submit a report to C4 whenever there was any development or his superiors asked for one. He would also file interim progress reports to keep colleagues in the picture, convince his bosses that he was doing some actual work, and provide material which—together with his notes and diaries—might be used by an eventual prosecution as evidence. Some of them were therefore pretty meaningless—such as "made contact, nothing of immediate relevance transpired, inquiry continued"—others amounted to only a memo for himself, but the rest contained the information that would be vital to detectives taking over a case from him.

The steady accumulation of scraps of information, even if much may seem useless initially, builds up the solid basis of detection, the vast combined knowledge of police—some three million records stored by the Criminal Records Office. The Registry keeps the files up to date and opens some 200,000 new files each year: the "serial number/year" will identify an offender forever. The general Crime Index is indexed, in turn, under various headings to achieve maximum usefulness. The Nominal Index lists each criminal's various aliases. Criminal techniques and specialists may help to identify a villain when the Method Index is consulted. There is a Wanted Index; a Check Index of stolen checks and credit cards; the Rogues Gallery contains the photographs of all with a genuine claim to criminal fame; the Drug Squad has a card index of drug offenders; C11, the Criminal Intelligence Section, collects and collates information on several hundred major criminals and thousands of their associates who may not be criminals themselves; banknotes, forgeries and stolen antiques and works of art are also indexed, and the Information Room has a Central Vehicle Index with anything up to thirty thousand cards referring to vehicles which have been stolen, missing, abandoned or suspected of being used by criminals.

Apart from the top brass who automatically have the right to study the records, all the four thousand CID officers of the Met are entitled to consult the files if they give some simple reason why they need them. When a detective draws some records, he has to sign for them, bring them up to date if he has anything to add, and return them with remarks concerning their use, even if saying no more than "no assistance" or "suspect not identical."

Every call for information from C4 must be recorded on the file itself. Unfortunately, this is not always done. Also, when one officer has the file on loan, another may consult it on his permission or by simply reading it over his shoulder without adding his signature. Irregular, but it happens.

And when it came to the "irregular," Bucken knew the routine better than most. Cutting corners had often kept him ahead of his colleagues, and he always found the way to talk even staff officers, who signed for files on behalf of an Assistant or Deputy Assistant Commissioner, into letting him have a peep. But irregularities would be no news to Allerton either.

"I leave it to you, Fred, if I may. You know best."

"Thanks. I'll let you know about the arrangements and you file only what you wish."

"And I hope it will be better protected than my reports and meeting arrangements with the Lad."

After a long pause, Allerton looked briefly at Bucken, then turned away and reduced his voice almost to a whisper: "Are you still talking about a leak?"

"What else? Apart from Maxine, only the top brass here knew that the Lad worked for me."

"Are you lodging an official complaint, then? Because that I'd want in writing."

What's the use, thought Bucken. Mere logic, suspicions and allegations without hard evidence... "No, Fred, no official complaint. Not yet." And he left before Allerton could play his customary "any-questions-lots-of-questions" signature tune. He returned to his room and jotted down a brief summary of the case and the lines of investigation he intended to follow. As all this would only be seen by anybody else if something happened to him, he added a note on the attacks on the Lad, himself and Maxine, and his thoughts about the tail, in case those suckers were not from A10.

He was ready to leave his office when a call came through from General Brammel.

"Are you on a scrambler?"

"No, I'm afraid not."

"Oh." The General sounded disappointed. "You think we can talk?"

"I don't know what you have to say."

"No. Well, I don't think it matters all that much, and I hope you won't think I'm a fusspot or a nosey parker or something, and I don't even know what this game is all about, but now that I'm involved one way or another ... I'm worried." Bucken swore silently, wishing that the man would come to the point. "Well, the gist of it is that I've received orders to stay put, continue the exercise but purely on a theoretical basis, and cooperate with you."

"And that worries you."

"Not quite. I'm a generous man, and I gave you the benefit of the doubt, and you came through well, if I may say so. But what does worry me is this old ammo ship right under my nose."

"What about it?"

"Well, to be frank with you, exercise or no exercise, I'd like to explore the possibility of salvage."

"Don't."

"Ah. That's what my Minister said, too. An odd coincidence. What?"

219

"Is that all?"

"Not quite. You see, before I suggested a salvage operation, I wanted to know where I stood. So I went along to the archive of the local rag, not too bad, really, I must say, though they haven't got much more than what I already have here, but they asked an awful lot of questions, why I wanted the file, et cetera."

"Journalistic curiosity, I suppose."

"That's what I thought. But eventually I got it out of them. They were puzzled by the fact that, only four or five months ago, some big sloppy Yank came to see the file, then yesterday a dumpy little fellow, and now me. Can you make head or tail of it?"

"No . . . not really, but thanks anyway."

"I thought you should know."

Bucken could not have agreed more wholeheartedly. He had no doubt who the big Yank was. But who was the little fellow? Was there one at all or was he an invention to help a clever scribbler interrogate the General? He decided that for the time being he would not follow up this lead: the little fellow could not have been inquiring on behalf of the Principal, and any police interest would only persuade the local editor to run a story in his paper or flog it to the national press—about the last thing Bucken wanted.

He packed a tape recorder and all the tapes marked C-S, for Cutter-Smith, and called for a car to run him home. The Saab was still there, and Maxine told him that it had been sitting on her tail all day. It worried Bucken that they were so amateurish. Did they intend to call attention to themselves so that some other tails could follow him more easily?

At 0340 in the afternoon, he locked himself in the bedroom and began to listen to the tapes. Maxine plied him with coffee and Bacardi, and just about managed to resist the temptation of offering him food when he did not want any. His first objective was to check C-S's consistency and soon he came to the conclusion that, if chummy was a liar, he was as good as anybody at it. On the tape with

Allerton, on several others with Bucken himself, before and after the disappearance of the money, his story never varied, not even in minor details, and Bucken was prepared to accept his words as the truth.

How did the Principal get in touch with him?

"He telephoned me and offered to help."

"Just out of the blue?"

"That's right. Though normally, I don't talk to any strangers."

"Why didn't you put the phone down?"

"I was interested."

"In what?"

"He said he was concerned about my fate. He said it was really rotten the way they treated me."

"How did he know?"

"He wouldn't say. But he knew all right."

"Did he say who he was?"

"He said I didn't know him, but I could regard him as a friend."

"You must have found this ridiculous."

"I did, but it intrigued me. I was dying to discover how he knew about me and what he wanted. Perhaps he could really help."

"You must have tried to guess who he was."

"I did. At first I thought it might be some stupid practical joker. Later I thought he was someone in the same predicament as me. Someone who worked perhaps at the Bank of England. Then finally, it didn't matter."

"When he convinced you that you could get away with this crime."

"No. It was when he spelled out what I always knew but was reluctant to put in practice, that I must take revenge. Be a man. Be myself. As he said."

"When did he spell out what he really wanted to do and what your role in it would be?"

"At the second meeting."

"Weren't you shocked?"

"I was. But I was fighting it."

"Why didn't you go to the police?"

"I didn't want to ... I don't know."

"Did he threaten you? Were you frightened?"

On every tape, Cutter-Smith tried to avoid answering these questions. Bucken believed that he was ashamed of being afraid of the man. Of anybody. Perhaps because all his life he was afraid of everybody.

All the meetings were at the same motel in the evening. The Principal would telephone C-S and tell him the time. The room would already be booked. On arrival, C-S would go into the room, turn the radio on but not the light, and wait. Eventually, a tall, big shadow would arrive on foot—no, C-S had never seen him or his car or what appeared to be some dark uniform. The Principal always brought a briefcase from which he produced drinks and glasses. No, he never used the glasses that belonged to the motel, even though he always wore gloves. "What impressed me most was that he was a truly cautious man, always well prepared for our meetings, never leaving anything to chance," said Cutter-Smith. "He not only knew everything about me, my ambitions and failures, yes, I admit, failures, but also that I drank large pink gins, when I could afford them, that is. Mind you, he wasn't much good at measuring the bitter."

"Didn't it bother you that you never saw him? Don't try to tell me that you weren't curious and didn't ask any questions."

"I never said that. I asked the questions and he had a perfectly good answer. The less I knew, the less I could give away, so the less I needed to worry about anything. He wanted me to end up in the blissful safety of total ignorance."

It was almost midnight when Maxine brought in more coffee and asked Bucken if the thought of sleep was repugnant to him.

"It's a dirty word."

"It's not a four-letter word, you know, and not a synonym of fuck."

"In my book and in your bed it is."

"That's why you look like somebody who has just

222

survived Gomorrah, brimstone and all, and committed sodomy not only with Lot's two salacious daughters but buggered the old man, too. So come and let me preserve your seeds at least and we'll bless the Lord."

"For God's sake, Maxine . . ."

"Watch it! Blasphemy against the Holy Ghost shall not be forgiven unto men. Fortunately, Matthew says nothing about women. So there."

The early hours of the morning failed to improve Bucken's looks. His intensive staring into some invisible void, the listening not only to words but also to tones, searching for the telltale tremolo of lies, drew black circles around his eyes until he resembled a film negative of a black-and-white minstrel. But displeased he was not. The tapes convinced him that it was the truth when chummy claimed, "I can't lie. But my memory is exceptionally good. I can remember every word he said." Bucken had asked the same questions over and over again. Yet he could not catch C-S out: whenever he quoted his Principal, hardly any word differed from the previous version. Of course he might have learned it all by heart. But it seemed likely that the text would have been written by the Principal because the style differed from his own.

Bucken now compiled a list of words and expressions which did not seem to belong to Smith's own vocabulary. He referred to "Old Bill" but thought it was a nickname for the Treasury. If the expression came from the Principal, he might be a criminal or at least a user of the underworld's language. There was a reference to "hotel," the hiding place to rest the loot or the men after a crime while the heat was on. C-S was also given the choice between taking a "fix" or a "corner." Yes, the Principal might be a star in C4 under some other alias, and nobody might ever suspect him because of his perfect choice of a front man.

In fact, Bucken would have been delighted to discover that the Principal was, indeed, "tasty" with a record as long as the Krays' and the Richardsons' put together. Because on his list, some other words began to point in the

223

opposite direction—the other side of the law. Cutter-Smith was thought to deserve "a commendation" for informing the authorities about the bomb. Officers' language. Might be a criminal's army background. But the references to C.O. were even more important. Only detectives, and within this only London CID men, refer to Scotland Yard as C.O.—the Commissioner's Office. Crooks and police-men might use other nicknames, such as the Big House, but C.O. is an exclusive one. Provincial cops might not even know what it is when "you get a posting on division" or a transfer to C.O.

And then there were the "wherebys," and the whole caboodle of report-writing vernacular that went with an admin man's job. The attacks, the Professor's tipoff, Lau, and now this police language. Allerton and Co. might fume or laugh, but this was too much of a coincidence for Bucken. If he was right, he had now found the Principal's first weakness: style. Didn't he realize how good his man's memory was?

Bucken hated corrupt policemen. Those who planted evidence, bricks or weapons or drugs on their suspects, disgusted him. But he retained some compassion and sympathy for them if there was a chance also to blame their superiors who encouraged the planters, praised their blind or even insane determination, and drove them on and on to fill in more "stop slips," make more arrests and achieve more convictions. And he blamed the law and the courts, too, which often deprived coppers of a fair fighting chance and so increased the temptation of cheating whenever the would-be planting artists felt sure that a suspect was guilty but the evidence was insufficient.

The thought of a rogue cop, and the possibility that he might have to go for a man of his own cloth, filled Bucken with painful apprehension to the brim as he decided to call it a day at a quarter past three in the morning.

But if he thought it was bedtime at last, he was wrong. He found Maxine crying silently and struggling violently in her sleep. The blanket was on the floor and sweat was pouring out of her. Bucken stood there, stunned by the fact that he had not heard a sound, staring at her wet face and all those tears—he had never thought she would know, let alone have use for that clean, nonalcoholic liquid.

He touched her shoulders to break the grip of the nightmare, but she fought back ferociously, kicking, screaming, "Don't! Don't! Please don't!" and when he leaned over to kiss and hush her, her head shot up and thumped him on the nose. Bucken jumped into bed and tried to restrain her gently but could not hold her strong, arcing, slippery body, so he had to pick up the blanket, wrap her into it, and hold the whole suddenly limp bundle in his arms.

As far as he could make out, she was refighting her attackers who had burnt her leg and the experience was somehow mixed up with another horror story of Maxine, as a child, witnessing her mother being beaten or raped by intruders. Bucken's questions and soothing words did not seem to penetrate the realm of the nightmare, but he could hold her now, still wrapped in the blanket, and she gradually curled up into a fetal position.

The entire scene and the reference to her mother were a shock to Bucken. Maxine never spoke about her past and claimed to regard everything prior to meeting him at the quayside as nonexistent. At first Bucken did not press her to tell him anything—it was just a light affair. Later it became more difficult to go back to basics and ask the questions when she volunteered no information.

Maxine lay now quite still in his arms which slowly grew numb under her weight, but he would not want to move because she was sobbing and muttering intermittently. He was not sure if she was still asleep or talking to him. "Mummy never swears. Daddy never swears. You must never swear, Maxi. Never, never, never. Why not, Mummy, tell me. 'Cause thou shalt not take the name of the Lord thy God in vain. But you didn't do that, Mummy, did you? And what was your reward? You were attacked. And where was your famous God when you buried Daddy? And why did he let you also bury two sons? Why? Only I was left to you and pain. So swear,

Mummy, swear, and cry out loud, and attack and let them have it and let me be shamelessly successful on this earth and stay on top!"

The doorbell woke them up at seven-thirty. Bucken was virtually paralyzed with pins and needles, and Maxine opened the door to Walsh. He stared stubbornly at the minute area of her body that was merely screened off by a corner of a blanket, and backed away mumbling about "wrong number, I mean wrong door number, sorry" until he heard Bucken's shout from inside asking Maxine who the caller was.

"I'm looking for . . ."

"Come in then."

His eyes revealed that he considered her too good for a cop, and her smile acknowledged the compliment. The mutual sympathy was confirmed when they became victims of a ten-second farce routine.

"I'm Maxine," she said and tried to hold out her hand but could not without dropping the blanket. Meanwhile Walsh struggled with two large paper bags and two smaller packets which were wrapped in newspaper and held under his arms, preventing him from shaking hands. They ended up touching elbows. "Ancient tribal custom," she said, and he apologized, indicating the bags: "Same here—I never go anywhere without a bomb" . . . which she found funny.

They both laughed as they entered the bedroom and saw Bucken's embarrassment at being found fully dressed in bed. They shared the natural early risers' cheerfulness which irritated him even more.

While Maxine grabbed a dressing gown and volunteered to make some coffee, Walsh tried to put down the paper bags, still balancing the packets precariously. Bucken took one from him: "What have you brought for me? Fish and chips?"

"That? Oh, just a pound of gelignite."

Bucken almost dropped it.

He led his visitor into the rather impersonal living room (he never found the time though always meant to do something with it) and Walsh emptied his bags on a coffee table. Apart from soldering iron and a few electrician's tools, most of his wares looked like pretty black building bricks for children. Bucken was not sure how or where to put down the gelignite and would have been happier to hand it back to Walsh who was already kneeling in front of the impromptu workbench.

"You asked me what sort of an underwater bomb I would construct if I was a fucking amateur knowledgeable enough to produce something better than a constipated poodle's first fart but not a premature bang which St. Peter might mistake for a 'knock, knock, who's there?' Right?" By now he had his tools and building bricks in a neat row. "Apart from the jelly, everything you see here can be bought over the counter. The little darling over there is of course a detonator and for that you'd have to buy a pint or two for a thirsty quarry man or pay a Welsh miner enough to keep him in laver bread for a year or go to a black market source if you want a good genuine ICI product in a presentation box."

He selected a few of the black toylike integrated circuit chips and lined them up next to the detonator. "And that's your timer. Better than the old alarm clock to arm your detonator. You can also buy it ready made if you're not work-proud." He picked up a small box, about the size of a cigarette package, which showed only the sockets on the side. "That's the baby, with built-in batteries. It has electronic circuits which can count the seconds, and when time's up, it closes a relay and switches on automated baking ovens, opens bank safes or activates a detonator. The advantage of the homemade pack of chips is that you can fit it into any shape . . . even a length of scaffolding for easy waterproofing." Walsh was tactful enough to make it sound as if the example had occurred to him purely by chance.

Maxine brought them some breakfast on a tray. She studied the odd collection on the table, then took just one look at the two men, and turned to go: "Don't try to keep me, I must have a bath."

Walsh was too preoccupied to think about food. "Explosive, detonator, timer, batteries—and that's it, unless that device on the buoy is anything to go by. Remember? There was a rubber disc or what hanging from that piece of scaffolding. I guess that might have been a receiver. Now if I wanted to make a device like that with remote control, I would avoid underwater speech transmission like the plague and would use a coded signal instead." His agile sausage fingers gathered up the rest of his chips. "And that's why I'd need the little darling I could put together from these—a decoder to go between the receiver and the timer. I'd insert a master code so that, each time a transmission is picked up, the incoming signal would be compared to the master and commands would be accepted only if the codes tallied.

"All this is routine stuff to anyone who knows a bit about electronics, somebody like a radio-controlled boat enthusiast, and you could then make it as sophisticated as you like. It could be programmed to change the code after each transmission or the timer could be stopped and restarted for a shorter or longer countdown period at will. Overall cost? Under a hundred quid, probably no more than sixty for the timer and the decoder."

So the price would be no stumbling block to any criminal, and no matter how many pairs of legs Bucken scrounged from Allerton, it would take decades to track down everybody who had bought or had access to such electronic parts in the past year or two. He would have to concentrate on sonars: there were only a few companies and individuals who needed and could afford very costly underwater communication facilities for a legitimate purpose; also, the number of specialist dealers was limited— Bucken expected some positive results within a few days.

Walsh was still busy building his bomb. Bucken watched the kneeling figure and in his mind's eye it transformed into the outline of the Principal: tall, probably lean and muscular and, although as yet faceless, a man whom Bucken was beginning to know intimately.

6

A PAINFUL DEATH IN SAN FRANCISCO

It promised to be a hectic, nerve-testing week for Bucken with only Saturday offering something to look forward to. Each year, he gave a combined birthday treat to the two Rattray boys, and this time they wanted to go to the Hendon RAF museum followed by a monumental hamburger nosh-in followed by Agatha Christie's *Mousetrap* which was becoming with its endless run something of a London schoolboy's theatrical graduation ceremony.

The "routine inquiries" Bucken was directing required a more generous supply of shoe leather than of ingenuity and seemed to lead nowhere. Diving instructors could always recall some peculiar would-be divers with mad schemes to recover galleons or capture the Loch Ness Monster, but this was no surprise to them and no lead to the police. Diving gear dealers were no more helpful. Bucken contacted all possible underworld snouts and put the word around that hefty rewards could be earned by those who led him to a very hot million, but there was no trace of the money, and no gossip about a new big spender in the playgrounds and gambling capitals of the world.

The Saab had disappeared and Bucken saw no sign of being followed, but he felt it in his bones that he was still being watched somehow, as if the tail was in front of him, knowing his destination and waiting for him on the spot. He admitted to himself that it worried him and gave him an unwanted urge to hurry because this might be a race, and a race he could not afford to lose. A race to where? And why? At C.O. he had his friends but nobody would confirm that A10 was interested in him. Rattray denied it most categorically. What if, through him, somebody wanted to find the Principal in order to exploit his setup on a far bigger scale? It would be a compliment to Bucken that they, whoever they might be, trusted him as a guide when he himself had virtually no hope of succeeding.

On Tuesday morning he shared a lift at the Yard with Inspector Linley who was now handling the immigration-racket investigation and helping the local CID with their inquiries into the circumstances of the Lad's death. Bucken thought the man's sugar-sweet smile and slimy compliments would soon make him puke.

"I hear you're handling the biggest job ever single-handed."

"Rubbish. You shouldn't listen to idle gossip."

"I understand. It's very hush-hush, they say. What is it? IRA? . . . Well, who else but you, of course . . ."

Bucken ignored it. "Any progress at your end?"

"No, not at the mo. Very, very difficult."

"I know. But you had enough to start with, surely."

"Sure, sure. But it's very big. I have a feeling there's so much money involved that they could buy anyb. or anyth. Perhaps they tried it on with the Lad, too."

"You have any serious suspicion?"

"No, nothing in partic. But I mean if they pay enough, nobody will talk to us. And if they offer enough, even I could be tempted, couldn't you?"

Corruption was oozing from the corners of his mouth and eyes. Bucken felt he would not be surprised if . . . but then stopped himself thinking about it. He would have to control himself. He must not see corruption everywhere. Disliking Linley was not a good enough reason.

In the evening, Bucken visited a dingy little man in a dingy little shop in Greenwich. It was an inevitable chore because the man was the foremost expert and had the greatest single collection of books and documents on World War II cargo ships. Bucken managed to survive a landslide of words about the Liberty ships and the *Montgomery* without revealing his lack of interest, and even tried to guess when the man asked him: "And why do you think people called them SAM ships? Ah?"

"Sam? Could that be Uncle Sam?"

"Ah! That's what most people think. Isn't it stupid?" He rubbed his hands with great satisfaction as he chuckled. "People think that the name shows that some of the Liberty Ships were American built or lent to us by Uncle Sam. The clever cookies even suggest that it's an abbreviation of Surplus American Marine. Isn't it stupid? Isn't it? Well, I'll tell you what it is so that from now on you can tell others. It was made up by Admiralty pedants for classification: Superstructure After Mast. Isn't it funny?"

Bucken expected to hear yet another description of the Principal, but the old man had had no inquiries. At least one good source the opposition missed, Bucken thought, as he made notes of a potentially useful remark: according to the old man, the Liberty ships were built in a rush and their welding was very poor. Some 12 percent of them had actual welding defects and most of these soon developed cracks. One in every thirty ships suffered major fractures in service, and there were a few which split open spilling cargo and passengers as they went, because "such bad welding runs like ladders in women's stockings when it cracks." So apart from the decks and the main fracture in the hull, somebody could have access to the *Monty* through a crack in the hull—a gap just wide enough to allow the insertion of something like a length of scaffolding. If then a rubber disc were wedged in the crack, the receiver would be right on the surface of the hull but well-concealed from blind hands groping in the dark.

The man promised to call him at the Yard if anybody else came to make inquiries about the Liberty Ships, locked the door behind Bucken, and dialed a London number. As soon as the phone was answered, he began to speak without introducing himself as if expecting to be recognized at once:

"You remember you came to ask a lot of questions about those SAM ships about a year ago. Well, now there was somebody else, right from Scotland Yard, asking very

231

similar questions, and I must warn you that if there's any monkey business going on, then friends or no friends I'll have to tell him that you were here. You understand? I just wanted you to know because I promised."

And he was very angry, too.

Bucken drove straight to the Sheerness circus to see Brammel whose patience was running out fast: "Find yourself a drink and a pew and then listen. I'm supposed to make contingency plans and serious preparations but the locals are not supposed to notice a thing apart from this bloody monster standing bang in the middle of their playground. Well, who will tell me how to do it? Then there's these divers reporting to me about the search that is not a search. Well, are they supposed to search anything at all and if yes, what the hell should they try to find? And then there's this bloody new lot you let loose on me."

Brammel summoned a cool Canadian who was acting as an adviser to the Ministry of Defence on underwater communications matters. He was fed up with repeating his complaints yet again, so he tried to get it out in one breath: yes, he had most of the equipment he needed to plant sensors and sow underwater bugs all over the Estuary which he could "wire up from end to end like a pinball machine so that if and when anything sails, slides, wriggles, lays eggs or collects them, all the lights will flicker and the bells will signal the biggest jackpot of them all, and yes, I can put in underwater floodlights and cameras which will be triggered off automatically by sonic devices sensitive enough to pick up the noise made by a winking eel, but I just cannot do any of this in any sort of complete secrecy."

Bucken stressed how important it was not to attract publicity or frighten and arouse the locals' curiosity, and the Canadian shrugged his shoulders: "Okay, but then it may take months or more to cover everything. I don't know what signals you're really looking for, but if it's anything like the one we picked up on Sunday . . ."

"Sunday? Why the hell wasn't I told?"

"There was nothing to tell, really. Now if we were fully operational . . ."

A few minutes later, Bucken had the full report. As the Canadian's team had to proceed surreptitiously, mostly at night, pretending to carry out some maintenance of telephone cables, only a few of their devices had yet been positioned around the *Monty:* "At the moment we're trying to cover both speech transmissions and telemetry, but to be really effective we must position many more hydrophones and I need more men to monitor them. What we did pick up was a coded signal, several short bursts coming in on Eight KHz, which is fairly standard carrier frequency under water, but the signal was weak which might have been due to many things. The transmitter might have been too far out or not powerful enough—or just that we weren't quite up to it. Anyway, we could never identify it. Probably that's why you weren't told."

Bucken arranged with Brammel top-priority facilities for the Canadian, but what he was told did not sound very promising: even with full preparedness and around-the-clock monitoring, when a signal was picked up, they could only determine a path which would cross the *Monty* in a, say, east-west direction. The transmission could come from any point on the left or right along this path. To catch the transmitter would require extraordinary luck.

And that was not Bucken's only problem: judging by the Principal's cautious, logical techniques so far, he guessed that the man would now simply switch off the timer's batteries at this stage. That would conserve energy and eliminate the risk of regular transmissions to stop and restart the countdown cycle. After all, if for any reason, including revenge for Cutter-Smith, he wanted to activate the device, he could do it any time.

On Wednesday morning Bucken invited Maxine to join him on the Saturday outing for the boys.

"All right. I'll meet you somewhere."

"No. We go together."

"There won't be enough room in the car."

233

"I'll borrow Mu's car," said Bucken.

She thought hard to invent more excuses and Bucken was anxious to parry them, but they both knew that the real dispute was about something completely different: she had never met any of the Rattrays. As Bucken had spent most of the year away from London, he saw them only infrequently and attached no importance to introducing her to the family. Mu on the other hand was never keen on meeting his girl friends whose very existence offended her no matter what the relationship between Sarah and Bucken: "If I invited all your popsies here one after another, neighbors would accuse me of running a disorderly house."

Maxine was determined: "I don't want to sneak into their home through the back door. Of course if they asked me . . ."

He knew that she was right but tried to argue. And that she appreciated. The fact that he thought about her meeting them at all might mark a turning point in their relationship.

Bucken spent the rest of the week mostly in Elstree. He talked to detectives who had watched Cutter-Smith and Winnie day and night since the Meeting in Bloomsbury, listened to all the tapes of every word spoken in the bugged Cutter-Smith home, examined all the recorded telephone calls to and from the maisonette—and the emerging pattern just would not make sense: chummy lived the way he had lived before.

The bank manager who held the hundred thousand for Cutter-Smith told Bucken that the money was still virtually untouched: only £5,002.30 had been spent so far, including the initial spending spree and cash withdrawal.

The real estate agent was very keen to promote his luxury apartments in Florence and wrote two letters to Cutter-Smith but received no answer.

Mr. plain-Smith, head of the Finance Department whom Cutter-Smith had described as his "superior with the inferior mind," first refused to talk to Bucken. Eventually, he yielded to "extreme pressure from above."

"We're not in the habit of discussing our employees' affairs with the police or anybody else, and I can only tell you that he's engaged on matters of Planning, Programming and Budgeting, known as PPB for short, and that his conduct as an officer of the local authority is satisfactory. He had a few days off on some important family business—I wouldn't know what exactly it was because the ratepayer does not wish us to pry into our officers' private lives."

Apparently, having concluded his "important family business," Cutter-Smith had returned to work and "mentioned only once, in the vaguest possible terms, that due to some changes in his circumstances, he might be obliged to seek a long unpaid leave—which we would, of course, consider sympathetically—but he did nothing further about it."

"Has he got friends in the office?"

"No, I don't think he has any friends at all."

"Does he talk a lot about his background?"

"Not really, no. Let me put it this way: he drops the occasional hint or two about some supposedly glorious past and special services to the nation, but not more than anybody else. You know how it is, we all like a bit of the old mystery and romance in our lives." Plain-Smith straightened his tie—and looked about as romantic as a mouthful of cold spaghetti.

The visits to Cutter-Smith left Bucken totally bewildered: who would know about, let alone choose, this man? The couple had simply no idea what to do with the money. They shared some old, cooling dreams about "exciting adventures" such as a fortnight's cruise to Tenerife and a Christmas with champagne for breakfast, and they would have done these, too, if Cutter-Smith's "compensation from the nation for his troubles" had been one, not a hundred, thousand. Winnie felt it would be immoral to fritter away that sort of fortune and she was incapable of making any decision, not even about going to consult the leading orthopedic surgeon in Harley Street, although, as a result of several years of inquiries, she always expected that he could perform outright miracles on her troublesome stump.

Cutter-Smith dreamed about retirement but dreaded the thought of having nothing to do: "What I need is a truly good and viable idea for a spectacular financial venture which would fully stretch my abilities, utilize my experience, provide genuine excitement, yet not without safeguards against Lady Fortune's whimsical moods."

"In other words, no venture at all," said Bucken provocatively.

"You're wrong, wrong and wrong again. A true financial adventurer should always retain the ultimate trump up his sleeve. And until I've found the right investment scheme for my money . . ."

"Your money? You're a fool, Smith. You're a fool not to run out and spend, spend, spend. 'Your money' won't last."

"Fortunately, your predictions have not been particularly accurate, so far, if I may say so."

"You don't even deserve that money. You just walk up and down Bond Street and buy nothing."

"It's nice to know that I have police protection against mugging. Besides, I have my fun. I get plenty of joy from the knowledge that I could buy almost anything."

"Except honesty. That you've sold, Smithy." Bucken knew that remarks like this really hurt him though he never quite understood why. Cutter-Smith was, in fact, still considering divorce from Winnie, proving to her that yes, she was right, he was bad, even rotten, deep down, and only she could have changed him if she had really tried to. . . . Except that he could not bring himself to turn her out at once, without a penny, as he had planned.

Although the couple adamantly claimed to be fed up with their home, they just could not imagine themselves living anywhere else. Yes, they would eventually have it redecorated because he hated all do-it-yourself chores, but they worried about what the neighbors might think because every one of them painted and papered and repaired and modernized their homes apparently nonstop.

"Yes, I suppose it is sheer, stupid inertia," she said to Bucken, "but you must understand, we lived in foreign countries, we tried different things, and we failed. So we wanted just a quiet corner, where we could live out our days, surrounded by friends."

She had nobody she could call a friend. The few people she knew in the neighborhood spoke about her as "the bloody cripple who thinks she knows everything better and takes advantage of being disabled." Yet everybody in the neighborhood seemed to know about her husband's glorious past and what an injustice it was that nobody gave him some high-powered executive position, because at the slightest encouragement, bitter complaints were pouring out of her. Bucken knew that any of these people might have been the vital link between her and the Principal.

At last, Saturday. Maxine spent the entire morning dressing, undressing, dressing. Although when Mu telephoned her it was obvious that this would be no more than a five-minute drop-in for coffee before museum, hamburger and theater—a rather odd combination to dress for—yet it was important to her to impress Bucken's best friend and his family however varied their ages and tastes might be.

She kept asking Bucken for advice, but all he could suggest was that she should "stop behaving like a fucking virgin" and be herself. She ended up wearing a full corduroy skirt with a jumper but in the car, she changed the jumper for a shirt with plunging neckline and the matching jacket of the skirt, all topped by the softest, floppiest cartwheel of a hat. Luckily, they were at the house by the time she decided that everything was a mistake after all.

As soon as they stepped inside, she became an outright winner with all the children. They grabbed her by the hand and she had to visit their rooms and inspect their toys and prize possessions, and Ron, the eldest at thirteen, cleverly maneuvered her into standing next to a half-nude calendar poster in his room because, as he would later confide to Bucken, "her figure would beat the pros hands down."

Mu made the correct noises but remained virtually invisible when standing near Maxine. So it was a good solution that she retreated and asked Bucken to help make the coffee.

"Not in the same class as Sarah," Mu declared. Bucken did not answer. "Very pretty, of course, no offense meant, Quint."

"Thanks for inviting her up."

"The least I could do—since you asked me to."

He asked her where Rattray was.

"With Aunt Oriana. He was very sorry that he would miss meeting . . . er . . . your friend."

"Well, there's always another time, I suppose."

"Oh yes. Anyway. He was anxious to go because Aunt Oriana is rather poorly these days and she's come to sort of rely on his Saturday visits."

"You mean . . ."

"Oh, yes. He has lunch with her if at all possible. He usually picks up some Chinese food on the way. Very decent of him, don't you think?"

"Yes, I suppose. I've never met her."

"You haven't missed a thing." She peered into the hall, then shut the kitchen door firmly. "Ring Sarah," she whispered. "She wants to talk to you."

He was about to say that Sarah knew his number, but heard the children coming and it was pointless to say it anyway.

The museum turned out to be a huge success. Maxine seemed to know everything about fighter planes and bombers, Battle of Britain pilots, dogfight tactics and ejector seats. Bucken suspected that she had done her homework. Timmy held her hand firmly, all the time, with the total lack of inhibition of a seven-year-old, while Ron, desperate to be recognized as a grownup, only touched her whenever he could to guide her this way or call her attention to something over there. Ron made meticulous notes in his diary about what they saw and what Maxine said. She produced the ultimate winner of lasting admiration when she casually mentioned that she had once flown in a friend's chopper.

"You mean he owned it himself?"

"Yes."

"But that's fantastic," declared Timmy. "Why don't you marry him?"

Ron sadly admitted that, apart from holidays, the nearest he had come to "real flying" was when once, fishing with his father, "something terribly urgent cropped up and a helicopter came to pick up Dad. But there was no room for me, so I had to go home by train. On my own."

Bucken remembered the day well. It began for him at the foot of The Long Man. "Yes, I spoke to your mother that day."

"And to me," added Timmy. "While Ron was still at Ramsgate."

"Shoeburyness it was if you must know, and Dad was picked up at a small airstrip outside Rochford."

Way back, in the more leisurely days of youth, Bucken used to go fishing with Rattray. He remembered the old dinghy well and was a little sad to hear that Rattray now owned a fiber glass one with a fast outboard motor. Ron appeared to have endless tales to tell in true fisherman's style and was obviously delighted with the fact that, whenever possible, his father would now slip away from work and weekend household chores to take the boys fishing. "Only last Sunday . . ."

Bucken listened to only half of it. He disliked coincidences and these were peculiar ones. Shoeburyness was opposite Sheerness and the *Monty,* less than three miles away. Rattray now kept the boat mostly in the outer Estuary area. It was last Sunday that the strange coded signal was picked up.

Bucken did not want to press the child about it, but he was disturbed and could no longer relax. Ridiculous, involuntary mental exercises ruined his fun for the day.

Before the theater, they had half an hour to kill. Timmy

and Maxine insisted on visiting an amusement arcade and there the boys continued to stare at this incredible Miraculous Creature: first with a pistol she scored one bull's eye after another, and later she shot down every moving duck, ship and airplane, firing her air rifle at machine-gun speed. "You see? I have secret talents," she laughed.

Throughout the play, Bucken's mind was totally preoccupied with what he had heard about Rattray's fishing. The same thoughts went to bed with him that night.

Maxine was silent for a long time and he concluded that she had fallen asleep. "I made a mistake," she said at last. "I shouldn't have tried to please her."

Bucken resisted the obvious "I told you so" and reassured her instead: "The boys fell in love with you. So did I."

"I don't know what came over me. I wanted her to like me. Why can't I ever succeed at anything I really care about?"

"You're a total success with me."

"That's different, isn't it?"

"Mm." That bloody, idiotic coincidence. And the one-in-a-million chance that he would hear about it. No. That was no coincidence. As he saw the boys from time to time, there was a better-than-even chance for the subject to crop up. Which would explain why Rattray was so keen to get him transferred to some other case.

Bucken did not try to pretend that the pleasure was his when Walsh treated him to yet another hearty "good morning" just after eight o'clock on Sunday.

"I know, I know, I'm just an ordinary bomb wallah and not a Spec. Branch genius, and I'm not trying to look at my bird droppings as if they were elephant dung, but I've been thinking."

"Must have been a shock."

"It was, it was."

"I'll help your recovery with a decent breakfast," said Maxine, "if you promise to leave Bucken here. We have plans for the day."

"Oh, it would be absolutely presumptuous of me to interfere with the Superintendent's plans and decisions..."

The frame survived the shutting of the door, and after the bang had stopped reverberating like naval gunfire in a fjord, Walsh's face resumed beaming with self-satisfaction: "Sound navigation and ranging, *sonar* for short. Relatively few dealers, selling mostly to old customers, firms, professionals because the stuff is too expensive for an ordinary diving enthusiast's pleasure. Right?"

"Right."

"Yet your inquiries produced nothing. Which didn't make sense: if you were rightly worried about what you seemed to be worried about, then some underwater transmitter would be necessary. So I did some thinking."

"Make a note of the date. It seems such a memorable occasion."

"While acting as a driver for you, another memory to be cherished and handed down to my children's children with pride, I overheard a thing or two. Accidentally, of course. Such as that your man paid cash to everybody he employed, including the bug-detector peddler, so why not the sonar dealer? In which case there would be no record, the tax fiddler is every honest man's alter ego, and your boys would get nothing out of him."

"So where did you get with your early-morning studies of human foibles?"

"To the tale of the rich treasure hunter. Big fat man with beard and toothache. Ordered and paid two thousand in cash for the latest German diver-to-diver set."

"Okay, let's go and see the storyteller."

"Wait. The set normally transmits speech, which is the easiest for divers, but it's no great problem to throw away the microphones and earphones and use the equipment for transmitting and receiving some coded signal. It can be as simple as switching the transmitter on and off a number of times for varying duration."

"Which solved the Principal's problem."

"Like an icepick solves chronic constipation, it did.

241

Your man bought trouble, sir, trouble all the way. The range is limited, depends on all sorts of circumstances, even water temperature. The transmission needs a direct line to the receiver which may still be confused by dozens of deflected echoes of the original signal which may arrive at intervals of fractions of a second."

"So he returned to the dealer and beat the daylights out of him."

"He did better than that. He returned and paid the dealer a couple of hundred for advice, and that's how he was told about a new American gadget which is still very much on the hush-hush list. It's part of SONUS which is the baby of the Navy-CIA marriage for sound surveillance of the sea, and which will fire automatically CAPTORs, the moored torpedoes that home in on Russian subs." He stopped to breathe in and noticed that Bucken was shaking his head to dispel giddiness. "Don't worry, sir, you don't have to digest it all. It will suffice to say that the gadget helps any transmitter to home in on the underwater receiver—and here's the address of Kowalski, the American specialist who was experimenting with the gadget in the North Sea in the days of the tale of the treasure hunter."

Maxine entered with the news of "breakfast ready" during the last sentence. "Who's Kowalski?"

"My new boyfriend in San Francisco. And he's waiting for me impatiently. Sorry, love."

It was a pity for such lovely bacon and eggs to land on the kitchen wall sunny side up, but Maxine could never be accused of being docile and this time she had even reason on her side.

After a quick check to see if CRO had anything on the dealer (negative), and some wrangling with the Yard's switchboard over the authorization of a phone call to San Francisco, Bucken sat in his office at half past nine waiting for connection.

"Your call to San Francisco, sir. Mr. Kowalski's on the line, go ahead please."

Due to British Summer Time, the difference was nine

hours, forty-five minutes past midnight in San Francisco, but Kowalski did not seem to mind. Bucken introduced himself and offered him the opportunity to call back, reversing the charge, if he wanted to check that it was really Scotland Yard.

"Let's hear the questions first."

"We understand you carried out some experiments with a new diver-com and a special range-finder attachment in the North Sea. Is that right?" There was no answer. "Hullo, are you there?"

"Yeah, I'm here."

"You didn't answer."

"Look, you say I carried out some experiments. What about it?"

"Were the experiments successful?"

"What if they were?"

"Have those attachments ever been freely marketed?"

"No. There're only a few sets as yet. The Navy has them all except . . ."

"Except what?"

"Well, one set was damaged beyond repair and was scrapped under supervision, the other was lost during the North Sea trials, but that you would know about."

"What do you mean?"

"Do your homework, sir. It was your own man from Scotland Yard."

"Not a big fat man by any chance . . ."

"Yeah. You know him? Some old English name . . . he was very proud of it being double-barreled . . . I could look it up for you . . ."

"Please do. Now tell me about the loss of the gadget and what checks you made when the fat man contacted you."

"Well, I just about came unglued when he started to talk about the project because it was very much on the secret list because . . . er . . . look, it's very difficult to talk like this. I don't know how much you know and how much you're supposed to know and how much I'm supposed to say, because, you see, I've left my job."

"We could get clearance, of course."

"Fine, that's fine. Do that, sir. And then pop over here and we can sure have a long chat about it. But we really must obtain clearance from the ... er ... you know who I mean."

"I do. But just now, you could tell me a couple of things which do not affect security. First ..."

"Look, sir, I wouldn't want to appear uncooperative or something, but it's well past my bedtime, and Sunday or not, I have a heavy day ahead of me, because I'm not on the payroll any more, if you know what I mean, and as an independent adviser I must really look after the business side if you know what I mean, sir. ... Are you there, sir?"

"How much?"

"I don't even know what or how much time you'll require. So why not pop over here and we could then discuss everything. It's not a telephone matter anyway, I presume."

"I'll need authorization, so I must know what you want."

It was no good arguing, and from the security angle Bucken fully agreed that this was not a subject for an open line, but he knew that to obtain an authorization and the ticket for a cop's "popping over" was another matter again.

Allerton was found at home—but in the bath. Then he called back but said that this should be authorized and paid for by Bucken's current "other masters." Call-me-Wade's number was answered by a message-recording machine. Rattray was out of town, and the DAC on duty felt that it could wait until Monday when the Commissioner or Carron, his Deputy, could be approached. Yes, for true emergencies Carron was available this Sunday, but would the Superintendent call his case a true emergency? It was past noon when Allerton told Bucken that, luckily, Carron had called him quite out of the blue, and promised to drop in for a brief discussion as he was passing the office anyway. In the meantime, Bucken was trying desperately to uncover the twists and turns of red tape so that, eventually, he would know which ticket clerk to track down to obtain cash or credit or whatever. He had a valid passport—though no American visa. This had to be dealt with when at last his flight was authorized. He sent a courtesy telegram to the San Francisco police department to warn them of his arrival. At three in the afternoon, he found Call-me-Wade who promised to help with intelligence clearance at least on a limited basis. But he still could not cable his exact arrival time to Kowalski.

Bucken studied the timetables and crossed out several departures with growing resentment. He had already missed the quickest flight by Jumbo on the most direct route via Los Angeles, and two other good ones which involved changing planes in New York or Chicago. He could just about catch the flight at 1700 to New York where his visa would await him, though it would be a mad rush without time even to pick up a toothbrush. Call-me-Wade was against it: it was easier to obtain clearance for Kowalski to talk if the Sunday duty officers of CIA and Naval authorities were given a little extra time. After all, Kowalski was not going to run away, particularly if Bucken had the authority to compensate him for his loss of time.

The 1700 to New York was not even half full. The middleaged Chinese businessman, who arrived at the "hand luggage only" check-in desk with only minutes to spare, found a good seat on it without any difficulty.

Bucken was driven home by Walsh to pack an overnight bag. Maxine was out. She had put a note on the bed: "Went sailing with friend. Will be back tonight or tomorrow night. Love M." Bucken left it where he found it and pinned another note to the cushion: "Went to the States alone. Will be back tomorrow night or soon after. Love B."

Here's one-upmanship for you, he thought, but it bugged him. With three hours to kill, he dialed Sarah's number at Windsor. She was at home.

"You wanted to see me."

"You make it sound as if it surprised you."

"Sometimes it does. Is it urgent?"

"The sooner the better."

"All right. I'm on my way to San Francisco..." he paused for effect.

"Oh, we *are* going up in the world, aren't we? Who's paying?"

"My girl friend. You're virtually next door to Heathrow. Can you get away from...er...whoever, and meet me in the Oceanic Building?"

She greeted him with the deadly combination of a coy smile and one of those "semen-curdling" glances, and kept her voice very low and intimate: "I want to make you a proposition."

"I love the sound of it. Don't stop."

"Ring Joseph as soon as you're back. He's about to retire."

"He isn't even sixty yet."

"It's on medical advice, quite out of the blue. Heart trouble." She put her hand on his as he was about to lift his cup. "Ring him. Please. It could be the answer to everything. And it was his idea."

"Suggested by you."

"No. Honestly."

It was an attractive proposition. Her Uncle Joseph's had been one of the most spectacularly invisible careers in British intelligence. It began in the Middle East during the war, and ended at the point of a long, heavy calibre .377 magnum bullet which shattered his nerves and left his right hand paralyzed at the age of forty. He learned to write with his left hand, and landed the biggest security job in the City. He looked after the worldwide interests of a major finance corporation, and traveled a great deal, always accompanied by his wife. It certainly was the nearest thing to a nine-to-five job Bucken would ever be interested in—a job that would satisfy Sarah's only condition of yet another remarriage. Yes, it was an attractive proposition.

"Thanks. I'll think about it."

"Do that, Bucken, and do it fast. Before one of your chums hears about it. Because the money is good.

Something like three times what Rattray is getting plus perks. In fact, Joseph thought about approaching him, too, but I talked him out of it."

"For my sake. How touching."

"He was second choice anyway. Joseph wants a real detective, not a would-be one."

"I'm most flattered."

"Besides, he's a cheat and I told Joseph."

"What do you mean cheat? I thought you liked him."

"I still do. But he's a cheat. He has a mistress. Some little bird tucked away in the woods."

"Rubbish."

"Mu doesn't think so."

"Come on, Sarah, give. What's going on?"

"Wish I knew. Not that it surprises me, not with what I think of Mu, as you very well know, but I'm sorry for her. It must be awful to live with the thought for months and months."

"But is there any proof? Has he admitted it?"

"No, my dear. Mu is much too civilized to ask for explanations and make scenes. But she thinks it's been going on for almost a year now. He's away quite frequently, seems to have night duty which is something rather new in their marriage, and although Mu never quite knew how much money they spent or saved apart from housekeeping, she's convinced that he had some heavy expenses."

"Sure, getting his clap cured and betting heavily on some international hopscotch competition."

"Well, it's none of my business, I only said I was sorry for poor Mu."

"Poor Mu is dreaming things up to color her wretched existence."

"Whatever it is, suspicions can be even more painful than the truth, believe you me."

Which was not the right sentence to act as a lullaby for Bucken on the first leg of his flight. Only to reassure himself that his own suspicions were the result of stress and exhaustion, halfway over the Atlantic he was tempted

247

to send a telegram to Walsh and ask him privately to watch Rattray. The knowledge that he could not do it to Rattray, certainly not in such a devious way, made it even worse. Then he went through all the scanty evidence he had collected, and again and again he concluded that all could still be coincidence. There was nothing, not a word against Rattray, nothing that would stand the test of being spoken out aloud.

Rod Connor, an American CIA agent, came right up to the plane to greet him in New York. Thanks to him, Bucken went through customs and immigration without a hitch, and although he had been warned that the one hour before the connecting flight might not be enough, he had in fact twenty-three minutes to spare.

"Someone from the San Francisco Police Department will meet up with us to take us to the place," said Connor who found it "kind of neat and most amusing" that Bucken drank just rum, not even rum and Coke. "You can fill me in on the way because I was just given a few skeleton facts."

Bucken could not possibly tell him all. So he invented a pack of lies hoping that he would still remember them in the morning.

Their plane took off at 2100 Sunday, local time—three in the morning and Monday already for Bucken with much sleep missing from his life. In San Francisco it was six P.M. Sunday. Kowalski looked through his books: the figures were not very reassuring. All the business his former government contacts had promised to give him never materialized. His wife was nagging him all evening to take her out, somewhere, anywhere, preferably to the Garden Court of the Sheraton-Palace because it reminded her of some glorified greenhouse for communal mastication in Krakow, but she had no idea that all his credit cards had been withdrawn or invalidated, and that the sucker coming from Scotland Yard would have to be milked and milked with the ceaseless intensity of a lifesaving blood transfusion.

It was 0117, Monday, local time, when a Chinese

passenger from London landed at San Francisco International Airport. Two young Chinese waited for him with an old Buick, and soon they were speeding down Bayshore Freeway, James Lick Freeway and Skyway, rounding the old U.S. Mint, and approaching Chinatown along Grant Avenue. Twenty-five minutes later the visitor checked into a relatively cheap hotel where he had a room with bathroom reserved on the second floor. He said a noisy good-bye to his companions, went to his room, turned on the television set full blast and ran both taps in the bath as well as in the shower stall, sang heartily, ordered sandwiches, and proceeded to make a general nuisance of himself. Eventually, neighbors complained and the night manager asked him to cool it. From then on, he gave no more trouble to anyone: he ran out the water, left the light and the TV on, stepped out of the window on the fire escape, and descended into a side street where the Buick was waiting.

At 0315, Kowalski's Doberman pinscher died instantly from a poisoned dart. Kowalski never heard a window being cut out and three men entering the house, so nothing happened to him until a pair of hands grabbed his shoulders, pinning him to the bed, while another pair of hands stuck a wide band of insulating tape across his mouth from ear to ear. His wife's mouth was taped in a similar fashion and she was then tied up and locked in a closet next to the main door in the entrance hall. Kowalski was trussed up like an oven-ready fowl. The man from London brought in a small canvas bag and emptied it on the bed. Everything he had asked for was there: several sticks of varying length, a few short metal spikes and coils of rope and wire.

A lieutenant from the Police Department came out to the plane from New York looking for Bucken and Connor. He suggested that Bucken should perhaps sleep for a couple of hours as it was only 0442. Alternatively, he could fly the party by chopper to the downtown heliport and lay on a good breakfast with a cheerful view of the defunct prison on Alcatraz island. Bucken settled for breakfast: why alienate Kowalski with a reveille at dawn?

"We'd better watch out for the dog," said Connor who knew Kowalski. "It's one of the two huge beasts he lives with." But as they approached the house at 0720, there was no sign of the Doberman. They knocked on the door several times. All they could hear was some sort of suppressed groaning which first they mistook for snoring. A figure moved behind a curtained window and they thought that Kowalski was investigating who the early callers were.

"It's Connor from Washington. I've brought you a visitor from London."

There was some more flurry inside. The groaning grew more distinct. "Open up. Police!" shouted the Lieutenant. Then the loud report of a single gunshot as the Lieutenant kicked the door in. The three men threw themselves through the opening and fell into the hall in a huddle. The groans were coming from the closet. Through the open door to the rest of the house, running feet could be heard.

"Cover the rear," yelled the Lieutenant who already had his gun out. To Bucken the whole scene appeared unreal: in his more than two decades of detective work he had never fired a gun in anger.

Connor leaped toward the broken front door. Two shots rang out. He fell against the frame with a thud. "Are you hit?" shouted Bucken.

The Lieutenant was not waiting for an answer. With his gun leading, he was through the door where the shots came from. He saw two men escaping through a window. They would have been sitting ducks if he had ever reached that window, but from behind a large desk, a shot hit him in his side just below the ribs. He spun around and his last bullet punctured his attacker's forehead at the same moment as Bucken brought the man down with a flying tackle. Blood sprayed Bucken as he held his victim, not yet realizing that the Chinaman in his arms was already dead.

The Lieutenant pointed at the window and Bucken

dived through. He caught a glimpse of two men jumping into a Buick. He heard a shot and threw himself flat on his face. He never saw the car's registration plate.

Connor was dead. The Lieutenant was losing blood and strength fast but his injury did not seem fatal and he remained conscious right until police cars and ambulances began to arrive with a crescendo of noise.

Bucken had already freed the elephantine Mrs. Kowalski from the closet. She was hysterical and had no idea who the attackers were or what exactly had happened.

Kowalski was in the bedroom, naked and strapped to a chair. Bucken had to force himself to check if there was any life left in the body that displayed the ghastliest collection of injuries he had ever seen. He guessed Kowalski must have been dead for some time. The heavy smell of blood mingled with the bitter smoke of black-burnt flesh. Handfuls of Kowalski's hair with patches of his scalp were scattered on the floor. His skull seemed to be held in one piece by thin wire wound round and round the temples, forming a metal band. Behind his nape, a spike had been inserted into the headband and twisted, tightening the all-around grip until the eyes began to bulge dangerously out of their sockets, and the skull cracked. Similar attachments were on his feet, hands and chest, and a rope band went round his right hip, down between his legs squashing his testicles against his thigh, and back up to the hip where a short, thick stick applied the increasing pressure.

The whole house was a mess. Every drawer and cupboard had been emptied on the floor. The attackers had searched thoroughly for something. Bucken was sure they had not been after money. Had Kowalski's death been due to a bullet or a stab, it would have implicated the Principal whose interest was to silence him. But this was clearly torture. There was nothing the Principal would want to learn from him. So who had attacked him and what were they after? And did they get it out of him? Bucken's guess was that they did not: long before the relief of such an awful death came, Kowalski would have told them everything they wanted. But above all, Bucken wanted to know when Kowalski had died. The police doctor estimated that it must have happened at least two, probably three or four, hours earlier. It meant that Bucken could not have saved him even if he had come to the house straight from the airport. But if he had caught at least the previous flight out of London and if . . . It was no good considering the ifs. Or to indulge in fruitless self-accusations. He could not possibly have known how urgent his visit was. But somebody did know. Somebody who knew that he was on his way.

He tipped off the Police Department that a passenger just in from London might have been involved in the killings. He was impressed by the fact that the majority of the night arrivals were accounted for within a couple of hours. A Chinese Londoner was among them, but his alibi of watching television and falling asleep soon after that noisy bath appeared to be unassailable. The purpose of his visit was stated to be "family reunion." He spent the day with relatives while police lifted his fingerprints from furniture in his hotel room, took scrapings from his shoes and examined his clothes. By three in the afternoon, they had matched the scrapings with soil samples from Kowalski's garden. That was enough to pull him in: even if he had tortured or murdered nobody, he must have been present when a CIA agent was killed.

Bucken listened to the interrogation for a short while and knew that the sus was in for a rough ride. He felt no compassion, and saw no reason to stay any longer: if the man was on a mission for the Tong in connection with the *Montgomery* ultimatum, as Bucken suspected, he would not be frightened into talking because of his loyalty to and superior fear of his own comrades.

At Kowalski's house nothing seemed to be missing and nothing could be interpreted as a clue to the reason for the savage attack. Bucken's presence was the only positive lead, but his explanations were much too vague, so he had to accept that he would not be very popular with the local police. Yet they let him go through all the papers in the house because they were watching him, looking for signs of special interest.

The entries in Kowalski's carefully preserved diaries were laconic and often meaningless to strangers. Under the eyes of policemen and two CIA representatives, Bucken ran through the period of the North Sea diver-com trials. It was easy for him to appear only casually interested until he read a peculiar name: Waltheof Stockton-Wright.

"You know him?"

"No ... not offhand." Which was a lie. Waltheof was Old English meaning "thief rule," a curse of a name to live with particularly if the bearer happened to be a police instructor at Peel House. But Stockton-Wright, now long dead, used to have the strength of character and good humor to bear his cross with dignity, and share the laughs when the trainees organized a Waltheof limerick competition. With a vicious entry, the contest was once won by a PC Rattray.

7

THE SQUEEZE

Bucken hoped to catch up a little on his sleep during the long homeward journey, but niggling suspicions about Rattray would not let him. It was ridiculous to doubt his friend's absolute integrity. It was ludicrous to attach any importance to mere coincidences and vague possibilities. But none of this was funny. He had to list and analyze the various points.

Waltheof himself could not have been interested in underwater gadgets because he had been dead for about ten years. Who would use his name? Would the choice be a sign of some macabre sense of humor? Rattray did like black jokes.

A tall, stooping figure with definitely no fatty bulk would fit him as a description. The whisper? Yes, he had a fairly distinctive voice, which had to be used sparingly to avoid painful coughing. He used many expressions typical of policemen of long service, knew the Estuary, could do all the necessary research quietly, would have access to confidential records and, if he really had a mistress and some financial problems, he would probably go for the big money with style rather than a bit of debt here and gap-filling borrowing there. He could use disguise, he was a good swimmer, and had some knowledge of electronics as well as explosives. He had the brains to work out and organize the entire project always retaining something up his sleeve. . . .

Bucken stopped. Who had recently mentioned to him the importance of always having something up one's sleeve?

Besides, Rattray would have the advantage of knowing police procedure and having access to progress reports on the investigation. Rattray had the opportunity, too. He was on the spot when the buoy blew up. That, on the other hand, might have been a time bomb. After all, he was with his son who had to return by train. But Rattray was in the area once again when the coded signal was picked up on Sunday. No wonder he would not want a family friend working on the case.

Bucken tried to be truly fair and objective: would he report to A10 or Allerton such faint suspicions about a stranger or a colleague he hardly knew? No, he would not. Would he obtain a confidential report on the suspect's financial status from his bank? Yes, he would, without any delay. Yet he could not bring himself to do it. It would have been an admittance of his own serious concern and his failure to clear a friend of all suspicions. And yet and yet and yet. Rattray would have access to Bucken's meeting schedules with the Lad. Apart from Maxine and Allerton, Rattray would be in the best position to monitor Bucken's every move. Then why use a tail? And why torture Kowalski? If somebody tried to follow the same trail as Bucken, Cutter-Smith could be the next target. . . . What defense would the front man have? But of course, it was he who had said it. "A true financial adventurer should always retain the ultimate trump up his sleeve." Did he stick to his own principle in dealings with his Principal? It could only be an escape route or an emergency procedure to enlist the Principal's help and backing by the renewal of the threat. That could be the only scrap of information Cutter-Smith would never give away, not under torture or even hypnosis. So he would have to be squeezed like a lemon for this last drop of the juice.

Bucken frowned. It would be a dirty job.

He did not tell anyone that he was back in London. He wanted to achieve absolute concentration. So he just booked into a hotel, took a fair dose of sedatives, and gave himself some eleven hours of uninterrupted peace. He woke up on Wednesday, at one in the morning, made a couple of telephone calls, finished what was left of a soggy ham sandwich, put on his relatively cleanest shirt, and ordered a cab.

He timed his arrival to coincide with the squad car's at Elstree. He was pleased with the police driver who, following his instructions, made enough noise to wake up half the neighborhood. Embarrassment could well be the first and most important step toward a man's final degradation. Curtains fluttered up and down the street, worried and sleepy faces appeared in the windows lit up intermittently by the flashing light on the roof of the police car.

Bucken stopped a burly Inspector and a young and eager Sergeant with his final instructions. He chose them knowing that they were the roughest, most heavy-handed types in the business.

"I cover you all the way. I want you to lean on them hard and really rattle both of them in there, no matter what."

At 0247, when the defenders would be at their most vulnerable, the raid began with hammering on the door: "Police. Open up. Open up!" Bucken stood back while the Sergeant kicked the door.

Cutter-Smith opened the door slightly, peering through a narrow gap, but fell back as the two detectives pushed their way in. Bucken entered behind them and gently shut the door. Cutter-Smith turned to him: "What do you want?" Bucken gestured toward the Inspector who took his cue:

"You know what we want. You just show us where it is and there won't be no trouble. Otherwise we'll have to search the premises and you might not like that."

Smith knew there was nothing to find in the maisonette and this helped him to recover his composure. "Have you got a search warrant?"

"They have my permission," said Bucken quietly with his most polite smile.

"And you're a judge or magistrate or what?"

"Under the Official Secrets Act 1911 and the Explosives Act 1875, if there's great urgency, a Superintendent of the Police may issue an effective search warrant to other officers in the form of a written order of search. I happen to be a Superintendent, and the Inspector has my order in writing. And I can also do this under the Prevention of Terrorism Act, and if you survive this little exercise you'll have an opportunity to check my facts with your lawyers and make complaints if you wish. But right now," and he suddenly raised his voice, "you just shut up, you piece of common shit." The whipping effect was unmistakable, though Bucken wondered whatever had made him commonize the shit.

The bedroom door opened fractionally. The Sergeant shoulder-charged it, not knowing that Winnie had only one leg. When he saw her stumble, his face went beet red and he was about to help her up when his eyes met Bucken's. The Superintendent swallowed hard—and shook his head. Cutter-Smith started toward her but Bucken held him: "She'll manage. But she must stay in there. For the time being."

The Inspector began to open drawers and cupboards, searching for something unknown to him. Bucken strolled over to him and with deliberate slowness pulled a drawer all the way out until it tipped over, spilling all its contents. The two policemen noted the hint. From then on, it became a "search and destroy" operation. Pictures and mirrors were torn off the wall, cushions and upholstery were ripped open, the doors of a sideboard were smashed in, and when Bucken pointed at the polystyrene tiles in the bathroom, the two policemen stripped the ceiling bare.

Winnie was brought in and made to sit with her husband on the uncovered and freed springs of a settee. She tried to hide the stump and began to sob.

"Let me go and get her leg," Cutter-Smith asked. Bucken swallowed again—and shook his head.

While the Inspector found a spade and used it as a lever to pull up floorboards, the Sergeant made some tea. When he brought it in, Bucken tasted it—and simply dropped the cup. There was a moment's silence, all of them watching the liquid's slow spread on the torn carpet, then she began to scream without becoming hysterical. She screamed continuously, at an even pitch, as if letting off steam.

"Make her shut up or we'll lock her into a cupboard," Bucken said in a cool voice to Cutter-Smith.

The bedroom came next, then back to the kitchen, and the bathroom where the toilet bowl was smashed "to check the base" and water flowed freely everywhere.

Bucken took Cutter-Smith into the bedroom alone. He slowly raised his hand, searching for a spot on Smith's face. He pinched the upper lip, holding it without hurting, just showing that he could do anything he liked. Smith trembled as if crying without a sound.

"Where is it?"

"Where is what?" The words came out with a lisp.

"You know perfectly well."

"I don't. Honestly."

"Honestly? You?"

"Please believe me."

"Why should I? Why should I help you when you're not helping me?"

"If only you told me . . ."

"Told you what, sweetheart?"

"What you're looking for."

"Then you'd tell me?"

"Anything. I'll tell you anything."

"Ah. Now we're getting somewhere."

"Are we?"

"Yes. You've admitted that you know the answer, but you're trying to force me to ask the question, to spell it out for you, to humiliate myself, before you'd tell me."

"Yes, yes, if I knew the answer."

"So you're going back on your word, are you, my pet?"

The prolonged physical contact and the degradation of being held by the lip were too much for Smith's nerves. Shaking violently, on the verge of vomiting, he could not answer any more.

The place was not a home any more. It looked like a

bloodless battlefield. "What a shame," said Bucken. "None of this would have happened, of course, if you hadn't put up a fight to resist the legitimate presence of the police. You're lucky, in fact, that we won't take you in with charges of assault. But we'll be back. I promise you that."

Opposite the house a small crowd had gathered to watch the police cars and wait for anything to happen. Bucken felt like spitting on them or chasing them away. But their presence was his doing. He had ordered the police guard, the noise, the flashing lights to attract the vultures and make them hover waiting for the crumbs of human misery. He felt too dirty to go home at all. He bought a shirt and some underwear, went to a public bath, met Walsh who brought him his car, and returned to Elstree where he listened to endless sobbing transmitted by the bugs to the surveillance van.

At half past eleven, the couple emerged from the house and started toward the bus stop. Bucken sent a patrol car after them. They were stopped and questioned because the officers had "reason to believe" that a wanted criminal's description fitted Cutter-Smith. Later that day Cutter-Smith was taken to a police station because he was suspected of "being about to expose himself." He was not booked but warned that if ever again ... He protested his innocence.

"You wish to lodge a complaint?"

No, he did not.

In the afternoon, Bucken heard them crying in the flat once again. They telephoned for a cab and left for a West End hotel with a few of their undamaged belongings.

A few minutes before midnight, Bucken knocked on their door and woke them up. He stayed with them, asking endless questions to which there were no answers, until four in the morning.

Throughout Thursday, the presence of the police increased all the time. An embarrassed hotel manager informed them that their checks were not acceptable, could they please pay cash. With the aid of a magnetic bug attached to the metal frame of a coffee table, Bucken monitored all the conversation in the room. Winnie wanted to leave at once for another hotel, Cutter-Smith convinced her that it would be no better there. He needed time to think.

In the evening he took her to the Savoy. Just as their meals were being served, two policemen came in and took them out, attracting as much attention as the staff would allow: the waiters gathered and formed a walking screen around them.

That night Bucken was back in their room well before midnight. He apologized for all the inconvenience he had been causing them. And he meant it, too. Whenever he had hit a suspect, it was a true sign of anger. Cold harassment of a suspect had never been part of his armory. "It's no more fun to me than it is to you, believe me."

"Then why not stop it right away?"

"I can't. You give me no choice." Bucken produced a flask of rum and poured some in the two glasses on the hand basin. Cutter-Smith watched him with suspicion, but when the policeman drank some himself, he accepted a glass. Winnie also drank it thirstily. Dry nerves, concluded Bucken, the beginning of the mental disintegration of a woman whom he disliked but pitied. About her husband his feelings were even more mixed. He refilled his flask top and raised it toward the couple: "To peace." Smith stared at him but without personal hatred. Bucken gave him that infectious smile: "Armistice? . . . All right, I'll settle for ceasefire. Cheers."

Smith smiled with him for the first time. Bucken was ready to change tack again.

"The one thing I fail to understand about you is the way you got involved in this. All right, I know, I said ceasefire, but this is purely personal. As you said, you're not a criminal. I accept that."

Winnie drank up and turned sharply toward the policeman: "Do you? Do you really?"

"I do."

"Then what do you want from us?"

"Help. Information in return for sympathy, leniency, call it what you like."

"And if we say 'no' to you?" Winnie snapped.

" 'We?' " Cutter-Smith was unable to believe his ears. "Did you say 'we'? You mean you side with me for once?"

Instead of answering, she held out her glass toward Bucken. He refilled their glasses and his flask top.

"Unfortunately, he or you, both of you, can't say 'no.' You'll lose whatever you do, but it's a question of how much and how badly you'll lose."

She drank up. "I know Johnny is a loser. I knew it when I married him and when he was a handsome man. But can't he ever be a winner?"

"I am a winner now."

"Are you, Smithie? Are you really, my pet?" Bucken rang room service and ordered another bottle, then gave Smith a truly sad look: "What sort of a winner are you? I could wipe the floor with you, spit in your eye, rape your wife, arrest you without any good reason, perhaps even shoot you, and you could do nothing about it. You couldn't complain, you couldn't sue me, you couldn't resist. What sort of winner is that?"

"I have nothing against you. You're trying to do your job and you're in a hopeless position, Superintendent."

"You're clutching at the last straws, Smithie. Why did you do it? How did you get involved?"

"I still don't know what he did," said Winnie very quietly, like a drunk talking to herself. "But whatever he did, he did it for me and for self-respect." Cutter-Smith took her hand and held it gently while a waiter brought in a bottle and Bucken poured out more rum. Then he took over. "It's a matter of record, if you press the authorities hard enough, they'll confirm it. I don't care whether you believe me or not. But I always helped Britain wherever I served. I and others did a few things for British interests in Uganda. Many of my colleagues were arrested, my best friends were killed. But they let me out after a few days' detention. Can you imagine the indignity I suffered by

261

coming out without a scratch to show? My country of course never recognized my services. But I never expected it. I only waited for a word of thanks.

"Then Hong Kong. Then I got a lovely job in Brunei. My chief cashier could not add up and the Finance Minister mostly cared for his own business alone. So I ran the show and the rewards were rich. Big house, servants, social status, bridge with the top people, Scottish dancing on Thursdays at the club, a lot of official travel, and whenever my Winnie and I came to London, we were guests of the government, stayed at Brown's and had free use of a hospitality Rolls.

"Tell me, Superintendent, do they ever give you a hospitality Rolls? Do they honor you with ... oh, well, never mind. When they approached me yet again and asked me for more favors, I was glad to do it. Out of loyalty. Even though I knew that it would ruin my future out there. But I didn't complain, I knew I'd get a fair deal when, eventually, I'd have to run for it. Anyway, while I was arranging all those illegal currency transfers to Britain via Brunei, the Government, your Government, offered me money. The Treasury offered to invest it all for me in Switzerland or open accounts for me anywhere. I turned it down."

"You were a fool," said Bucken and refilled the glasses.

"Perhaps I was. But I accepted the promise of a really good job on my return home. I chose the Bank of England. And they promised it to me. You know something? They never even gave me a reason why I didn't get it. And I was out in the cold. Have you ever been on the dole, Mr. Bucken? Have you ever seen friends, relatives and neighbors turn away from you believing that if you're out of work for so long then you can't be any good? You argue, but then comes the 'something must be wrong with me' syndrome. When you can't imagine that everybody is wrong and you alone are right, that all the cards are stacked against you through no fault of your own. That is the point where you begin to see everything in a new light. When your wife turns away from you at night, you don't woo her any more, you stop asking, begging, fighting for sex, you accept that you're not entitled to sex any more because you've not done right by her. And believe me, when you cannot seduce your own wife, and a cripple at that, any more, then you begin to doubt if anyone would want you ever again."

There was a long silence broken only by Winnie's violent hiccups. "I thought ... uck ... I thought you had little girls on the side ... uck ..."

"I wanted only you."

Bucken turned away. Like it or not, he had a job to do. He wondered if Nazi henchmen were created that way. Except that the threat of the *Monty* would have to be removed at any cost. This couple and his own self-respect were expendable items. He knew he would have to hurt Cutter-Smith: "You realize, of course, that you're being used again."

"I do."

"You're a sucker."

"I'm loyal. If that means sucker in your world, all right, I'm a sucker."

Bucken shuddered and found it hard to control himself. Are we trying to be loyal to the same man? He fought to stamp out the suspicion. "You're set up as a loser, sweetheart. Your Principal's got what he wanted. Why should he risk anything for you any more? He doesn't pose a threat any more. We're not even concerned with him directly any more."

"Then you wouldn't let me be free or even live any more, would you? Yet I have the money ..."

"You haven't. Your account has been frozen for the time being."

"You couldn't ... no ..."

"I could. I did. Think about it until tomorrow morning. Then you can check with your manager. And that's only the first step. Yes, I'm sorry for you."

"All right, then arrest me."

"I can't. I need you outside. Because somebody else also seems to be interested in you and I wouldn't be surprised if it turned out to be your Principal himself. So you see, I need you as bait. But I cannot guarantee your life ... unless ..."

"Unless what?" Winnie urged him.

"Unless I could make a deal with you."

"No deal."

"Think about it. The trouble you've caused should be sufficient revenge for you. If now you help me, I'll let you run away with the money. The full hundred thousand. The day we arrest the Principal and his associates with your help, the Treasury will guarantee ..."

"Don't you see the irony of it?"

"It doesn't matter what I see. The fact is that you can help us and make our job easier and quicker, but he can't help you any more. He wouldn't even know what happened to you. I can arrange for your disappearance to look like a successful emigration with the cash. Your Principal will believe that this is a happy end for your involvement."

Cutter-Smith sadly shook his head. The Principal must have frightened him more than Bucken. Or must have convinced him that he would know of every development and back him against any threat forever. Bucken had already exceeded his authority. He was not supposed to risk retaliatory measures.

"Think about it, my pet. The offer is unrepeatable. Tomorrow morning may bring the beginning or the end of a beautiful friendship."

Which did not really make sense, and he knew it. But it sounded good, like common shit. The way he felt. He had not been home since leaving for San Francisco.

On Friday morning, while Bucken bought another shirt and change of underwear, Cutter-Smith was at the bank right on opening time. Shamefaced tellers told him he could not draw a penny until further instructions. The manager refused to see him. The manager's clerk handed him a sealed envelope. Inside, on a large sheet of paper, there were only six words:

"How about the deal? Love, Bucken."

On his way out, he threw it away. A policeman stopped

him at once. He was to be prosecuted for being a litterbug. Then within two hundred yards, he was stopped and searched three times under Section 66 of the Metropolitan Police Act 1839, because he was "noticed to be acting in a furtive manner" and his behavior "gave rise to reasonable suspicion" that he might be "having or conveying something stolen or unlawfully obtained."

The harassment continued throughout the morning. After lunchtime, he telephoned his office to make arrangements for his return to work. None of his superiors was available to talk to him. In the evening a stone was thrown through his window. At midnight, four detectives arrived, and a second search-and-destroy operation ruined most of what was left after the first visit. They searched for drugs—and did produce something, allegedly heroin in watertight packing, from the bottom of a U-shaped waste pipe in the bathroom. The search ended at half past four, Saturday morning.

Cutter-Smith did not go back to bed. Winnie asked no questions as he sat for six hours, staring at his toes, without a word. They then had breakfast, and the conversation sounded so normal and relaxed that Bucken, listening in, became convinced that Cutter-Smith had either gone mad or had come to some important decision.

Police reinforcements were brought in. Two radio cabs with police drivers were on standby. Telephone tappers were ready. A vanful of electronic gadgets from the "tricks section" were on hand. Bucken borrowed the helicopter once again, and stationed fast patrol cars at various vantage points all over London. This time he would not lose Cutter-Smith from sight even momentarily or miss a single word chummy chose to utter.

Bucken fully realized the enormity of his gamble. If it misfired, the Principal might retaliate by exploding the *Monty* and Bucken alone would be responsible. He fought back a weird hope, something like a death wish, for the disaster: it would at least clear Rattray who would never be able to make the final decision and actually explode the bomb that would kill and devastate on a vast scale. He just

265

couldn't do it. But then it was also inconceivable that Rattray should ever become a criminal.

It was too late to philosophize. Bucken called Brammel's command post and asked the General to prepare for a maximum evacuation of the entire area at short notice though he should "forget" to notify his Ministry. Walsh was dispatched to Sheerness to supervise and intensify the physical and electronic surveillance of the wreck and the Estuary.

At 1405, Cutter-Smith picked up the phone, hesitated, replaced the receiver, then lifted it again. He must have known that the line would be tapped and so it was unlikely that he would make an important call from his home, but Bucken was catering even for madness. The dial tap, inserted on the line between caller and the local exchange, began to count the pulses each time the dial on Cutter-Smith's telephone returned to normal position. At the same speed as the pulses selected the suitable switches via exchanges along the required route to the caller's destination, the tap gave a readout of the numbers dialed by Cutter-Smith.

In the surveillance van, a Post Office telephone engineer mumbled: "Five ... eight ... zero ... Bloomsbury district..."

"That's it!" yelled Bucken and alerted all available patrols in Bloomsbury, the area where the circular underground garage was also situated. As soon as all seven digits were displayed by the tap, the number had to be found in the registers to be matched with the subscriber whose telephone had just begun to respond with the ringing tone. Bucken knew that the identification would take only about forty seconds because of the special facilities he had arranged, but that was forty seconds too long for him.

Luckily, the telephone was not answered immediately. Ten, twenty, thirty seconds... Cutter-Smith was waiting patiently. Perhaps the number he had called was totally insignificant from Bucken's point of view.

Forty, forty-five seconds ... Subscriber Section called

Bucken: "Bassani, Marcella, number seven, Museum Mansions, Bloomsbury ..."

"You heard that?" Bucken shouted into his master microphone to all cars. "Seal that place and wait for instructions."

At the same moment, Cutter-Smith's call was answered by a hoarsely whispered "Yes?"

"I'm in trouble." Bucken heard Cutter-Smith swallow hard to remove the nervous lump in his throat.

"Be brief and precise."

"Are you sure we can talk?"

"I told you so. But not for long. So carry on."

Bucken's palm was squirting sweat all over the receiver. He had cars near Museum Mansions. With a bit of luck, the first could be there in less than two minutes. The delayed answering of the phone gave him the edge. It just seemed incredible that, after all the careful planning, the Principal could be caught like this. "Nobody is to leave the building. Arrest all occupants of number seven."

Cutter-Smith was complaining endlessly and shouting for help down the line. "They froze my money. They're after me. You must do something, you must!"

"Calm down, Johnny. We haven't much time before they trace the call. You tell that Superintendent to piss off ..."

"How did you know his rank?"

"Shut up. Tell him to piss off because there will be another warning explosion somewhere on the river within a day or two. I hope he's listening. This will be the last warning. After that, we'll have to apply some sterner measures."

"They won't believe me."

"Trust me, Johnny. Haven't they always believed us right from the start?"

The first patrol car with four officers had just reached Museum Mansions. "Entrance B for BROTHER leads to flats numbers six to ten, inclusive," reported the driver.

Bucken closed his eyes so as to envisage two officers racing up the stairs, to encourage them and help them go

267

faster.... He was still listening to the Principal on the telephone: "For the first time, we've found loyal partners in each other. So don't panic, Johnny ..."

The two officers reached the door of number seven on the first floor. One of them reported on his walkie-talkie to the driver outside:

"There's no answer. Shall we break down the door?"

The driver radioed the question to Bucken who answered an immediate "yes." At the very moment when the two officers burst in, Bucken was still listening to the final reassurances and good-byes on the telephone. It was peculiar that he did not hear the officers or the Principal shout, nothing of the sound of the fractured door, only the telephones being replaced in the normal way, and the sound of the "line free" signal returning ...

A few deafeningly silent seconds later, the patrol car reported: "Two officers have searched the premises but the flat is empty. There was nobody on the blower when they got in. Nobody could have left through the entrance or the front windows. One bedroom has a window toward the small courtyard at the rear but that was covered by Inspector Mann at the time the door was broken down."

It seemed impossible. The tap dial could not have made a mistake. Bucken quickly dialed the detected number. The call was answered immediately by the two officers inside flat number seven. They confirmed the driver's report.

Bucken drove furiously into town. On the way he radioed all units to call off the emergency operation. It was pointless to keep them all on duty now. With special services and overtime pay and running expenses, his investigation must have cost already almost a million.

He found the five-story Museum Mansions only a few minutes' away from the underground garage. The red-brick building had six entrances, each serving five flats, with no connecting corridors between these sections, and no elevators. The block occupied a corner site so that three of the entrances were in a Victorian street, and three in a laboriously mock-Gothic square. The officers—and the dozen others who had arrived as reinforcements—were perfectly justified in claiming that nobody could have disappeared from number seven or any of the other flats sharing Entrance B. Nobody had been permitted to leave before Bucken arrived, and even the walls of number seven had been scrutinized for concealed doors that might communicate with other flats.

"If we are looking for a ghost, sir, we must have come pretty close to catching him. Pretty close," said Inspector Mann and from the reaction he concluded that Superintendents sometimes lost their sense of humor.

Bucken telephoned Allerton to arrange urgent legal cover for his unauthorized breaking into number seven, then set up office in the caretaker's flat, where he first quickly interviewed the occupants of flats using Entrance B. Most of them appeared to be reasonably well-to-do, staid and innocuous types; all who were at home at the time—with the exception of a teen-age boy and an octogenarian Colonel—were elderly women. Bucken "asked" them all "to stay indoors for a short while." It was easy to detect what they all thought of Miss Marcella Bassani when they told Bucken that "she's never at home before ten at night and she's a rather late riser. But then, of course, she's a 'dancer' or something like that by profession." (She was located, eventually, at her bedbound sister's home, where she had spent every day of her last five years. She was reluctant to admit her real age, but assured the Superintendent that "I'm a dancer, indeed, by profession, except that unfortunately, I had to break off my career fifty-one years ago, almost to the day, for that matter.")

Bucken ordered full background checks on all occupants, but what really bothered him was yet another apparent coincidence: if the dial tap made a mistake, why would it put its finger on such a very regularly unoccupied home of all places?

He called in Hefty Solomon from "tricks" once more and the bug man swore all the way from yet another messed-up family weekend to Bloomsbury. But he looked delighted and went totally silent when Bucken told him about the problem.

"No way, guv, no way to trick you, not unless chummy conjured up some miracle or the pulse counter cheated you, and that's more than unlikely ... or ... but that's too crazy for words ..."

"Start with the crazy bit."

"Pooled wire technique. Cheese box. Do these say anything to you?"

"Come on, Hefty, give."

"It's an American specialty, really. Pooling is a bit of messing about with the telephone lines so that when you dial one number, two phones will ring and the call can also be answered on another subscriber's set. The cheese box uses a timer for pooling the wires automatically for certain set periods."

"Could it be done here?"

"I'll have to see the distribution frame."

"If you're right, Hefty, you can choose the time and the place and the menu."

"Like tomorrow, around the corner, bangers and mash, guv?"

With the caretaker's help, he soon located the panel under the stairs of Entrance D in the square. That was where incoming lines were distributed to pairs of terminal points representing the individual lines in the entire block. "That's it," nodded Hefty, "the phone number of each flat is marked on the side of the frame, but we'll have to test them all and perhaps do a physical trace to see if they're still mixed up."

"What do you mean 'still'?"

"Chummy might have pooled any two pairs, then he could take the call to number seven in another flat, then readjust the frame while your men were breaking doors down and sealing the wrong entrance. It would only take seconds to loosen a couple of screws, correct the connections and walk out unseen."

It meant that the Principal had to know about the always-deserted Bassani flat (if, by any chance, the call

270

was answered there, he could simply replace his own receiver) and, even more important, he needed an accomplice in, or regular access to, one of the flats. For all Bucken knew, he might still be there. The detective ran faster than ever, dragging the caretaker with him. In a single sweep, he glanced through the register of all tenants, and the answer stared him in the face: "... Number sixteen: Mrs. Oriana Ketteringham ..." It just could not be yet another coincidence. Aunt Oriana. She is rather poorly these days, Mu had said, and she has come to sort of rely on his Saturday visits. The day was Saturday. Flat number sixteen was on the ground floor, of Entrance D—facing the stairs under which the distribution frame was sited.

There was no proof, but Bucken, for private purposes, did not need any more than confirmation. He gazed at the entry in the register with eyes burning, with thick saliva rolling like tears down his hard-working gullet. "What now? What do I do?" he kept asking himself. There were no answers. So he allowed routine to take over.

He called out the "dabs" squad for a thorough fingerprint examination of the terminal points on the distribution panel. He expected it to be found abnormally clean.

His knock on the door of number sixteen was answered by a tall woman who wore old age like a set of precious jewels and who oozed the sort of grandeur Mu could never attain. She told him he had missed Rattray by about half an hour: "He had an urgent telephone call and had to leave, but he'll call me up later on. So if you tell me your name ..."

"Bucken. Superintendent Bucken." He was still trying to choose the excuse for staying to talk to her, but she solved all his problems:

"Bucken! Come in, Bucken, you've just missed the little rascal, but I'm so pleased to meet you at last. I've heard such a lot about you." Before he could answer she was already leading him by the hand into a room full of the soft smells of green apples and old cupboards. She wore a full skirt and Bucken noticed that she walked with a slight limp. "Now. Let me take a good look at you ... yes, I can see why he likes you so much. You have good bones, a strong jaw and honest eyes ... I'm sorry, I didn't mean to embarrass you, I'm just a silly old chatterbox."

Honest eyes. Bucken felt like crying. He could only nod when she offered him tea and tiny ginger cakes. "You can't imagine how much I know about you, Bucken," she carried on and on. "It's like talking to an old friend, because I know about your Sarah, and your successes with work and women, yes, if I were a few, say, fifty years younger, or if you were ..." She winced with pain and touched her left knee for a second. "More tea? ... You must stop me talking, but I'm so delighted to see you here. It's as if I've known you all my life. Which of course would make me guilty of being ungrateful."

"To me?"

"Who else? After all, you saved his life by risking yours and nobody thanked you for it."

"I'm sorry, but ..."

"Now don't you deny it. I know it all. He never lies and he told me how he was attacked as a young constable in Cable Street by a bunch of drunken hooligans who were determined to kick him to death as revenge for something or other, and how he begged you to run for help, but you wouldn't, because by the time you returned he could be dead, so you fought them and risked your life, but luckily you both ended up with nothing worse than a couple of broken bones. How's that in one breath?"

"You're doing fine, but you got the story upside down."

"La-di-da, la-di-da, don't give me that. You're too modest, that's your trouble, he always tells me, otherwise you could be a general by now, like my nephew."

"General?"

"What I mean is that he's high up in his profession, and his profession really ought to be the Army like most men's in my family. After all, policemen are all constables or perhaps sergeants. Except that he forever wanted to be a detective and always thought that the police force is the greatest thing God created since the Rocky Mountains. Do you agree with him?"

"Not always."

"I mean about the police."

"I suppose so."

"You're not sure."

"No."

"Am I talking too much?"

"I wouldn't know, because I love it."

"You do?"

"I never had an auntie."

"Will you accept me then as a substitute?" She winced, and as she touched her knee again she noticed the worried look Bucken gave her. "Don't worry, it's just that the weather is about to change. My stump is the best meteorologist ... Oh, you didn't know. I always presume that everybody notices it or at least hears about it because even the doctors and technicians like to show off with me because I had my amputation at the age of sixty-one, and I learned to walk again more quickly than most young men. In fact they say I run too much and that's why I need such frequent repairs and adjustments, which usually take all day at Roehampton, but I don't mind, because there's always a partner there for a good natter which I enjoy, as you must know by now, and for which old hags like me who live alone don't find many opportunities. Mind you, I'm a good listener, too, when it comes to that, and at Roehampton it always seems to come to that with us regulars. You know why? Because when they take your leg off, you feel more naked than in the bath. Naked, and exposed and helpless, that is, but without shame, because we all sit like that in the fitting room."

It needed only the gentlest steering from Bucken, and soon she was confirming all his painful suspicions and worst fears by talking about her Roehampton friends— and Winnie.

"Now there's a poor dear I'm really sorry for. Not enough that she lost her leg as a young girl and never knew what it was like to hop about with a lover, but she's also full of grief for her hapless Johnny who was apparently given a rough deal by our government, and he keeps seeking revenge and hankering forever after some job with the Bank of England. She told me all about it and more, but I think he's better fixed up now one way or another."

Yes, Rattray had promised to do something about it and told her later that it was being looked into. There was not much more Bucken could hope to learn from her. He was anxious to leave quickly before his acute embarrassment and growing agony began to show. If only he had some experience in stabbing friends in the back. If only Rattray had achieved his transfer from this case. Nobody would ever have known.

He was already standing in the door, saying good-bye and promising to come again, when the policeman in him put a final sentence in his mouth: "I'll make sure not to come on Saturdays because then you have company. He does come only on Saturdays, doesn't he?"

"Mostly yes. In the past few months or so he's certainly come only once on another day."

"Oh, yes, I remember that it was a Monday. He told me about it. Yes, definitely a Monday, at about two in the afternoon, when we were doing a job round here ... at Bloomsbury Square ..."

"That's possible, because he wanted to park his Mini in the garage that goes with the flat and I said just help yourself because I never use it these days. Haven't even got a car for that matter."

Bucken spent the rest of the afternoon pub hopping aimlessly, stupefied with mental anguish, numbed by wind and rain, and not quite knowing hot from cold and right from wrong any more. What would Rattray do in a reversed situation? Would he turn him over to Allerton right away? Would he resign from the job and let others put in the knife? Would he complete the case against him by collecting the missing factors of material evidence? The answers eluded him and soon he recognized that if the basic question—what would he do in my place?—was the acid test of their friendship, then their friendship had never gone deep enough to seek and identify the most crucial factors. And yet he was sure that deep down he knew all the answers which his brain instinctively exiled into the subconscious in sheer self-defense.

He ordered another rum, buttonholed a deserving little old lady whose elbow had scraped slight dents in many a London bar, bought her another gin and it, and explained to her in baffling detail why a friend-is-a-friend-is-a-friend no matter what. He then tried in vain to track down Rattray on the telephone.

Every detail seemed to tally, every finger seemed to point to Rattray, and every double rum failed to suppress the lifelong honest copper in Bucken.

Kowalski! Rattray never had a chance to know in time about the emergence of the name and Bucken's trip. Not unless Rattray had one or more associates. Like Allerton, Carron or even Maxine. But that would be out of character. Besides, why would Rattray want to get information out of Kowalski?

Bucken decided that all his facts, reasoning and deductions needed the cold objectivity of the written word in the unemotional setting of his room at C.O. He was brave enough to admit that he would be digging for excuses for Rattray. But he saw nothing wrong with that. He had done the same many times for suspected strangers.

He was so surprised to find Allerton in the office that he almost blurted it all out in a spasmodic effort of his mind to relieve itself. Luckily, Inspector Linley was also present.

"Anything on the Lad?" asked Bucken.

Linley shook his head without even pretending sadness or disappointment: "Nothing in partic."

"We're handing it over completely to the local chaps," said Allerton.

"How about the immigration racket itself?"

"That's just it. The clues you gave us haven't led anywhere, guv," said Linley. "Something of a false alarm if I may say so."

"False alarm? Your tinkling balls, that's what! Wasn't I

attacked? Wasn't there a contract out on me? Wasn't the Lad killed at the right moment? What the hell are you all talking about winding up the investigation? Are you suggesting that the Lad hanged himself by the foot and drove his thought-controlled car at his own head in a sudden onslaught of momentary amentia? Are you . . ."

"Bucken, please!"

"You call them clues. I'd call them evidence, what I gave you. Enough to go on at least. And I bet I'd be there by now. Rattray was right."

"In what?"

"In wanting to keep me on the case."

"He wanted you transferred."

"Rubbish. He wanted someone else on this . . ." Bucken looked at Linley, "on my current case."

"That's what you think." Allerton's cold voice sliced every word thin. He knew he was stabbing a friendship in the back. "The AC wanted you on this hopeless task. I told you at the outset that I was sorry for you, that I didn't want you or anybody else in the Branch on this case, but I had no choice. It was only at the AC's insistence that you got lumbered with it."

Bucken was backing out of the room. He only half-heard Allerton going on and on: "I mean he made out a good case for it, you were the right man with experience and maturity and integrity going for you . . ."

Which would explain it all. Rattray evaluated their friendship more correctly than he. Bucken's handling the investigation was the Principal's final insurance policy. He knew that Bucken would not report him. He reckoned that in the fight between Bucken the policeman and Bucken the friend the latter would be the winner. But then nobody else would have recognized some of the crucial clues, nobody else would have natural access to the children, no other copper would spot the significance of a name: Aunt Oriana.

It was ten o'clock and still nobody answered the Rattrays' telephone. Hadn't they mentioned something about a family outing? Or was he busy preparing the next warning bang?

Bucken drove to Elstree. There was not much else he would want from chummy, but he wanted to take a signed statement from Winnie about her visits to and chats at Roehampton.

The street was dark and quiet, everything back to normal. The surveillance van had gone—after the discovery of the pooled line there was no reason to keep running up the costs. The bugs and the various gadgets would have to be recovered from the maisonette to avoid all the fuss, raised eyebrows and, above all, tons of paperwork that was the real penalty for the loss of equipment, anything from bent paperclips to smashed squad cars.

The curtains were drawn and no light came through at the edges. They must be watching the box or have gone to bed. Before he approached the door, Bucken looked around for the remaining two men assigned to watch Cutter-Smith. He could not see them anywhere. He drove around the block and saw no parked car. Even if one of them had gone with the car to find a loo, the other would be there. They would never leave together unless . . .

Bucken stepped on the accelerator and three seconds later, he just avoided a motorcycle, mounted the curb, and almost drove into the house. He did not bother to knock. The door opened easily from a single kick. "Anybody home?" There was no answer. Somewhere the water was running. He tried a light switch, then another, but nothing happened. He was already in the living room. Suddenly he was pushed. As he stumbled backward, trying to regain his balance, an upturned chair tripped him up. The curtain moved and two figures jumped through the window. He wished for the first time that he carried a gun. But he could only run and shout after them, and they had an invaluable fifteen seconds' advantage. He saw them mount a powerful motorbike. The engine roared to explosion, and he knew he had lost them.

As he reentered the room, he recognized the acrid smell

of blood. He drew aside the curtain so that the street lamps gave him some light. Winnie was just a heap in the corner. Her throat was severed almost to the nape, her head hanging loosely to the right.

A faint groan came from the kitchen. The sink was full of water, blood and foam. Cutter-Smith had slumped under the sink. His head was in a wire band with a spike inserted at the back. He was naked from the waist down— the rope band tight on his hip. He moaned and foamy blood and water spurted from his mouth. Bucken quickly moved him to try some artificial respiration when he noticed the two big, deep chest wounds. Cutter-Smith must have been stabbed when Bucken kicked the door in. He ran out to his car to radio for help, but there was never a chance to save Cutter-Smith.

While the photographers and the dabs men and the entire "murder circus" swung into action, the Yard's Information Room tracked down the two detectives whose job it would have been to watch Cutter-Smith. They claimed that they had been ordered to leave together with the surveillance van and the rest of the Elstree show. It might have been a genuine mistake, but Bucken would not believe it. Somebody, somewhere along the chain of command must have inserted a slight "error" in the transmission of his orders. Would it be Rattray? Would it be whoever else seemed to be so closely watching Bucken and his cases? Rattray had no need to kill the man. But he might want to know if Bucken had found out something valuable from him.

At a quarter past eleven, Rattray's telephone was picked up by Timmy who was so full of stories about the outing and the meal and what Mummy said and what Daddy said and what the waiter said and what Ron said and what was not said by anybody, that he was quite irrepressible for three full minutes. Mu apologized for him and Bucken assured her it was a pleasure to listen to him, and he meant it, too. Timmy proved that Rattray himself could not have been to Elstree. At last he took the phone from Mu.

"What's up, Bucken?"

"Must see you."

"Must? Come over then."

"No. You remember Spooky's hotel? You can make it in forty minutes."

"Look, Bucken, we had quite an outing so if . . ."

"I've been to Aunt Oriana."

"Oh."

"Forty minutes?"

"Get stuffed."

Spooky not only looked like a ghost but was also proven and known to be one—a specialist in disappearance tricks for wanted criminals. In London's dockland, he ran a so-called boarding house with a difference: nobody had ever been seriously blamed for mistaking it for a brothel, an outpost of the United Nations, the stray wholesaler of the Karachi bazaar or the live section of the Museum of Uncommon Insects.

Spooky's face revealed genuine delight and toothless gums as he greeted Bucken: "Where have you been, guv, all this time? It's good to see you again."

"That's good. Because I need a hotel."

"A room you said, guv?"

"I didn't. I said hotel."

Spooky was astonished that a Superintendent should look for a hiding place, but he knew better than to show any sign of his reaction. He did some favors to Old Bill, and in return, his protégés were sometimes spared while staying with him. He soon led Bucken to a back room where they moved a cupboard to uncover a trap door. A stepladder took them via a crumbling drydock inspection tunnel into an unoccupied warehouse with all doors and windows boarded up against squatters. The current "hotel" in there was relatively comfortable and a half-stubbed-out cigarette butt told Bucken that the room had just been evacuated for his sake.

"I appreciate that," he said.

"How long?"

"A day. Two at the most."

"You need the blower?"

"Yes. I just wanted to ask." Bucken remembered the telephone arrangement: from some legitimate subscriber's line, Spooky's friends would run a temporary "private extension" which could be disconnected any time. Bucken knew that this was not one of Spooky's "top security" hotels, but it suited him. "Will do. Just bring me some food, a bottle of rum, the number on which I can be called, and the visitor who'll ask for me by name."

Spooky returned with all four fifteen minutes later. He recognized Rattray, the visitor, and grew more and more uneasy about his distinguished guests, but managed to control himself and recede like a cunning spirit during exorcism.

Rattray pulled a crate to the table, sat down, finished one black cigar and lit another. "Hasn't changed much. Spooky, I mean."

"No."

There was a long pause. Rattray refused the bottle but then changed his mind. "The arrangements are different, though."

"Yes."

"The clients must feel safer and happier this way, I suppose."

"That's right."

Rattray was waiting. Bucken did not know how to say it. Would Rattray keep cool and simply deny it or go berserk and attack him? Would he kill him or himself? Was he armed? Would he plead with him? Would he run for it?

"Remember when we once picked up Spooky for questioning?" Rattray coughed violently but never took his eyes away from Bucken. Was that a sign of defiance? A show of innocence? Readiness for self-defense? "Remember?"

Bucken nodded.

"The station sergeant screamed 'get him out of here! get him out!' He was afraid that the station would be haunted forever...." He watched Bucken with the bottle. "You drink too much."

"Do I?"

"Like that same sergeant, remember? He drank sherry!" Rattray laughed and Bucken heard that the sound was false and hollow. "Sherry at any time of the day! Except that he would never order 'medium.' Superstition, I suppose, wasn't it?"

"He asked for 'in between,' didn't he?"

"Yes, that's right ... Oh, well, we did have a lot of fun together...."

That's it. He was definitely pleading now. As good as an admission of guilt.

"You look tired, Bucken. Are you well?"

Bucken tried to make his tone as ominous as possible: "I've been under a lot of pressure lately."

"Oh, yes, I know. I'm sorry I failed to keep you away from this rotten *Monty* job. I tried to spare you but it was impossible. Pity."

"Stop it, Ratts." Desperate to control his temper just for once, he was crushing the edge of the table with white flat fingertips.

"Stop what?"

"Allerton told me how hard you fought to have me assigned to this one."

"So suddenly you choose to take his word against mine."

"Wouldn't you? I mean if you were in my place?"

"I don't know, but if I were you and if I did choose to believe him, I certainly wouldn't be sitting here. Why are you hiding here anyway?"

"I'm a bad liar and I don't like to lie. And here I won't meet colleagues and superiors to whom I would have to lie about you until I was ready to move."

"You're talking in riddles."

"Am I? Then why did you come here at once when I mentioned Aunt Oriana?"

"I thought she was in trouble. Or you were."

281

"Or you were. Do I really have to spell it out for you?" Bucken was choking on every word. He did not plan to hold a conversation. Or give explanations. Or go into details and make accusations and listen to denials or even more painful admissions. He just wanted to give Rattray a fair warning—the golden handshake at the end of a long friendship. "Do you know that Cutter-Smith is dead?"

That shook him. He obviously did not know. He looked pale in the yellow light that battled through a dirty plastic lampshade. He reached into his pocket. For another cigar even though one was still burning in the corner of his mouth? Or for a gun? It was a cigar. He stood up, walked round the room slowly, then stopped with his back to Bucken. "Are you accusing me of something?" He lit the new cigar from the old one.

"What do you think?"

Rattray was still offering Bucken the chance to attack from behind, implying "look, nothing to hide, no resistance."

"Are you drunk, Bucken?"

"No. And you may turn around. I won't stab you in the back."

"Why should you?"

Bucken drank again and offered the bottle to Rattray. "You're a bad liar, chum, like me. And I respect you for that. You were not born rotten and now you don't know what to do. So you're playing for time."

"Rubbish."

"A better liar would scream at me or hit me, run out or protest his innocence, we've both seen it many times. But you know that this case is special. And that I must think of your kids, too. And that's exactly why I'm giving you twenty-four hours. Like shouting 'draw' before the shooting."

Rattray spun around: "Draw!"

Bucken shot him down with a sad smile. "I know, it's not easy for you either. But twenty-four hours is all I can give you. It will be your choice. You can run for it, kill

282

yourself, salvage whatever is left of your pride, even give yourself up for the sake of your family. You must know what would be best for the children. Twenty-four hours, that's all."

"And then you charge me or report me or arrest me or what?"

"There won't be charges and accusations, and your children won't be dragged into court. I'll track you down and kill you. It will be in self-defense."

"You're mad. You really would do it."

Bucken nodded slowly as if too tired to hold his head up.

"Even if I were innocent."

"Even if you were innocent in law. Because I know you're guilty. Otherwise you'd already have tried to beat the hell out of me."

"Couldn't it be that I'm only sorry for you?"

"Nope."

"All right then, take me in."

"I wanted to. But I can't do it."

"Then you're a cheat, Bucken, because at the final reckoning, you're a cop above all. You must be. I know."

"You think you know the answers, but that's because you've never been more than a nine-to-five detective. You never understood the loyalty of the CID."

"I understood it better than anyone else. That's how I came to loathe it. While you just accepted the facts without ever thinking about them. You knew you were fighting wrong and thought that this would automatically make you right. But you're wrong. All of you."

Bucken stood up to face him. "You ... yes, you're trying to provoke me ... Why?"

"Don't ask questions. Not from me. I'm the accused, remember? The accused who's not worth even an outright accusation! So let's go, make your report. You'll be doing me a favor, believe me."

"Because you're a better friend than I thought. You want to spare me from tomorrow and the hardest move of my life."

"Don't give me that mouthful of sentimental shit, Bucken."

"Why? I'm not ashamed of it. People who believe in virtually nothing, the skeptics and the cynics, are perhaps outright sentimental somewhere down the line."

"But they don't necessarily fail in their duty."

"Neither will I. In my own way . . . I'm sorry, Ratts. I wish I knew a better way."

Rattray stood up. Bucken pressed the bell for Spooky to come and collect the visitor.

"Bucken . . ."

"Yes?"

"If I . . ."

"Yes . . . go on . . ."

"You accuse me of something, yet you didn't even ask me why I did it."

"You must have had your reasons. Money, madness, I don't know. Don't even care. Your excuses make no difference to me. But if you want to tell me . . ."

"Bucken, you're bluffing."

"Please yourself."

"If you had proof you'd take me in. Well, do me a favor. Take me in now. Or report me to the Commissioner. Just do your bloody job, for God's sake!"

"Sorry, Ratts. It's not on. Because you're ready for it and you'd wriggle out of it somehow. But you mustn't be allowed to. And besides, I can't do it to a friend. Even a shitty friend. I can't drag your family through the courts and the front pages of the press. I can't."

"Then you've failed. And I thought you were the absolute copper."

"Then you were mistaken, Ratts."

Spooky came in. Bucken turned away: "You can reach me here for twenty-four hours in case you need me or want to tell me something concerning Mu and the children. Spooky will give you the number," he shouted as the two disappeared down the inspection tunnel.

284

8

THE LONG NIGHT OF THE SKIM-OFF

Hefty Solomon was not particularly pleased when Rattray woke him up at four in the morning: "Can you trace and tap an unregistered extension line for me without anybody knowing about it?"

"Without Post Office help?"

"Just you and me."

"It will take longer."

While Hefty dressed, Rattray called Mu and told her that he would not be back for a day or two.

By the time Hefty had traced and tapped the line to the seemingly deserted warehouse near West India Dock Pier, it was past three o'clock. The streets around were Sunday-dead, and the rain was as steady as an ugly girl friend. "Why the hell do I do it? Why the hell do any of us do it?"

Rattray was waiting in a ramshackle café where the table could just about support his writing arm:

... So how could I say anything? Because we both were bad liars, it had to be for real from beginning to end. You'll see the logic of it. I'm sorry.

"Won't be long," he said to Hefty, wrote another few lines, and slipped the paper into an envelope. "I want you to monitor and tape a few calls I must make. And somehow, one day, I'll show you how grateful I am for everything you've done for me."

At 1547, Hefty noted that Rattray called a Harrow number from a public telephone booth.

"Carron."

"Rattray here. Sorry to trouble you with this but I'm in

an extremely invidious position and I need your help."

"Go on."

"You know that Superintendent Bucken and I have been friends for a long time."

"Yes."

"He must have gone mad or something."

"What's up?"

"Well, to put it in a nutshell, he's solved, at least partially, the case he's been working on. You know what I mean?"

"Of course I do. But what's wrong with success?"

"Nothing. Except that Cutter-Smith is dead."

"And you think that Bucken's killed him."

"No. Bucken got there just as he was dying."

"And?"

"He squeezed some information out of him in his last minutes."

"About the attackers?"

"Bucken refused to tell me that."

"But you think that's what he's got."

"I don't know. And it doesn't worry me too much. But what does matter is that he may know the whereabouts of the money."

"And?"

"He wants to get away with it. He contacted me because he needed help and, well, not in so many words, but offered me a deal."

"What? Fifty-fifty if you help him or something?"

"I didn't ask about the details. He's already gone underground. And there isn't much time."

"I understand. If it were anybody else, you'd move yourself. But in the circumstances, particularly after all the gossip that you were hounding an old chum, you don't want to be involved. Is that it?"

"You think I'm wrong?"

"I'm not your judge, it's not for me to say. So I'll just keep it to myself."

"Thanks. I appreciate that."

"You know where he's hiding?"

"I only have a phone number . . ."

At 1558, Rattray dialed Allerton's home number. It was engaged.

"Guv . . ." Hefty's voice was unusually soft.

"Yes?"

"Why don't you let me have a word with the Superintendent before you talk to Commander Allerton?"

"Because it's not your fucking business and you'd be wasting your time. Bucken is mad. It's really terrible."

At 1559 Allerton answered the telephone. The conversation followed the same lines as the previous one with Carron. When Rattray told Allerton that Bucken had squeezed some information out of the dying Cutter-Smith, the Commander jumped to the conclusion that Bucken would have to be stopped: "I spoke to the chaps who went to the scene. Bucken had never mentioned such information to them. It could only mean that he wants to go it alone one way or another."

"What do you think the one way and the other are?"

"He might want to chase the attackers and kill them because he's a good detective but an impetuous bastard— or he wants to muscle in on the act, and pick up enough cash to get out of The Job and away from you, sir, if I may say so."

"From me?"

"Well, from the treatment he's had lately."

"You think he's ready to become a crook?"

"I don't think so. It's just a possibility and it's happened to better men than him, too. For if he knows who the attackers were . . ."

"I didn't say he knew."

"Well, I presumed . . ."

"So did I. But he wouldn't say. On the other hand, he knows about the money."

"He told you that?"

"Yes."

"Did he . . . oh, this is too repulsive . . . he must have offered you a deal, right?"

"Right. He's lying low and wanted my help."

"Then why didn't you ... I mean ... oh, I see ... old friends and all that. But he must be stopped."

"You have a free hand."

"I see ... Any problems? Lots of problems. For me to solve them. Where is he?"

"Probably on his girl's four-berth cruiser, moored behind the Tower for the last few days."

"St. Katharine's Wharf. Got it."

At 1612 Teng, the chef of the China Duck, Cantonese restaurant, received an urgent telephone call. He gave some instructions to his staff—his wife, daughters, sons, cousin and nephew—and left via the back door that led through an alley in Soho where, not very long ago, an old man had been murdered in a most horrible way.

At 1616 another entry in Hefty's makeshift logbook: "AC ordered Yard Duty Officer to report any new major operation in the coming 4 hrs. Gave our number in phone booth."

At 1643, the phone rang in Spooky's back room. Bucken picked it up at once: "Ratts?"

"No, this is another friend." The accent was faintly Chinese, but the voice was occidental and also familiar. "I hear you have some information to trade."

"Do I?"

"Let's not play games. Not on the phone, please."

"What would you suggest, then?" The call had to come from Rattray one way or another. What was the game?

"We could talk, perhaps?"

"Talk about what?"

"A deal perhaps? You have something that can be of great interest to us and we have something that might be useful to you."

"Concerning what?"

"Don't try to play hard to get, Bucken. I give you a key word: wreck. Will that do?"

The voice called him Bucken. No Mister, no rank, no "guv." In his experience, even the crooks among the Chinese were too polite or too sly, Bucken never knew which, to do that. Sounded like someone to whom it would come naturally. A superior. But it was not Rattray.

"Yes, that will do. Shall we meet?"

"Why not? We can't go on, not meeting like this in any case."

"When?"

"Tonight, perhaps? At nine?"

"Okay. Where?"

"Ah ... Just a minute, please ... There's an echo on the line, can you hear it?"

"Faintly. You think we're ..."

"What do you think?" And after a pause: "I'll tell you what. You remember where your old friend, the Professor, used to get his stall repaired?"

"Yes. How do you know it?"

"It's empty now. We could meet there. It's unlikely that anyone listening in would know the place, right?"

"I'll be there."

"Alone, Bucken, alone, if you please. No tricks, no mistakes, make sure you're not followed. Or else no deal, okay?"

The caller rang off, but Bucken still held the receiver for a few seconds. As the purring "line free" sound returned, he waited to hear if there was an echo. There was. It might have been Spooky. Or Rattray. But why? For the first time he doubted the wisdom of the course he had chosen to follow, but now he saw no other way. After all, he still had no hard evidence that would satisfy the Director of Public Prosecutions in a case like this. Besides, Call-me-Wade might even want to stop him if there was any risk involved. He decided to sweat it out.

At 1647 the Yard Duty Officer called Rattray in the phone booth to report preparations for a major raid at St. Katharine's Wharf.

At 1723 a second call came through: "Result of the raid negative."

"If you don't mind my saying it, sir ..." Hefty said, scratching his head, "I know the Superintendent rather well and perhaps I could ..."

"When I need your opinion I'll ask for it."

"Whatever you say, sir. Except that..."

"That will do. And you'd better go now. I've had enough of your wisdom. Thanks for everything you've done for me."

"But..."

"Shut up."

Hefty could not understand. He was a civilian working for the police, and nobody had ever been rude to him, least of all Rattray whom he regarded as a "real gent" and for whom he had done enough, more than enough favors privately. "As you wish, sir."

"And don't be cheeky with me."

"Shall I leave the recording stuff with you, sir?"

"Yes. And forget for the time being what we did today. Understood? One day, perhaps, you'll be asked about it, and then I'll expect you to remember. But until then, just shut up, will you?"

Hefty never claimed that he was a great thinker. "I'm a real doer," he would tell anybody interested in his self-appraisal, "and when it comes to electronics, I just go click-click-click." Now he wished he could work out things in his head more readily. He was confused. The AC's personal involvement in an investigation worried him because it was nonroutine. The AC's conflicting information for Carron and Allerton baffled him. It did not make sense that Allerton would immediately raid the place where Bucken was expected to be, but Carron would refrain from any direct action. Who would then make that peculiar call to Bucken? And Bucken's fate above all... If there was one officer Hefty really liked and respected, it was Bucken. If the Superintendent was in trouble, he ought to warn him. Which would be wrong... Only a few hours earlier, Hefty would have sought Rattray's advice—after all, the AC was Bucken's friend. Yet both Carron and Allerton had mentioned on the phone that the AC had given Bucken The Treatment.

At seven in the evening, when Rattray telephoned Hefty's home, an irate Mrs. Solomon told him that her husband was not home yet, and left him in no doubt about what she thought of the prolonged duty hours of the Yard. Hefty was not the sort who would stay away from home on a Sunday evening without a good reason. He should have got back more than an hour ago. It worried Rattray, who would have liked to go and look for him. But he had to watch Spooky's hotel and man the telephone tap.

Bucken decided to give himself at least an hour to lose any tails before going to the warehouse. Who the hell would know about that small repair shop? Another of the Professor's friends? Another stall keeper? The old mechanic was a keen but clumsy chess player. Like Carron, who had once joined Bucken and the mechanic at the warehouse to play against the Professor on three boards. What a crazy idea! Yet the caller's voice, minus the odd accent, was not unlike Carron's. Why would he call? What sort of deal? Why had Cutter-Smith called Carron's Harrow number when the payoff had been agreed? Was it another stratagem devised by the Principal? But how would Rattray now involve Carron himself?

It would have been good simply to call him and ask. But Bucken decided against it. He would have to let the current carry him. He only wished he had some help, someone to trust. He was quite used to playing a hunch single-handed. For various reasons he often steered a lonely course even against his bosses' wishes, and his devious tactics frequently depended on the absolute secrecy that would be immediately halved by sharing with even one man. But this was different, like working in a vacuum, where it would be no use whistling for reassurance because the sound would be lost. Just as well. He felt he could not trust anyone any more. Pity he had sent Walsh back to Sheerness.

He tried to list various people he had worked with over the years. He assessed and discarded each name. The conclusion depressed him: when you can trust nobody in your organization, perhaps they cannot trust you either—that must be the time to resign.

To chase away these bitter thoughts, he telephoned his flat. There was no answer. Maxine must be out. Or gone for good. He had disappeared for too long this time. He could visualize one of her cryptic notes pinned to the pillow. He dialed Sarah's number. She answered at once. He felt he could not open his mouth. She shouted hullo after hullo down the line, then lowered her voice, saying to somebody there: "Not a word, but I can hear breathing . . . Hullo!" There was only one thing to say, just two words. "I resign." Or six words. "I'll take the job you mentioned." She would then send away whoever was there with her, come to the flat to clear out Maxine and everything that would remind him of her, and all would be well. But he could say nothing. So he put the phone down and asked Spooky for some food. He had another twenty minutes to spare.

Hefty was not sure that he had made the right decision. He apologized profusely on the doorstep, and was quite ready to back out and leave when the Deputy Commissioner told him that he had guests.

"Still, now that you're here, you'd better come in." He led the way to a small study, and Hefty was always thoroughly impressed: the best-dressed copper also lived in style, surrounded with what seemed to be fine antiques—although, admittedly, antiques in Hefty's book began with a twelve-inch black and white television set.

"I don't quite know how to put it, sir, but something seems to be wrong somewhere and I need some advice or at least the opportunity to tell somebody about it, though I don't even know where to begin."

"Start at the end, Hefty, that's always the easiest," said Carron with a fleeting glance at his watch just to remind Hefty of the guests.

"Well, the end is that Mr. Rattray has been very rude to me. Something he's never done before. But then he has never misled you, sir, has he?"

"Me?"

"Yes, sir. When he telephoned you, he told you something, but when he called Mr. Allerton, he told him something quite different, didn't he? So Mr. Allerton then goes raiding the boat where Mr. Bucken is supposed to be hiding out but finds nobody of course because Bucken, I mean Superintendent Bucken, is to be found somewhere in the East End on a phone number which you had, if you know what I mean, sir."

"Go on."

Hefty was pleased with himself: the Deputy Commissioner was now listening to him intently. "Did I do the right thing then, when I came here, sir?"

"The very best. But get on with it because we, I mean you, haven't much time."

"Oh, yes. Because that phone call about the deal to Mr. Bucken. It was to be nine o'clock, wasn't it?"

"Nine. I mean, how would I know? I wasn't there, was I? But how do you know about it?"

"That's what I was coming to, sir, right now. Mr. Rattray asked me to trace and tap that line before he called you, you see, so if he wanted to check Mr. Bucken's whereabouts he could have called the number himself, right? So you understand that I find his behavior, well, odd, to say the least."

"So what do you make of it?"

"I wouldn't really know, sir. That's why I came to you. For advice. Because you can think it out. Because if you want my honest opinion, sir, I think that Mr. Rattray's off his rocker, I mean something's wrong up there, no offense, of course, because otherwise a real gent like him would never do things like that and would never treat me like a dog, not after all that I've done for him."

Carron's mind was working fast and only half-picked up the last sentence. "What have you done for him?" he asked lightly, just to keep Hefty going.

"Well, you know, sir, the usual things. The stereo installation in the house, fixing the telly one Sunday night, just like for you once, remember, sir?"

"Of course, of course, I'm most grateful."

"That's what Mr. Rattray always said and he was very grateful, too. He even arranged extra pay for me when I made the demonstration model for the lecture. Though I think the lecture never came off and it was lost, in fact."

"What model?"

"Well, you see, he was planning to give that seminar or something at the Home Office about underwater detonators and remote-control devices . . ."

"Say that again."

Hefty repeated it.

"And he asked you to make a model?"

"More like a prototype I'd say. First it was a simple thing, really. A sort of very small underwater bomb with remote sonar control, but it wasn't easy to choose the right carrier frequency and I stuck out for using telemetry rather than speech because the commercially available units we started with, and based it on . . ."

"Skip the technical details, will you?"

"Well, without the technical details, there isn't much to say, sir, is there? It was just a favor but more or less in the line of my duties."

"There's no question about that, Hefty, don't misunderstand me, please. I'm most interested. But you may well be right, I mean about his being off his rocker and all that, and then there's some urgency, you see."

"Of course. Sorry, sir."

"So what happened to the unit you made?"

"Which one, sir?"

"How many were there?"

"Two, sir. Anyway, it's not all that important. I'm sorry I mentioned it, but you see it was part of the picture. Because ever since I made the prototype, he came to chat with me quite frequently, and he was always very kind, and always said that, one day, in a most unexpected way, he'd show his full gratitude to me, and I said never mind, sir, but he was always showing that he meant it—until today."

"Quite. Perfect reasoning, Hefty. Did he ever say that you must keep quiet about all this?"

"Of course, sir. But you know how it is. When I'm doing sort of private favors, people always say that."

"Sure. I'm with you. Now, just briefly, what happened to those models?"

"Well. The prototype itself, which is in many ways superior to Number Two, is still in my shed, complete with transmitter, receiver, decoder chips, timer, detonator and waterproof boxes for various amounts of explosives which can be attached by an ordinary socket and clips system."

"And that's in your shed."

"Yes, sir."

"What about the other model?" Carron was growing quite feverish with impatience but, like others before him, he began to discover that Hefty must not be hurried too much.

"It was very similar to the prototype, but the difference was that Mr. Rattray had received an American experimental gadget to increase the range and the precision of direction of any underwater transmission. So the new version had to accommodate this device."

"And where's that?"

"Lost at sea, I believe, sir. Mr. Rattray or somebody at the Home Office experimented with it and it was lost from a boat. Which is a bit strange, really, losing not only the receiver end but the transmitter and all, but strange things do happen when somebody's just dabbling in something he doesn't quite understand, and after all, the transmitter must be actually under the water when operated . . ."

"You've been most helpful, Hefty. Most helpful."

"So can I leave it with you, sir?"

"Of course. But I might need more information, so please stay for a short while. I'll get you some coffee, and you let me think it over for a minute or two. Just wait here, will you? Anything to eat?"

As Carron ran toward the living room where his guests were waiting, he heard a church bell ringing the half hour. Not a chance to contact the reception committee, already at the deserted warehouse, before the nine o'clock rendezvous.

*

The rain was still trying to take revenge for the long dry summer, and Bucken left a damp patch on the seat when he got out of his car. He had gone through all the schemes of deception in his armory against a tail, and although occasionally he had the feeling that somebody might still be behind him, he enjoyed the certainty that his final trump was the ace itself. He put on the old Bogart, locked the door, and walked down a gradually narrowing side street—no more than a footpath toward the end—off Cable Street. The tail who did not want to lose him in there would have to expose himself and run or wait and watch from the entrance of the alley. Halfway down, however, he stopped and pulled his handkerchief with the big bunch of keys out of his breast pocket. One of those keys would open the door of number eighteen—a door to nowhere, one of the relics of the war, and the product of easy profit-taking in a crowded city.

At the height of the Blitz, the area had taken a particularly heavy belting, and many houses in this seemingly endless terrace were left in ruins. Some of them were rebuilt eventually, others were turned into muddy car parks. Number eighteen and the house behind it in the parallel street had received three direct hits and their collapse also weakened the walls of numbers sixteen and twenty. When the ruins were demolished, the front wall was retained as a support for the two neighboring houses, and heavy wooden beams were wedged between the two exposed walls just below roof level. Number eighteen ceased to exist: the car park behind its front wall could be approached from the parallel street. When these quarters used to be part of Bucken's beat, the young PC discovered that the lock still worked and he made a key for himself. Sometimes it was a joke he could play on people, sometimes he could surprise suspects in the car park by coming in through the wall, sometimes it was his last trump in a chase.

He opened the door, ascertained that he was not followed, locked the door behind him and turned to pick his way through the mud. That was when he was hit hard on the head. The blow was not particularly vicious but the effect was worse because the wound from the O'Leary affair had not yet healed properly. So his knees buckled instantaneously, and he sank into the mud without a groan.

When Carron returned to Hefty, his voice and taut lips quivered from obvious tension. "I'm sorry about the delay, my wife is out, so I had to make some coffee for you myself. But it gave me a chance to think. The most important thing is for me to straighten out Rattray while you bring over that prototype or whatever because it's unsafe to leave it in your shed."

"It's all right, sir, nobody could ever find it."

"Still, I must insist. It should never have been left there in the first place. It could be a hell of a weapon in the wrong hands." He raised his hand. "No, don't argue, please. You have a car?"

"No. Not here."

"Never mind. It so happens that Inspector Linley is over here, he's brought me some urgent papers to sign, and I'm sure he wouldn't mind giving you a lift there and back. You know the Inspector?"

"We've met."

"Good. He's waiting outside. You could be back ... what ... in an hour?"

"Just about."

"Excellent. Just one other thing: congratulations. You're a good man and you did the right thing coming here straight away."

"Thank you, sir."

"But now you must be even more careful. I don't want anyone to know, too soon I mean, that you've told me all this and that you'll bring the device. Can you get to your shed without even your wife knowing about it?"

"I think so, sir, at least I know how to neutralize my

various toys which would raise a hell of an alarm if anybody touched anything. That's why I was saying that..."

"Yes, Hefty, I know. Just hurry now. Please."

The tall, slightly stooping figure in the long Bogart coat parked the MG and approached the cul-de-sac on foot. The man watching his arrival identified him and his car easily, let him turn the corner, and walked behind him toward the warehouse. At the entrance another man waited for him.

"Mr. Bucken?"

"Yes." A savage outburst of coughing shook him.

"Will you step inside, please?"

"I'll discuss the deal only with the top man, is that understood?" he whispered with an effort.

"Of course, Mr. Bucken. Will you step inside, please?"

As he went through the door, the upturned collar of the Bogart reduced the ferocity of the blow at the top of the nape but the difference was a mere theoretical question strictly for pedants only. Teng the chef who had delivered that blow with a shiny blob of metal at the end of a six-inch steel spring was not particularly fastidious outside the domain of his kitchen. With his shoe toe he poked at the lifeless body on the ground, then turned to his assistant: "Ready?"

The other produced a ridiculously small piece of plastic explosive and a crude detonator-timer contraption. He, too, checked that their victim was fully unconscious, then attached the homemade bomb with sticky tape to the right temple and cheek.

"Give ourselves three minutes, please." Teng checked the tape. "Good-bye, Mr. Bucken. Sorry no deal today."

They waited at the top of the cul-de-sac. The bang they heard was not much bigger than a few balloons bursting in unison at a children's party. But they knew it had demolished the top third of a man.

*

Carron answered the telephone right away, giving his number. He recognized Teng's voice:

"Oh, I'm sorry, sir, wrong number. But I was sure I dialed the right number. I was quite, quite positive."

Carron heard Linley's car returning as he replaced the receiver. He went to meet the Inspector in the hall, and gave him the thumbs-up. Hefty entered carrying a not-too-heavy duffel bag.

"This device is quite ingenious, sir, a most dangerous weapon," reported Linley. "And I must say that Hefty is an incredible teacher. Although we made the return journey in record time, the lucidity of his explanations has already made me an expert. I could use this bomb and control it with the help of this simple sonar or whatever right away."

"Well done, Hefty," said Carron.

The tricks man, already drunk with shameless flattery, blushed and muttered something about duty and the pleasures of being useful. He was asked to stay for a little longer in case more help was needed from him.

"The only problem is that your report has started something and there may be a great deal of coming-and-going and you shouldn't be seen by some of these people too soon," said Carron softly, as if only thinking aloud. "So the question is . . . oh, I know! Come with me." He led Hefty into an old air-raid shelter in the garden: "It's not the Ritz but it has a bunk bed and a table . . . my children used to camp out here when they were young. I'll get you some food and a radio to help you while away the time, and I'll bolt the door from the outside in case anybody should stumble on you accidentally."

Hefty was not sure that he understood all these elaborate precautions but as a result he reached an even more dizzying height of elation where even prepositions sounded like compliments that could be questioned only with unseemly immodesty.

Linley carried the duffel bag and asked Carron on their way toward the living room: "Is she here?"

"They both are."

"How did she take it? I mean the decision about Bucken."

"What do you expect? And she doesn't yet know about Teng's report."

"Went all right?"

"It always does with bloody Teng. He blew Bucken's head off just to be on the safe side."

"Oh, well, couldn't be helped, could it?"

"No," Carron said and looked away. "We were cornered."

"I wouldn't go that far . . ."

"I would. We had no room to maneuver. And I don't like that."

"That sounds like her opinion."

"It is. That's why she understood. But I'm worried about her. When she hears the final confirmation, she might crack up."

"But what else was there to do? After Rattray's call it was obvious that either Bucken was in collusion with Rattray or else he had discovered something about Rattray which could be only one thing: that Rattray is the Principal. So then we could do a deal with him or else . . . well . . ." Linley shrugged his shoulder. "It would be nice to skim off that million, but if not, we have here something just as valuable." He began to swing the duffel bag—which annoyed Carron.

"I have a feeling it may be a final payoff, too."

"You're a pessimist, Carron, you've always been."

"That's what kept us in business."

Intensive shivering helped Bucken to regain consciousness, but it seemed to take ages to clear his mind and try to remember. Rattray. It had to be Rattray. Only he would know about number eighteen, only he would not need to follow Bucken, only he could be ready with an ambush on the far side. . . . Why had he not killed him?

Cold dampness was chewing through his sinews to the

bones. The warm Bogart had gone. He was covered by a plastic mac. Like the one Rattray had been wearing. Startled, he sat up but the pain stopped him half way. He could not move his right foot. His ankle was held firmly to the wall. He made a second, much slower attempt to sit up. It hurt less now. He felt his ankle with his fingertips and identified a very tight handcuff.

The darkness was near-complete. Two parallel, string-thin strips of light suggested a boarded window. He shouted a couple of inarticulate noises and listened to the faint echo. The sound told him that the room was probably small and bare. A cellar? Somewhere near the wharfs? Tried his foot again. Not a chance to free it without help or a saw. Might take hours or even days before anyone came near enough to hear him.

His brain began to yield to his will to marshal facts, figments and recollections in some logical order. If Rattray had taken the Bogart, he might want to impersonate Bucken. Perhaps replace him at the warehouse rendezvous. And complete the deal? What deal? Why would Ratts want any deals when he was already winning?

He wrapped the mac around his shoulders. The left hand side was heavy. A flashlight. How thoughtful of Ratts. Yes, the room was small, the window was barred as well as boarded, his ankle was handcuffed to a large metal ring firmly embedded in the wall. He tried all his keys on the handcuff but he knew that it would be no use. He stuffed them back into his top pocket, then searched the pockets of the mac. There was a denim cap. The underground garage attendant had mentioned that the bearded driver of the Mini had worn one like that. Bits of paper, receipt from a shoe shop, a crumpled envelope, a couple of tapes, some notes in what looked like Hefty's handwriting. He was about to throw them away when he noticed that the envelope was sealed. It was addressed to him.

Quint. Fortunately, it won't be long now. By dawn or so you will understand. I had to make sure that you'd be safe whatever happened because you might have to finish the job for me.

I intend to be back with you by eleven o'clock if not before. I'll tell you everything and supply the evidence. Then you and I together must make the decision about my fate. Suicide will have to be the probable verdict because too many things have gone wrong, too many things I'll be unable to live with.

If I don't return in time, it's probably because I'm already dead. In that case, chaps from C.O. will be there. It's already arranged.

I'm sorry about everything that's happened to you but I had no choice. It was more important than you and I. That's why I was so furious when you failed to do your bloody duty. I was counting on it. Now suddenly, I had to improvise and that might turn out to be rather unsatisfactory. It's on the tapes and in Hefty's notes. I was tempted, of course, to tell you everything at Spooky's. But I couldn't. There was not much time and your reaction was not fully predictable. After all, I couldn't trust anyone and, lately, that seemed to include you, too. Or somebody around you, somebody who knew your moves and plans or could guess them. So how could I say anything? Because we both were bad liars, it had to be for real from beginning to end. Soon you'll see the logic of it. I'm sorry.

My bank will hand over a note to you in case of my death. But there may not be enough time. So please, please, PLEASE obey the following instructions precisely! If I don't return, as soon as you're freed, take my car—parked where you left yours, keys under rear nearside wheel. DO NOT LOOK FOR ME. Drive to Mailers Ltd. at Paddington, and find the missing Andrews Sister. The rest is entirely up to you. Be my judge and tell Mu and the children what you like. R.

Bucken pulled on the handcuff with a wild jerk. It hurt. The ring held it firmly. Almost fifty minutes to wait. Bucken felt sure his hair would grow white by then. When the police cadets at Peel House once staged a Christmas concert, Ratts had been the director and three young men came up with a passable impersonation of the three Andrews Sisters. Then one of them went missing ten minutes before the show. The most frantic search Peel House had ever seen began. The missing "sister" was found in a toilet where the lock had jammed. His name was Waltheof Stockton-Wright.

Lei Wong, a fragile Chinese with a crumpled face, aptly nicknamed and known by the international gambling fraternity as Meester Lemon, looked up slowly when the door opened. Linley walked in and put the bag on an ivory-inlay card table. This irritated Carron who quickly removed the bag, wiped the top gently with his elbow, took a deep breath, and turned at last toward the darkest corner of the room. He opened his mouth, changed his mind before saying anything, pouted, let his shoulders droop, then just nodded. In the silence they heard Maxine swallowing hard. She stood up, walked into the light, stared at each of them in turn, then squeezed out an "excuse me" and left the room.

"Couldn't be helped, could it?" said Linley aggressively, but nobody cared to take up the challenge. "All right, what now?"

"We'll wait. Rattray gave us the tipoff about Bucken, he'll be in touch. Or we'll contact him when we, too, have a bomb down there. We could make a deal if he really has the money and needs help. Any better ideas?" Carron asked.

"Not at the mo. Though I must say, Rattray's the last man I'd have expected to be involved in something like that."

"I thought I was the last man you or anybody would suspect."

Lei Wong turned away from them: "The last but one. Meester Rattray has apparently suspected you, Meester Carron."

"Me? Of what?"

"I don't know. He had his reason for giving you and Meester Allerton different information. We'll have to watch this Meester Rattray very carefully."

Linley smiled: "We can always bump him off, you know."

"Not always." Carron was more and more irritated by Linley. "Any time. That's what you mean, I think. And even then you're mistaken. How long do you think this can go on? Bucken, the Lad, a few others on the side. To take the skim off crime is one thing, killing high-ranking cops is another."

"Thank you for telling me. You should have warned me way back in Kowloon, when the business began to go sour over there, when you kindly tipped me off about the investigations by the corruption squad, and you offered to set me up first in Singapore, then here. That's when you should have warned me that in London you had grown so very proper and squeamish."

Lei Wong pressed his face to the large patio door and stared out at the neat, upward-sloping garden, the low bushes which hardly concealed Maxine's rented sports car in the service road beyond, and the church spire further up the hill. He waited patiently until the others noticed his long silence. "Greed. That was the problem. We always knew how greedy we were when we abandoned our old principles and went after this one."

"It looked too good to miss," said Carron. "But I agree."

"And I don't," snapped Linley. "It still looks the perfect crime and"—with a gesture toward the bag—"we'll get our share one way or another. Or even more ways than one. I have the diver who can do the job, all our beloved Deputy Commissioner will have to do is to secure access to the wreck. Any ideas, sir?"

"Yes." He looked very tired now. "We'll have to use Maxine. Just once more."

"You think she'll help?"

"If we ask her, yes," said Lei Wong. "But I don't like it. We've already promised to let her go, Meester Carron."

"It's the last time, I promise. But it's the only way because Bucken alone had the authority around the *Monty*. She'll only have to telephone Walsh and say she has a message from Bucken who had no time to call him."

"Clever. It could lead to a superpayday."

"More than that. It's an insurance policy. In case something goes wrong with Rattray."

"But can we trust her?"

Carron and Linley gazed at the narrow bony back at the window and had to wait for an answer.

"Yes, we can. She and I have never cheated so we trust each other."

"Even after Bucken?"

"Our bond is deeper. And she knows that. I promised her mother to look after her and she knows that I always did."

"In a way . . ."

"You mean my way, Meester Leenley? Because if yes, you're right. It's the best way I know. And she knows that, too."

"Just don't forget how furiously she reacted to that sergeant's death at the foot of the Long Man. Not to mention the attack on Bucken," said Linley.

"Don't you think it was understandable, Meester Leenley? She was in love with the guy, only we didn't know it at the time. She was doing a good job, picked up the man in charge of the immigration racket, gave us the information, and made only one mistake—she fell in love."

"And it seems it still bugs all of you," she said as she quietly returned. Her eyes were red, her skin an empty bag containing only bones with all the flesh and muscles scooped out. Her voice was flat and spent, her body only wanted to collapse and shake but she controlled it with a superb display of willpower. "You must be pleased now. Relieved?"

"I thought you understood," Carron's voice was cold ' but the compassion in his eyes contradicted it.

"Of course I did. Naturally. I've always been a fucking saint, haven't I? I understood everything and condoned everything so I bloody well had to forgive you for everything. Perhaps I should also have turned the other cheek, or my other leg to be precise, when those morons came to burn me!"

"We were very sorry about that," the crumpled lemon face produced something that could be mistaken for an apologetic smile. "Those boys could have never guessed that you were on their side. They had a job to do and they went about it as they always would. They had to find Bucken. And you did a good job, too, when you never told them anything about our association."

"They wouldn't have believed me anyway."

"No, probably not. But at least that attack, wicked as it was, ensured that you'd always remain above suspicion whatever happened."

"Bucken trusted me a hundred percent. And I trusted him. No questions about the past, no questions where the other was away for a few days, no questions about motives if it ever came to breaking it off altogether."

"How touching, what a very, very moving story!" cried Linley, sobbing and dabbing his nose mockingly.

Maxine picked up a chair and threw it at him in a single effortless sweep with perfect aim.

"Bloody bitch!"

Carron restrained him but could not stop him shouting at her: "It was the proof of your love that you went on helping us."

"It was virtually nothing," said Lei Wong to pacify her.

"Whatever it was, it was part of the deal," she said quietly. "In return you were to let Bucken live."

"And to let him trust you," Linley sneered, struggling free from Carron's grip. "Trust you even when you 'forgot' to mention to him that the Professor telephoned the night he died, even when you questioned him about his work, even when you tipped off Carron about Kowalski and alerted us that your great love might go to San Francisco! Shall I go on?"

"Don't," said Carron.

"Let him." Maxine's voice was sharp, tinged with menace.

"No. And that's final." Carron now did not even raise his voice. He knew he did not need to. Beyond all the discussion and argument it was his show. "Right then. It

306

was my fault and your fault that against our better judgment we let Maxi carry on after she had frankly told us everything. It was too convenient, there were excuses, but it was a mistake. We could have done it all without her. All right. So what now? You already wanted out, Maxi, for quite a while. You still want to leave us?"

"Yes."

"I thought this ... I mean what's happened tonight might change your mind."

"It doesn't." She turned to Lei Wong. "What do you think?"

He shrugged his shoulders. "It's up to you. It's only that ... well, doesn't matter."

"Only what?"

"You always said you wanted to be successful at something. Anything. Didn't you?"

"I did."

"And now you are. You wanted to do something, achieve something that wasn't handed to you on a silver plate. Now you can achieve anything. What else do you want?"

"I don't know."

"It's no good, don't you see?" Linley was full of cold contempt. "It was great fun to her for a while to make money the dirty way instead of drawing it from the bank. But now the bored little rich bitch wants another doll to play with. She doesn't even deny it."

"Usually I don't bother to take any notice of you. But this time I just don't know the answer. Perhaps my mother was right. Perhaps my father and I should have been ashamed of the desire to seek success in this life. It's none of your business, I know, and you don't care, I know that, too, but now that you've asked ... no, never mind ..."

"You don't have to explain anything," said Carron and again his eyes and voice were full of warmth. "I hoped it would work out in some better way, but we shouldn't complain. You've been helpful, you've played fair, so if you really want to go ..."

"Please."

"As long as you're no risk to any of us."

"You must know me better than that by now."

"I think I do. Have you prepared everything?"

She nodded. The three men were still waiting, so she explained: "Maxine is already finished. The cruiser has been moored at St. Katharine's for more than a week. I left a good-bye note in Bucken's flat three days ago. In the last few weeks several people warned me in Seaford and Newhaven not to go diving when drunk. There will be witnesses to say that I just refused to listen. I was last seen at Seaford two days ago, going out with the new speedboat and making an absolute nuisance of myself with that roaring sixty-five-hp monster. Right?"

"By now you must have been reported missing," said Carron.

"Probably. The speedboat will be found with some of my diving gear at sea by tomorrow or the day after."

"If not found already."

"That's why I'm flying out tonight."

"Under what name?"

She ignored the question. "So it's about time to say our warm good-byes."

"As it is, presumably, a private aircraft, you could delay it until dawn, couldn't you?"

"No."

"Just one last favor," said Carron.

She looked at the Lemon who nodded but avoided her eyes: "The last. A going-away present?" He managed a smile.

"And an invaluable insurance policy for your future love life, too," a leering Linley added.

"Stop all this!" Carron banged the table—then quickly checked to see if he had caused any damage.

She sat down and closed her eyes.

"I don't care who loves whom and what your hangups are. I have a business to run, people to take care of, a man in my air-raid bunker to dispose of, and our biggest single deal to see through. So get on to your diver, Linley, and call me when you reach Sheerness. Meanwhile we'll find the way to contact Walsh and get his cooperation."

Bucken read and reread the letter and studied Hefty's laconic logbook entries until the paper began to look like parchment in the fading torchlight. Rattray was late. He had never been late before. He was a compulsive clock-watcher. Bucken now counted the seconds to make the minutes pass faster. Ten past eleven, eleven past ... twelve past. The men from the Yard were late, too. Where the bloody hell... Somebody was kicking the boarded window.

"Hey! Anybody down there!"

"Superintendent Bucken!"

"Who?"

"Hurry up, for God's sake!"

It seemed to take ages for them to find their way in. They carried a set of skeleton keys and while working on the handcuff they tried to cheer him up with jokes about his predicament. It did not go down well so they soon stopped. They knew nothing about this job: they had been given brief orders early that evening without any explanation. They gossiped idly about a fresh murder case.

"What, where, how?"

"Wouldn't know the details, guv. I heard it's a male and it's somewhere around here."

"Identified?"

"Not a chance yet. No papers, nothing on the body, I mean whatever is left of it. They say most of it was blown away from the chest upward. Ugh. They say the walls of some warehouse are covered with bits and pieces."

That was when Bucken decided to obey Rattray's instructions to the letter for once. He found the Mini. The keys were under the wheel. He then dismissed the two men. Rattray's identity papers were in the glove compartment. He drove to a telephone booth, checked the address of Mailers Ltd., and called them.

"What service, sir?"

"How long are you open?"

"Twenty-five hours a day, sir."

It was the same humorous switchboard girl who greeted him at the office.

"Do you have somebody called Stockton-Wright working here? Or do you take messages for that name?"

"No, I don't think so, sir. Most of our subscribers are wrong not wright."

The sleepy supervisor sat up when he heard the name. "First name, sir?"

"Waltheof."

"Your name, sir?"

"Bucken."

"Any means of identification?"

They allowed him to use a bare, quiet box room with a desk, and brought in seven large bundles of neatly stacked and dated letters. They also gave him two notes.

"This one is special instructions, sir," explained the supervisor. "And this one hasn't been entered in the register because it only arrived by messenger this afternoon."

The instructions were brief:

Quint (or whoever the reader is). From time to time I prepared a summary for myself in red. Look for these first if you're in a hurry.

The latest letter began with a warning:

Read this when the rest of the picture is already clear. Then you'll understand why I had to go about it this way . . .

Bucken's eyes slipped down the lines.

. . . of course if I'm dead, this proves who knew where I was this evening, apart from you, of course, because you were otherwise engaged . . .

Bucken hoped he had died cheerfully.

The notes began in the form of a diary. Many pages were missing, presumably thrown away as irrelevant.

Some entries were almost four years old and referred to corrupt policemen mainly in Singapore and Hong Kong. Rattray was disgusted and worried:

> A few are caught and although their crime is serious (and the payoff running sometimes into hundreds of thousands), the sentences are light. Most of them must have gone underground to wait for the storm to blow itself out. What then? Can they ever resurrect their protection racket for brothels, gambling and opium dens? What will happen to the remnants of the Tong? Who will use them? Where will they crop up?

Bucken winced as he recalled the Professor's warnings. "The Tong. The police is in their pocket." Could he have done more about it?

There were several references to conversations with senior policemen at a time when Rattray was already recognized as a potential high flier, enjoying accelerated promotion to become the youngest postwar Assistant Commissioner of the Yard. Way back at the Ryton police college, the predecessor of Brams Hill (when Rattray was only twenty-five years old and already approaching the rank of Chief Inspector) a Commander told him: "There's more corruption in the police than you'd dream of. The higher you rise the less you'll know about it because you'll be the odd man out, the Brammer, the college cop. But you must try to see and try to hear because if there's one thing that can chew away the force, it's corruption." Then Rattray's comment on recalling this remark several years later:

> The more I learn about the CID, the more I admire and fear them. They're the toughest, most capable lot any police force can wish for. With all their excesses and underhand methods, they're a superbly disciplined band, and immensely loyal to each other. Too loyal to expose and eject the cheats. That dirty job waits for an outsider. Me?

Bucken looked at his watch. Half past midnight. At this pace it would take days to get through.

Rattray had begun to learn more and more about the extent of corruption. He spotted likely suspects; and saw a

few potential cases against bribed detectives and uniformed cops whose palm had been greased to overlook
minor offenses. Then he heard about the "skim-off." And
he was clearly worried:

> Apparently, there may be a protection racket for crime. From
> raids that ended in failure, I get the impression that the
> villains were warned well in advance. There are rumours that
> when we have tips from informers about pending bank
> robberies and other major crimes, the villains also get the
> tipoff that they should change plans because the job may be
> ready-eyed.
>
> During the stage when the villains are already known to us
> and arrests are delayed only by the chores of collecting the
> final pieces of evidence that will satisfy DPP, the villains seem
> to receive a warning to run for it or make witnesses disappear
> or prepare better alibis or destroy some evidence. According
> to some wild accusations against the police, such warnings are
> available only to perpetrators of major crimes for a very
> sizeable share of their takings. We have no proven case
> against anybody at C.O. or even out on any Division, but I
> wonder how much truth there may be in it . . .

It was almost precisely four years before his death that
Rattray decided to set up a regular record of his suspicions. He chose the safe of Mailers Ltd., with duplicate
summaries deposited at his bank.

> This decision is forced upon me by the monstrosity of the
> suspicions I harbor. . . . Chinese involvement and cruelty (like
> torture used by the Tong for disciplinary purposes) seem to be
> increasing considerably in London at a time when the
> corruption investigations grow more and more successful in
> the Far East, and when a large number of senior men are
> returning from those parts to C.O. . . .

From there onward, Bucken began to detect Rattray's
changing mood from the notes. Vague suspicions and
worries gave way to anger and fury alternating with
despair, frustration, blind determination, and a touch of
madness in the totality of the obsession to stop the rot.
The letters now referred to the numerous enclosed
documents, too. These were individual cases, mostly with

fairly convincing evidence, against corrupt detectives. Rattray maneuvered to have these cases shelved temporarily.

I'm not interested in small fry. Even if they do belong to the big skim-off game, I must consider if their prosecution would help lead us to the heads of what I believe to be a superb organization built on power, financial resources, ingenuity, inside information and the use of professional frighteners—or if it would only warn them to be more careful, slow down and cut out the cancerous member before the disease spreads.

Rattray decided to wait and build up his case with infinite patience. He was now in charge of A10 and exploited well this tremendous vantage position, but the vast mixture of gossip, hearsay, malicious allegations, doubtful criminal intelligence reports and proven facts began to overload his mental sifting processes. He noticed the faint outline of what he termed as the "Hong Kong takeover," a villainous bid for the control of Scotland Yard, and the enormity of this elusive ghost led him gradually to distrust everybody. The life-style of some senior officers, their hobnobbing and holidaying with rich unsavory characters, and their excuses—"I can't help it if so-and-so is permitted to join my golf club: one is not supposed to be nasty to fellow members" or "Fraternization with criminals has always been the secret of my successes: now I'm doing it at the top, hoping for more spectacular results"—made him see a potential villain in everybody. He sought backing from the ailing Commissioner and suffered a plain rebuff from the man who had not improved police reputation but, being "a noisy dog with no bite," suited successive Home Secretaries admirably.

You often call me a nine-to-five cop, Quint. It's a joke, I know, but it hurts. You say that college has only taught us to be paper cops to detect expenses-fiddlers and think like maiden aunts of the fucking, glorified laborers on the beat. But even you fail to realize that this one is a job strictly for a desk detective, like me ...

It was soon after the date of this letter that Rattray grew convinced that "the Hong Kong lot either runs or thoroughly skims all the fortunes made by the increasingly successful south-coast immigration racket." Reading these notes, Bucken realized for the first time that his hopeless assignment had not been a form of exile. No matter what some people at the Yard might have thought, this was not Rattray's way of pushing an old friend out of the way:

> ... I have to do it, Quint. There's no choice. As you will see from some of these documents, I have evidence that several officers involved in the investigation are actually concealing information, and there are certain indications, more, suspicions, that they've been bought by the racketeers. So I must have a man there who has the necessary tenacity and cannot ever be bought. You.

The frustrating months and months that followed had slowly driven Rattray to the breaking point:

> My nets are bursting with small fry, and I'm inclined to throw them back into the water without fuss. Yet I may be making a fatal mistake. Perhaps I'm crazy. But it's gone too far. I cannot call it off any more. Wish I could talk to you, Quint. But it would be unfair to involve you, to unload my troubles on you, to make you a party to the greatest potential error in police history. Besides, how do I know that you won't stop me somehow, out of sheer goodwill. If I tell you everything and you disagree with me, I may still be right—yet be prevented from further action. You've already accused me of doing nothing about your allegations concerning some leaks at the top. If only you knew that I do nothing but chase such menacing shadows, and that my own suspicions go not only to the top but the very top ...
>
> Even you look a little suspicious from up here, Quint. The slowness of your progress at Newhaven, the things known at C.O. about you, your plans and moves—wish I could warn you to watch over your own shoulder ...

The supervisor brought in some coffee for Bucken who looked pale, drawn and shaky: "Are you all right, sir?"

"Fine. Fine. Thanks for the coffee."

"If you need anything else ..."

"Perhaps another pair of eyes, thank you."

Maxine's telephone call woke Walsh up at half past two in the morning. "Remember me?"

"How can I forget you? Have you decided to leave your Superintendent? Have I any hopes?" He kept staring at his watch incredulously.

"Not yet, but if I ever leave him, it will be for you. At the moment, I am only to pass on a message." She could not force herself to say Bucken's name.

"From the guv?"

"Who else? He was in a frightful rush and asked me to call you ..."

"And he gave you this number?" He was not sure if Bucken would have this number: it had just been installed for him at General Brammel's command post circus.

"Well, after some telephoning around, yes ..."

"And what's the message?"

"That he was in an awful hurry, but he'd call you as soon as he could. Until then, a diver will go to see you about something. You are supposed to know what. Does that make sense to you?"

"Go on."

"I don't understand what it's about but he said you will. The diver is some sonar expert—is there such a thing?"

"Yes."

"And he should be allowed to make a special examination as soon as he gets there. You should meet him on the waterfront. But it's most urgent and you must help him in every way you can."

"I see."

"All right? I hope I haven't made a mistake. Let me just check once more his written instructions ... yes ... he says it's absolutely vital that there should be no delay."

"It's very odd. Can I reach guv anywhere?"

"No ... not just now ... He'll be in touch ..."

Rattray's letters, even his cool lines of reasoning and pitiless self-examination, began to amount to a painful epitaph for a shadow boxer. Bucken had already seen the documents that could start scores of prosecutions and cripple respect for the Metropolitan Police for several generations, and now he could only hope that his friend's self-sacrifice was a service not only to the demonic thoughts that seemed to possess him.

By the time Bucken's Newhaven investigations had begun to justify some hope for positive results, it was too late for Rattray:

> I must face the facts. With all the evidence I am withholding from the Commissioner and DPP, I am signing my confession to being a failure as a policeman. Yet I must weigh the value of strategy against tactical advantages, the importance of winning the war at the cost of losing battles. My father always told me that he could not weep for every soldier, every battalion, the life of an innocent bystander or even a town, and now it's my turn to exercise the cruel kindness (or is it the kind cruelty?) of a general. My only possible justification is that I am ready now to put myself into the firing line ...

During a fishing trip in the Estuary, Rattray conceived "an idea for The Perfect Crime, an absolute blockbuster," which had to be big and irresistible enough to attract the mastermind himself behind the Hong Kong takeover. "The secondary purpose will be decent enough in itself," he wrote in one of the longest letters, "because, quite inevitably, it must lead to the disposal of the *Montgomery!* My ultimatum will force the Government to stop living with the criminal risk, the monster of Sheerness ..."

He thought about seeking Bucken's cooperation. Then he realized that both of them were bad liars: short of actually arming his bomb in the wreck, it had to be for real if cunning schemers were not to see through it. Giving Carron's phone number to Cutter-Smith was a red herring planted in the hope that Bucken might be made extra-cautious with the DC. He knew how Bucken's mind would work. He knew that the few "mistakes" in the plan would be noticed only by Bucken, so it was imperative that Bucken should immediately be transferred to the case.

And then the long wait began:

Sometimes you seem slow, Quint, particularly now, near the end. Wish I could give you more hints or ask you what's holding you up? Could it be that you resist your own findings and reasoning?

He thought that as soon as he was even slightly implicated, Bucken would report it to someone at the Yard. Rattray's two chief suspects—Carron and Allerton—would certainly find out about it, and one of them would make the fatal attempt to take the skim off the million:

I have monitored all senior men's actions. Enclosed you'll find a full record of their moves throughout your investigation. You'll see who drew what documents from Records, who had what contacts with all the other corrupt cops known to me, who has been eliminated as a likely chief suspect and why, who could have anything to do with all the snooping into your work, who wanted you followed at all times... Only Carron and Allerton could have acted in time to interrogate and kill Kowalski. But think, Quint, think. They must have had an early warning about your interest in him ... Then the death of poor Cutter-Smith. The removal of your guards was made to look like a potential error by you or a misunderstanding. But it could have been made only by Carron or Allerton. Wish I could have them watched. But it might frighten away the guilty ...

Toward the end, Rattray seemed to live in a state of complete mental disarray concerning everything unrelated to his obsession. He paid no attention to his deteriorating health, his rather elaborate handwriting grew blurred with long wavy lines representing anything from double Ns to ONSUM and ION in the word CONSUMPTION, as if living in a constant hurry. He worked out various schemes to deal eventually with members of the Hong Kong conspiracy.

The approach to them must be careful and well-prepared. It should never be forgotten that the aim is to cleanse the Met—

not ruin it ... They must be forced out quietly. Spectacular trials and long jail sentences must not be regarded as the only way to justice. In this case, justice must be done, not seen to be done. All who are thought to be guilty must be driven to see that all is lost. They must be convinced that suicide is preferable to any other fate that may await them ... If that was the only way, I'd gladly join them in a suicide pact ...

You poor, poor madman, whispered Bucken. After a lifetime of detection of crime and fighting for the punishment of the truly guilty, Rattray was now talking about those "thought to be guilty." That was how he had come to think of his own guilt as part of his duty, something inevitable, not worse than the guilt of the generals; that was how he came to regard a few deaths incurred on the way as painful running expenses of a major campaign.

Bucken looked at his watch. 0427. There was no time to stop and think. No time to realize that some of Rattray's ideas were infectious, and decide whether the notes and letters had begun to influence his own thinking. He just drifted along to let his next move be governed by gut reaction.

A hasty, special note reflected Rattray's anxiety for the wreck:

My friend in Greenwich told me all about the risk, but my success is too complete. The Government yields to every demand too readily. I thought they'd buy time to raise the wreck. But they want to buy peace. Perhaps that million—you must have an inkling where it is—should never be returned. Perhaps it should be used for helping victims of bad government, protecting Sheerness, tracking down the really big criminals instead of the petty parking offender, supporting families of jailed policemen who had been corrupted and convicted by our system ...

Are you pleading, Rattray? Pleading guilty? Pleading for Mu?

And then the last letter.

... so you failed, Quint. At Spooky's you failed as a cop, you failed me no matter how good a friend you are, and if now, as a result, I fail, too, then it was all in vain ...

318

Rattray reasoned that his own name and direct involvement would force a hurried, avaricious response from his principal quarry. Allerton chose the correct path and raided the boat. Carron made the phone call (Rattray, like Bucken, suspected that it was Carron himself on the line with the phony accent). The trap was about to be sprung. Rattray foresaw two main possibilities:

   a) Carron may want to make a deal with Bucken, knowing full well that I must be involved in some way—why else would Bucken make me an offer as I claimed, and why else would I contact Carron? So I must approach them as Bucken, to avoid some mistake by a surprised and trigger-happy gorilla when I appear; but then I can reveal myself, claim that Bucken was on to me, I needed help, and in return I can offer, in fact, a much better deal than Bucken . . .

   b) Carron is keen, no doubt about that. He's hooked on skimming that million. Otherwise he wouldn't have made the risky approach. But there's a chance that his logic and criminal experience will persuade him to seek a shortcut and eliminate the third party to the deal—Bucken. In that case, I, as Bucken, may be killed on sight, and Carron will start a search for Rattray. If I'm dead, Quint, the tapes and this letter will help in the demolition of Carron's empire. After all, nobody wants or needs trial-tight evidence. Just don't approach him, Quint, not directly. Do it through your Downing Street contact . . .

Bucken skipped the rest of the warnings and instructions. His instinct and pride took over. He dialed the number for Call-me-Wade.

"Mr. Wade is away, sir. Is it quite exceptionally urgent?"

"Why else do you think I'm calling him at dawn?"

"Sorry, sir. I'll try to reach him at once. Can he ring you back?"

While waiting for the call, Bucken scribbled a brief note that he was about to visit Carron in Harrow and try to make a deal. "If I succeed, your case will be that much stronger. If I fail, I'll be dead, and that, too, should complete the case." He would have liked to take somebody with him or get the local station to back him up. But

319

under Rattray's too fresh influence, he could not trust anyone. Allerton? What if Ratts was wrong? After all, they both might be involved . . .

"Wade here."

"I must see you, sir, and hand over something right away."

"What's it all about?"

"Can't tell you, sir. Not like that. You'll have to read a great deal to be convinced and there's no time. Where can I meet you?"

"Do you realize that I'm in Edinburgh?"

"Oh." Of course. He had read about it. The PM was busy wooing Scottish votes. Fighting a criminal takeover or the *Montgomery* ultimatum would not win him any seats. "Please trust me, sir, and return to London at once. I must have your backing. The papers will be waiting for you at Downing Street."

On his way from Whitehall to Harrow, Bucken passed his flat. He was shiverish in his soaked clothes and decided to give himself the moral advantages of changing into fresh underwear and kissing Maxine good-morning. The air in the flat was stale. The sort that tells the place is unlived-in. The two notes were still pinned to the cushion. "Went sailing with friend . . ." "Went to the States alone . . ." He had been away for eight full days. So had she. It felt like a lifetime.

It was only after changing, and on his way out, that he noticed another message on his desk. "Went away alone. Love you, I do, but it hasn't worked out this time. Perhaps we'll meet again. Love M." The note was held in position by her personal paperweight: an empty Armagnac bottle. She must have been through one of her nightmarish though luckily infrequent drinking nights. He stuffed the note into his pocket and ran. He later remembered that in the top right hand corner she had written "Thursday." She never dated her notes. This "Thursday" must have signified finality in her mind.

*

Maxine sat at the card table and rolled a cigarette.

"That's the sort of thing you'll have to give up," said Carron. "That's how the best new identities break down. On little things and unimportant habits like this."

She chose not to hear and completed the rolling with a lizardlike flick of her tongue.

"Your move," said Lei Wong. He was fingering the corner of the ivory draughts board so as to annoy Carron.

"I know, I know, but I also have other things to do, haven't I?" Carron glanced at the six-inch TV screen—a fine free favor job by Hefty who had once devised the closed-circuit security system to view all approaches to the house, and built the screen and the control console into a bowfront corner cabinet virtually without any damage to the old wood.

The phone rang twice, then stopped. It rang again after a pause and Carron answered it. He recognized Linley's voice.

"Oh, I am sorry, sir, wrong number. Sheer, sheer stupidity on my part, I'm sure. But I was quite, quite positive that I dialed the right number."

Carron smiled as he put the phone down. "Seems to be going all right." His smile froze into tension and his eyes narrowed as he stared hard at the small screen. A Mini could be seen in the distance. He adjusted the controls. The car was approaching slowly, the headlights searching for numbers on the well-separated houses in this spacious suburb.

"Rattray's," said Carron. He turned to Maxine. "You'd better leave now if you still want to keep your appointment for that flight. Thanks for the last favor."

She stood up and Carron opened the patio door for her. She lit the cigarette, stuck it in the corner of her mouth, and was about to say something to Lei Wong, but he was already switching over to another camera. The screen now showed a close-up of the Mini in front of the house. She walked out without a single good-bye. Her car was still in the service road behind the bushes. Lei Wong's back shielded the screen from her all the time and he wanted it that way: he had already seen that it was Bucken who was driving that Mini.

The two men hesitated only for a second. Then Carron went to open the front door.

Bucken began with a hearty "good morning, sir" but Carron silenced him with a gesture and repeated it when Bucken almost greeted Meester Lemon, an old acquaintance, in the living room. Carron then indicated that he wanted Bucken to remove his jacket. Bucken's eyes laughed as he handed it over to Carron who now demanded Bucken's other clothes.

"What? Everything?"

Carron nodded.

"All right, I'm not shy."

They searched every piece thoroughly for arms and hidden transmitters.

"Don't worry, I'm clean," said Bucken and sniffed twice, and then again. His nonsmoker's sensitivity had detected a faintly familiar scent. His puzzled expression revealed that he had failed to identify it, but the sniffing was noted by the Lemon.

Carron gestured: turn around and bend down. He was not taking chances. Bucken complied with the order. "Okay?"

"You may dress now. And good morning to you. The two of you have met, I suppose."

"Yes," said Bucken as he started to dress, "in slightly more formal circumstances where clothes were not optional extras."

Lei Wong walked nearer the patio door. His head was slightly tilted in an effort to pick up any noise. He had not yet heard Maxine's car leave and it worried him.

"So what do you want?" asked Carron.

"My shirt, please."

"Let's not play games, Bucken."

"All right. I want a deal."

"What for what?"

"I'm offering you a share in nine hundred thousand pounds. Cash. How's that for starters?"

"Why us?"

"I don't see . . ."

"Doesn't matter what you see. You'll have to explain."

"Okay. I discovered that Rattray was the Principal. I needed money and offered him a deal. But he had another idea. He said he had proof about your little organization, the Hong Kong mob and the skim, and he thought that if he and you and I got together, we could really go places. But, apparently, he changed his mind halfway. He was with me when you called, then left to meet me at the warehouse, and that's when he must have had new ideas. He ambushed me, knocked me out, and prevented me from keeping the rendezvous. Did he go himself?"

"I wouldn't know."

"It won't do, Carron. In a partnership, you must give as well as take."

"Have I mentioned a partnership? Have I agreed to any deal? I haven't even shown any interest in all this gibberish."

"Oh yes, you have. On the phone."

"I didn't call you."

"You did. And I have the tape. Your voice can be printed and identified, I'm sure. I thought this could be kept on a friendly basis."

"All right. What's your proposition?"

"I have the money. If Rattray remains in the deal, I'll take a third. If you can arrange to leave Rattray out, I take sixty per cent."

"You take forty," said Lei Wong.

"I didn't know that you were also a full-fledged negotiator. But let's not squabble about it. Fifty-fifty it is."

"Why?"

"Because I'll need help to cover up my tracks and show that my investigation hasn't led to anything, and I'll need help to get the money out of its hiding place and out of the country. If Rattray was right, you'll know how. But if he wasn't right, we wouldn't be talking here, would we?"

"Anything else?"

"Yes. I want to share your other takings from any future

action. I could be a very useful member. And I can tell you something to start with: I know how Rattray controlled the bomb, I can continue the operation easily, and then there's no end to some handsome regular revenue."

"Well, it sounds attractive," said Carron, "but not as attractive as you think. Mainly because we, too, have an entirely independent claim to the *Monty*. Yes, Bucken, you should look startled. But it's a fact." He looked at his watch. "By now it's fully operational, I would say, and a friend of ours can start the timer by sonar without any trouble. So you see, we don't need you all that much."

"I don't believe you. The wreck is under my control and you wouldn't get anywhere within . . ."

"Ask your friend on the spot. Mr. Walsh, yes, phone him if you wish. But if you do, and he confirms my claim in some way, then you promise to get the whole sum here, with my help, right away. Then you'd take a share, twenty percent, and then at last we could see what other sort of deals we may consider to be mutually advantageous."

Bucken hesitated. He shook his head and looked from one man to the other. He only hoped that his acting would be convincing enough. "Thirty percent. I won't take less than thirty. For seventy percent any casino would give me a check for the rest showing that I'd been lucky at the roulette tables for once."

"Okay."

"With you, too?" Bucken sniffed again.

"Okay."

"But only if Walsh can confirm and I have a share in any future action."

Carron gestured toward the table in the corner beyond the ivory-inlay card table. "Just be very, very careful what you say to him."

Bucken started toward the telephone.

"Wait." Lei Wong's voice was uncharacteristically sharp.

"Why?"

"Because I say so." He stepped nearer the table.

"I didn't know that you were in command here. And frankly, I don't care."

The Chinaman was faster. He produced a snubnose Smith & Wesson Model 38, known as the Bodyguard, seemingly out of nowhere, and held it lightly in the general direction of Bucken, but pointing at the floor.

"One should never point weapons at people unless one is ready to shoot," he said. "But don't let this give you foolish ideas." He stood now with his back to the small table, which was loaded with precious knickknacks. Bucken saw that his free hand was searching frantically for something behind him. The irrelevant question also supported Bucken's suspicion that there was something on that table he was not supposed to see—something worth pulling a gun on him for:

"What do you want to find out from Meester Walsh?"

"Just checking."

"Don't you believe us?" It seemed an almost impossible task to locate that small green packet of cigarette papers left among Carron's treasures by that foolish girl. Inch by inch he searched the table blindly. His eyes were on the target but the Superintendent saw that those eyes were glazed and empty, looking, in fact, inward. "What sort of a partner are you?"

Bucken was sniffing again. "I'm sorry, but something's irritating my nostrils and making me sneeze . . ." His nose began its well-rehearsed contortions. "Ha . . ." and another abortive half-sneezed "ha . . ." with his fingers wandering toward his breast pocket and touching the white cotton overhanging its edge.

Lei Wong had had enough of his groping about. Silly girl.

"Turn away," he ordered Bucken.

The Superintendent's face was sneezebound. He nodded to acknowledge the order, moved slowly as if complying with it, and fought yet another "ha . . ." At last he grabbed the handkerchief, lunged forward, and swung the keys toward the man's eyes. The Lemon never knew what hit him. The gun went off and fell on the floor. Bucken followed through the attack, ready to hit him again, kick the gun out of his reach and grab whatever was meant to be hidden from him, but Carron's quiet voice stopped him:

"Don't!" He held a huge 7.63mm Mauser automatic, once a favorite among the S.S. He aimed the almost foot-long pistol with a steady, two-handed grip. It seemed to be his turn to shield that card table. "Turn around, Bucken, and don't try the same trick on me."

Bucken turned toward the bowfront corner cabinet. The small screen still showed the entrance. Above it he saw the reflection of the patio door in the curved glass. Lei Wong was groaning. Carron swore at him: "Idiot. You holed the Chesterfield and bloodied the old Shirvan rug."

Bucken slowly craned his neck to catch a glimpse of the small table. Carron was there, still aiming at him. The curved glass glittered for a second. As if something had moved behind Carron—perhaps in the graying shadows of the garden. Then a sharp report and the sound of breaking glass shattered the silence. Bucken ducked and dived toward the door believing that Carron or Lei Wong had shot at him.

With a small, well-defined hole in the back of his skull, Carron had already collapsed. Bucken noticed him as he rose and dived again, this time with a twist to reach relative safety at the back of the Chesterfield. He popped his head up for a second and saw the hole in the patio door which was now open. The Chinaman slipped out, taking something from the small table with him. His gun was gone, too. Bucken ran after him but a shot, ricocheting at his feet from the stone path, forced him to seek cover. Then another shot from further away. The engine of a sports car kicked to a flying start. Bucken ran across the empty garden. The profusely bleeding Chinaman had left his marks all the way to the hedge beyond which the rear lights of a car were just disappearing. He turned and almost tripped over something. An American semi-automatic sniper rifle with a night-viewer attachment.

Carron was very dead from a perfect shot. So perfect that it could not have been a clumsy accident caused by somebody aiming at Bucken and hitting Carron.

Bucken walked toward the telephone but distant, muffled shouts stopped him. He switched off the lights, picked up the rifle by the barrel and followed the sounds to the bunker. Hefty was quite hysterical and Bucken had to slap his face before he could extract a sensible sentence from him. As soon as he learned about the second bomb and Linley, he knew he had no time to waste. He ran back to the phone. Hefty followed him and produced a second round of hysterical antics over Carron's body.

"Turn away if you can't stand blood, but stop behaving like a fucking virgin just released by a bunch of marooned sailors!"

Bucken had to get some help from Hefty. He pulled Carron by the leg out of the room, poured a drink for the electronics wizard and made him write down a few instructions and telephone numbers: "First you call Allerton and make him come here personally and at once with no more than one or two men. He must put out a general alert for Linley and Lei Wong immediately. The latter has facial injuries and might try to leave the country. On this other number, you leave a message for a Mr. Wade to contact Allerton here or at C.O. And finally, you call Walsh on the third number. Tell him I'm on my way to meet him at the command post ... don't interrupt me. Command post, yes, and never mind what sort. Right? He should have diving gear prepared. Got it? Good. Now tell me quickly what the device you gave Linley looks like."

"You don't mean to imply that ..."

"Never mind the implication. Just describe it."

When Hefty mentioned the word "slim" as a main characteristic—"Mr. Rattray actually insisted on this despite the technical disadvantages..."—Bucken felt he knew enough. A dingy little man's words in a dingy little Greenwich shop echoed in his ears: Superstructure After Mast ... 12 percent had welding defects and soon developed cracks ... such bad welding runs like ladders... A "slim" bomb would fit and could be concealed easily in one of these surface cracks.

For a second he toyed with the idea of calling Walsh and ordering him to dive at once. He could not do it. He himself would have to be there if anything went wrong.

Linley dialed Carron's number a few minutes after six. It rang once—then it was answered. Carron would not break the agreed code. A strange, panicky voice shouted "hullo" after "hullo." Linley put the phone down. What could have gone wrong? Planning and reasoning were not his forte. He only wanted to report that his duties had been discharged. Obtain explosives, attach them in the correct way to Hefty's waterproof box of tricks, take the diver to Sheerness, try to watch the dive from a safe distance, report any snags—none so far—or completion, and call again in the usual manner for further instructions after six A.M. All done. Except no further instructions. He recalled that, just before leaving Carron's house, there had been some talk about the bomb that would be both a goldmine and an insurance policy. If something went wrong at the house, he would have to make his own demands. But how? To activate the bomb would be easy. He needed time to work out his next move: first activation and then the demand or the other way round? And he would have to find the diver who had not yet turned up at the rendezvous...

Walsh was adamant, claiming that he had spoken to Maxine. Bucken knew that this was impossible. He had not talked to Maxine for eight days and she would not lie about it. She would not know how to find Walsh's new direct line and why on earth would she try anyway?

"Somebody must have impersonated her."

"I swear I spoke to her, I swear on everything sacred to me, on the seaworthiness of my dinghy and on my gift to burp up surplus gases at will, I swear!"

"How would you know?"

"I recognized her voice, I recognized her chitchat, her easy style."

"You met her only twice." But Bucken did not want to press him too hard. He knew Maxine better and that was a satisfactory answer to him. He was determined not to let himself be dragged down by this case to the level where nobody and nothing was sacrosanct except Walsh's belching ability. Besides, he had no intention of making Walsh a scapegoat: all right, he had been taken in, he had made a mistake by accepting orders in this unusual fashion, but these were unusual circumstances and, above all, at least he had the good sense to keep the diver there, locked up at Brammel's command post, waiting for Bucken.

General Brammel asked no questions apart from the single essential one: "How much time can you give me?"

"Preferably not more than five minutes," said Bucken and tried to smile.

"In five minutes I can't even reach the corners you want me to cut."

"Half an hour?"

"I'll do what I can."

Brammel did not bother to call his Ministry or any of his superiors. His instinct rather than orders told him to trust this Superintendent who had already had the courtesy to alert him on Saturday. Evacuation was, of course, impossible. If he tried to raise some form of general alarm, people would flood the streets and panic might cause a disaster even if nothing happened at the wreck. He chose to begin moving in his units already on standby. Ambulances and fire trucks in the first place. Lorries to be positioned at strategic points to take over the evacuation. Parachutists to do a traffic job: not a single private vehicle must be on the road. Remove all obstructions that might delay movement in the sole bridge area. Additional ferrying facilities to be lined up. Ensure that anything that floats will carry people.

Brammel would never have admitted it to anyone, but he was rather enjoying himself. Apart from having dodged family occasions and a world tour with his wife, he had not had a ball like this since working on Eisenhower's staff before D-Day. A thought which reminded him: medical units should have air transport to move them in and fly casualties out. A few helicopters would have made all the difference on the beaches of Normandy.

According to the clock the sun should have been up by now, but heavy skies fought to prolong the gray dawn. The diver—an ex-professional, sacked by a North Sea oil company for excessive venery—looked frightened enough to tell the truth. Both Bucken and Walsh chose to believe him when he claimed that the man he knew as "Cooper," and whose description fitted Linley accurately enough, had asked him "to position a new, perfectly harmless experimental hydrophone in the wreck."

"Didn't you know that this was a restricted area?"

"I did. But try to see it from my angle, sir. I was hard up, needed some quick cash, and couldn't be too choosy. After all, it didn't look too black, did it? I only had to say that this was a job for a Mr. Bucken, and I had to report to the fuzz, sorry, I mean to the law. Now how would I know that there might be something fishy when I was doing it with, how shall I say, police cooperation?"

"How much did you get?" The diver hesitated. "That's how you should have guessed," snorted Bucken. "But let's forget that. Your 'hydrophone' must be recovered at once. If you help me, I'll go easy on you."

The diver was ready "to do anything to put the record straight" but Bucken had reservations about his trustworthiness: in the boat, on the way to the wreck, he opened the valve of the diver's air bottle.

"What are you doing?"

"I just want to be sure that if you try to leave me alone down there, you won't get far underwater. And if you happen to surface without me ... well, God help you then."

Bucken had decided against using the naval divers. He was not sure about their chain of command and he wanted no reports, no delays, no interference. If eventually heads were to roll, it must be his own and perhaps Walsh's. So they settled for the police launch and relied on Sergeant Elms's advice and experience. "Another good breakfast down the drain," was his only command when Walsh summoned him and his two Wilsons for "a little extra fun."

They rowed the last leg of the journey to the wreck as usual, and tried to position the launch at the spot where Linley's man had dived.

"Mr. Cooper, or whatever his real name is, gave me this sketch," said the diver. It showed roughly the area where Bucken knew there were several welding cracks in the wreck. Hefty's slim design would just fit in. . . .

Elms jumped in first. He would remain in the water as a standby, holding the communications cord, in case the professional diver and Bucken needed help. "Usual signals," he said and repeated them to be on the safe side.

"Let's hope we can beat Linley to it," said Bucken before he would bite on the mouthpiece. In the distance he saw rows of vehicles moving into Sheerness. People gathered on streetcorners and stared at the pointless military exercise on such a scale.

The water was cold but, apart from his codiver, Bucken's main concern was to prepare himself for the earache and avoid the panicky fear of bursting eardrums. Now he knew what to expect but the lack of visibility and the inevitable claustrophobia worried him. He remembered how he had once sworn never to dive again. Never. And it should be a job for the professionals in any case. But they might not do it at short notice, just like that, on his authority. And in all fairness, he could not ask them.

The diver was descending faster than Bucken, pulling jerkily on their buddy line. Perhaps he was afraid that his air bottle might run out too soon. Bucken knew that he had probably been unfair. It was too late to do anything about it. Something touched his cheek at the edge of the half mask. Something slimy. He recoiled with disgust. Bloody fish moving about.

He worked his fingers along the sharp edge of a crack in the hull. The diver's hands were only a fraction ahead of

331

his. Slowing down now. The surface became smooth—must be some rubber solution filling the crack and holding the device. Bucken felt a short piece of cable leading to a rubber disc ... the ear of the bomb. The diver's hand moved away. He must be reaching for his knife to cut the device free. Bucken could see only vague outlines. He braced himself for an attack. He would try to grab the diver's mouthpiece and give the "four bells" emergency signal on his lifeline to Elms at the same time. But the diver would probably stab him and go for his mouthpiece. Perhaps it was a mistake not to reduce his own air reserve, too. All he could do was to wait.

A pull on the buddy line. Oh, yes, his worries and utter concentration on preparing himself for self-defense had made him forget his duties as well as that awful throbbing in his ears. He quickly ran his fingers down the smooth surface until he touched the diver's hand and felt the knife. It was for him to hold the bomb as the diver was freeing it, and make sure that the currents did not push the receiver-timer and the explosive unit inward where they might be lost irretrievably.

Back in the boat, it looked such a harmless little gadget. And the whole recovery operation had taken less than twelve minutes. Bucken could not believe that, apart from some mopping up and the seizure of Rattray's boat and transmitter, it was all over.

Nobody spoke on the way back. For once not even Elms bothered to criticize the two Wilsons. The morning was still reluctant to begin in earnest.

Elms and the two Wilsons took the diver to the station. Bucken just sat in the launch, massaging his ears, staring out toward the insignificant silhouette of the *Monty*'s mast.

"My wife, my former wife that is, once warned me that if I didn't resign this bloody job in time, I'd die a lonely old man," he said.

"That would make bloody two of us," said Walsh and spat into the water to add his lot to the incoming tide.

*

332

Upstairs, beyond the White Boudoir, in the already familiar small room permeated permanently by the odor of yellowing dossiers, Bucken was asked to wait, and he welcomed every minute of delay. Encouraged by Call-me-Wade, he had slept for almost twenty hours, had a leisurely bath, prepared late breakfast for one with loving care to kill time and fill the emptiness of the flat with sounds of activities, left his car behind and walked all the way to Downing Street—and he still did not know what he would eventually say to Mu, and he still could not decide how to tackle the even more immediate task of discussing Rattray with Wade. He wrote, rewrote, scrapped and recreated an imaginary script for that scene. I hope you realize, sir ... sounds menacing. You do realize, of course, sir ... too presumptuous. I assume, sir ... don't. Well for God's sake, it's immaterial what we think of the course Rattray chose! We know he meant well, we know how dedicated he was, surely you can't let his family suffer beyond the actual loss and the disgrace!

By the time Wade entered the room, Bucken had worked himself into quite a state.

"I am sorry, Mr. Bucken, I'm not quite with you. What exactly are we talking about?"

"Pensions, sir. As simple as that. All I am saying is that whatever our opinion of Rattray is, we can't let his family starve. He gave a life's service and you can't just cut off all due benefits."

"I can't imagine whatever made you think that any such action could even be contemplated concerning a hero not only of the Metropolitan Police but also of the nation. In fact, depending on the magnitude of the posthumous recognition of his most outstanding services, the widow will be entitled to special considerations over and above the usual pension and special awards ..."

Now and again Bucken tried to surface for a breath of air, but the flood of words forced him back every time into the depth of silence.

"I recognize the numerous errors I've made in the

333

course of my investigation and I'm prepared, naturally, to face the consequences. And of course the Commissioner will have my resignation today."

"Would you mind telling me what errors we are talking about?"

"I knowingly withheld information about Rattray."

"So? What's wrong with that? You don't quite see it, I'm afraid. If Rattray is a national hero, you could not possibly have any defamatory information on him."

And the real shock was yet to hit Bucken. Rattray did not die in vain—and he did not die alone at the hands of ruthless villains. Carron, too, was to be given the full treatment.

Bucken's objections were swept aside: "The man is dead! He can't do any more harm, but he may damage the reputation of the police and through that all our institutions. This country is not geared to Watergates. No country is, if you ask me, but that's beside the point. Don't worry, the rest of the men will be squeezed out, forced to resign, prosecuted if possible on various other charges."

"What if somebody talks?"

"It's against their interest. Besides, nobody has any proof."

"Except me."

"That's right. But you're bound by loyalty and the Official Secrets Act, and I expect you'll know and do your duty."

He almost said it. Bucken was still waiting: your Queen and country need you ... But it did not come. Bucken heard the ceaseless waffle of big words through a cloud. Ours is a low-disclosure society ... what do you want? do you want to undermine authority? ... only because a few tiles are crumbling you don't have to change the whole roof, let alone demolish the building ...

"I'm sorry, sir, but I'll have to think about all this. I'm no social reformer, but somehow I fail to see how this kind of falsification and secrecy increases the value and respect for authority."

"Good God, man. Are you accusing us of practicing clandestine government?"

"I don't know, sir."

"Right. So let's stick to facts. You don't want to ruin the Met. Right? You don't want Rattray's dependents to live in shame and poverty. Right? You want to carry on and complete the demolition of this Hong Kong takeover, and do it in a way that is harmful to them and beneficial to us. Right? Well then. All that is left for us to discuss is not the what but the how and when. Agreed? Sometimes, my dear Bucken, we must make certain concessions to the truth to achieve a higher level of fuller truth."

"I'll have to think about that, too."

"Do, by all means. Take a long holiday. You deserve it. And don't worry. Your devotion and superbly conducted investigation will be fully recognized and rewarded."

"Which reminds me of the money."

"Fortunately it's still missing, I presume."

"Fortunately?"

"Well, recovery may create certain administrative problems. How can we repay what has never been paid out in the first place? As for the payment to the foundations, well, I think it would create a dangerous precedent if research establishments and the like suddenly decided to refund their surplus allocations instead of finding new ways of spending them in order to increase their requirements for the next financial period. But, if it comes to that, the bookkeepers will have to find a way, I suppose."

"Nine hundred thousand pounds could go a long way toward the recovery of the *Monty . . .*"

"Are you suggesting that you know where the money is?"

"Nnno . . . but I could venture a shrewd guess . . ."

"Oh."

"I could, of course, keep it. And put it to various uses, accepting the guidance of our new national hero, perhaps."

"Well, do you or don't you know where that wretched nuisance is hidden?"